Praise for Alison Larkin's *The English American*

"*The English American* is a funny, charming and poignant book—the kind that you can't resist reading in a single day. It's impossible to dislike this scatterbrained Brit, who overstuffs her suitcase and then ties it together with nylon stockings. But the book, based on Larkin's one-woman comedy show, has a serious heart."

—*Chicago Sun Times*

"*Vogue* labeled it as one of the most powerful books of the season. And there's really no doubt Larkin can deliver onstage at readings and book signings. The buzz is on. Who wouldn't like main character Pippa Dunn, a vulnerable 28-year-old Brit who hails from the American South but doesn't know it? Both poignant and funny, the story rings true. Larkin has a winner on her hands."

—*The Oregonian*

"Marvelously light-footed, hugely entertaining."

—*The Times* (London)

"Larkin's debut novel takes a comedic but heartfelt look at issues of identity, heredity, and self-acceptance. Pippa is a complex, compelling character and readers will root for her as she uncovers her roots and finds herself."

—*Publishers Weekly*

"Drawn from Larkin's own life, this debut novel—like Pippa herself—is smart, funny, and utterly charming."

—*Booklist*

"Deceptively simple in framework, the novel successfully veers between poignancy and outrageous humor, with Larkin having great fun with English and American cultures as Pippa navigates her way through the culture clashes and extended families to recognize her unique, quirky self."

—*Library Journal*

"An engaging, highly readable tale of one woman's search for love and a place in the world."

—*The Newark Star-Ledger*

"Alison Larkin has written a book that makes you laugh and cry at the same time. Not only that, *The English American* is a story that you've never read before. You'll be a most appreciative reader."

—Gail Parent, Emmy Award-winning writer for *Tracey Takes On, The Golden Girls,* and *The Carol Burnett Show*

"Alison Larkin has written a book that is not only hilariously funny, but poignant and deeply moving as well. She gets the absurd complexity of an adoptee's life down perfectly. Our heroine Pippa Dunn cracked me up, then broke my heart over and over. I was cheering for her the whole way."

—Susan Ito, co-editor of *A Ghost At Heart's Edge: Stories & Poems of Adoption*

The English American

ALISON LARKIN

Simon & Schuster Paperbacks

NEW YORK   LONDON   TORONTO   SYDNEY

Simon & Schuster Paperbacks
A Division of Simon & Schuster, Inc.
1230 Avenue of the Americas
New York, NY 10020

First Simon & Schuster trade paperback edition November 2009

SIMON & SCHUSTER PAPERBACKS and colophon are registered trademarks
of Simon & Schuster, Inc.

For information about special discounts for bulk purchases,
please contact Simon & Schuster Special Sales at
1-866-506-1949 or business@simonandschuster.com.

The Simon & Schuster Speakers Bureau can bring authors
to your live event. For more information or to book an event,
contact the Simon & Schuster Speakers Bureau at
1-866-248-3049 or visit our website at www.simonspeakers.com.

Designed by C. Linda Dingler

Manufactured in the United States of America

1   3   5   7   9   10   8   6   4   2

The Library of Congress has cataloged the hardcover edition as follows:
Larkin, Alison.
The English American : a novel / by Alison Larkin.
p.   cm.
1. Adoptees—Fiction. 2. Birthmothers—Fiction. 3. Mothers and
daughters—Fiction. 4. British—United States—Fiction. I. Title.
PR6112.A745E65 2008
823'.92—dc22   2007025431

ISBN 978-1-4165-5159-1
ISBN 978-1-4391-5653-7 (pbk)
ISBN 979-1-4165-6566-6 (ebook)

For my husband

We shall not cease from exploration
And the end of all our exploring
Will be to arrive where we started
And know the place for the first time

—T. S. Eliot, "Little Gidding"

SPRING

Chapter One

I THINK EVERYONE SHOULD BE ADOPTED. That way, you can meet your birth parents when you're old enough to cope with them. Of course it's all a bit of a lottery. You never know who you're going to get as parents. I got lucky. Then again, if I'd been adopted by Mia Farrow, rather than Mum and Dad, today I could be married to Woody Allen.

As far as the side effects are concerned, I discovered early on that the key to dealing with a fear of abandonment is to date people you don't like, so if they do leave you, it doesn't matter. Either that, or guarantee fidelity by dating people no one else wants.

Which is why, at the age of twenty-eight, while my friends are getting married to men who look like Hugh Grant, I'm still living with my sister.

Charlotte and I are sharing part of what used to be a Georgian house, before it was turned into flats, in West London, opposite Kew Gardens. The Kew famously referred to by Alexander Pope, on the collar of Prince Frederick's new puppy:

> *I am his Highness dog at Kew;*
> *Pray tell me, sir, whose dog are you?*

On the morning of the day everything will change, but I don't yet know it, I jump out of bed half an hour after the alarm goes off, wolf down a bowl of cornflakes, and scrabble about in the bottom of the broom cupboard for an umbrella. It's raining, of course.

"Charlotte, have you seen my brush?"

"Try your sock drawer," she says.

My sister is a buyer for Harrods. She's looked the part since she was three. She emerges from her room, impeccably dressed, blond bob perfectly in place, handbag over her shoulder, car keys already in hand.

"Pippa," Charlotte says, "you're a gorgeous woman. Positively Titian. I wish I looked like you, but—how can I put this? Today you look like a plumber."

I'm wearing overalls, which I enjoy very much. Put a different colored T-shirt under them and it looks like you're wearing an entirely new outfit.

"I suppose you want a lift to the tube too?"

"Thanks," I say. God knows how I'm going to get to work on time when Charlotte moves in with Rupert.

We're almost out of our front door, which has been opened and shut by Londoners for nearly two hundred years, when Charlotte spots a tiny piece of cornflake on my shirt. She takes her hanky out of her pocket and starts jabbing at it with the precision of a woodpecker.

Ever since I can remember, my sister, friends, parents, and occasionally even complete strangers have taken it upon themselves to wipe spills off my clothes. Without asking. They simply assume I feel the same way as they do about food stains. I don't. I think it's absurd that anyone thinks they matter.

But I also don't like to hurt anyone's feelings. So when people start wiping food stains off my clothing, I act surprised that the stain is there and thank them profusely.

It's all about what interests you. If I spend a whole day with you, and someone asks me afterward how you are, I'll know what you're feeling, i.e., sad, happy, preoccupied, pissed-off—whatever it might be. I've always been able to tune in to people in that way. But ask me what you were wearing, and I'll draw a blank.

Charlotte will not only be able to report on exactly what you were wearing, down to the color of your socks, she'll somehow know about the hole on the inside of your shirt, even if you've tucked it into your trousers. She'll know the name of your hairstyle, the brand of your lipstick, and the make of your car.

Charlotte was born a year after me. I was adopted. She wasn't. It happens a lot, I gather. People think they can't have children, adopt one, and then, *bam*, a few months later, the mother gets pregnant with a child of her own.

Like Mum, Charlotte thinks before she speaks, makes pros and cons lists, and is content with her life the way it is. She's practical, grounded, solid, sure.

I, on the other hand, interrupt people because my thoughts fly out of my mouth. My handbag's full of rubbish. And I want to do something that matters with my life. Right now I'd like to write plays, sing in musicals, and/or rid the world of poverty, violence, cruelty, and right-wing conservative politics.

I've tried to be happy leading the kind of life that makes Mum and Charlotte happy, really I have. But pretending to be interested in things I am not is becoming more and more difficult. Take Scottish dancing.

If you've ever been to any kind of Scottish dancing evening in the south of England, you've probably met my dad. He's the Scot at the microphone, with the shock of thick white hair, barking out orders. He's never happier than when he's marching up and down a drafty church hall in his tartan kilt and sporran, teaching the English a new Scottish dance.

There are more than three thousand of them. To date he's checked off two hundred and fifty-two. He keeps his dance list in the right-hand cubbyhole of his desk, next to his spare golf balls and his paper clips.

"Set to the left!" he shouts. Dad's lived in England so long his Scottish accent is barely detectable most of the time. Except when he's trying to teach the English to Scottish dance. Then his Scottish burr becomes much more pronounced.

"Now set to the right! Turn your partners. Very good, Charlotte. No, Pippa! Wrong way! This isn't the Dashing White Sergeant!"

I've always felt restricted by Scottish dancing. You can't do your own thing. If you twirl to the left and jump in the air when everyone else is turning right during the Eightsome Reel, for example, you'll spoil the dance for everyone else.

I think it's one of the saddest things in the world—don't you?—when people are upset because the direction they're going in feels all wrong for you—and you know you just have to go the opposite way.

Chapter Two

CHARLOTTE'S SPENDING THE WEEKEND with Rupert in Paris. She's hurrying toward her light blue Saab because she doesn't want to get her suitcase wet.

"He's going to ask you to marry him, you know," I tell her.

It really is bucketing down with rain now.

"Get in!" Charlotte says.

Her car is clean and dry and smells of leather and lavender.

I know that Charlotte will accept Rupert's proposal, because he's perfect for her. He loves going to dinner parties with his fellow commodity brokers in the City as much as Charlotte does. They'll get married after a long engagement. Then she'll give up her job, and they'll move to somewhere like Bath. They'll have at least two children, and go on annual skiing holidays to Verbier and Val d'Isere in the winter, and somewhere hot in the summer—as long as it has all-day child care and inexhaustible supplies of wine.

"So here's to you, Mrs. Darrington!" I lift up an imaginary glass of champagne.

Charlotte laughs again. Her blue eyes light up just like Mum's when she's utterly happy.

From what I've told you so far, you're probably thinking that Charlotte's the grown-up in our relationship. The one who looks after me. But it also works the other way around. I've protected Charlotte for years. Without her knowing it. By not telling her what's really going on with me.

Charlotte and I share the same parents, but we don't share secrets. I actually don't think Charlotte has any, and I hate to burden people. Which is why Charlotte doesn't know the truth about Miles. She thinks I broke up with him because I'm being fickle, wanting to play the field, because that's what I want her to think. She doesn't know that, for me, falling in love is terrifying.

And I haven't told her about the dream that's started haunting me at night. The one about the mother who gave me birth. If I let anyone in my family know how much I've been wondering about my other mother, they might feel displaced. As if I don't love them anymore. As if I don't need them anymore. And I do.

Charlotte drops me off at the tube and kisses me on the cheek. "Don't get into too much trouble while I'm gone, Pip!"

I always feel a tug when I say good-bye to people I care about. Even if it's just for the weekend. Especially this time. Perhaps a part of me already knows that everything is about to change.

Half an hour later, I get off the tube at Embankment, stop at the newsstand to buy a packet of Maltesers, a box of Ribena, and some prawn cocktail crisps, and walk down the Strand to work. I work for Drury Lane Publications, selling advertising space on the telephone in *International CEO* magazine.

The setting isn't exactly salubrious. Thirty salespeople sit in cubicles in a large room in a white building opposite the back wall of the Theatre Royal. But I don't mind. It gives me flexibility, and I can dress however I want.

It's probably a combination of what Charlotte calls my "absurdly un-English enthusiasm"—and the fact that I have a posh accent—that makes me the top salesperson in the company. The rest are men.

I call Europe in the morning and America in the afternoon: "Hallo. My name's Pippa Dunn. I'm working with Tony Blair."

This isn't strictly true. Someone from Tony Blair's office told our editor that of course we could reprint one of his speeches in the magazine, because it was already in the public domain. But it gets me through to the right person.

"Our current goal is to help American companies break into the European market."

This isn't true either. Our current goal is to make as much money in commissions as possible. But I get caught up in my own pitch and, *ping:* I've sold another double-page spread for nine thousand nine hundred and ninety-nine pounds.

Ever since I started calling America, I've wondered if I'm speaking to someone who knows the parents who gave me birth. Maybe my real father is the governor of Virginia? Or doing something to help the poor people in New Orleans? Or doing what he can to bring the soldiers back from Iraq? He's a Democrat, of course. He must be. We share the same genes.

And my real mother? What about her? Maybe she's a senator? Unlikely. There are more women in the Iranian parliament than there are in the U.S. Senate—but you never know.

In London, in 2007, people in their twenties are supposed to hate everything. Especially America. And American foreign policy. And British foreign policy. And optimistic, successful people, like Richard Branson, who I swear the British only tolerate because he consistently fails to get round the world in his hot-air balloon. But I love America. I always have done. And not just because, despite my British accent and upbringing, I am, myself, really an American. I've always known I was adopted. But I didn't find out my birth parents were Americans until I was fifteen years old.

Charlotte and I were home on summer holidays from our separate boarding schools. Charlotte went to Pelsham Abbey, because she was good at sports. I went to St. Margaret's, because I was good at music.

While sending your children off to boarding school is considered barbaric by every American I've ever met, in England it's still considered a privilege. It's especially common if your parents live abroad, as mine had ever since Dad joined the Foreign Office. Important to give the children a solid base in England while one's moving from post to post, and all that.

Anyway, I'd gone upstairs to Dad's office to try to find what the British call Sellotape and the Americans call Scotch tape. It wasn't where Mum said it would be, so I started rummaging about in the drawers of Dad's desk to look for it. In the lower right-hand drawer, I noticed a file with my name on it.

I took the file out, and, inside it, found my old school reports— the ones I used to take on the plane with me, when I traveled from England to Kenya, or Hong Kong, or wherever Mum and Dad were stationed at the end of each term.

ART 11

Instead of drawing the fruit bowl still life everyone else drew in art class this year, Phillippa drew a rain forest. This rain forest, which comprised little more than an untidy mess of orange and green flowers, has now appeared in exercise books, on note pads, and, I am sorry to say, on the inside cover of Art History Explained. *Phillippa will not be permitted to borrow any more books until she has replaced the one she defaced.*

Valerie Eason, Art teacher

MUSIC

Pippa rose to the position of head of Junior Choir because she has an unusually beautiful voice and clearly has a gift for performance. When she asked if she could teach the choir a song from a musical, as a surprise addition to the end-of-term concert, I agreed, assuming we would be treated to a song from one of the musicals Pippa is so fond of singing. "Oh, What a Beautiful Morning," perhaps. Or "How Are Things in Glochamorra," which she sings quite beautifully.

Fortunately I attended the dress rehearsal and was able to stop the theme tune from the television program Shaft *from being performed on*

*Parents Day. These are not suitable lyrics for twelve-year-old girls, even
if the song is performed in six-part harmony, and with perfect pitch.*

Miss Dunk, Music teacher

LATIN

*Phillippa's essay on "My Family Tree, How I Came to Be Me" was
not supposed to be a work of fiction. Even if it were true that Pippa is
adopted—a popular fantasy amongst girls in the Lower Fourth—her
real father could not possibly be King Lear. Even if King Lear were
not a fictional character, he only had three daughters. And Phillippa
was not one of them.*

*On the eternal subject of Phillippa's untidiness, I'm sorry to say
her essay on the fall of the Roman Empire had more crossings than the
Waterloo Line. She is, at times, very immature.*

Miss Possum, Latin teacher

Well, of course I was immature. I was ten.

HOUSE REPORT

*Phillippa drives us to the point of despair in her dormitory—and by
leaving her belongings scattered abroad. Alas, she will never make a
needlewoman—and her work suffers because of her appalling untidiness. The universal distribution of her belongings entails much work
for other people. Please note, when I say she is appallingly untidy, I
am not exaggerating.*

Miss Steel, Housemistress

The reports of my untidiness alarmed my neat-as-a-pin parents far
more than anything else. Ashamed of myself for disappointing them
so terribly, I'd return to school at the end of the holidays, determined to be tidy. No matter how hard I tried, I never managed it.
Within days I'd be hauled up before the headmistress with ink on

my hands, or my uniform, or both, and told, once again, that I was a grave disappointment to the school.

I blocked out memories of the aptly named Miss Steel and kept flipping through.

There were papers from the British school I went to in Hong Kong before boarding school, and from my prep school and nursery school in Zimbabwe. Then my baby weight, height, that sort of thing.

Then I came across a thin file with a label on it. It read: "As supplied by the adoption agency, non-identifying information about Phillippa's biological parents."

I'd always known I was adopted. But we'd never talked about who from. I held on to the file tightly. There, in my hands, fifteen years since I was born, I was holding a file that held the facts about my long-lost mother. I was holding the key to my true identity.

Feeling like a criminal, but unable to stop myself, I got up and shut the door. Then, guiltily, heart beating extra fast, I opened the file and I started to read.

For Phillippa when she is ready:
Non-identifying information about Pippa's biological parents

Mother: 5' 8", 110 lbs. Very pretty. Writes excellent poetry. High achiever. Well-spoken, lively, highly intelligent. Born in ▮▮▮. Educated at ▮▮▮. American.

Father: 6 ft., 180 lbs. Born in ▮▮▮. Varsity football team. Excellent speaker. Politically ambitious. Married. American.

Mother relinquished baby so as not to ruin father's political career.

I held my hands to my heart, which was still beating at double speed. I shut my eyes.

I knew it. I just knew it. My real parents were brilliant people. They were remarkable people. They were famous people.

And they were American!

I took a deep breath.

"Relinquished baby so as not to ruin father's political career."

Of course. This explained everything. No wonder I had been given up for adoption. Why, if the press found out about me, it could cause a nationwide scandal, maybe even bring down an entire American administration! Why else would the adoption agency black out all the details?

I carefully put the file back in the drawer, exactly as I had found it, left Dad's office, and ran down the stairs.

"Couldn't find the Sellotape anywhere," I said, in as casual a tone as I could manage.

"I'll go and look," Mum said. She returned a minute later. "Oh Pip, you are a silly billy. It was on top of the desk. Right under your nose!"

"Sorry," I said, somehow managing to hide my excitement.

Thank God I found the papers. Now that I knew the truth, I would never have to upset anyone by asking questions.

I mulled over the information I now had until it sunk in, repeating it to myself, over and over again.

I'm descended from remarkable people.

I'm an American.

My father was in politics and unfaithful to his wife.

I have red hair . . .

Of course. I am a Kennedy.

I selected the people I told this information to very carefully. With my best friends I'd say, "I've got a secret to tell you. I am not what I seem. I was adopted at birth, and my real father is a famous politician, probably a Kennedy."

I'd wait for the fascinated expression that invariably followed this revelation.

"And," I'd say, "there is evidence to suggest that my real mother is Emily Dickinson." Or, when I read *The Bell Jar*, Sylvia Plath. Or, when I decided my true vocation was to become a playwright, Wendy Wasserstein.

Chapter Three

It's still raining as I leave work, and London smells of damp coats and bus fumes and cigarettes. A thousand feet are walking along the Strand, and down the hill toward Embankment tube. I'm high as a kite after winning top salesperson of the week again, and for the first time in the three months since I ended things with Miles, I feel my usual optimism return. I hold soft, sweet-smelling daffodils, my prize for selling the most, which dance against my face, kissing me as I walk. I'm full of joy and I feel light again.

If I were hip I wouldn't tell you that I can whistle the tune to just about every musical ever written. The great ones uplift me as no other music can. But I'm not hip. I care even less about my hip factor than I do about the stain status of my clothing.

So I leave work whistling "Singin' in the Rain" and walk at a healthy pace toward Trafalgar Square. Dad spent hours teaching me how to whistle when I was about eight. I've been a world-class whistler ever since. As I whistle, people on the street around me start to smile.

Today I look at each face as I pass by. Who are these people sharing the street with me? What is going on in their worlds, inside their heads? Are they in love? If so, is it the kind that Mum and Dad have? Based on having things in common, like raspberry picking and a love of dogs, and Shakespeare, and long country walks? Or is it the knock-you-out, eat-you-up, set-you-on-fire kind of love that I have longed for—and avoided—all my life?

Are they looking at me and wondering the same thing? Or are they just going home, not thinking about much in particular? Is it quiet inside their heads? Still? Peaceful?

A thousand thoughts compete with one another in my head, every day. They always have done. I sometimes wonder what it would be like to have just one thought at a time. Like Mum and Dad and Charlotte.

When I get to Villiers Street, where you turn left off the Strand to get to the Embankment tube, I stop at the light. There's a woman next to me. I can tell, from the way she is standing, and the look in her eyes, that she's terribly unhappy. She's about thirty, I think. Tall and thin, like me. In her shiny black boots with big silver buckles she looks like an elegant buccaneer.

It's impossible to smile and whistle at the same time, so I turn my face to her and whistle the rest of the song in an attempt to cheer her up. The tune is almost lost in the traffic, but not quite.

Her response to my whistling is quite different from everybody else's. The woman turns her pale, tightly drawn face toward me. Then she says, in a voice that's both shaking and sharp: "People like you—Christ! You just have to draw attention to yourself, don't you?"

Then she turns her head away and gets ready to move as soon as the traffic light turns green.

She seems so miserable, and I know what that's like, because I've been feeling unhappy recently too. Bursting with the desire to make everything all right for her, I turn to her and say, "I'm sorry you're having a horrible day. I'm sorry for annoying you. I—well, I hope these will cheer you up." Then I hand her my bunch of daffodils.

The woman holds the flowers slightly away from her, her attention on the traffic light, which is about to change. Then, as a London bus revs up its engine, puffs warm exhaust into our faces, and rattles on down the famous London street, she drops the flowers on the ground and walks away.

If this happened to Charlotte, or just about anyone else I know, they'd brush it off and carry on with their day. But for me it hurts terribly. For me, any kind of rejection hurts terribly. It always has done. I'm even sensitive to little rejections—like the butcher giving the last chicken to the lady in the gray coat, even though she was behind me in the queue.

It's the real reason why I've never actually auditioned for a singing job of any kind—or applied for a job somewhere like Amnesty International. I'd rather be accepted for a job I don't care about than risk being rejected by one I do.

It's the same with men.

When I'm on my own with a boyfriend, everything's wonderful. But when we go into the outside world, I find myself on red alert, terrified the object of my affections will be making a date with the waitress if I so much as go to the loo. I never let on, of course. Because everybody knows the bloke stays with you if the chase is still on.

I thought I'd found the solution by dating the men least likely to leave me: Dull Blokes Only. That's why, when Charlotte introduced me to Miles, I thought he'd be ideal.

He absolutely wasn't my type. He loved to spend hours looking at old buildings, and he thought Benny Hill was funnier than Ricky Gervais, for God's sake. He was big and spotty and laughed too much at his own jokes. Miles, I knew immediately, would never leave me. I would be the one to leave him. Thus I accepted his invitation to dinner with absolute confidence in my ability to stay in emotional control.

But Miles was kind, and even sexy in his own way. Before I knew it, to my surprise and dismay, I was in love again.

We settled down. In the morning, Miles rode his yellow moped to work and spent the day designing corporate websites. We made love in the evenings, sometimes on the floor of his office, sometimes at my flat, once in the ladies' room at the Tate.

The more time we spent together, the more afraid I became that he would go off with somebody else. And, as usual, everything became about trying to make sure that didn't happen.

Once we bumped into an attractive friend of mine on the street, and she invited us to a dinner party. I couldn't make it because it fell on the same night as Hanif Kureishi's playwriting workshop at the Royal Court. I'd been looking forward to it for months.

"Why don't you come anyway, Miles?" she offered.

"Not without me!" I said, instantly on the alert.

"Why on earth not?" they said together, turning to me in unison. My heart was beating twice as fast as it had been seconds before, but I smiled quickly, pretending to consult my diary.

"What an idiot," I said. "Got the date wrong. The playwriting workshop is *next* week. I am free on Friday after all." And so Miles and I went to the dinner party together, and I spent the evening checking to see if he showed any interest in other women, but pretending not to. And, even though I knew we weren't really "right" for each other, I flirted conspicuously with the bloke sitting next to me, to make Miles jealous. So he'd love me more. And never leave me.

When we got back to his flat Miles held me tightly, all night, his bearlike body wrapped around mine. I felt utterly at peace. But in the morning, when his body left mine . . . All I can say is that it's all-consuming, the panic that sets in. And I know it's all in my head, because no bloke has ever gone off with someone else.

"Oh Pip," Miles said one morning, "I don't want to do anything else. I just want to be with you. Always."

For a second, my heart eased. But as soon as it did, I started worrying about the next time. So I said, "I think we need a break." I told Miles, and myself, we were completely wrong for each other, returned the matching yellow moped he'd given me for my birthday, and took up smoking again.

It's awful. I'm awful. And it's been going on for years.

Recently I've begun to wonder if it might have something to do with the fact that I was adopted.

Maybe if I found out that my mother gave me up for adoption because she had to—and not because she took one look at me and went "yuck"—I'd no longer have a fear of rejection. And then I might finally be able to fall in love totally, absolutely—maybe even honestly—without the panic that sets in. Like normal people.

When the woman rejects my flowers, the feeling of joy disappears. By the time I get to the ticket counter at Embankment, the sense of despair that's been haunting me recently returns. London isn't beautiful anymore. It's dirty. The smell of stale piss that I didn't notice the first time I came through the tunnel hits me, now, as strongly as the stench of rubbish on the street and the vomit on the wall. I can see, now, that the other people are just tired and want to go home. I no longer care who they are or what's going on in any of their lives. I just want to go home too.

I don't know where my long-lost mother is. Or who she is. Or how she is. Or whether or not she'd want to have anything to do with me. But in my mind's eye, she's with me on the tube, which is thundering through the underground tunnel toward Kew.

She has a lovely, serene face. She's singing to me now. Soothing me.

She understands the joy. She understands the terror. She understands everything.

Chapter Four

I GET OFF THE TUBE and walk up the ivy-covered stone steps to my flat and into my room. I wade through piles of clothes, some dirty, some not, and climb up onto the window seat in my bedroom.

The Abbey looks almost ethereal at night, bathed as it is in murky yellow light from the street lamp on the corner.

A group of Benedictine monks lives on one side of the Abbey, and a group of Benedictine nuns lives on the other side. I used to tell people that if you looked very closely, in the middle of the night, you'd be able to see the monks and the nuns sneaking up onto the roof of the Abbey and dancing together in the shadows.

I lie down on the comfy maroon and cream window-seat cushion that Mum made me for Christmas and fall asleep. I dream that the nuns and the monks are dancing their nightly dance. The wind is up and the branches of the huge oak tree at the end of the road are swaying furiously. The dancers have a wildness about them I've not seen before.

Then one of the nuns and one of the monks lift their habits and become the parents who gave me birth. I'm watching them from inside my room. All the lights have gone off, and it's pitch black. They can't see me, but I know they're there. They come to the bay window in my bedroom. In unison, they reach out their hands and open the heavy curtains. Then I wake up and, in that state between wake and sleep, make the phone call that changes everything.

The call itself doesn't last more than five minutes. But it has the power to catapult me out of the world I know, into an in-between world, from which the "me" I thought I was can never return.

It's nine thirty. I dial international directory enquiries and ask the operator for the telephone number for the adoption agency in New York City where my parents collected me when I was six weeks old.

I'm not expecting anyone to pick up. I'm expecting an answering machine.

"Post-adoption services, can I help you?"

"Oh. Hallo," I say. "Um—my name is Pippa Dunn. I'm calling from London. In England."

Shut up, Pip. Of course they know that London's in England.

There's a pause and the sound of rustling paper.

"Yes, Pippa, I remember you well." The woman's voice is nasal and efficient and American. "You called a few years ago, didn't you?"

"Well, yes, I did," I say.

The last time I called the adoption agency I was in the same state I'm in today, when I just do something, without planning to. It usually happens when I'm tired either due to lack of sleep or to the sugar crash that follows an excessive consumption of Maltesers, chocolate buttons, or if I'm particularly hungry, a large bar of Cadbury's Fruit and Nut.

About three years ago I'd called to make a general inquiry about what I would need to do if I ever decided to trace the woman who gave me birth. The woman at the other end of the phone asked me if I had any siblings and I'd said, "No, I'm not married." And then I felt like a complete idiot later when I realized what she meant.

"Oh yes," she's saying now. "It's Judy. I remember you well! We don't get beautiful British accents calling here every day, you know!"

She sounds excited.

"Something unusual happened," she's saying. "The day after you last called, your birth mother came into the agency. The very next day! Isn't that something? We all thought it was just such an extraordinary coincidence . . . "

There's a long pause, this time at my end. Mum's maroon and cream curtains are moving slightly in the breeze.

I was expecting a bland recorded message, on which I would probably have hung up. I wasn't expecting this. Sparks of adrenaline are shooting off, like tiny fireworks, inside my chest.

"So she's all right?" I ask. "My mother . . . she's all right? I mean she's alive? And . . . and real?" I sound like an idiot again.

"Oh yes," Judy says. "She's certainly real. And it says here—yes—she's open to contact."

I take a deep breath in a futile attempt to calm myself down.

"Why?" I say. "Um, why did she come into the agency? And what should I do, if I wanted to maybe meet her? Or find out more about her? Or reassure her she did the right thing, and thank her, for . . . for giving me up to the most wonderful life?"

"I'm sorry. I can't disclose any information over the phone," Judy says. "You need to write us a letter."

"What sort of letter?"

Judy has gone back into practiced mode now.

"Oh, you know, a letter saying who you are and why you want more information. It may take some time for us to respond. There are only two of us here at post-adoption services and we're getting requests like yours every day."

Poor Judy, she sounds tired. I feel guilty taking up her time.

"I'll write to you," I say. "Thank you so much—thank you, thank you, thank you."

I put down the telephone. I'm shaking, and my heart feels tight.

The mother I have dreamed of and wondered about all my life is alive, and real, and—oh, best of all—"open to contact"!

The excitement is accompanied by a thud of guilt. How can I do this to Mum and Dad? The maroon and cream bedspread that Mum made to go with the curtains reproaches me from the floor.

I look around my room. My orangutan washing bag is still stuffed full of dirty laundry. The Oriental carpet I brought back from Kashmir is still desperately in need of a clean. The Abbey is still standing in the shadows under the moon, which is still full. Everything looks the same and yet it is not the same.

Minutes ago my mother was a ghostly figure, asleep in the back of my mind.

Now she has become real.

I sit down and write the letter Judy asked for. Miraculously I find an envelope, stick far too many stamps on it—better safe than sorry—and run down the end of the road to post it before I can change my mind.

The next morning, I clamber into Typhoo—my beaten-up old Renault 5, named after my favorite tea—and drive along the familiar road to Mum and Dad's house. My mind is still racing.

I was afraid she wouldn't want to see me.

But she does want to see me!

As I drive, badly and fast, past the house Mum lived in as a child, which is now a teashop, I try to think of moments in my life that might have caused the feeling that has overtaken me. I can't describe it as anything other than longing.

Mum first told me I was adopted when I was about six years old. We were living in Hong Kong at the time, in a lovely, light four-bedroom apartment that looked over the Star Ferry. I could watch it chugging back and forth across Hong Kong harbor from my bedroom window. Mum had just finished reading *The Hundred and One Dalmatians,* and I'd asked Mum how the puppies were born, and she was explaining that they came out of Perdita's tummy.

"Is that how human babies come?"

"Yes," Mum said. "Human babies grow inside their mummy's tummies too. Only with human beings, there's usually only one baby at a time."

"I see."

I loved this time of day, just before bedtime, when Mum tried to bring some kind of order to my unruly red hair, by brushing it and brushing it, with her cool, carefully manicured hands. I secretly wished I had smooth blond hair, like Mum's and Charlotte's, despite the fact that Mum was always telling me how pretty mine was. I bent my head back so she could brush from the top of my head down.

"So Charlotte and I came out of your tummy?"

The brushing stopped for a second, and then started again.

"No, darling."

"No?"

"Charlotte came out of my tummy."

There was a pause in the brushing. Then it started again.

"Didn't I come out of your tummy too?"

"Well, no, darling. Before Charlotte was born, we thought there was something wrong with Mummy's tummy. We thought we couldn't have a baby. We wanted a baby very much, so we came and got you from the adoption agency. As soon as we saw you, we knew you were the perfect baby for us. And so we brought you home. You were chosen, darling," Mum said gently, smiling at me in the mirror, with tears in her eyes.

Within a second my worldview shifted. I was special. I had been chosen. But my poor little sister. She wasn't chosen, like me. She just came. From that moment on, I was as kind to Charlotte as it's possible for a six-year-old to be.

The first time I remember actually picturing the mother who gave me birth was in the middle of a freezing February night at boarding school. I was eleven years old and in deep trouble for shoving the clothes under my bed that I was supposed to have folded and put away.

I was sent to see Miss Steel, who was not at all happy at being called out of bed to discipline a student. Especially Pippa Dunn, again. The phrases Miss Steel used in her school reports were tame in comparison with how she spoke to me in person. Miss Steel's face was almost as white as the pictures you see of Queen Elizabeth the First.

"Your punishment," she said, standing ramrod straight in her buttoned-up dressing gown, "will be to stand under the clock in the cloakroom until it strikes twelve. You will not speak. You will not move. Upon the stroke of twelve, you may return to bed."

It was dark under the clock, and the cloaks took on scary shapes. I shut my eyes tightly. There was a draft coming through the cloakroom door, so I pulled the sleeves of my dressing gown over my hands like mittens.

I tried to think of anything but the scary gray cloaks, which looked like monks' habits. The harder I tried not to think about the scary cloaks, the more like faceless, heaving monsters they became: hanging on their hooks in menacing rows, waiting, challenging me not to look at them.

So I looked above the cloaks, not at them. And when I did, I thought I saw my long-lost mother, looking down at me from above the racks. She was there and yet not there. She was sort of transparent, and she was smiling right at me.

She was beautiful, and delicate, with red hair, like mine, only hers wasn't springy. It was long and smooth and cascaded down her back like a mane. And her eyes were gentle and kind. The sight of her filled me with warmth and made all the fear go away.

And that's how she's come to me, over the years. Until now.

I'm driving through Fenhurst now. The Spread Eagle Hotel— yes, that's its real name—stands in all its glory, bridging the road in the middle of town, as ugly today as it was when it was first built over six hundred years ago. I spent a night there with Miles once. Wooden beams, white walls, a bed covered in a pink floral bedspread that sloped too far to the left, karaoke in the bar the night before, and no air-conditioning.

I drive toward my parents' house in Peaseminster heavy with guilt. The adoption thing was something that happened a long time ago that Mum and Dad put right. But now here I am, about to bring up the one thing that can only cause pain to the people I love most in the world.

Chapter Five

Mum and Dad's house was built in 1470 and used to be a farmhouse. It still has parts of its original thatched roof and all its dark wooden beams, a long oak staircase, and large, lovely windows that look out onto a massive maple tree, a glorious green lawn, and a large greenhouse, inside which are rows of tomato plants and a small swimming pool.

The house, called Little Tew, sits alone, surrounded by wheatfields, about three miles from Peaseminster. If you climb up the stone path to the hill at the back of the house, you can see Gately Castle nestled amidst miles and miles of Sussex countryside—flat farmland, with bales of hay neatly dotted around in squares, green trees and hedges on yellow ground in the summer.

There's a chalk pit on the South Downs, behind the house, where I used to go and smoke cigarettes when I was sixteen. Men in checked caps and green Wellington boots breed pheasants up there in the spring, so they can shoot them dead in the winter.

The house itself is surrounded by a four-hundred-year-old gray stone wall, with moss growing between its bricks. The wall is high enough to block out the occasional car that drives past on the country road outside. But it's not high enough to block out the horseback riders, who can be seen from the neck up, trotting up and down, backs straight, hard hats perfectly in place.

I drive down the last two miles of narrow country lane and

through the wooden gates into my parents' driveway. It's a warm day and I'm not wearing any shoes. When I get out of Typhoo, the sharp gravel stones hurt my bare feet, as they always do.

Mum and Dad are on the porch, talking to my cousin Neville, who is staying for the weekend.

It's Neville who will think nothing of making an eight-hour drive up to Scotland because I have a sudden longing to stand on the ramparts of Edinburgh Castle and take a walk up Arthur's Seat. It's Neville who bought me a keyboard with volume control when I was at university so I could get out of bed and play without disturbing anybody in the middle of the night.

Neville's parents are currently living in Pakistan, and we're the only family he has in England, so Mum and Dad have practically adopted him too.

"Hallo Pippadee!" Neville says, hacking away at a fat, stubborn carrot. He's been helping Mum with the vegetables for tonight's beef stew. "I heard you had a spot of engine trouble on the M25," he says, referring to my latest car fiasco. I'd called the tow chap, insisting the engine had fallen out, because I heard a clunk. It turned out I'd run out of petrol.

"I need to talk to Mum," I say.

"Ooooo. Boyfriend troubles."

"Maybe," I say. "Whatever it is, it's private."

Mum laughs. Her eyes light up when she laughs. "Go on. Off you go," she says, pushing her six-foot nephew off the porch.

"Miles, Miles, it's always about Miles," he says. "He loves you, you siren, he hasn't eaten in weeks . . ."

"Go *away*!"

Neville makes a kissy-kissy face and retreats into the sitting room.

Mum brings two cups of tea and a plate of Swiss rolls on a tray from the kitchen. My heart is beating wildly. I have no idea how to begin.

"I can't believe how warm it is," I say.

"Daddy and I nearly went swimming last week," she says. "Unbelievable."

The teacup clicks back in the saucer. I can hear the low hum of the swimming-pool heater in the corner of the porch. I can smell sweetly scented wallflowers through the screen window.

I devour a Swiss roll, crumple the wrapper into a little gold ball, and flick it into the plant pot.

"Oh darling, I do wish you wouldn't do that. Boris knows exactly where to find your wrappers, and you know silver foil isn't good for dogs."

"Sorry," I say.

"Well, take it out. Honestly."

"Sorry," I say. I reach to take the wrapper out of the plant pot and send my teacup flying.

"I'm sorry!" I say. "Oh God, I'm so sorry!" The tea has spilled all over the carpet. Mum rushes into the kitchen to get a cloth, as she has so many times before.

"I'll do it!" she says. "Just sit down, Pippa, so you can't do any more damage."

I sit in the red armchair that belonged to Granny H. before she died. I watch Mum clean up the mess, feeling guilty and incompetent.

"I'm sorry," I say again.

"It's all right, darling," she says. "Really."

It's not. I still drive Mum crazy with my clumsiness. I hear Charlotte's favorite quip in my head: "Pippa can't walk across a room without spilling at least something." It's said with affection, and without exaggeration.

The tea cleared up, Mum and I sit for a moment, looking out over her lovely pink and yellow rose garden. Every third evening or so, Mum deadheads the roses. Then she puts them in a red plastic bowl and throws them on the compost heap, in the northeast corner of the garden, where the stone walls meet.

I've never been so nervous. Mum looks so content, sitting on the porch in her sunglasses, taking the tea cosy off her Brown Betty teapot, and pouring in more hot water from the stainless steel jug she's used for this purpose ever since I can remember.

"Gemma! Gemma!" Dad's voice calls in from the sitting room, where he can often be found, earphones on, conducting an imaginary orchestra with a pencil when he thinks no one is looking. Today he's watching the rugby. "It's Scotland five, Wales nil!"

"Wonderful, darling," Mum says. Then, turning toward me, she asks, "What is it, Pippadee? What's wrong?"

"Well, nothing's wrong exactly," I say.

"Is it Miles?"

"Oh no," I say. "I'm over that. Really." And I am. Sort of.

"Scotland seven, Gemma! Can you believe it? Scotland seven!" Dad's voice again. Mum stands up, gently shuts the door, and sits back down again.

She is waiting for me to speak. I'm trying to relax, but in truth I can hardly breathe. Mum takes a sip of her tea and waits.

"Last night . . . ," I say, finally. There's a pause.

"Yes?"

I can't speak.

"Last night . . . ?" Mum repeats, looking at me intently over the rim of her teacup.

"Well," I manage to say, finally, "last night, on a sort of impulse, I called the adoption agency you got me from in New York."

I take in a deep breath and let it out again.

"Oh yes," Mum says, utterly unruffled.

"Well, I called just to find out what I'd have to do, if ever I wanted to find out who my biological parents were. And, well . . ." I don't want to hurt her. God, I don't want to hurt her. "Well . . . ," I say.

And then it comes out. All of it. I tell her about my conversation with the agency and about the non-identifying information they said they'd send. Mum sits there, listening carefully. I can't see into her eyes. She's still wearing sunglasses.

"Oh, Mum, I won't do any of this if you'd rather I didn't. If you'd be upset by it in any way. But I did want to tell you what happened," I say, unable to stop the tears.

"It's fine, darling," she says. "Don't worry. It's fine."

"I won't do it if you have any problem with it . . ."

"Of course you must do it," she says. "Of course you must! If you and—and this woman . . . Darling, listen to me. Good heavens, there isn't enough love in this world as it is, Pippa. Why would it matter if you and this woman love each other? Nothing can replace the years we've had together."

"Of course not!" I gush. "Of course not! And, anyway, I might hate her, if she's still alive . . . which it appears she might be. Oh Mum!" I look at my mother across the porch. "Is it really okay with you?"

"Of course it is, darling, don't be silly. Anyway," she says, pouring another cup of tea, "it shouldn't really matter what Daddy and I think."

"But it does," I say.

"Well that's nice, darling. But you're a grown-up now. You can do what you want. And it's fine. Of course it is."

The next day, we go on a walk around Siddenton, a small fishing village by the sea. I walk on ahead, along the path by the sea, looking out over the Mirrors and Lasers and Toppers sailing about in the harbor. I've never liked sailing or had much in common with the people who love it, including my father, who is now walking beside me.

He's wearing the light green Pringle sweater I gave him at Christmas, his favorite shorts, and dark green socks, pulled up to just under his knees. Despite the fact that he's two inches shorter than I am, he walks fast, in long strides, like I do. But there the similarities end.

"Mummy told me about your decision last night, Pippa."

My heart feels tight.

"Have you really thought this through? I mean, think about it, Pip. What kind of a woman would give up her child?"

I look at my father's worried face. I want to cry and tell him it has all been a dreadful mistake and I don't want to pursue it at all. But I can't.

"You're opening Pandora's box," Dad says.

"I know, Dad," I say. "But unless I do this I'm never going to know why I am who I am."

He looks at me in the slightly baffled way he usually looks at me.

"But you're Pippa."

"Oh Dad, you know I'm different from you, Mum, and Charlotte. I always have been."

Before he can answer, something wet and smelly dashes past us.

"No, Boris!" Dad says, chasing after the dog. "Not in the mud! No, Boris! No!"

As Boris and Dad charge along the path above the sea, I walk behind them, breathing in the sea air as deeply as I can. A gull swoops past us and out over the ocean. Dad returns, holding Boris by the collar.

"I had a dream last night," he says, straining to keep Boris at his side. "I dreamed that Mummy had her head chopped off."

"Oh Dad!" I say. "Dad! I'm not looking for a replacement mother! Nothing could replace Mum, ever! I just need to know."

Dad pulls Boris toward the car.

I know he's right. I will be opening Pandora's box. But I'm utterly relieved he hasn't asked me not to do it, despite his obvious misgivings.

Because I know that, for me, not doing this would mean a kind of death.

Chapter Six

FULL OF GUILT, I return to London and wait with intense anticipation for news from the adoption agency in New York.

Days, then weeks pass.

I can't make any sort of order out of the chaos in my head, my heart, or my room. Each night I have to slog through piles of clothes and chocolate wrappers to get to my bed. As each day passes, the waiting gets more and more difficult and the stacks of debris get higher and higher.

Always trying to drag me into his and Charlotte's never-ending social life, Rupert invites me to a drinks party. I go, because, as I predicted, he's asked my only sister to marry him, and she's said yes. When she calls me with the news I tell her I'm thrilled for her. Because that's the appropriate response, and she seems so happy about it.

Actually to me the whole concept of marriage is even more alarming than falling in love. I don't want to have to spend my precious life doing everything I can to make sure the man I've married doesn't leave me. Looking at Rupert and Charlotte holding hands under the chandelier, I try to imagine what it might be like to be able to trust someone completely. But I can't. I try to picture myself having children. But I can't. It does occur to me that it might be nice, one day, to produce children with someone. Children that come from you. And him.

But first you have to find the "him."

And in my case, if you want to know anything about the people whose DNA your children would share, you have to find the "her" as well.

The party is excruciating, but I've promised Charlotte I'll behave myself and stay as long as I can stand it. The girls are all called Fiona and spend the evening drinking Pimm's and eating warm prunes wrapped in bacon, talking about Becks, Kate Moss, and Princess Diana, who one of the Fionas' mothers shared a dormitory with at West Heath School.

"Mum says she wasn't shy at all! She was really bossy! She used to refuse to dole out pudding to people who didn't kowtow to her."

"Prince Charles will make a fabulous king," Fiona says. "He's sooooo funny. I heard him give a speech once, at school. He flew down onto the games field in his red helicopter—very glam. And his opening line—wait for it, Fiona—was 'I hope you infants enjoy your infancy as much as we adults enjoy our adultery.' We all thought it was very daring, considering Camilla and everything."

Aching with boredom, I leave as soon as I can and run home to eat chocolate, have a bath, and read my book.

Everyone knows that law, don't they? It applies to the job you've been waiting to hear about, the phone call you've been waiting for from the boy you're obsessed by. Apparently it applies to the letter from the adoption agency you came from too. The moment you stop thinking about it, *plop*, there it comes.

It's been five long weeks since I made the phone call, and I've just finished savoring the chocolate sludge at the bottom of a glass of Nesquik—when I pick up the pile of mail and see the airmail envelope from America.

Inside is a letter, yellow with age, dated April 25, 1978, the day before I was born. My heart leaps when I see the handwriting, which slopes energetically to the right, with the *f*'s and the *p*'s curling down past the next line and back up again. Some people might have trouble deciphering it. But I won't. The handwriting that covers the paper looks very like mine.

All identifying information has been deleted, but, in my trembling hands, I hold my first ever communication from the woman who gave me life.

April 25 1978

Dear ███,

You're not due for another three weeks, but they've put me in the hospital anyway and they're making me lie down. Generally I hate to stay still, but I don't really mind today because my feet have been aching so. I've swollen everywhere, and I look like a ball.

I hope you get my skin, because I'm famous for having soft, smooth white skin. That's because I've never been in the sun without a hat. Not ever. Today my skin feels like leather, but that's just water retention. As far as my feet are concerned, well, Mother says her feet grew a size with each child. Mine feel like they've grown to a size ten.

They keep talking in hushed voices, and I don't know why. They just brought me a tray and a pen and a paper and said they wanted some information about me to give to you after you're born.

Mother insisted on getting me a private room. She said she thought it would be easier than sharing a room with a woman who's keeping her child.

I need to try and stick to the facts because they say it's important for you to know the facts. They say they're going to black out any information that will enable you to identify me.

It's hard to concentrate because the nurse keeps coming in and taking my blood pressure, but I'll do my best.

Let me try to tell you a bit about myself. My name is ███. I was born in ███. You're a direct descendent of ███, honey, so you're descended from ███, who, as you may know, played an important part in forming ███. Daddy's a very successful businessman, and Mother came from a highly cultured, musical family. She's very creative and beautiful, but not an organized person. Daddy always used to say, "Honey, you can't walk across a room without leaving a trail of litter behind you."

I have lots of interests. Most of all I love music, writing and art. Mother is a painter, and her mother was a wonderful piano player and the daughter of a composer.

My dream is to work with artists in some way. I'd like to maybe own my own art gallery one day. I'm interested in a lot of things and don't see why I should do just one.

I always thought that I'd marry when I was about thirty, and then have children and write or paint from home. Then I met your father.

Ours has been the kind of love you read about in books. The kind of love that is far too powerful to resist. He's asked me to marry him. And there's nothing I'd like more. I've told him that I will marry him but only if, first of all, he tries to make things work with his wife.

And we can't start a marriage with the handicap of a child.

The next two paragraphs have been blacked out.

One week later.

You started to come as I was writing. They put me under, so I didn't feel anything at all. When I came round they told me they nearly lost me. And you.

Something achingly sad happened when you were born, my sweet baby. They won't let me tell you about it here. I hope to be able to tell you about it in person one day.

Even though your father and I could not be together, we love each other as much as it is possible for one human being to love another. There isn't time to tell you everything. I have to give this to them before I sign the papers. But know, always know, you were the product of a great love.

██ came to the hospital and I saw him through the glass standing in the corridor, holding you in his arms so tight. He was crying and telling you something I couldn't hear. And it looked like you were listening to him closely.

Then they brought you to me and they had to hold me up so I could hold you. I'd lost a lot of blood and I was still weak. And you were tiny. And fierce. And you had red hair, all spiky, standing up straight, like a little baby bird.

I believe that the most important thing for a woman is to be engaged in work she loves, surrounded by people she loves. Please know there will always be room in my heart for you.

They tell me a couple who cannot have children of their own are coming for you now. This brings me peace.

I stare down at the paper and then up at the reflection of myself in the mirror on the back of my bedroom door. I see a young woman with a pale face, large green eyes, and long, wet, unbrushed copper hair. She is naked—apart from a towel wrapped around her bottom half.

She's holding a letter. Her cheeks are wet with tears, and her body is shaking. We stand there, the young woman and I, staring at each other, for what seems like an age.

Then the young woman and I smile ever so slightly, still shaking, still rooted to the spot, and speak together, in perfect unison.

"Blimey," we say, at exactly the same time.

Chapter Seven

I READ THE LETTER OVER AND OVER AGAIN. Even though she wrote most of it before I was born, and she doesn't even know me, I feel understood. Connected. To my own kind. "I believe that the most important thing for a woman is to be engaged in work she loves. I believe that the most important thing . . ."

I haven't done work I love in seven years, since I was twenty-one, just out of university, when I tried to write a play. The moment I had written a rough first draft, I rushed home to Little Tew and, over a Sunday lunch of roast lamb, roast potatoes, Brussels sprouts, rhubarb crumble, and custard, I told Mum and Dad that I had found my true vocation. I just knew it. I was going to be a writer.

"What have you actually written?" Dad said, eyebrows raised, cutting into a piece of Brie with military precision.

"Loads of things, Dad. Poems, plays, music. I'm writing a play at the moment," I said.

"What's it about?"

"Well, it's a two-handed comedy-drama, set in a womb," I said, thrilled that he'd asked. "I've got all sorts of ideas for the next draft. It's going to include a lot of satire. About politics."

Despite—or perhaps because of—his top-notch education, Dad has never been a supporter of the Conservative Party in England. He's not really a Labour Party supporter either. He thinks all politicians are crooks and says so whenever a politician appears on the telly, regardless of whether or not there's anyone else in the room.

"Lots of people want to be artists," Dad said. "They end up disillusioned and broke. Even the talented ones. Look at poor Van Gogh!"

Sometimes I really wonder.

"I haven't shown it to anybody yet," I said, taking my play out of a plastic blue and white Tesco's bag and handing it to Dad. "You will be the first."

I knew that when Mum and Dad read the play later that night, they would understand that playwriting was something I was meant to do.

The next morning I went downstairs to the kitchen at 10:05. Time for Mum and Dad to take their milky coffees out of the microwave. *Ping* went the microwave. Up Mum got. I waited for her to put a spoon of Nescafé into each mug, one with sugar, one without. Then I came to the point.

"I've decided to go on the dole, so I can devote myself to my writing."

"Don't be ridiculous!" Dad said, not looking up from his crossword.

"I'm not being ridiculous!" I said. "If I go on the dole for a month I can take the time I need to finish the play. Then I can submit it to the BBC."

Dad stopped doing his crossword and looked up at me, utterly perplexed.

"But your play is set in someone's tummy!"

"It's set in a womb, Dad. Not a tummy."

"No one's going to want to pay good money to sit in a theater for an hour and a half looking at someone's tummy!"

"It probably won't have a set."

"No set!"

Mum and Dad looked at each other.

"What would the BBC pay, anyway? If they did accept something like this."

I had no idea. "Two thousand pounds," I said, plucking a figure out of the air. "And that's just to develop it! If it becomes a television play I'd get much more."

"And how long could you live on that?"

It was the end of the conversation. Or it was supposed to be. Dad picked up the *Peaseminster Post* and started reading. Mum started putting the dishes away. I got up to help.

"Oh, Pip," Mum said, "how many times do I have to tell you? Scrape the remains of the Weetabix into the bin before putting the bowl in the dishwasher."

Mum sounded tired. Of me.

Dad's favorite hobby—after Scottish dancing, crosswords, and Sudoku—is writing letters to the newspaper, complaining about various things. At the time, he was on a crusade against litter.

"They've put up the littering fines in Fenhurst," Dad said. "About time too."

"I wonder if they got your letter?" Mum said.

"Must have done. Now that's the kind of writing that makes a difference," Dad said, looking at me pointedly from behind his half-moon glasses.

I wasn't going to give up. Not this time.

"But did you like the play?" I said. "Did you?"

Mum stifled a sigh. Dad didn't look up from his crossword. Mum turned to me with candor in her pale blue eyes.

"No," Mum said.

"Not really our sort of thing," Dad said. Then he looked up at me impatiently and said, "I like playing golf, but I don't delude myself that I can make a living at it. I spent years doing a job I hated in order to earn the money to do what I wanted to do. It's called *work!*"

I wanted to shout, You don't understand! I'd rather be broke for the rest of my life and spend my life doing something I love than spend my life trapped in a job I hate! It's part of who I am!

But I couldn't. We don't shout in our family. It's just not done.

So I picked the blue and white striped milk jug off the breakfast table and filled with a sudden, irrepressible fury, poured the milk onto
the kitchen table. It splashed off Mum's blue and white checked
tablecloth and onto the floor.

All was quiet, apart from the sound of the dripping milk.

"I'm sorry," I said, finally. Utterly ashamed. "But I just—well—I
just. We just . . . We're so different. Who we are. What we're like in
every way . . . Everything . . . everything's different. I'm different. We
just don't like doing the same things."

Mum and Dad were completely still.

"What do you mean?" Dad said finally. "What don't you like
doing?" He looked like he really wanted to know.

"Scottish dancing, Dad," I said, unable to stop the words from
tumbling out. "I don't like the dancing, or the music. I especially
hate the bagpipes."

"You hate the bagpipes?" Dad said, astonished. To the Scots the
bagpipes are sacred. But the truth was on its way out.

"Yes," I said. "I'd—I'd rather listen to fingernails scraped against
a blackboard!"

Shocked, Dad and I stared at each other from either side of the
kitchen. Charlotte had come down the stairs and was standing stock
still, watching Dad and me. She looked utterly stricken. She followed me to the car.

"You okay, Pip?"

"No," I said, my face crumbling.

"Just go," she said. "I'll talk to them."

And nobody said anything more about it.

But Dad's words about not deluding myself kept ringing louder
and louder in my head until I could no longer hear the voice inside
me that had been urging me to write.

So finally I put my play back in the Tesco's bag and put it in a
box under my bed. And the next day I got a job selling advertising
space over the telephone.

. . .

The night I get the letter from my mother, I take the Tesco's bag out from under the bed again and take the coffee-stained script out for the first time in seven years. After I have read the letter from my mother ten more times, I read my play all the way through.

My mother loved writing too.

With the first flicker of confidence I've felt in years, I start the rewrite I'd planned to make seven years earlier.

When I'm concentrating on something I'm interested in, a bomb could go off in my bedroom and I wouldn't notice.

I stop work at six o'clock in the morning when I fall asleep at my desk, cradling the script in my arms. Not because it's particularly good. But because it's a part of me.

Chapter Eight

IT'S BEEN A MONTH since I got the letter from my mother and told Judy I'd love to meet her, and I have heard nothing. All sorts of unwelcome thoughts have been crashing violently through my brain.

Perhaps my mother called the agency and told them she changed her mind and doesn't want to have anything to do with me. Perhaps she died in a sudden, tragic accident? What if all the papers and files in the agency burned in a fire, before they had the chance to contact her, meaning that I will never, ever find out who she is? Ever?

In my mind she goes from being the most successful business-woman in New York, to being a brilliant playwright, to being a drunk, obese, one-eared artist, disillusioned and broke, lank hair plastered to the side of her face, rolling around in a pile of empty beer bottles, muttering incoherently about how much promise she had in her youth. If only she'd known she would never make it as a writer, she'd have pursued a sensible career selling advertising over the telephone.

I've been going through the motions at work, but my sales fig-ures are at an all-time low, and my boss is less charmed than usual by the origami elephants I make out of yellow Post-it stickers and place in rows along the top of my cubicle.

I make just enough sales to justify my presence there. When my boss is in the other part of the room, I sit in my cubicle, furtively working on my play and dreaming about my mother.

The invisible Judy is the only person in the world who can grant me the key to my identity. Even though my mind is churning and I'm feeling desperate, I know I must be careful not to piss her off. And so, on Friday mornings, when the sales manager meets with the managing director, I call New York, casually, just for a chat, to keep her up to date with what is going on with me.

"Pippa," she says again, rather sternly, "there are only two of us here at post-adoption services, and we're getting more and more requests like yours every day. We will inform your birth mother of your interest in meeting her by letter, as protocol dictates, and we will write that letter as soon as we have time."

"I'm sorry for the inconvenience," I say. "I'm sorry . . . well, in general. I do appreciate your help."

My heart hurts and I stop eating and shake a lot as I wait for Judy to write to the mother who gave me birth.

It's odd how the mind works. Memory, I mean. When you're feeling utterly desperate, and you can't think of what do to, sometimes you remember someone you haven't thought about in ages. And if you're desperate enough, or religious in some way, you'll half-believe that person has come into your head for a reason. And, so, on impulse, you'll get in touch with them again. Which is why I decide to contact Nick.

Nick and I only met a handful of times, when I was twenty-one, but Nick is not the kind of man you forget. Particularly when you connect in the way we did.

But it's not just the memory of our intense mutual attraction that's pulling me to find Nick again now. Or the fact that he's been visiting me in my dreams at night. It's the fact that we share something I've never shared with anyone before.

Now that I might be about to find my mother—well, Nick could be the one person I know who will truly understand.

I google "Bank Global" and learn that Nick's still with them.

Nick's a high-flying international banker. He works in India and the Middle East mostly—and is rarely in one place. But, thanks to the Internet, time differences and schedules no longer stop people reaching out to each other from across the world.

DATE: June 6

TO: NickDevang@bankglobal.net

FROM: pippa-dunn@hotmail.com

Dear Nick,

Hallo. Pippa Dunn here. I know. It's been seven years. How are you? How's the banking business?

I don't know if you remember that I was adopted? Well I've set the ball rolling and am hoping to meet my birth parents. I haven't met anyone else who has done anything like this—apart from you—so thought I'd drop you a line.

I think you met your father soon after you left Oxford. I think meeting your father changed your life. Is that true? Do I remember it right?

One of the only pieces the adoption agency let slip about my mother is that she works with artists. Painters, specifically. Or used to. Are you still painting? If not, why not?

Hope to hear from you. Bye for now, love, Pippa Dunn

Chapter Nine

IN THE TWO MONTHS since I made the first call to Judy, I've been in a daze, treading water, waiting. Needing to get away from London, one glorious Saturday morning in June, I drive down to Peaseminster to spend the weekend with my parents.

Dad stopped smoking when we lived in Singapore. He now considers people who smoke to be unutterably weak and coughs dramatically whenever he thinks he can smell cigarette smoke. This is why he absolutely refuses to set foot in France. This is also why I have to lean two feet out of my bedroom window if I want to smoke a cigarette indoors.

Dad is safely upwind at the bottom of the garden, so I can take a puff of my Silk Cut and inhale deeply before blowing the smoke far away from him. Unfortunately the wind changes. Seconds later, Dad's standing at my bedroom door in his floppy gardening hat, sniffing like a furious beagle. I stub my cigarette out on the wall of the house and pretend to be closing the window.

"Where are they?" Dad says, breathless from having run up the stairs at top speed. "Come on. Where are they?"

He prowls around the room, searching for my cigarettes.

He spies them out on the window ledge.

"Got 'em!" he says. He crushes the packet in his hands. Then he holds them above his head, like he's the Statue of Liberty or something, and says, "I'm going to throw these in the rubbish."

Then he storms out of my room.

Later, I overhear him talking to Mum. They're sitting on the porch. The skylight is open, to let in the sweet summer air. From the room above I can hear everything.

"Ever since Pip decided to go on this ridiculous quest she's fallen to pieces. Did you know she was smoking again?"

"She certainly didn't eat much lunch," Mum says. "And she usually loves Scotch egg."

"It's just an excuse, that's what I think. For not getting on with things. She's completely incomprehensible."

In truth, any understanding Dad ever had of what's important to me ended the day I turned down his invitation to go on a family sailing holiday in Greece when I was eighteen. Mum, Dad, and Charlotte spent three weeks swimming in the sea, sailing from island to island, sunbathing and relaxing on a yacht. I chose to spend the summer playing a troll in a new opera at the Edinburgh Festival, which involved writhing around on the floor in a body suit for a month for no pay.

"She should be building her career in advertising sales! Not airy-fairying about writing letters to America! And what if she doesn't come back? Hmm?" A slight pause and then, "Goodness knows what she'll find."

There's an ominous silence.

"More tea?" Mum says.

More silence.

"Why can't she bloody well leave it alone?"

"I think she would if she could." Mum's voice is calm. "But I don't think she can."

"It's typical bloody Pippa," Dad says. "Drops a bomb and leaves us to deal with the debris."

I can hear Dad stand up and march back into the house.

"Make sure you put the right crossword in the right envelope Alasdair," Mum calls after him. "You don't want to send the *Times* crossword off to the *Independent*!"

My parents still laugh at the memory of Dad's Great Crossword Sending Mistake six years earlier. He's been sending the *Times* crossword off to the weekly competition for fourteen years. So far he's won a bottle of olive oil and two tickets to *The Pirates of Penzance*. It made him very happy and I understand why perfectly. How I wish he could at least try to understand me.

The hum of the swimming pool heater reaches me through the porch window.

"And what if she doesn't come back? Hmm?"

The guilt is heavy and thick and instant. I want to run to Dad and reassure him that of course I'll come back. Of course I will. I love him fiercely and always have done. I've just never known how to talk to him honestly about things that really matter.

So it's going to have to be Mum who reassures him. And she will. She's good at that.

As afternoon turns to evening, a light English rain starts to fall.

"Bring the deck chair in from the garden before you go, darling!" Mum says.

I listen to the sound of the raindrops splashing on the corrugated plastic roof of the swimming pool, and when I hear the sound of Dad's car driving away from the house, I get out my secret supply of cigarettes from behind the bookcase and head into the rain.

As I walk up the path to the top of the hill behind Little Tew, I turn my face to the sky. I've always loved the feel of rain on my face. This time it takes me back to my first real rainstorm.

When I was eight years old, we lived a few miles outside Nairobi, Kenya, in a yellow house on loan to us from the embassy. We called it the upside-down house because the bedrooms were downstairs and the kitchen and dining room were upstairs. We had a cook, and an ayah, and a day guard, and a night guard. It was during the few years I spent with Mum and Dad before boarding school.

One Saturday morning, when I was riding my bicycle to the local shop to spend my weekly pocket money on a giant bar of Cadbury's Fruit and Nut and a *Bunty*, I met a little Kikuyu girl called Agnes. She was about my age and height, with a round, shiny face and hair braided in a hundred little braids. I thought she was beautiful. When she learned that we lived opposite each other, she invited me to come and visit her at any time, and I said I would. Agnes lived in a hut made out of leaves and sticks, in the banana plantation on the other side of the dirt road from our house.

The drought was unusually long that year, and there wasn't a green blade of grass or leaf in sight. All you could see along the murum roads was brown dirt and, occasionally, a dead or dying animal.

Charlotte and Mum had taken to lying down in the heat of the day. On the day the rains finally hit they were asleep in their respective bedrooms, with the ceiling fans whirring above them.

I didn't ever want to lie down, in case I missed something. A dung beetle pushing dirt laboriously up the hill behind the kitchen door. A chameleon scuttling up the pawpaw tree, stopping suddenly on a leaf, and turning yellow. The cat on the wall, trying to catch lizards.

That afternoon, I stood on the veranda, looking up at the darkening sky. The wind was strong, and black and blue clouds were blocking the sun. I was watching the skies the moment they broke for the first time in months, with a violent crash. Lightning and thunder tore through the air, and torrential rain came pouring down, suddenly, on the hard, dry ground.

Rain like this is incredibly loud and hits the ground like long silver bullets. I just had to feel it against my skin, so I ran outside, held out my arms, and threw back my head. As the hard raindrops hit my skin, I marveled at how different they felt from English rain, which, to me, seemed insipid by comparison. Then I heard drums beating and music coming from the direction of the banana plantation, where Agnes lived.

I ran down the long dirt drive to the bottom of our property, across the road and up the path that led to the banana plantation. Agnes had pointed her hut out to me many times. I knew it was

the third tallest hut from the left. The music was coming from that
direction, so I headed straight for it.

As I ran toward the music, I saw Agnes and what must have been
her entire family dancing together in the rain. They wore rows and
rows of orange, blue, red, and yellow beads around their necks, and
brightly colored cloths, and they were holding one another's hands
and dancing and shouting with joy. Agnes's face was thrown back so
she could drink the rain, just like I had, and she was laughing with
the others.

When she saw me standing completely drenched in my yellow
sundress and flip-flops, she held out her hands. Before I knew it
I was dancing with Agnes and the others—children, grown-ups—
about twenty people with open faces, who welcomed me with much
laughter. And we all danced in the rain, in a big circle, Agnes, her
family, and me.

"It is called a rain dance!" Agnes said.

The drum beat faster and faster and I whirled faster and faster. I
had never felt so free or so alive.

After about half an hour, we stopped dancing and sat under
the eaves of one of the huts. Agnes had taken my wet clothes and
wrapped me in a rough orange cloth, which smelled of must and
dung. I know that might sound unpleasant, but it wasn't. The combination of cloth and dung smelled sweet.

Agnes sat me down and started braiding my hair in tiny little
plaits, just like hers. Several children stood around touching my
hair.

"Ngumba santi mtoto mari!" they said. "Her hair is made of red
and gold."

I was sitting on a wooden stool eating a banana, Agnes's swift
hands working on the last of my braids, when I heard my mother's
voice.

"Pippa! Pippa!" There was Mum, her blond hair tied neatly back
in a black velvet scrunchy, completely dry, thanks to the large black
umbrella a worried-looking Juma was holding over her.

"Here Mummy!" I said, waving at her. "Come and meet everybody! I'm over here!"

In perfect Swahili, Mum graciously thanked Agnes for looking after me. Then she grabbed me by the hand and pulled me away from my new friends.

Later, much later, after I'd been given a hot bath, scrubbed down, lectured for hours about not going off on my own, and sent to bed, I heard my parents' voices, hushed and low.

"Charlotte would never go off like that and play with the Africans. Charlotte is perfectly happy indoors, playing Snap and drinking mango juice with the Morton-Pecks. You know how much I love Pip," Mum was saying. "But sometimes—well, sometimes I just don't understand her at all."

The crickets were high pitched and cricketing away at top volume. I heard a howl in the night. And more rain. Then my mother's voice, clear and matter-of-fact, seemed to echo throughout the house.

"You don't know what you're getting when you adopt a child."

Twenty years later, the English rain is still cold and light and it still spits. As I walk to the top of the hill behind Little Tew and look out over Peaseminster, with its dark gray cathedral and tidy little houses nestled in the valley below, my tears mingle with the rain.

That night I get an e-mail from Nick.

DATE: June 14
TO: pippa-dunn@hotmail.com
FROM: NickDevang@bankglobal.net

Dear Pippa,

So there you are. I've been wondering when you would resurface. I knew you would. Odd that it should happen now, at a time when I am clawing my way out of the very dark place I've been stuck in for the past year, cut off from the part of me that makes me feel alive, my ability to paint in shreds.

I was lying on the floor, literally and metaphorically, when your e-mail arrived, written in the dead of your night, which I have just reread again in the dead of mine. And I find I am able to pull myself up from the floor and think, for the first time in weeks, of something other than the agony within me.

Namely, you.

At last. There is movement in the air.

You remember correctly. I did indeed meet my father for the first time when I was an adult. It did, indeed, change everything.

I hope your meeting with your parents casts you out of all safe places and into the great adventure that should be your life.

I'm here whenever you need me.

Love, Nick

SUMMER

Chapter Ten

I'VE BECOME TWO PEOPLE. When I go to work or to the shops to buy food and cigarettes, I chat cheerfully to people as usual. I talk to my friends and family as if there's nothing going on.

The rest of the time, I sit in my room with the curtains drawn, waiting for the agency to call. When I sleep, I dream fitfully of a woman whose face I can only half see.

And then, finally, three months after it all began, the phone rings.

"I have spoken to your mother," Judy says. "She is delighted."

"Really?" I say, my heart filling instantly with pure joy.

"Yes."

She is delighted! The joy is coupled with an enormous sense of relief that the tortuous waiting period is finally over.

"She said the news couldn't have come at a better time. She's in Georgia, to be with her father, who is dying of cancer. And it's her greatest hope you will be able to come and meet him before he passes away."

Georgia? And—oh! Her father is dying. My poor mother.

"Uh—should I call her, or should she call me?" My hand is shaking.

There's a pause on the other end of the line.

Then: "Oh, I can't give you her number."

"Can you give her mine?"

"Oh no."

What cruelty is this?

"Why not? I mean, you've just told me she wants to meet me before my grandfather dies, so . . ."

"It's the law."

"What law?"

"Adoption law in the United States. It is against the law for me to give you identifying information. It is against the law for me to give you her name. If you want the information, you'll have to petition the courts."

"Well, how long will that take?"

"It could take years."

Years? I can't wait years!

"Well, if I write to her, will you send on a letter? Please?"

"Yes, but we will need to remove any identifying information."

I want to shout in frustration, but I dare not. Judy holds all the power.

"What can I call her?"

Judy's voice softens.

"You can call her by her nickname. You can call her Billie."

I can't move. I lie on my bed, shaking. I can call her by her nickname. I can call her Billie. Billie, Billie, Billie.

My hand is shaking. I start to write.

July 5

Dear Billie,

Thank you so much for your letter you wrote just before I was born.

Unfortunately it took longer than you would expect to be delivered—twenty-eight years actually—but you can't rely on the postal service these days . . .

I can't say that.

any parents, the good ones do what's best for the kids, and they're trying to get the records opened. The ones who are fighting to keep the records closed are scared."

"Of what?"

"Losing their kids to the birth parents."

"But I'm—they're—not looking for a replacement mother! They just need to know who they came from! I mean in my case—well, nothing can take away the fact that Mum and Dad are my parents."

"It's not just some of the adoptive parents," Pete says. "It's also the Catholic Church. They're deliberately distorting the facts. They know that in the states where records are open, abortion rates have actually dropped, but they pretend it's the other way around."

"But why would the Church do that?"

Pete's laugh is tempered by something else.

"Some say the bishops are nervous that priests who have been birth fathers will be in a whole lot of trouble if the birth mothers are found. Not just the bishops, either. There's a lot of more-moral-than-thou political types who'd look pretty bad if the adoption records were opened. Find the birth mothers and that leads to the name of the fathers."

Of course.

"America is full of adopted kids who will die earlier than necessary because they're being stopped from finding out the truth about their own medical histories. Heck, it makes me mad!"

"Yes," I say, "I can see that."

The injustice of it takes me away from myself for a moment as I listen to this low American voice talking to me from the other side of the Atlantic Ocean, in the middle of the country from which I came.

"And the crazy thing—the thing the people in power and the people who make money from adoption are trying to keep quiet— is that ninety-eight percent of birth mothers actually want to be found!"

"There's a relief!" I say. I'm sipping a cup of Darjeeling tea. My head is spinning as I try to take all of this in.

"The two percent of birth mothers who don't want to be found—well, they have the same right as any other American citizen to take out an injunction if they don't want contact."

My heart tightens at the thought of it. My God. Treating an adopted person who just wants to meet her mother like a stalker would be the greatest cruelty of all.

"I'm a Christian," Pete says. "I read the Bible. And it says in the Bible, right there, clear, pure and simple: 'The truth shall set you free.'"

After I hang up the phone, his last words ring in my head as I drift into the first full night's sleep I've had in weeks: "They think they're doing God's work in keeping you and your mother apart. But really they're doing the work of the devil."

Chapter Eleven

I'M NOT GOING TO WRITE what happened next, bit by bit. I could go into great detail, describing the trembling that just won't stop, not even when Pete calls giving me Billie's details, telling me he's given her mine. The standing in the middle of the room unable to move. The whirlwind in my head. All that.

People don't want to know about the darkest bits, do they? They don't want to know about the banshees dancing like furry black demons through your dreams in the night.

I will say this: It nearly kills me, the waiting. The uncertainty. The fear that she will change her mind.

But I'd rather write about the elation when she sends me an e-mail. Finally, at last, for the first time in twenty-eight years, I know who, and where, and how she is.

DATE: July 25
TO: pippa-dunn@hotmail.com
FROM: BillieP@earthlink.net

Dear Daughter,

I named you Courtney when you were a tiny baby in my arms. Pete says they renamed you Pepper? It's hard for me to think of you as anything other than Courtney, after so many years picturing you as Courtney, but I'll do my best.

I am trying hard to hold myself down long enough to write to you, but it's hard, honey. I have a daughter! How blessed I feel! How full! How healed! I am so excited I can hardly breathe. This kind of excitement used to take me over when I was your age. It gets easier, I promise. People of our nature have difficulty in concentrating for a long time when we're going through something intense—and this certainly qualifies as intense!

I have longed for this moment my whole life, and now it's finally here I feel so happy I'm going to have to be careful not to expire of ecstasy.

It sounds as if your creativity knows no bounds! Writing plays, playing the piano, singing! I used to be an art agent, but I was spending all my time dealing with contracts. I wanted to work with the artists themselves, nurturing their talent, helping them be everything they could, and so I left the mainstream art world and set up a company called Art Buddies to do just that! We're growing steadily and have already helped launch the careers of some very successful people. As you can imagine, when I learned that you had written a play, I was all the way to thrilled.

I have one son—Ralph—by my husband. He's nineteen years old and will be thrilled to meet you.

I am fifty years old (which you must know) and I have never in my life received a message as welcome as the one that you have arrived in a state of readiness to meet me. I am here to be near my father. "Here" is a very beautiful spot in the Blue Ridge mountains of north Georgia. Other than the fact that the cancer's only giving him two months or so to live, your grandfather is in fine fettle. Into the midst of all the sadness I feel at losing my beloved father, comes you.

Oh Courtney, if you could come before he passes, it would mean so much to him, and to me. Would you come here? Before Daddy dies?

Please put me out of my misery and just come.

With all my love, Mother xxxx

There is only one person with whom I feel I can share what I feel when I read this letter.

DATE: July 25
TO: NickDevang@bankglobal.net
FROM: pippa-dunn@hotmail.com

Dear Nick,

She's alive and well and wants me to come and see her. I can't eat. I can't sleep. There's a whirlwind in my head, circling round and round at top speed. I wish, wish, wish it would stop.

I feel numb, then joyful, then afraid. I can't move. Help me.

And, because on this night everything is falling into place, he writes back immediately.

DATE: July 25
TO: pippa-dunn@hotmail.com
FROM: NickDevang@bankglobal.net

Pippa, hang in. Once I had made the decision to find him, I had no peace until I was able to actually touch the phantom father I'd longed for all my life. Only then could he move out of my imagination and become real.

Go to her. As soon as you can. I'll be thinking of you during the day, and no doubt dreaming of you at night as you embark on your adventure.

Let me leave you with a few lines from Ayn Rand, if I may:

"I'm waiting."

"For what?"

"My kind of people."

"What kind is that?" . . .

"I can tell my kind of people by their faces. By something in their faces."

Chapter Twelve

ONE OF THE PROBLEMS for a girl meeting her mother for the first time as a fully grown adult is what to wear. Billie's the owner of a company. I don't want to put her off. So the next day—another rainy London day—I go to Laura Ashley, where I settle on the dark blue dress with the white lace collar, as per Charlotte's suggestion.

When I get home, I find Mum in my kitchen. She has been at the flat all day, throwing out stale food, washing and ironing my clothes, and cleaning dirty ashtrays. Unspeakable chaos has been transformed into order.

I'm so grateful, for a moment I can't speak.

Mum's wearing the shiny plastic apron she gave me for Christmas, which she must have found at the bottom of my cupboard. It's got a bowl of fruit on it.

"Oh, darling," Mum says. "You're absolutely soaking wet. Don't you have a raincoat?"

"I couldn't find it, and I was running late, so . . ."

"It was under the bed," she says, "I hung it up. You can wear it tomorrow if it's still raining. Oh, darling. Come in, for goodness sake."

I don't move. My throat aches with the strain of trying not to cry. I know this thing I have to do is hard for her, whatever she says.

"I'm so sorry, Mum, about the birth mother thing," I say finally. "I'm sorry I have to do it. You do know it doesn't mean I don't love you, you do know that, don't you?"

I long to hug my mother, but I know she won't like that. She's wearing her light blue cashmere jumper, and I'm dripping all over the rug.

Mum goes to the airing cupboard, gets out one of the towels she folded an hour before, and hands it to me. Then she goes into the kitchen, puts on the kettle, and takes out the roast chicken she's cooking in the oven. Hugged or not, I feel calmed by her presence, and I eat my first full meal in days.

"You did this when you were a baby, you know," Mum says.

"What?"

"You stopped eating."

"Really?"

"Yes. Soon after you were born. They took you to a foster home, because they weren't sure you'd make it. Apparently there had been some sort of trauma at your birth, and you were reacting badly, and they didn't want to give us a baby that might die, because it could be upsetting. It was probably nothing. You know how dramatic the Americans can be."

I smile. So does she.

"Anyway, for whatever reason, they took you to a foster home and said we could either wait for you or apply for another baby if we preferred."

"God, I'm glad you didn't take them up on that!"

"So am I, darling." Mum smiles at me and pats my hand across the table.

We sit quietly for a moment. I've never heard this story before. I don't want her to stop talking.

"What was the trauma, Mum?"

"They wouldn't tell us," Mum says. "Only that it was life-threatening. We didn't feel it was our place to ask what happened. I told Mrs. Dillard that we would take our chances, and she said that in that case I could go and visit you at the foster home. I went every day."

"What was the home like?"

"Small. And there were several babies, all lying in cots in the same room. I think the foster mother, who was very nice, had rather too many babies to look after, so she didn't have time to pick you up much."

It's dark outside now. The English rain is drizzling into the plant pot containing a long-dead cactus. The Abbey bell rings. The fridge hums.

"When I first saw you, you were all scrunched up and you looked as nervous as I was. You were so tiny, and I felt so big, and I had no idea what to do with you. But when I did pick you up, it felt quite natural, and we both calmed down."

Just like today. I look across at the still, kind, wise face of the mother I've known all my life, and my heart hurts.

"I went to the foster home every day after that, and fed you your bottle, and you'd stare at me while you were drinking your milk. I told you that everything was going to be all right, and you hung on to my finger for dear life.

"Each day, when it was time for me to leave, I gave you a little kiss. And you clung to me, and I held your tiny heart against mine and felt it calming down until you fell asleep. Then I'd lay you down in your cot, creep quietly away, and come back at the same time the next day. The foster-care people said your condition started to improve after I started coming to visit you. Within six weeks you were home and our new family had begun."

As Mum talks, she's a young woman again. She's not with me in the kitchen. She's with the baby that was.

"Once a week, Deidre Martin, Sally Thorne, and the other expat wives would get together at somebody's house and have tea. You wouldn't let anyone pick you up except me, you know! Once I left you with Deidre while I popped out for five minutes. You were so cross, you turned blue and were sick all over the Dutch ambassador's wife."

Her laugh is clear and young. I laugh too.

"But then," she says, "on your first birthday, something happened, for no reason I could ascertain. It was as if, after weighing everything up, you decided that the world was a safe place after all, and you stopped fussing and clinging whenever I went out and simply decided to be happy. You were a very easy child after that, and not just with me, with everybody."

I ache with love for this woman I can't quite reach. Mum and Charlotte have always managed to click quite naturally. But not Mum and me. Perhaps it's because Charlotte grew in her tummy and I didn't. I don't know.

"Darling," she says, "nothing can affect our feelings for each other, whatever happens."

We don't say "I love you" in England. Not like the Americans do. I think the British find it embarrassing, generally speaking.

Right now I wish Mum and I were American so I could tell her I love her. Straight. Just like that. But we're not. And Mum would hate it. So I don't.

"The woman at the agency said I should take it slowly, not jump in."

"Nonsense!" Mum says. "You're a jumper! Just like at the swimming pool. You've always preferred to plunge right in." In some ways she knows me better than anyone.

I don't say anything—we both know that she and Charlotte pussyfoot around the sides of swimming pools that are eighty-five degrees, dipping their toes in and out, taking half an hour to get in up to their waists.

I grin at her. She smiles back. She looks sad, for a moment.

I rise and scrape the chicken bone off my plate. Mum puts on a pair of plastic yellow washing-up gloves, picks up the Fairy Liquid, and starts on the dishes. I dry and put them away in the cupboard. When we're finished, there's no clutter to be seen. The kitchen looks cleaner than it has in months, and I am greatly comforted by it.

Chapter Thirteen

FIVE DAYS LATER, Dad is driving at top speed down the narrow country roads that, after an hour or so, will lead to the M25 and Heathrow Airport. He doesn't speak. Mum is reminding me to keep my passport zipped inside my purse, so it doesn't get stolen, like it did when I came back from Rajasthan.

Dad switches on Radio 4. Libby Purves is interviewing a man who crossed the North Pole on his own.

"Must have been bloody cold," Dad says.

"Yes," Mum says.

We whiz past the post office in Pease Pottage, where I used to buy large round sherbet lollipops that lasted for hours.

"I might hate her," I say.

"Libby Purves?" Mum says.

"No, Mum," I say. "Billie."

"Nonsense," Mum says. "Of course you won't hate her."

Libby Purves's end-of-program theme tune fills the car.

"I hope Marjory stops patting you on the back," I say, trying to make a joke of it. Ever since Mum told her friends at the sewing club that I was about to meet my birth mother, people have been cornering her in odd places and asking in low tones if Mum's "all right."

Mum's voice has an unusual edge to it. "I think it's best if we don't tell anybody else. Do you know, Jilly actually came up to me in Waitrose and said, 'You've been a terrific mother to Pippa, she'll be back.' I wanted to clock her!"

I need some fresh air. I open the window a crack.

"Don't open the window!" Dad says. "You'll let the cool air out!"

Dad's finally bought a car with air-conditioning.

"Sorry." I close the window again. Hedges, trees, green fields with cows and sheep in them seem to zoom past the window, like a film in fast-forward.

"Everybody seems to think I'm feeling hurt and rejected," Mum says. "Including you, Pippa. But I'm not! Honestly, darling. I'm not. You need to go and do this. You're in a terrible muddle, and if going to find this woman helps you sort this muddle out, I'm all for it. Besides, you're only going for two weeks! You traveled around India for six months!"

"Sssssh!" Dad says. "I want to hear the cricket!"

If you think cricket is dull on television, try listening to it on the radio. Mum and I shut up anyway.

The plane is delayed, so Mum, Dad, and I sit at the airport drinking lukewarm tea from Burger King cardboard cups. A man lights up in the smoking section, twenty feet away. Dad wrinkles his nose and coughs, loudly.

"Alasdair!" Mum warns.

It's too late. Dad's up and moving. He marches over to the smoking section, heads straight for the young man with a crew cut, cigarette, and face that looks like a bulldog, and says, "Can't you point that thing in the other direction? We're choking in here!"

The man is capable of knocking Dad into the next room. Instead, a kind of miracle happens and he stubs out his cigarette.

Then, as if it's news, Dad barks, "Don't you know those things cause cancer?" and marches triumphantly back to our table.

We drink half our tea and then carry my bags over to the check-in counter. My squashy red suitcase bursts open as soon as I put it down.

"For God's sake, Pippa," Dad says. "How many times have I told you? If you pack your suitcase too full, the zip will break!"

"Never mind, Dad," I say, in a merry voice. Rummaging about in the bag I bring out a pair of striped tights. "These'll do the trick." I tie the tights around the bag and lift it back onto the scale.

Mum takes Dad aside and talks to him quietly.

Fifteen minutes later, we're standing at the customs gate on opposite sides of the metal barrier.

I turn to Mum, kiss her on the cheek, and pat her on the back. I can't speak. She responds by kissing me on the cheek, patting me on the back, and saying, "Good luck, darling."

Dad is trying to smile. He reaches into the pocket of his maroon shirt with the lion on it and, patting me on the shoulder, hands me a bar of Cadbury's Fruit and Nut chocolate. "Here you are," he says.

"Thanks, Dad."

"It's for the flight, darling." Dad's voice is gentle. "And Pippadee," he says, "try not to eat it all at once."

His eyes are twinkling and he's smiling now. He knows the chances of the chocolate bar lasting for more than ten minutes after take-off are nil. I smile back.

"Thanks, Dad."

With a lump in my throat, I sling my handbag over my shoulder. I turn around to blow them a kiss, but they're already walking toward the car park, with their arms criss-crossed behind each other's backs.

I watch them go. They're so happy with each other, Mum and Dad. They only met four times before they got married, and they're still happily married after thirty-four years.

Lasting love. Isn't that what everyone longs for?

I once asked Dad if he thought he and Mum are soul mates. It amused him immensely. He doesn't believe in soul mates.

But I do. And I hope, more than anything, that the journey I have just embarked on will somehow make it possible for me to recognize and truly love mine. I find myself thinking about Nick as I head toward the plane.

• • •

I met Nick in the summer of 1999. Neville had somehow made Steeplehurst School's first eleven cricket team and Mum, Dad, Charlotte, and I were summoned to cheer him on.

Women in lovely dresses and large English hats sat on blankets, next to wicker picnic hampers and teenaged boys in scarlet uniforms, devouring Marmite and cress sandwiches, with the crusts cut off. And sponge finger biscuits with strawberries and cream.

I get restless if I have to sit still for too long, so after a respectable amount of time, I took off my shoes and my hat and headed off on my own down the path to the left of the ivy-covered school building that has housed the sons of Britain's most privileged families for generations.

I walked past a lush green field and into a wood. I passed a stream with a waterfall on one side and green bracken and endless bluebells on the other.

Through a gap in the trees I noticed a man leaning against a fence on the other side of the wood. I watched him put out a cigarette as he stared out at an empty paddock. He was wearing an expensive-looking brown leather jacket and a pair of blue jeans, and he was about thirty or so. I was wearing what Charlotte called my "wood nymph dress"—a light, sleeveless green cotton number, with a swirly skirt, which I liked because it was soft and comfy.

I walked up to the fence he was leaning over and leaned over it with him.

"Hallo," I said.

The man was shockingly handsome, with dark skin that made me wonder if he might be half Indian. He was taller than me, and when he stood up straight, he held himself with absolute confidence, like a prince. He had an extra energy coming out of him that made it hard to look away. There was something about him that I recognized, I wasn't sure what.

I bent down, picked a buttercup from the thick green grass at our feet, and handed it to him.

He took the buttercup in one hand and smiled. Then, without saying a word, he lifted my chin, cupping my face with the palm of his other hand, and stared at me. I couldn't look away.

"You do like butter," he said finally. I was surprised to hear that his accent was as English as mine. He was holding the buttercup under my chin. I couldn't move.

If he had been anyone else, I would have said something witty and pulled away. But I couldn't. It's hard to explain, but it felt as if the man could see me. All of me. And I wanted to lay my face in his palm and rest it there, breathing in the smell of him.

"Who are you?" he said, finally.

"I'm Pippa," I said.

I couldn't think of anything else to say. I couldn't stop looking at him.

Slowly, he bent down and kissed me on the mouth. His lips were soft at first, and he tasted of Polos.

And then the kiss, which began gently, became something else. Within seconds my body was pressed hard against this complete stranger who I somehow knew. I wanted to make love with him for hours. The rest of the world had already gone away.

His arm was pressing hard against the small of my back. He was leading me toward the trees, and I was going with him.

And then I wasn't.

If I let myself love a man like this, surrounded by bluebells, in the wood, I knew I would experience the greatest passion I had ever known. But that kind of connection could only bring heartbreak when he left me, as a man like this inevitably would. And that would destroy me. I needed to protect myself. And so I did.

I managed to pull away from him. I managed to hide everything I was feeling. I managed to step aside, tap my watch, smile, and—giving the impression that I was amused, but indifferent—walk back through the woods to the safety of what I knew.

A shot of adrenaline hits me as I walk onto the plane. I wonder

again if this journey to meet Billie will finally free me to love someone at a level that's soul deep. Without any kind of fear.

An hour later, I curl up under my blanket on seat 23B and pretend to be asleep. These are the last eight hours of my life as I know
it, and I must savor them.

Chapter Fourteen

I AM HIT BY A WAVE of intense heat and humidity as I step across the gap between the air-conditioned plane and the air-conditioned terminal building at JFK. These are my first footsteps in America, and I am taking them toward my mother.

After twenty-eight years, it isn't the agonizing red tape, or the guilt, or comments like "But why would you want to *do* something like this? Did you have a bad adoption?" that brings me closest to breaking point. It's something as mundane as a delayed suitcase at the airport.

My mother is less than forty feet away, and my luggage doesn't come through and doesn't come through. I watch every other passenger pick up their bags and head toward the exit. Mine still doesn't come through. I try taking deep breaths to calm myself down, but it doesn't work. I'm terrified my bag will take so long she'll think I changed my mind about coming.

I leave my body. I'm watching myself from afar. I'm wearing a baseball cap with my hair pulled through the back as identification. It doesn't exactly go with the Laura Ashley dress, but Charlotte isn't around to be upset by this. I watch myself, waiting to pounce at the first sight of my luggage, like an impatient hawk.

Finally, a red squashy bag tied together with a pair of tights comes bumping through the hatch. I watch myself run toward it and walk at top speed toward the gate.

As I walk through customs, and the final barrier between us comes down, I return to my body again. The adrenaline has subsided. Nothing can stop us now.

A tall, extremely pretty woman with short, curly strawberry-blond hair is waving enthusiastically at me from amid a five-foot-deep wall of men holding up taxi signs. From a distance she looks about thirty-five. She's wearing a T-shirt and overalls.

Now she's coming toward me at top speed.

Now she's standing in front of me. Her perfume is strong and sweet. She's got a gorgeous smile and the whitest teeth I've ever seen.

First she says, "You didn't need the hat."

Then she says, "My God. I didn't expect this! You look exactly like your father."

"Thanks," I say, grinning. "I travel all this way, across the years, and the first thing you say to me is that I look like a fifty-year-old man."

Billie laughs loud and long.

"That, dear daughter, is exactly the kind of thing your father would say."

Her accent is soft and pretty, and sounds even more southern than it did during our one brief phone call. I like it.

Billie picks up one of the handles of my bag and, with me holding the other handle, starts walking quickly toward the gate. "We've got to hurry," she says. "I overshot temporary parking and parked the car in the tow-away zone."

She catches sight of the tights holding my bag together.

"Pantyhose tied around your bag!" she says. "What a brilliant use of your resources!"

She gets it. We grin at each other.

We arrive at her red Chevrolet seconds before the traffic cop, who shakes his head and waves his pad and pencil at us as if to say "Next time!"

Billie ignores him and looks at me.

"Same eyes as your father," she's saying, shaking her head. "I didn't expect this."

We climb into her car. And I do mean climb. Not having been in America since I was a baby, I don't yet know that, in America, a car you don't have to climb into is probably French.

When the engine turns on, so does the music, at top volume. I know it well.

"The Bach fugues," I say, surprised.

"Yes," she says. "They help me think. They've done research. People of our nature are real right-brained; it's good for us to listen to Bach. It helps us develop our left."

People of our nature. At last.

The lady at the exit barrier smiles at us and we head out onto the road that leads north from JFK to Adler-on-Hudson, where Billie has lived for the past twenty years.

I'm thinking: She's real. And she's here. I can reach over and touch her if I want. She's not a phantom anymore. Oh Nick, I tell him in my heart, I know what you meant.

I watch my hands at the end of her arms turning the steering wheel.

"Your brother Ralphie wanted to come with me, but I said, 'No, honey, this is something I need to do on my own. I waited until he turned eighteen before I told him about you. Weird, that you should show up less than a year later."

"Yes."

I have never heard the word "weird" uttered by anyone over the age of eleven before.

While talking, Billie looks at me and then back at the road and whoops loudly. "Honey, I did not expect this! You look like your father in a Laura Ashley dress!" And then she laughs. It's my laugh, coming out of someone else.

Billie turns to the right, at top speed, down a big American freeway. She drives even faster than Dad, and that's saying something.

"Ralphie spent the whole day vacuuming in your honor. He's never picked up a vacuum before in his life."

We drive for an hour, my long-lost-mother-now-found. And me. By the time we turn off Route 10, we're the only car on a country road with enormous trees on either side of it. Billie tells me we're going to spend the night at her house in Adler-on-Hudson. I'll meet Ralphie, and then tomorrow we'll hit the road for Georgia.

People love to ask, "Yes, but how did you *feel* when you met your birth mother?" And they clearly expect a satisfying answer.

The truth is, I went completely numb. People do go numb, I've been told, when they're in shock. In order to protect themselves from the intensity of what they're feeling.

So what feelings was the numbness protecting me from? Part of me is hoping that as I finally tell the truth about all of this—the truth that has been trapped inside me for years—somehow I'll be able to figure it out.

There are people who don't want me to tell the truth about any of this. There's a lot at stake. But you can't stop the truth from coming out, any more than you can stop kin from finding kin.

There's a natural law with secrets. It's the same law that applies to kettles. If you block the ventilation hole, there will, eventually, be an explosion.

Chapter Fifteen

Billie's house is made of dark wood and is built on stilts. It looks out over the Hudson River. You could park a car in the garage under the house, if it wasn't full of furniture, a motorbike, and other stuff Billie's bought from garage sales over the years. Collecting other people's junk is obviously genetic. I've been shopping from the boots of people's cars for years.

If you're English you'll know all about the car boot sale. If you're not, a car boot sale is exactly the same as the garage sale, only the secondhand Tupperware is sold from the trunk of someone's car, in a remote field, by English people—standing next to dozens of other English people—drinking cups of tea from plastic Thermos flasks in the pouring rain.

"We're here!" Billie's voice rings out loud and strong.

At the top of the steep staircase leading to the sitting room is a young man in torn jeans and a black T-shirt, with long blond hair tied back in a ponytail. He doesn't look remotely like me, but I like his face. He's smoking a cigarette. He's my brother Ralph.

"My God!" I say. "I have never ever walked upon such a clean carpet in my life!"

He's got a sweet, high laugh. Quite different from Billie's and mine.

"So, Ralphie, do you think she looks like me?" Billie says.

"Kinda—without the hat," Ralph says, smiling. "But then I

don't look a whole lot like you either. You must have weak genes, Mom!"

"Ralphie's father plays the cello," Billie says. "He ran off with a violinist when Ralphie was five. I raised Ralphie on my own. But we've done okay, haven't we, Ralphie?"

"I've got the coolest mom on earth," Ralph says. He picks up the bags. "I'll just take these to your room."

Sitting rooms in England are usually filled with antique furniture: old drapes, carpets handed down from generation to generation. When I walk up the stairs and turn left into Billie's sitting room, I am struck immediately by the fact that everything—and I mean everything—looks new. By new I mean modern, by which I mean as if it's been bought within the past fifty years.

At the center of the sitting room is a cream-colored leather couch, a beige rug, and a large square glass table. To my astonishment—nay, delight—I note that her home is as messy as mine.

A furry blue sweater with a cat on it is thrown over a chair, one shoe is at one end of the couch, another on the floor. The room is cluttered with piles of newspapers, magazines, books, coffee mugs, ashtrays, cigarettes, and, in an oddly shaped rose vase, a small bunch of purple flowers.

"Those are pretty," I say.

"Mary brought them for you. She lives down the road. She's a recluse, and her son's a kleptomaniac, but she's just wonderful with flowers."

I'd be willing to bet that a sentence like that has never been uttered in England.

Hanging on all the walls are original paintings. Some of people, some of plants, all vivid, remarkable in their own way.

"These are from my art-dealing days," she says. "Here's the Marfil! Oh that was a heady time, discovering Marfil! The whole of New York was talking about it."

She told me she worked with artists, but I didn't know she discovered one of the greatest artists of our time. I can't wait to tell Nick.

While Billie makes us some coffee, I stare at a print of Marfil's most famous painting, hanging above her piano. It's a small oil painting of an old woman walking down the streets of New York. She has a craggy face and bright blue eyes that penetrate my soul. I've seen the painting hundreds of times before; I'd found it so compelling I hung it on my bedroom wall at university. How amazing to find out that my own mother was partially responsible for getting it there.

Nick was right. There's magic in the air.

I read an article, framed, on the wall leading to the kitchen, about Billie. It talks about how she first met Marfil, then a street painter. The article says Billie had a gut feeling about him, knew he was a great artist and felt she just had to do something about it. And so she beat down doors until people took notice. Then she became a well-known art dealer. "After that," Billie says quietly, "I became an alcoholic and dropped out of the game."

"People drink for all kinds of reasons," she says. "Mainly because it's in the blood. In my case, after years of therapy, I came to realize I was drinking to drown out my grief." Then, "Losing you was real, real hard, honey."

I look over at her. There are tears in her eyes. I find myself responding instantly and instinctively by crossing the room and hugging her.

"I'm so sorry," I say. She hugs me back. She doesn't smell of alcohol. She smells of sweet perfume.

"What sort of drink do you—er—drink?" I say, finally.

"I haven't touched a drop of alcohol in eleven years," she says.

"Oh good," I say.

"I take it one day at a time," she says.

"How sensible," I say. We laugh as we pull away.

Soon the adrenaline is back. I'm looking at another painting I know. Only this time it's mine. It's the forest painting I was thrown out of art class for drawing again and again. I've been doodling it on telephone pads ever since. The leaves are orange and green, and in the rain forest scene in front of me they look like teardrops. They're my leaves. Bursting across a canvas, in a sitting room on the other side of the world. Almost legible, in the bottom right corner, are the initials ND.

"Who's ND?" I ask.

"Your grandmother," Billie says. "That was one of hers."

"Was she a painter?"

"She didn't start painting till she was forty. She always got so into her work, she was scared that if she started before we were old enough to be left on our own, she wouldn't notice if one of us kids fell off a ladder or something. It's called hyperfocus. It's in my nature, too, and probably in yours. It's common in artistic types."

I come from artistic types. My heart soars.

"Is your mother still alive?"

"Yes. And no." Billie's movements are quick, like my own. In under three seconds she's left the room and come back into it, lighting an unusually thin cigarette with a sparkly pink lighter.

"Mother has Alzheimer's now."

"Oh. I'm so sorry."

"Turns out it's got its advantages," she says. "Each time I tell her you've found me, she's all the way to thrilled."

I smile with her. "What was she like before—well, you know . . . ?"

"Real creative and beautiful, and she just adored your father. But, as I told you in my letter, she was not an organized person. Most highly creative people are that way. Einstein used to leave his house wearing odd socks. God, who'd want to be neat!"

I start to grin again. She's everything I dreamed she would be. And she thinks I'm wonderful too. I tell her about the rain forest I drew again and again at school, and for years afterward. Billie listens intently.

"Honey," Billie's voice is low and quivering with intensity, "you're highly intuitive. It's not something to be scared of. It's a gift. Mother has the gift. I always swear your father does too. Just make sure you trust your instincts and let them lead."

I try to picture Mum, Dad, or Charlotte telling someone to "trust their instincts," but I can't. I try to picture Mum, Dad, or Charlotte moving across a room as fast as Billie is now, but I can't.

Billie brings out a photo album and tells me about each and every relative. I've never seen anyone related to me by blood before, and I stare, fascinated, at photographs of strangers who look like me.

Chapter Sixteen

B Y NINE IN THE EVENING we're sitting on the sofa in Billie's bedroom eating chocolate chips out of a bowl. I've been up for nearly twenty-four hours but I'm wide awake. Billie tells me we're descendents of Governor McKay of Georgia, and about her childhood, growing up in Georgia. Her happiest childhood memories are of long summers spent on her grandfather's estate, where she and her brother and sisters would run wild through cotton fields and drink sodas from their grandfather's soda fountain.

For half a second I remember my own happiest childhood memories—camping in the Serengeti, getting up at six o'clock in the morning to see the hippopotami in the river, making mud pies with Charlotte in the African bush. Then Billie's voice brings me back.

The unhappiest moments of Billie's childhood took place at dinnertime when her parents were fighting. Billie's mother was the daughter of a composer, who loved musicals and her father. Her father was a successful businessman, and an alcoholic.

"When he'd had nothing to drink, Daddy was one of the most intelligent, enjoyable men I have ever known; after even one really stiff drink he became belligerent and cruel. It runs in the family," she says again. "Alcoholism."

"Oh."

Billie is looking at me in a significant sort of way.

"I don't drink," I say. "I'd rather have a glass of chocolate milk than anything else. I've never liked the taste of alcohol much."

"That doesn't mean you're not an alcoholic," Billie says.

The phone rings. Billie picks it up, slipping seamlessly from her role as long-lost mother to businesswoman. As she talks, I pick up the bowl of chocolate morsels, put it on my lap, and drink in every detail of Billie's room.

On the wall behind the headboard of her bed are four bookshelves with hundreds of books I am not at all familiar with. My bookshelf in London is filled with the complete works of Jane Austen, Ibsen, Strindberg, and A. A. Milne. The titles on Billie's bookshelf range from *Do What You Love, the Money Will Follow* to *You Mean I'm Not Lazy, Stupid or Crazy?! A Self-Help Book for Adults with A.D.D.*

As soon as Billie is off the phone, she continues talking as if there has been no interruption. She tells me she was twenty-two when her father left her mother for his secretary, to whom he is still married. Later the same year, Billie met Walt. Something in the way she says the name "Walt," with a slight lilt to her already musical voice, tells me this is important.

"I was interviewing for a job in New York City, and Daddy called saying he was going to be in town, and did I want to go with him to hear this incredible new speaker, Walt Markham, who was speaking for the young conservatives? I was a rabid young conservative myself at that time—oh, don't look so horrified!"

"A young *conservative*?"

"It's okay, honey," she laughs, "I became a libertarian later. But at that time . . . well, I wanted to change the world. And so when I heard your father speaking—well, he was so charismatic and I was just blown away by him, and I said, 'Daddy, I have to meet this man.' And when I did—oh."

She takes another handful of chocolate morsels and turns her back to me, looking out over the river. With the light from the Adler Bridge behind her, in profile, she looks breathtakingly beautiful.

"He was tall and handsome as all get-out, with thick copper-red hair, just like yours and so full of life. Oh, honey . . ." She turns toward me now. There are tears in her eyes. "Your father was, without a doubt, the most exciting man I had ever met."

I can see the memory is causing her pain. I wish I could soothe her, but I can tell she doesn't want me to interrupt.

"We knew what we were doing was wrong, and we tried to stay apart, but we just couldn't. He was married. He had a child. His wife's name was Margaret."

Her face changes for a second. There's something tough underneath the softness of her tone. "Walt and I recognized each other, honey. We knew we were meant to be together. We could not be in the same room without touching each other."

I think of Nick.

Then Billie looks at me for a long moment with tears in her eyes and says, "Your father was a very athletic lover, honey."

At a moment like this, most Brits will look away, change the subject, and/or head straight for the kettle. But Billie has me mesmerized. I have a feeling she knows this. Her voice is low again. Husky.

"We saw each other as often as we could for almost a year. That time in my life was the most wonderful, and the most terrible."

Billie seems lost in the memory. "Granddaddy cut me out of his will, of course. Up until then he'd always loved me the best, but this . . ." Billie looks too sad to speak. Eventually she sits down next to me.

"I'm sorry it was all so hard for you," I say, reaching for her hand.

The lights from the cars crossing the Adler Bridge half a mile away hit the mirror above her dresser. Her voice is soft and sweet. "It was hard. Very. But we got through it. And now—well, we get to meet you as an adult. How fascinating is that? We knew you'd be special beyond belief. You do have our genes." She reaches out and tucks a strand of hair behind my ear. "And you are special," she says. "You are, you are."

I like being called "special beyond belief." That, too, could never happen in England.

For a moment Billie looks exactly like the young Billie, the one in the painting on the wall behind her. Twenty-eight years have gone by but she doesn't seem to have changed. A few lines around her mouth and at the corners of her eyes perhaps. An extra ten pounds or so. Nothing more.

Billie's black cat, whose name is Heathcliffe, has come into the room. He slinks over to Billie. Billie laughs. "Heathcliffe's an under-the-cover cat. He lays his silky body against my chest and kneads me all night long. Isn't that right, Heathcliffe?"

The cat sits on her lap purring loudly as if to say, She's mine.

"Are you still in touch with Walt?" I say, not ready to change the subject.

Billie's hand is moving across Heathcliffe's body with long, steady strokes.

"Oh yes," she says. "I hear from him every year. On your birthday."

A warmth spreads instantly across my chest. I picture my father, picking up his phone faithfully, every April 26, calling the love of his life. And wondering about me.

"We talk every year. Hoping you'll come and find us. 'How could she not?' we say to each other, 'with our genes?'" Billie takes my hand this time. "And now here you are."

"Have you told him yet?"

She looks at me. Her voice is soft. "Not yet, honey."

Up until this point I hadn't given my father much thought. Everything was about finding my mother. Up until this point.

"Do you know how to find him?"

Silence in the room.

"Do you know how to find him?" I say again.

Billie smiles at me.

"Honey, we've both had a long day, and I'm real tired, I've got to

go to bed. Why don't you have a hot bath in *my* bathtub? Now there's
a treat." And she leads me to her bathroom, which smells of perfume
and other sweet things. The towels are purple and red. There are rose
pink light bulbs all the way around her bathroom mirror.

"Look!" she says, holding up a bottle. "I got you some *foam!*"
She pours several capfuls into the bath and then she's gone.

After saying good night to Billie, I put on my pajamas and knock
on Ralph's door. He's playing the guitar and smoking a joint.

"Want some?" he says.

"No thanks," I say. "I don't."

Ralphie looks at me blankly.

"Someone gave me some bad stuff at university once. It turned
out to be opium. Everything went blurry and I got totally paranoid.
Worst of all I couldn't feel my nose. Haven't touched it since."

"Your nose?" he says.

"No," I say, laughing. "Pot."

There's a pause. "You know you said your mom was the coolest
mom in the world?"

I'm careful to pronounce it "mom" rather than "mum." And I'm
careful to refer to Billie as *his* mom. I don't want him thinking I've
come to take her away from him.

"What kind of cool things did she do?"

Ralph takes another drag from his joint. He's thin and looks as
if he hasn't been out in the sun for a long time.

"Well, she never got on my case about things, like other moms,
you know? Like she never forced me to go to bed at eight o'clock and
stuff. She's never, like, interfered or cramped my style in any way.
You know what I mean?"

"I think so," I say, sitting on his black comforter and accepting
one of his Marlboro Lights.

"Would you play me a song?" I say.

Ralph looks pleased, as is my intention, and plays me a song by
Steely Dan. I try to look as though I enjoy it, but I don't really. I

prefer musicals to just about any other kind of music. Except Rach-maninoff, of course.

But it's not the time to break this news to my newfound kin, so after clapping enthusiastically I go to my room, just down the corridor from Ralphie's, lie down on the daybed that's been made up for me, and fall into a restless sleep.

Chapter Seventeen

I WAKE UP EARLY and pad upstairs. No one seems to be around, so I open the wall-to-wall sliding glass doors that lead out of Billie's sitting room and on to her wooden deck. The Hudson River is black and wide, the air above it humid and thick. Trees far taller than any I've seen in England line the banks.

I can hear Billie talking on the phone.

"It's like falling in love!" she's saying to whoever's on the other end of the line. "And I feel so healed!"

As I look out over the river, tears crawl down my cheeks. I don't have anything to wipe them away with apart from my sleeve.

Later on, I go into Billie's office and dial Mum and Dad's number. It's one thirty in England. Mum and Dad will be sitting at the kitchen table, having a mini Kit Kat and a post-lunch cup of coffee before taking their afternoon nap.

"Hallo, Mum," I say.

"Darling! Alasdair! Quick, it's Pip!" I hear Dad run into the sitting room and pick up the other phone.

"This has got to be quick because it's Billie's bill—lots of *b*'s there." I try to make my laugh sound natural. "I just wanted you to know I got here safely."

"Good."

"Good."

There's a pause.

"Our voices are overlapping I think."

"Sorry, yes." There's a pause.

"Good flight?" Dad says.

"Yes."

"Good film?"

I don't want to tell them that I couldn't possibly concentrate on a film, so I say, *"Mrs. Henderson Presents."*

"That is a good one," Dad says.

"Judi Dench," Mum says.

"Yes."

There's a crackle on the line. Mum's voice now, faint and far away.

"I'd better go now," I say, feeling tears welling up again. "Can't hear you very well. Bye Mum, bye Dad."

"So glad everything's all right!"

"Yes Mum," I say. "Everything's fine."

I put down the phone. Billie is standing at the door in a pair of shorts and a green T-shirt with little gold sequins on it.

"I hope you don't mind," I say. "I just wanted to let Mum and Dad know I'm here safely."

"That's fine, honey." She's distracted, looking for her purse.

"Here," I say, taking ten dollars out of my pocket. "This is to cover the cost of the call."

"Put it on the dashboard of the car, honey. We can use it to pay the tolls. Now, you go get the cat box, and I'll call the cat."

"Heathcliffe!" she calls from her front steps. "Heathcliffe!" The image of Emily Brontë's Cathy on the Yorkshire moors passes through my mind, as it is no doubt supposed to. Billie's laugh joins mine as the cat trots dutifully in.

"Is he coming with us?"

"Of course, honey!" she says. "He *lives* to be close to me."

I marvel at the fact that Billie clearly thinks nothing of traveling the eight hundred plus miles between Adler and north Georgia on a regular basis. A twenty-mile drive is considered long-distance in England.

She picks the cat up and puts the black, green-eyed feline into the car.

"Does he sit in the cat box?"

"Oh no, honey," Billie says. "Heathcliffe likes to be able to see out of the window when we're on the road."

I climb into Billie's car, delighted by the eccentricity of it. We do what we want to do, regardless of whether or not it's the norm— Billie, Heathcliffe, and me.

For someone used to driving around an overcrowded island in a Renault 5, there's something very exciting about being on a big American road, in a big American car. I'm so high up, I can see everything.

So can Heathcliffe, who sits atop a bed of cushions, between Billie and me, next to the coffee holder. Back straight, he looks like a little sphinx.

"The key to not getting caught while speeding, my dear daughter? Get yourself a radar detector, drive behind the fastest car on the road, and never speed past clusters of trees, 'cause that's where the cops hide."

We pass the International House of Pancakes, which is an intriguing name, when you think about it, whatever nationality you are. And we pass the Wise Trading Company, outside of which I am appropriately horrified to see a sign offering cash for guns.

"You can't just walk into a shop and buy a gun in England," I tell Billie. "If the British want to kill someone, we have to put on uniforms, invade another country, and call it a war. Either that or go to a football game and beat the crap out of the French."

Billie can't reply because she's holding the ticket for the tollbooth between her teeth and scrabbling about in the glove compartment for some change.

I've never used a tollbooth before, and Billie lets me throw the change into the basket. When I miss, I have to get out of the car, pick up the coins, and put them in by hand, but I don't mind. I've never done this before and it's fun.

I have chocolate around my mouth and have spilled some on my T-shirt. I look over at Billie. She has done the same.

As we drive, Billie tells me all about her love life, her sex life, her brilliant career, her recovery from alcoholism, and the reason she never travels anywhere without a vibrator. "Regular orgasms are essential for people of our nature," she says. "It helps us relax."

I sit next to her feeling conventional and dull in comparison, but hopeful too. Billie is my mother after all. She leads such an interesting life. Perhaps mine will turn out to be interesting too.

Once over the Virginia border, four hours into our journey, we stop at a roadside café. The diner has almost no one in it.

A woman with ink-black hair piled high on her head and long blue fingernails comes over to our table.

"My name's Connie and I'll be your waitress today," she says.

"Pleased to meet you, Connie," I say, holding out my hand.

"Well, listen to that accent!" she says. "I just love it! Where are you from?"

She's so excited when I tell her I'm from England she knocks over the milk.

"It's okay," Billie and I say in unison. "We're spillers too."

We all roar with laughter.

Connie brings us our all-day breakfast within five minutes.

"Can you cook the eggs a little longer?" Billie says.

"Sure," Connie says.

The British would rather risk salmonella poisoning than do something as embarrassing as sending a plate of food back to the kitchen. I'm astonished to note that Connie doesn't mind at all.

"I just love England," Connie says, putting the new plate in front of Billie. "The movies. The books. Mrs. Slocum. All those buildings being so old!"

"Indeed," I say.

"How come your accents are so different if she's your mother?"

"Well," I say, unable to resist. I take a bite out of what the Americans call a biscuit and the British call a scone, look Connie directly in the eye, and pause for dramatic effect. Then I say, "She gave me up for adoption when I was a baby, but we were reunited yesterday." Connie clasps her hands to her mouth and gasps.

"Praise the Lord!" Connie says. "Bernie! Carly! Come hear this!"

I glance at Billie, who is as pleased as I am to be creating such a commotion.

A huge man in a stained white shirt comes out, holding a plate of grits and eggs, sunny-side up, swimming in grease, followed by a tiny woman in a faded floral dress and apron. They stand by our table, staring at us, riveted by our tale.

"Was your adoptive mother jealous?" Connie asks, when we're done.

I hesitate for a second. I've never thought of Mum as my "adoptive" mother before.

"Was she?" Connie is saying. "Your adoptive mother, was she jealous?"

"I don't know," I say, drawing my hands into my lap.

"Bet she was!"

"Course she was!" Bernie chimes in. "Had to be! Why, look at you two! You look so alike! Apart from the hair, of course. Does she get her hair from the father?" he says, turning to Billie. And then, to me, "You got your dad's hair?"

Billie is enjoying herself immensely.

"I love that you think she looks like me too! The more I look at her, the more I see it. Oh, yes! She has her dad's hair. It was just like hers. Only shorter, of course."

Dad doesn't have red hair. He has white hair.

"Hey, Betty Sue," Connie calls to the other waitress, who is setting a table across the room. "Ain't that what happened to Mary Lynn? Got knocked up by a married guy, had a kid. Didn't her sister raise it?"

"Sure did," Betty Sue calls back.

"No one in your family could take her, huh?"

Billie is busy mopping the gravy up with what's left of her biscuit. I suspect she's pretending not to hear the question. Poor Billie. Why should she be judged by these strangers in a highway diner?

"Oh, Billie did the right thing," I step in quickly. "I've had a wonderful upbringing. A wonderful life."

"And now you're back home." Connie has tears in her eyes. "Well, c'mere." I'm made to stand up. Connie's mighty arms pull me to her ample bosom and hold me there.

We eat for free on the road to Georgia.

Chapter Eighteen

BILLIE'S CABIN ON BUCK MOUNTAIN, Georgia, is twenty miles from the nearest shop. You get to the sitting room through the deck, from which you can look out over the mountains and a huge front lawn that has seen better days.

Billie tells me that my grandfather saw the land from the air one day, while flying one of his little planes, and fell in love with it. After building himself a log cabin, which he calls his "getaway place," he built this house for Billie right next to it. Billie says it was his way of giving her some of his money before he died and "it all got into the hands of my greedy stepmother."

It's a wild but peaceful spot. I spend most of the evening sitting in a large bamboo chair on Billie's deck, with Heathcliffe on my chest purring loudly. The air is cool, sweetened by the flowers growing wild in the uncut grass. The evening light fades to a soft orange and yellow, while Billie chats away about our genetic ancestors and the *fact* that creative talent is in the genes.

"Honey!!!" Billie's voice wakes me suddenly at eight o'clock the next morning. "It's time to meet your grandfather! Hurry! He's here!"

I leap out of bed, throw on a dress and my Marks and Spencer cardigan, and run out to the deck. A silver Lincoln purrs up the narrow white drive and stops next to the creek. Out comes a tall old man wearing buckled boots, black pants, a black suede jacket with long tassels, and a big black cowboy hat that hides his face. He moves slowly toward the house. Halfway up the steps to the sitting room, he lifts the hat and looks up at me. His face is old and white and his eyes are startlingly blue, and full of laughter.

"Hallo, Granddaughter," he says. "How's the queen today?" He speaks slowly. His voice is resonant and southern and I feel like I've heard it before.

"Well," I say, "last time I spoke to her she had a bunion."

He stops walking.

"And where is this bunion?" he asks, poker-faced.

"On her left foot," I say solemnly. "But it's doing better now. I'll tell the queen you asked after her."

He walks up the last three steps. Then he holds out his arms and I walk into them. His jacket feels rough against my skin and smells of tobacco. I feel comfortable in his arms.

"How are you?" I say.

"Well, I've only got another three weeks or so to live, but apart from that, I'm fine."

I start to laugh.

"Well, who'd have thought it. My long-lost-grandbaby's got a million-dollar smile," he says, laughing with me.

We walk into the sitting room, arm in arm, my grandfather, Earl Joe Stanford, and I, both of us direct descendents of Governor McKay of Georgia and proud of it. We sit down on the shiny tan leather sofa that stretches L-shaped across half the room, while Billie makes us all a cup of tea. The American way. Which means she sticks three coffee mugs half full of water in the microwave for thirty seconds. Then she dunks the same Lipton tea bag in all three mugs until a nasty brown swirl appears. Then she adds a squidge of lemon and tells us to "come and get it."

If you are English, you will know how I feel about this. If you are not English, let me take this opportunity to tell you how to make a drinkable cup of tea.

First, you warm a teapot. Then you put in tea leaves—Earl Grey,

Lapsang, or Darjeeling, ideally. One teaspoon for each person, and one for the pot. Then you pour in water that has been boiled. In a kettle. After waiting a few minutes for the tea to brew you pour a little milk into the bottom of a teacup. Then, using a tea strainer, you pour in the tea. Then, if you take sugar, you add sugar. Then you drink it.

If you are English and have the misfortune to find yourself drinking tea with an American who has made it incorrectly, you do not give any indication that the tea is anything other than delicious. Instead you say something like what I say to Billie, which is, "Thank you. How lovely. Do you by any chance have any milk?"

When your American watches you pour in the milk and declares that next time she'll put the milk, the sugar, and the tea in the teapot all at the same time, because it'll be so much quicker that way, you do not flinch. Instead you smile, politely, and pretend to drink the mug of tea in front of you. You can't of course, because apart from everything else, the lemon has made the milk curdle. So you pour it down the sink when no one's looking.

"She's got Mother's legs, don't you think, Daddy? And she's got my arms," Billie says.

"And my father's breasts?" I quip.

"Honey, your father had no breasts at all," Billie says, taking me literally. "Mother was flat-chested too, which mean clothes hung on her just beautifully. Which reminds me!"

Billie disappears and comes back in a flash, carrying an electric-blue dress made out of something silky on a hanger.

"This is for you, dear daughter of mine. It was one of Mother's favorites."

She hands me a pair of high-heeled shoes and white silk stockings to go with it. "Try it on," she commands.

I hate trying on clothes as much as I always do whenever Charlotte begs me to try on something of hers. But I go into the bathroom and, alas, it fits. I come out. "Ta da!" Billie says to her father.

"Don't you look just as pretty as a picture! If I were thirty years younger . . ."

"Oh, Daddy," Billie says, with tears in her eyes. "She looks *just* like Mother. Don't you think?"

Earl's voice is soft.

"I do," he says.

"Oh, Daddy!" Billie says, suddenly laughing in delight. "What is Molly Alice going to say when she sees this?"

Chapter Nineteen

DURING THE EARLY AFTERNOONS, while Billie is napping, I walk through the trees to Earl's cabin, to sing to my long-lost-grandfather-now-found, at his request. Unlike Billie's house, Earl's cabin is ordered and clean. Actually it feels a bit like being inside a boat because it's tiny and the walls and floors are made of dark polished wood.

Earl has one of those chairs that recline backward at the touch of a button and are so comfortable you never want to leave. As I sing, he lies in his recliner with his eyes closed, dressed in a pair of white cotton pajamas. Everything about him is white, apart from his toenails, which are yellow with age.

After I've finished singing, I tickle his feet with the long white feather he keeps for that purpose on the shelf by the door.

"Thank you for granting the wishes of a dying man," he says.

I smile. Billie has already told me he's been cajoling people into tickling the soles of his feet with a feather for the past thirty years.

"Now, listen up, Granddaughter," he says. "I want you to remember something." His voice is frail and old, but his eyes are clear.

"You sing like an angel, which confirms my suspicions. You, dear granddaughter, have got the family gift. It's an artistic gift and it comes out in different ways. Your grandmother had it too. I wanted her home, loving me and my family, so I stopped her using that gift.

Hell, I treated her gift like it was her lover, and that was wrong. A little higher now."

The skin on the instep of the feet that have carried my grandfather for eighty years is as smooth as a child's.

"Make sure you use your gift. And don't go and do something stupid like getting married. But if you gotta marry, whatever you do, marry the kind of man who will let you do everything you gotta do."

Someone who understands the artistic spirit. Someone like Nick.

Mum and Dad's parents died in their early seventies. I haven't had grandparents past the age of ten. How I would have loved this man had I known him growing up.

When Billie joins us, our conversation turns to the subject of Earl's wife, Molly Alice. The wife he left Billie's mother for. Billie calls her Malice for short.

"Biggest mistake I ever made," Earl says. "Lost a great secretary and gained a lousy wife."

"Daddy couldn't understand why she was so mean about me until I sent him an article I read, entitled 'When Paranoia Comes Home,'" Billie says. "It makes it much easier to have compassion for her, knowing she's mentally ill. Malice is not going to like Pippa's arrival one bit," Billie says happily.

"Oh dear," I say. "I didn't want my arrival to upset anybody. Maybe I could talk to her and try and help?"

Billie looks at me with a gleam in her eye.

"Now, Daddy, what do you think? 'Course she'll say no if you *ask* her, so why don't you just . . . I know, Daddy! Why don't you take Pippa with you when you go down the mountain and surprise Molly Alice with her?"

Earl shakes his head slowly. Molly Alice's hatred of Billie goes back many years. Seems to me there's a fierce competition going on for Earl's affections, which Billie is winning hands down.

"Weelll," Earl says slowly, "the situation can't get much worse than it is already . . ."

An hour later I am driving Earl down from the mountain.

"It's the right side of the road in America," Earl says. He's gripping the door handle tightly.

"Sorry," I say, hunched up at the wheel, concentrating like mad. "I do know that. It's just that the road is so thin."

I hit a rock.

"Sorry," I say.

We drive past the trees and the mountains, down through Main Street, which looks clean and pretty, with old-fashioned dark yellow traffic lights hanging from a wire above the center of the road. We drive on to Pine Drive and pull up outside a pretty old colonial house painted white and light blue, with a swing on the porch.

"You stay back," Earl says. "And when I signal to you, step forward and give her a hug."

I get out of the car and stand by as a tiny, reed-thin, immaculately dressed woman with jet-black hair scraped off her face in a tight bun hurries out of the house.

"Earl, you're late," she says.

"Well, yes I am, Molly Alice," he says, "but look what kind of a reason I got."

She squints at me. "Who's this?" she says.

"This," my grandfather says, pausing theatrically, "is Pippa Dunn. My granddaughter." She looks blank for a second and then it dawns upon her.

"No! Not Billie's . . . not the one she . . ." Her voice is sharp and thin.

"Yup," says my grandfather, signaling for me to make my move with the arm bent behind his back.

"Which makes me your step-granddaughter," I say, coming toward her and holding out my arms with a smile, waiting for the usual reaction. I'm getting quite fond of being hugged by everyone I meet.

Molly Alice stares at me open-mouthed and just as I reach her, she jumps back.

"Keep away from me," she says. "You just keep away from me!" And then, "What d'you want? The money? That what you come for?"

"Of course not!" I say, horrified. "Of course not!" Apart from anything else, money is never, ever discussed in England.

Earl is a wealthy man, and part of the battle between Billie and her stepmother is over who will inherit that wealth when he dies. I am mortified by the thought that anyone would think I wanted anyone's money.

"I'll be back in a while," Earl says, getting into the driver's seat of his Lincoln. "You two girls have a nice talk now." And suddenly he's gone.

Molly Alice and I watch the dust from the Lincoln settle back on the road and look at each other.

"What you come for?" she says. She's standing on the porch steps, so we're almost the same height. "If it ain't the money, what you come for?" Molly Alice's face is white with fury. "She thinks she's really got me this time, pulling you out at a time like this, her little English trump card." And then, bringing her face an inch away from mine, she says, "Don't you ever forget what they did to you! They abandoned you!"

Along with most English people, I have spent a lifetime perfecting the craft of hiding what I am really feeling, particularly when it's something strong and difficult. But at this moment, my years of training fail me.

"Your mother back home, she's your real mother. Not *her*."

I feel as if I've been punched in the stomach. Suddenly I'm crying.

"I know that!" I say. "Of course Mum's my real mother, I just wanted to find out where I'd come from. I didn't want to hurt anybody."

"Why'd you surprise me like that? Was that her idea? Was it?"

"No," I lie. "It was my idea. It was very immature of me. I'm sorry."

"Well, it was immature," she says. "Don't use your sleeve, I got tissues somewhere here."

She reaches into her handbag and takes out a small packet of Kleenex.

"Thank you," I say, blowing my nose loudly. "I'm sorry," I tell her. "I'm so sorry. This must all be so hard for you, Earl being so ill."

"It's more than hard," she says. "It's more than hard. It's been terrible, living with an alcoholic. Then when he finally stops drinking he gets cancer, then she comes to the mountain and starts doing her usual, making everybody crazy, interfering in people's lives. Ruining people's lives." Her eyes are black with fury.

"Ruining people's lives," she says again. "Make no mistake, she's not a good woman. She'll sweet talk you all right, till you think you're safe, then she'll hurt you real bad. That's what she does. That's what she's always done."

She believes what she is saying. Poor Molly Alice.

"He's only got three weeks, they say. Time's special. He should be with his wife, not up on that mountain with that no-good daughter of his."

During the hour we spend together, which I shall never forget, I watch this strange little woman struggle with her innate good manners and her hatred of my birth mother. I've never seen hatred face to face before. Its hardness disturbs me.

When we're not talking about Billie, Molly Alice seems almost normal. When we are, her eyes narrow, and she tenses and a completely different expression crosses her face. Then she relaxes again.

"Earl Grey?" she says, almost smiling, making the tea the English way, perfectly.

"Thank you," I say.

Silence, apart from the sound of the antique grandfather clock ticking in the corner of her beautifully decorated early American sitting room.

"You had a good life?" she says.

"Oh yes," I say. "I've had a wonderful life. I have wonderful parents who I love dearly."

"Well, I'm glad about that," she says.

"Oh yes," I say, finally on familiar ground and holding a decent cup of tea, to boot. "And we lived in Africa and Hong Kong, and they live in the country, and I have a sister, and we're very happy. I just came to find out where I'd come from, that's all."

"Well," she says, "I can understand that." We sip our tea in unison.

"I'm pro-choice," she says, suddenly. "I marched in the pro-choice rally they had in Mapleville last month. You pro-choice?"

"Oh yes," I say. She still needs reassurance. "If they had pro-choice rallies in England I'd march too, but there it's really not an issue."

"You're prettier than she is," she says as I am leaving. To me Billie is beautiful. But I feel warmed by the compliment.

And then: "You poor child, you don't know who you've found, do you? She's . . ." Her face has tightened again and I am astonished to see what look like tears of pity in her eyes. "She's . . . You poor, poor child . . ."

Chapter Twenty

BILLIE AND I GO OUT BIKING and stop to have a sandwich by a small farm owned by a man who really does make moonshine, just like in the *Dukes of Hazzard*. He's old and gray and gives me a sip from a tin bucket in a small shack with a dirt floor attached to the side of his house. It tastes like turpentine. When we leave his house, Billie starts telling me about her sisters.

"Octavia's three years older than me. She's a poet, I think. Or she might run a store, I'm not sure. We haven't seen her in a couple of years. But I talk to my sister Marcie all the time. She's the one you most resemble. Only she's obese. And a manic-depressive. And she's married to Otis, who's obsessive-compulsive, but he plays the banjo beautifully, and you can't have everything."

"Oh," I say. I saw a film about a manic-depressive once. I can't remember much about it—except the man stood on a rooftop and tried to fly.

"What about your brother?" I say.

"Your Uncle Irv? Well, that's another story. It's not so much that he's mentally ill, he just has an impulsive personality and a serious drinking problem . . . I wish to hell he'd get some help."

"Is he unhappy?"

"Very." We're riding two feet away from each other. I can hear every word, despite the noise of the tires hitting the rocks on the long mountain path.

"The thing that frustrates Daddy so much about it is that Irv had so much. In addition to gifts of intelligence and good looks, Irv has good business sense. He was making more money than he knew what to do with as a financial consultant. I think the real reason he turned to illegal pursuits was because the edge wasn't there."

Illegal pursuits?

"What sort of . . . ?"

"The last time he got into trouble was for masterminding an illegal animal liberation operation. I don't know whether he's been freeing animals recently or not. He probably hasn't. He really hated it in jail."

"He went to jail?"

"Oh, yes. The year the circus came to Dawsonville. He'd have been fine if the lion hadn't torn through town and snacked on that poor little boy."

"When did he get—um—set free from jail?"

"About three years ago. It's really been a long time. I had some hope for him when he came up and visited Daddy at my place a few months ago, but my instinct was 'Don't feel good about this. You'll be disappointed again.' Probably what it is is that he's drinking again."

"Oh."

"Irv is very much the kind of alcoholic who, unless he hits a really low bottom, will never get it right. And even then he may not, because the program is based on honesty. And I just don't think he has the capacity to be honest. They think his kind of personality may be in the genes."

My heart's pounding. I'm thinking of Dad's sister, Auntie Laura, living in her stone house in the south of France. Of the childhood summers we spent there, jumping into bales of hay in the barn, being chased by geese, playing Snap with my cousins who had never heard of manic-depression. Auntie Laura, who won the Florence Nightingale Award for her work as a nurse in Cyprus during the war. And tall, handsome Uncle Magnus, whose bravery won him the Légion d'honneur for rescuing Jewish people from the concentration camps. Uncle Magnus, who taught me how to swat flies and catapult cheese across the table with the cheese scraper. At the big, wooden dinner table, in the stone house which he built himself, in the heart of Provence.

Auntie Laura and Uncle Magnus are my aunt and uncle. Were my aunt and uncle. Are my aunt and uncle.

Billie's voice comes back in again.

"Seeing Irv turn out this way just breaks Daddy's heart. And Daddy has the additional burden of never quite being able to shake the idea that if your kid turns out bad, you didn't raise him right."

We're biking downhill next to the creek that's become so wide it's more like a river.

"Most people who are very sophisticated about parenting, and who have read all the books and studied behavior and so forth and so on, know damn well that you're not responsible for the way your kids turn out."

I don't know if Billie is aware—really aware—of what she's saying, or if she's actually trying to tell me something about myself. But if it's all in the genes, then according to Billie, Mum and Dad and my upbringing had nothing at all to do with who I am.

In that moment, something shifts inside me. Before I know it, I've started biking as fast as I can. I'm hurtling down the mountain at top speed, away, away, away from the stranger who keeps calling me her daughter.

The road is steep and winding, and my head is spinning as fast as the bicycle wheels. I have to get away, I need time to think.

"Honey! You're going too fast! You're going too fast!"

I am going too fast, tearing down the mountain, desperate for just a moment away from the chatter. I don't know what to do, but I know I have to think, I just have to. And then I ride up on the bank next to Deer Lick Creek—the deep part, lying cool and still to the right of the road before me. I jump off my bike and, fully clothed, dive into the water. There's silence under the water. For the first time in almost two weeks, I hear nothing. I come up for air behind a rock. Billie is calling me from the bank.

"Pippa? Where are you? Pippa!"

From behind the reeds, which are tall and green and still, I watch Billie standing on the creek bank. With her hands on her hips, calling for me in her purple shorts and T-shirt, from a distance she looks like an indignant Shirley Temple. The air feels cool against my wet skin.

The sun is setting against the mountain, which has turned blue and orange in the evening light. I duck under the water again. My body feels light. I watch the bubbles from my breath make their way to the surface. I come up for air again and look at her, through the reeds. The sunlight makes her curls look like burnt gold. I feel as if I am looking at her from a long way away.

Where is the sense of peace I've been longing for? Will it come tomorrow?

I look up at the sky. It will be dark soon. I take a deep breath and start walking toward the creek bank.

"Sorry," I say, coming out from behind the reeds.

"What are you doing? Pippa, honey, your shirt's all wet! We don't want the mountain boys looking at your nipples. Here. Put on my sweater."

But I'm already back on my bike and riding off again. This time Billie manages to stay close behind me.

"Let me tell you about the time I wore a shirt that was almost see-through to a Christmas party at the Whitcombs. Daddy nearly had an angina attack . . ."

In England, it's considered polite to wait for somebody to stop talking before you talk yourself.

I've been waiting for the moment when Billie will stop talking and ask me more than the basic facts about my life. So I can tell her all about Mum and Dad and Charlotte and my life in England. And me. But the moment hasn't come. And it doesn't come now, either.

Chapter Twenty-one

THE DAY BEFORE I am to go back to England, I tell Billie I really, really want to speak to my father.

"Well of course you can speak to him any time you want. But—well, we haven't had that long together, just you and me."

"It's been wonderful, Billie. Really it has, it's just that, well, he is my father."

Billie has been vague about the whereabouts of Walt's number ever since I met her. Now she reaches into her poppy red handbag, takes out her address book, and reads Walt's number to me.

"It's his home number on Marsama Beach," she says. "You'll probably get his wife, but she'll know where he is. Why don't I make the call?"

"Please let me," I say to Billie. "Besides, I've got an idea."

Quickly, before she can change her mind, I call Walt's number. A woman's voice answers.

"Hallo," I say, in my most authoritative voice. "My name is Pippa Dunn. I am calling from the BBC." No one would refuse to talk to someone from the BBC. "I'd like to speak to Walt Markham, please." I'm so convincing, I half believe I am from the BBC.

"He's not here," the woman says. She sounds friendly. "He's in Kabul."

"Kabul, Afghanistan?" I say. God, how stupid. Of course Kabul's in Afghanistan. Everyone at the BBC knows that.

"Yes," she says.

"What's he doing there?"

"Well, I don't really know!" she says. She sounds intrigued and curious herself. Like the mother of an adored child who knows her son is in some kind of mischief, but that's just the way he is, and—oh—she'll just have to live with it.

I can tell from the way she speaks that she loves him, and I feel guilty for deceiving her. But the voice inside me is becoming more and more insistent. I need, need, need to meet my father.

"Do you know when he'll be back, Mrs. Markham?"

"Well, you can never be sure with Walt," she says. "It could be weeks."

I can't wait weeks. It would kill me.

"Do you have a number for him in Afghanistan?" I say. "I'm wanting to interview him for an upcoming piece on the World Service."

I pronounce "Afghanistan" with a long *a*, just like someone from the BBC World Service would pronounce "Afghanistan." I half expect to hear "Lillibullero" chiming out behind me. I used to hear it every day, blaring out from Dad's black shortwave radio, announcing the arrival of *News Hour*. He kept the radio next to his bed, no matter which country we were living in.

"I'll go get the number for you," Walt's wife is saying.

When she gives it to me, I thank her and put down the phone.

I jump in the air holding the number. "I've got it Billie! I've got it!"

"Afghanistan?" Billie says.

Before she can raise any objections, I start dialing. Afghanistan is eight and a half hours ahead. It'll be six in the evening in Kabul.

I take a deep breath as I listen to the phone ring. He has to be there. He has to.

In my mind's eye, I can see my long-lost father in a room with a desk and a phone and a tall, dust-covered window, in the heart of downtown Kabul. He's looking out onto a dusty street. There's a boy, kicking a can along a dusty road next to a white boxlike building. And American soldiers and tanks. Everywhere.

Now I can see a telephone on my father's desk, covered with papers. It's ringing now. A faraway sounding ring, but it's definitely ringing. Walt's hand is reaching for the phone.

The line is surprisingly clear. He picks up right on cue, as if I willed it.

"Markham here." The voice is gruff and sounds very American. No matter. He's there.

"Hallo," I say. I swallow. It's all happened so quickly I've had no time to think about what I'll say. I find myself stammering. "Um, my name's Pippa. We—uh—we last met twenty-eight years ago. I was very small."

There's another pause. Then he says, "Oh . . . my . . . God."

And then, shaking, I hand the phone to Billie.

"Walt? It's Billie."

"Oh . . . my . . . God," he says again. I can hear him from two feet away.

"Yes," Billie says softly. "She's finally here."

They're both silent for a second.

Then Billie is talking fast, with lots of excitement, telling him all about how I found her, what we've been doing, everything.

"If I had to describe her in just one word what would it be? Delightful. I've experienced her that way. Everyone who's met her has experienced her that way. And she's beautiful! Yes! I know! And she's got so much energy, and she bounces, Walt, be warned! . . . You heard it? Of course you did."

When Billie speaks again, the pitch of her voice has dropped low. For emphasis, I think. She's mesmerizing when she speaks in a low voice. You can't not listen to her when she does this.

"Walt, honey," she says, "I just hope that when you meet your daughter you don't feel so much you just expire of ecstasy."

Billie is sharing the receiver with me now, so I can hear what Walt is saying.

"I've been fighting the biggest battle of my life. But I'll be leaving soon."

"Are you in any kind of danger?"

"Not at all," Walt says.

"Are you going to tell me anything more about it?"

"I can't. Now put her back on, Billie."

Billie hands me the phone.

I can't say anything. My throat has constricted. The anxious feeling that kept gnawing at me, insisting I connect with Walt, has stopped. The numbness has gone. I'm filled with a sense of utter relief. I'm afraid that if I loosen my grip, he will go away. He doesn't.

"So you've come," he says, finally.

"Yes," I say.

"I will rearrange my flight and fly to London on my way back from Kabul," he says. "I'm almost done here. It shouldn't be long now."

"Good," I say. He's coming to see me. Thank God.

Walt feels the relief I feel. I know he does, because just before he hangs up, during a few seconds of silence between us, I hear Walt exhale. And it sounds like air is being let out of a bicycle tire.

Billie and I talk about Walt long into the night.

"Could he be with the CIA?" I ask.

Billie shakes her head. "There's no knowing with Walt."

The Pippa who left England two weeks earlier would have been shocked and appalled that there's even a possibility that Walt is working for the U.S. government in Afghanistan. But at that moment I don't care what Walt does for a living. I don't even care that he's a conservative—or used to be. I'm just grateful he's safe, and alive, and coming to see me in London.

When I go to his cabin to say good-bye to him the next day, Earl is on his third bowl of Froot Loops. This may or may not have something to do with the fact that he's been smoking marijuana.

"He lost his appetite," Billie says. "So I got him some pot. Everybody knows pot gives you the munchies."

Earl may be eating more than he has in a while, but he looks tired and old and his arms feel like twigs when he hugs me good-bye. As I leave, he looks me directly in the eyes. "Even when you're hurting so bad you can't move, and you will," he says quietly, "welcome the pain, Granddaughter. Because, when it really hurts, when the difficulties are truly difficult . . . What I'm saying is, welcome the difficulties. 'Cause it's them you learn from."

As I sit on the plane, flying from the mother who gave me birth back to the family that raised me, I understand completely how Pandora must have felt. Now the box is open, there can be no closing it again.

Chapter Twenty-two

WHEN I RETURNED FROM AMERICA that August, Mum, Dad, Charlotte, and Rupert were all at Heathrow to meet me. I was so happy to see them, I almost cried. But I stopped myself. I wanted them to think that the visit had brought me the peace of mind I hoped it would.

On the way back home in the car I regaled them with the tale of the man with moonshine and my encounter with Molly Alice, keeping to the periphery.

And then Charlotte asked, "What's she like?"

I couldn't tell them she's fun and creative and thought my striped-tights-around-my-suitcase solution was genius. Or that it felt so right to learn that I had come from a family of artists, or how thrilled I was to learn that she had worked with creative people all her life.

I couldn't tell them that I was longing for some time to be quiet and alone. So I could try to absorb everything that just happened.

And so I said, "Well, she talks a lot. I mean, a lot."

"Hah!" Charlotte said, laughing.

"And she's a terrible cook. And she's very untidy."

I looked at their faces in the car, bursting with love for all of them. "You see, Dad? My untidiness is genetic!"

"That's no excuse," he said sternly.

I smiled, crammed between Charlotte and Rupert in the back-seat.

And then Charlotte and Rupert told me they're moving to Bath.

And Mum and Dad told me how Rupert's little cousin pushed Boris into the swimming pool while I was away. And about how Dad tried to fish Boris out with the swimming pool net and almost drowned him. And all about how Dad and Rupert jumped into the pool fully clothed to rescue him.

I sat back in the car, listening to their voices, knowing that enough had been said. For them, it was done. Over. It was a journey someone they knew and loved went on. And then she came home.

Only I wasn't home. Not at all.

I waited weeks and weeks for my father's visit to London. Until his arrival, nightly e-mails to and from Nick kept me sane.

DATE: September 12
TO: NickDevang@bankglobal.net
FROM: pippa-dunn@hotmail.com

Dear Nick,

You're right. I have been in a daze ever since I got back from Georgia. Pictures of my long-lost relatives balancing spoons at the end of their noses, pouring lemonade in my grandfather's cabin, his prayer before Billie fed us: "Of what we are about to receive, may the Lord make us truly tolerant. Amen."

Something deep within me has clicked into place. I feel ready for full life as opposed to half life.

I've doubted myself for so long. Probably because the essence of who I am is so completely different from the family that raised me. But now—well, I'm finally starting to trust the instincts that told me to find Billie. And Walt.

And then there's you. And the fact that Billie works with artists. And the fact that you long to leave the banking business and become a full-time artist yourself. Tell me more about your paintings.

The end of an English summer. The air is crisp. I have an old gas fire in my room. It's on low. Orange light. Lovely.

Love, Pip

P.S. My mother has told me to ask my father what he remembers about their time together. I asked him. He says he remembers everything, and he's going to tell me when we meet. I hope it will be soon. We speak on the phone every third day or so. He's going to come as soon as he can.

I thought it was supposed to be the other way round. Women remembering everything, men being fuzzy on the details. Which led me to wondering what, if anything, you remember about me?

My heart beat a little faster as I pressed Send. His answer told me everything.

DATE: September 13
TO: pippa-dunn@hotmail.com
FROM: NickDevang@bankglobal.net

Pippa, you intrigue me. You open your soul for a second, so it touches mine. And then you end your letter in a way that reminds me you are also a flesh and blood woman, wanting to know what I remember of you.

What will you think of men now, or of me, when I tell you?

I was half drunk and mildly depressed, leaning against a rail watching an excessively dull game of cricket at Steeplehurst. I was home on leave from Singapore and wondering, as I always did, why I bothered coming back to England when absolutely nothing about it ever changes.

And then I noticed you. You were sitting on a blanket, next to a picnic basket and a woman in an absurdly large hat, trying valiantly not to look as bored as I was. Your hair was long and tied back in a ponytail. It caught the light in a magical way. And your face, which, as you must know, is quite beautiful, took my breath away.

Then I saw you get up and walk toward the woods. I went to school at Steeplehurst for ten years, so I knew you'd come out, eventually, by the paddock. I ran around the school and positioned myself by the fence.

So it wasn't a chance meeting. Clever Nick.

To my delight, you saw me, as I'd hoped you would. The moment you handed me the buttercup I knew you would be an important player in my life. I didn't know how. Or when. Just that you would be.

I could tell you were quick-witted, full of life, and utterly charming. But there was something else there too. Something I recognized. Your eyes gave you away. Even at twenty-one. There was a depth there. A sorrow that I knew you weren't aware of yet. An understanding. An empathy. I knew, the moment I met you, that you were one of the few.

And I knew, from the moment I saw you, that I wanted you. And when you walked away from me, the first time you walked away from me, I felt ripped apart, my love.

Me too, my love.

A month or so later we met by accident outside my building in the City. It was bucketing down with rain, and I was standing with the suits and the umbrellas, waiting for the rain to stop. And there you were, standing outside on the pavement, your head turned toward the rain, completely unselfconscious, without a waterproof, I might add. Whether you knew it or not, you were rebelling against England in general by being completely yourself.

You clearly loved the rain and refused to wear protective clothing just because everybody else was. It made me feel rather stuffy for a moment, watching you standing there, a genuine free spirit, simply not caring about getting wet.

When you saw me you grinned at me.

"Hallo," you said. "Let's have lunch."

"I haven't got any money on me," I said.

"I have," you said.

Then, irresistibly, you took me by the arm and led me to the third floor of the Wong Kei restaurant in Gerrard Street. We were the only non-Chinese in the place. You were a child, but you lit up the room. And even the usually unspeakably rude Wong Kei waiters smiled as you came in.

You took your jacket off, and your shirt was damp with the rain. You were very wet. Your nipples were erect, my love. And so was I. We shared a bowl of roast duck noodle soup and a plate of shrimp lo mein. You paid the bill with great panache, producing a crumpled ten-pound note from your very wet pocket.

Two weeks later, I invited you out, to reciprocate. I treated you to lunch at Boulestin. You made it clear you'd have much preferred to dine at the African restaurant next door—but you tolerated the fifty-pounds-a-dish menu in sumptuous settings as best you could.

That's when we exchanged histories.

"Avoid safe places," I said to you. "They are so very hard to escape from." You seem to be following my advice to the letter.

The next time I saw you, you asked me to bring you some of my paintings, and I did. You were wonderfully encouraging about them and you told me to paint all night if I didn't have time in the day, but paint. I adored you for it. And then you said that, in the unlikely event that you ever came across an art agent, you would make sure to put them in touch with me.

It's true. I had. And I'd meant it. I've always been good at putting people together. I hooked Sally Pearse up with the photographer's rep I met on a plane. She's just had her first exhibition in Paris. And I hooked the president of the Sharton Shipping Company up with an actor friend of Neville's who was fed up with being broke. He made his first million two years ago. With Billie's help, I will try to do the same for Nick. I can't wait to introduce him to Billie. Once you've seen a Nick Devang painting you don't ever forget it.

The next time I met you was in a lovely outdoor pub restaurant near Arundel, I can't remember its name. It was a perfect summer's afternoon. Everybody else had gone, and we were the only people left in the garden. Our table was discreetly placed behind a willow tree. You were wearing a short white skirt, which showed off your ir- resistible legs beautifully. Your hair was down, this time, and catching the light and—God, I wanted you.

You were holding an ice cream in one hand and a cigarette in the other. There was a small piece of ice cream trickling down your neck that I wanted to lick off, before burying my face in your gorgeous bosom. I am not above suggesting such an operation to just about any other woman. But not you. I didn't want to flirt with you. I wanted to kiss you on the mouth again, and so, when you'd finished the ice cream, I did. Gently. Carefully. A brush, no more. So you wouldn't pull away.

Our table settings were close together. There was a large white linen tablecloth over a tiny table, with pink roses in the center of it. I wanted to touch you. I needed to touch you. Unable to bear the tension any longer, sensing you couldn't either, I reached under the tablecloth and put my hand on your leg.

Below the table you were absolutely still.

Above the table, your hands were tearing the tops off packet after packet of artificial sugar and pouring the contents into the ashtray. Then you stopped tearing off the tops of those silly packets of sugar and turned your hauntingly lovely face toward me. I moved my hand farther up your thigh, which was cool and soft and I kissed you again.

Then you opened your eyes and for half a second you let down your guard. And in that half second I saw what you'd been hiding

ever since I first kissed you in the woods. A longing, a passion, the
like of which I've not sensed in a woman before or since.

I had you in that moment. You. Naked, without camouflage. I knew
I did.

"What are we going to do, my love?" I said.

"What do you mean?" you said.

You knew precisely what I meant. You knew. But you were terrified. And I knew why. And so I watched you reach the part of you that
wasn't you. And in a voice that wasn't really yours you said, "Nick,
you've read me wrong."

I'd have felt rejected. I do easily, you know. But I knew you were
lying. And I knew why. It would have been schizophrenic of me not to
empathize. We shared the same pain, you and I. Only you were still
too young to know that old wounds, however painful, can have no
real power unless you give it to them.

And then I let you go by saying, "I'd like to meet you again when
you're thirty." I saw the relief cross your face as I knew it would.
We're frighteningly similar, you and I.

Later, after I'd left London for Singapore, you sent me a letter
telling me that you were going to challenge government corruption by
writing political plays. It was so student-ish of you, so predictable.

I told you I was going into the Year of the Dragon. You then wrote
me a note saying "The rest of the world goes with you into the Year
of the Dragon." It was delightfully done, for a twenty-two-year-old. I
hadn't the heart to spoil things by replying.

And now, here you are again, on the brink of the greatest adventure of your life, writing to me once more. I am honored, my lady.

There aren't many of us around you know. Those of us who were
abandoned and have the courage to go back to our source to face
whatever we find there. I wish you luck in your adventure. You did the
right thing finding me again.

What do I remember about you? Everything.

                                                        Love, Nick

P.S. I've started painting again. Not sure if they're any good. Perhaps your mother would know?

P.P.S. I'd like to leave you with some lines by Pound which he wrote just before he moved to Europe.

> *I am homesick after mine own kind,*
> *Oh, I know that there are folk about me, friendly faces,*
> *But I am homesick after mine own kind . . .*

Nick remembered everything.
And so do I.
Our time is coming. I can feel it. Our kind's time.

FALL

Chapter Twenty-three

WHILE I WAIT FOR WALT, I show up at work, because there I can call Billie and my grandfather courtesy of Drury Lane Publications. But I haven't sold an ad since I got back from America, and my bank balance is getting dangerously low.

I tell my friends and family that the reason I can't see anybody is because I am the sole emotional support for an Australian girl I met traveling, who just returned from Rajasthan with a mysterious, debilitating disease.

But each night, as soon as work is over, I head for the bedroom in my flat as fast as I can and sit, smoking, with the curtains drawn, waiting for Walt's calls.

Walt says e-mail's not safe and that he can only call at certain times. His calls from Afghanistan usually come in the middle of the night.

"This place is a wild, double-dealing, malevolent, ungovernable cesspool," he says. "It's run by a bizarre conglomeration of unimaginably ruthless warlords, tribal chiefs, and religious fanatics. Few Westerners have lived here long enough to fully understand it."

"Are you sure you're safe?" I ask for the umpteenth time.

Walt laughs, as he has every time I've asked that question. I know his laughter is meant to reassure me. And it does. Sort of.

"I'm safer here than I would be crossing the street in Washington, D.C.," Walt says. "I'm surrounded by the U.S. Army."

I picture the huge Americans dressed in heavy combat gear that I've seen on the news surrounding my father, who for some reason, in my mind's eye, is wearing a linen suit and yellow bow tie.

He tells me the battle he's in the middle of fighting has something to do with winning a contract to help rebuild the country. Walt has devoted the last eight months of his life to the project and has invested every penny he has.

"The game's over, kid. You have to pay baksheesh to operate effectively in Afghanistan. But I'm working for a governmental organization, and the U.S. Foreign Corrupt Practices Act prohibits paying bribes. It's a catch-22."

I don't fully understand what he's talking about, but I don't want him to think I'm stupid, so I say, "Oh yes," a lot and hope whatever he's doing allows him to come to London soon.

On November 6, Neville rings my doorbell over and over again.

"Pip? Are you in?" he says.

The kitchen is buried in dirty dishes, cereal packets and empty boxes of Jaffa cakes. If I let him in he'll know something's up.

"No!" I say.

Neville rings the doorbell again.

"All *right*! I'm coming!"

Neville looks unusually dapper tonight, and I'm surprised by how glad I am to see him. So the outside world *is* still there.

"This is bad, even by your standards, Pip," he says, wrinkling his nose at the debris.

"I know."

"Where's the Rajasthani?"

"She's not a Rajasthani! She's an Australian girl just back from Rajasthan."

Great. Now I'm insisting on accuracy regarding the ethnicity of a girl I've completely made up.

"Well, where is she? Under the table? Nope. Under the chair? Nope."

"She's not here!" I say, laughing.

"Good. Then you can come out with me."

Neville can be bossier than Charlotte on a bossy day, and there's no point in arguing with him, so I jump into the first shower I've had in days, throw on my velvet trousers and the only clean blouse I can find, and head out the door.

Looking across the tube at the cousin I love most, I wish I could tell him what's going on inside me. But even if I understood it myself—I don't—I certainly have no idea how to articulate it.

We are headed for Dial a Date, a new bar in the city. Every table has a telephone on it and a number above it. You sit at a table, buying expensive drinks, and telephone people at other tables if you fancy them. We've been there two minutes when the phone at our table rings.

"You've got—let me count here—one call and four people on hold," I say to Neville.

"They're not calling me, you idiot."

I look around me. It's not that the men are bad looking. I just have zero interest in being picked up by anyone at a bar. So I pretend to go to the loo, invite the blonde at table nine to take my place opposite Neville, and spring for a taxi home. So I can lie, curled up by the fire, as I have done every night for the past three weeks, waiting for a call from my father.

That night I get home to Walt's booming American voice on my Ansafone: "Hi there, kid, it's me. I'll be arriving at Heathrow from Kabul at three fifty p.m. tomorrow on Indian Airlines flight twelve fifty-four. Can you be there to meet my plane?"

Chapter Twenty-four

I WEAR MY GREEN MARKS AND SPENCER cardigan with a leotard under it, a knee-length skirt, and a pair of sneakers. I wait at the rail, with the taxi drivers holding up signs for businessmen coming off the flight, which is two hours late. I keep peering at the people coming out at arrivals, adrenaline running wildly. I tell the minicab driver on my left that I'm meeting my father, but I'm not sure that I'll recognize him.

"When was the last time you saw him?"

"When I was five days old."

"That's different," he says. Then he tells me that he's "mightily pissed off" because the plane is late and he wants to get home to his tea.

I'm looking at the entrance when, amidst a stream of chattering Afghanis in long white robes, pushing heavily laden baggage carts, I see a tall man in a dark blue suit headed in my direction. He's pulling a large suitcase. He has a strong, confident presence, and, like Dad, he has a full head of hair. Only Walt's hair isn't white. It's the same color as mine. And he looks like me. I mean, he really looks like me!

He stops and looks at me.

Is it you? I mouth. He nods. Then he stops.

I climb under the rail and run into his outstretched arms, in the middle of the arrivals lane, surrounded by streams of people speaking Arabic. I hug him tight. Here he is, at last.

Instead of the numbness I've felt ever since I met Billie, I suddenly feel very much alive. I know—in my knower—that this is the parent I have been waiting for. Finally. He is here.

His breath smells of whiskey. I pull back.

"You're not an alcoholic, too, are you?" I say.

"Good God no!" he says, laughing. "I had a bourbon on the plane to help me sleep. Haven't had a drink since I got to Kabul. Whiskey's hard to come by there. So I ate a lot of ice cream instead."

"Do they make good ice cream in Kabul?"

"Not as good as Ben and Jerry's." He's smiling broadly, staring at me. "You look exactly as I thought you would," he says.

We laugh. I babble. We get into Typhoo, which has never looked so clean, and I start driving. I can't remember much of what we talk about. I know that we both keep taking deep breaths. I know that I feel wholly comfortable, and relieved. I know that there is something that feels undeniably right about his being there.

He keeps looking at me, laughing and saying, "Oh . . . my . . . God." I ask about his children. He tells me that his daughter, Ashley, "does good" working with people with special needs, and that his son Edwin sells advertising space on the telephone.

"But that's what I do!" I say.

He looks at me again. "Oh . . . my . . . God."

Ashley and Edwin are definitely not names you'd call a Brit. Any more than you'd call an American Phillippa. Or Nicola. Or Hamish. Or Fiona. Or Tarquin.

"My family all disapprove of me," he says. "They want me to settle down and get a nine-to-five job. They spend all their time praying for me."

"Oh dear," I say. "I mean, I believe in God and everything, but—"

"But what?" Walt looks like he really wants to know.

"Well, whenever I meet a religious person, it makes me want to say 'fuck.'"

Walt roars with the kind of laughter that keeps coming back once it's died down.

Somehow I drive him safely to the hotel I booked for him to stay in—the Cone Court in Holland Park—very pink, cozy, and full of eccentric antiques and prints on the walls.

"This is my father," I say to the hotel receptionist. Walt laughs and says, "Nobody's going to believe that with our accents being so different."

I say I'll wait in the lobby while he has a shower and changes. He says, "No, come up with me, I don't want you out of my sight for a second."

We go to his room. It's tiny and as pink as the lobby, but he doesn't seem to mind.

"Should I change my shirt?" he asks.

"No need," I say. "I mean, you don't smell or anything." He starts laughing again.

"But if you want to . . . ," I say.

While he's unpacking he takes a baseball cap out of his suitcase. "Have it," he says. "I've had it for years. It's something that is truly mine. It's my Orioles hat." I look at him blankly.

"That's the baseball team we support," he says.

"Oh," I say, putting it on. It's slightly too big, so I pull my hair through the back and tighten the clasp. "Thank you."

I give him the cricket sweater I bought him, and also the thermal underwear from Damart, which I reckon he might need, London in November being particularly chilly this year.

"I'm not that old and frail you know." He's laughing again, putting the sweater around his shoulders.

We walk downstairs to the lobby, looking at each other every few seconds, sometimes catching each other in the act. The autumn leaves are swirling in the wind as I walk him toward Holland Park where we find a pub that, to Walt's delight, is called the Frog and

Firkin. He buys me a gin and tonic and buys himself a beer. We sit opposite each other, in a little wooden alcove, on benches with maroon cushion covers on them.

We talk and talk. I tell him how strongly I needed to find him—that I knew, as soon as I met Billie, that it was terribly important. We talk—and then stop—and then look at each other with recognition.

"You're beautiful," he says.

"No, I'm not," I say.

"You are," he says.

I want to cry. I do cry. He looks at me.

"I'm sorry," I say. "This is completely out of character. I'm usually pretty sensible."

"Sensible!" he says. "God, I hope you're not!" I roar with laughter this time.

"Well—I try to be. Sometimes," I say. "But it's not all that much fun." We're both holding our glasses at the same angle, smiling, like children.

"What were you thinking we'd do tonight?" he says. "I could take you to *My Fair Lady*."

I remember going to see *My Fair Lady* with Dad when I was about eight. I loved it so much, I learned all the parts on holiday in Scotland one year and performed a two-person version of it with Sally Gibbs, to our parents. Actually we performed it in the bathroom of the farmhouse we were staying in, because it was the warmest room in the house. The grown-ups all sat around the heated towel rack, and Sally and I performed the entire musical for them on the ledge in front of the bath. It's my favorite musical, and it's Dad's favorite musical. Thinking of Dad, for a second I feel guilty and disloyal.

"Aren't you tired?" I ask, bringing my attention quickly back to Walt. "It was a long flight, and with the time change and everything . . ."

"Good God, no! The night is young!"

"How long are you staying for?"

"I'm here on a twenty-hour stopover," Walt says. We fall silent.

"Can I put in a request to just go out to dinner and talk?"

In the taxi, on our way into the West End, Walt tells me that my grandmother ran a marathon at seventy-two. And that my great-grandmother, who's ninety-two, drives a red sports car with the top down and was recently photographed in a leather pantsuit on the back of a Harley-Davidson. He tells me that her mother was half Cherokee Indian.

Thank God, I think. Longevity—and sanity. Eccentric old ladies on Harleys I can deal with.

"You have Billie's laugh," he says.

"I know," I say. It still feels odd, suddenly sharing parts of myself—that I used to think of as unique—with somebody else.

We walk past Trafalgar Square, along the Strand, past the Savoy Theatre, where my friend Rachel is playing the oboe in *The Three-penny Opera*, and end up in Bertorelli, an Italian restaurant in Covent Garden. We talk for an hour and a half before ordering anything but cocktails, which I explain to the waiter aren't "cocktails" but a predinner drink.

And then I have to ask Walt about Billie. He takes a sip of his drink. Then, in a soft voice, he says, "Billie was magnificent. No one could come close.

"I first met her in New York. In the lobby of the Waldorf. I was twenty-two years old. I'd just delivered a speech for the Young Conservatives and was in the lobby, talking to her father—your grandfather—who shared my views on communism. I had heard wonderful things about him and was glad to meet him."

I picture my grandfather and my father meeting as much younger men. Tough, smart and valiant—the best of their respective generations—they would have impressed anyone.

"Suddenly this extraordinary woman walked up to me," Walt says. "She was alight with life and beautiful and all I could see. Her eyes were full of wit and intelligence and laughter. And her fragrance—oh . . ." He takes a deep breath and leans back in his chair, remembering.

"That night the great Pearl Bailey was in the Cedar Room. Just after her last number Frank Sinatra surprised everyone by walking up on the stage, and the two of them brought the house down with 'A Little Learnin' Is a Dangerous Thing.' It was an unforgettable night. In every way."

He stops. He looks at me.

"From that night on, we saw each other as often as we could, usually when I was in New York, staying at the Waldorf.

"When we found out she was with child, I went to Margaret and asked for a divorce. In half a minute, the gentle woman I married turned into someone I didn't recognize."

Walt takes another sip of whiskey. There is silence between us.

"Mother flew in," Walt says, finally. "She played every card she had. 'There has never been a divorce in this family,' Mother said. 'You will bring disgrace upon the family, upon Margaret, upon yourself—and you will ruin your political career.'"

He tells me that when he and Billie "hit town" people would whisper, "Who are they?" And before they knew it, they'd be at the center of a crowd.

I watch my father across the dinner table. I can see he is still under Billie's spell.

"Do you enjoy living in a big city, Pippa? Do you enjoy going out at night?"

"Yes," I say, "But I hate nightclubs. They make my ears hurt."

"It's no fun unless you're with somebody exciting," he says.

I've never met anyone anywhere near as exciting as Billie and Walt. Except Nick.

Walt watches me while I'm eating. He looks at my arm. "The way your arm bends is exactly the same as Billie's," he says. He looks at my hands. "Billie's hands," he says.

"Yes."

He tells me a little about his wife, Margaret. "She's very good," he says. "Billie isn't 'good.' But at bottom there's pure diamond. Real strength."

He tells me that Margaret was very beautiful when she was young, and that when Jackie Onassis walked into a room, followed by Margaret, all eyes would be turned on Margaret. He also tells me that Jackie was always photographed from the waist up, because she thought she had thick ankles and big feet.

"Did you love your wife?" I say.

"Hold out your hands, Pippa." I hold my hands out across my linguini. "Now look at them."

I look at my hands.

"Now, if you had to, which hand would you cut off?"

I understand. I can't eat anymore.

I ask him whether or not the stability and lack of passion in his marriage enabled him to go out and fight the dragons he has fought in his life. That if he had been wanting to be at home with his loved one all the time, maybe he wouldn't have achieved so much. He looks at me closely and does not deny it.

"Do you really think that if you and Billie had got married that your marriage would have lasted?"

"Of course," he says.

I am not so sure. Neither is Billie. I remember that Billie told me one of the reasons she doesn't think their marriage would have lasted was because they were too alike. They both had so much energy, if they'd tried to make a life together, there would have been an explosion.

I think of Nick again.

Walt asks me what I think about the Iraq war. I tell him how profoundly wrong I felt it was, right from the very start. I tell him that I think America as self-appointed international policeman is terrifying. I tell him how sickened I am that millions of people, including myself, sit riveted to news about the war while eating cheese on toast in front of the television.

"And as for George Bush? I can't bear thinking about him. To paraphrase Samuel Johnson, 'The fellow seems to possess one idea, and that idea is wrong.'"

Walt doesn't say a word. But when I am finished, he leans back in his chair, smiles broadly, and says, "So this is what happens when you're raised in a country teeming with socialists."

I have no idea whether or not he means what he has just said, and he has no intention of enlightening me. He seems to be enjoying himself thoroughly.

And then, in a serious, ponderous "this is how I talk about war" sort of voice, he says, "The mistake we made—and it was a colossal one—was to react before taking the time to understand why 9/11 happened. Those Saudi Arabians did not fly those planes into the World Trade Center to protest the Bill of Rights. They flew those planes into the World Trade Center because they wanted us to get the hell off Muslim soil. It was a huge mistake, and we'll pay for it for the next hundred years."

"But I thought you were a conservative?" I say, surprised by how relieved I feel by his answer.

Walt laughs. "Daughter of mine, I am a conservative. And so are you."

"Oh no I'm bloody not," I say, pointing at him, my brows knit together, in what Charlotte has always called my "contradict me and die" look, which I now realize I inherited from the man sitting opposite me.

"You are." Walt's pointing at me, leaning toward me in exactly the same way I'm leaning toward him. When we realize we're mirroring each other exactly, we get the mad laughs, after which Walt orders two glasses of port.

"Conservatism is in your genes." Walt's teasing me now. I won't rise to this. "From what you've told me about it, your play's about socialism killing the individual spirit."

"No, it's not! It's about fascism, about what will happen if the conservatives have their way in Europe! I'm not a bloody conservative, Walt."

"It's George Bush who isn't—as you put it—a bloody conservative."

"What do you mean?"

"The whole concept of preemptive war takes America as far from the wishes of our founding fathers as it is possible for us to go."

"Exactly!"

"Exactly!"

Walt looks at me, squinting.

"You remind me so much of myself at your age. I want the Iraq war to end as much as you do, kiddo. You're right to call it a terrible war."

I think of the number of times Dad has shushed me when I've tried to engage people in the subject of politics over Sunday lunch at Little Tew. Then I try to picture Walt sitting at the lunch table at Little Tew. I can't.

At about one o'clock in the morning, we leave and take a taxi to my car, which is parked outside his hotel. He holds my hand in the taxi. I feel his strength running through his hand into mine. Running through my hand into me.

I hand him the letter I first wrote to the adoption agency, explaining how important it was to me to meet my birth parents, and drive home, feeling terribly sad that he's going away again the next day.

Chapter Twenty-Five

I WAKE UP AT THE CRACK OF DAWN, give Walt a little time to sleep, and arrive at his hotel at 8:40 ready to drive him to the airport. He is already in the lobby. Before saying good morning, he hands me his plane ticket and says, "Go upstairs to my room and do whatever you have to do to have the airline defer my return trip to Washington until tomorrow."

The weight of sadness lifts, I fly up the stairs, happier than I have ever been, and call Virgin Atlantic. The woman says they'll have to charge him to change the ticket.

"But you can't!" I say. "He's only staying the extra day because he's my father and we need some more time together. We haven't seen each other since I was born, when he held me in the hospital, before I was given up for adoption, which I was, a few days later, only I didn't go straight to my parents, I went to a foster home first, though he didn't know that . . ." I explain the situation to the lady at Virgin Atlantic, who waives the fee and bumps Walt up to first class.

We walk off arm in arm to Tootsies for breakfast. I show him a few pictures of Billie from my visit. He looks at each one once, filled with emotion. He doesn't say much. He hands them back to me and says, "Thank you."

When I tell Walt about Miles he says, "good."

"You weren't really in love with him, were you, Pippa?"

"He started growing on me," I say.

Walt is peering at me from behind his glasses.

"Gro-wing on you?" he says, slowly.

"You don't understand," I say.

"I do," he says.

"No, you don't," I say. "You don't understand what it's like to be too frightened to let yourself really fall in love, because then—"

"Because then you might be left," he says. "And it would hurt way too much. To be abandoned by someone who really mattered."

"Yes, goddammit!"

Walt's very still. I'm not sure, but I think he might be trying not to cry.

"There are heroes in the world," he says, "believe me. Don't settle for anything less."

"Are there?" I say.

"Courage, kid. You have courage. You will know."

"Yes," I say. "I will. One day. Hopefully you're right." I want to believe him.

"I am right," he says. And then, "There can be no courage without fear."

After breakfast we go to Sloane Square. I ask him what his favorite songs are.

"The Lady is a Tramp" is one of them, he says.

I start: "I've wined and dined on Mulligan stew and never wished for turkey . . ." He starts singing too. We carry on as we start walking down the King's Road. There's a strong wind blowing. We sing into it.

"Oh boy," he says, "the energy level is on its way up."

I thought it was just me who got surges of irrepressible energy. But no! Battling against the wind, we sing, while walking, for a quarter of a mile. Then I start singing "My Favorite Things" just as we're getting to Man in the Moon pub.

"Stop," he says. He looks at me, stunned.

"What is it?" I say. He speaks slowly, emphasizing his words.

"That is the song Billie sang the night we met. We were walking around New York City in the snow. I kept leading her into doorways and kissing the snowflakes off her face . . ." He's obviously feeling something painful, so I stop.

"Come on!" I say. "You're in London! Let's go to the top of a double-decker bus!"

We climb up the stairs to the bus and sit, like children, leaning against the rails at the front.

Unlike Billie, Walt wants to know everything about me. And he really listens.

"It's so difficult," I say. "Because Dad is my father. Mum and Dad are my parents. That is what it has been. And yet. And yet. And yet they tell me to be sensible, beg me to get a 'proper' job, which I can't do, not without dying inside. And I love them, but I feel in here that you are my father. My God. You are my father."

I feel something lift.

"You're a good listener," I say.

"No, I'm not," he says. "I'm a talker. But if I don't listen to you—well I want to know all about you. It's the only way I can find out." Later, he says, "I didn't expect this. I expected to feel a quiet affection."

"It's not a quiet affection, is it?" I say.

"No," he says. "It's not."

We drive to Kew so I can show him my flat.

"Have you ever thought of spending time in the States?" Walt says.

"Not really," I say. "I mean, apart from fridges with ice-makers, what have you got that we haven't?" It's a weak joke, but he's going, and I'm feeling sad again.

"You're living in a country where success and enthusiasm are frowned on," Walt begins. "That will, eventually, destroy someone like you."

"That's not true."

"It is," Walt says. "And you know it. Come to America, kid. In America, you can be who you are."

I grin at him. "Whoever the hell that is, now Billie and you have been thrown into my mix."

"We've always been in your mix."

We climb up the steps to the flat. The postman has arrived. I pick up the airmail envelope.

"This must be from Billie," I say. My address is written in Billie's trademark bold red ink.

I read the letter quickly and hand it to Walt so he won't feel left out. It's a short letter telling me she misses me and can't wait to hear all about my meeting with my father, about whom, she says, she has been dreaming again. At the bottom she has drawn a large red heart with the initials *B* and *P* in the center, surrounded by *x*'s.

Walt's hand shakes as he reads it. I say nothing. Then I ask him if he'd like to see what Billie wrote just before I was born, about the two of them, the letter I received five months before.

"No. I can't," he says.

I show him a photograph of Mum and Dad. "I feel so grateful to those dear people," he says, looking at it. His eyes are moist. "So very, very grateful."

Walt says he'd love to read my plays and sits on the sofa, drinking a mug of lumpy Horlicks. I kneel on the floor, watching him closely as he reads the part of the nineteen-year-old secretary in my first play. He speaks in a high-pitched voice, with an appalling British accent.

The play is called *Odd Behaviour*. It's about two social misfits and a middle-class couple who set up a company designed to remove odd behavior from the streets of London.

He laughs and laughs and laughs. At the end of it he looks at me and says, "My God, you've only picked the most important theme of our time. You're the real stuff, kid."

He says again that, now he's read it, the play definitely proves I'm a conservative. It doesn't at all. It's a play about individuality under threat. We banter back and forth about it, but I know he thinks it's really good. I know he's not just being kind, I know he's excited by it. And the specific tightness in my chest that comes from a fear that Mum and Dad are right, that I am deluding myself about wanting to be a playwright, loosens a bit more. I love him for reading it with me. And for laughing.

"Are you writing anything at the moment?"

"Well, yes—I'm trying to finish a play I started a few years ago."

"What's it about?" he asks.

"Well, there are these two characters. Talking to each other. In a womb. They're twins, obviously."

"Twins?"

"Yes, twins."

He's looking at me intensely.

"It's called *Womb Mate*." I wait for him to laugh; I thought that was a clever title. I'm fossicking around in the box, trying to find page five when, in a quiet, insistent tone of voice Walt says, "Did they tell you?"

"Who?"

"The adoption people . . . anyone . . ."

"What?" The pages collated into some kind of order, I look up. Walt looks old suddenly.

"Did they tell you about your twin?"

The air in the room has changed. I can't hear anything. Then I can. I sit down. My body is tense.

"I have a twin?"

"No," he says slowly. "You had a twin."

"I had a twin." I repeat his words because I want to be sure I heard him correctly. Walt's voice, when he finds it, is gentle.

"He died, Pippa. In childbirth."

I had a twin. And he died. In childbirth. The sorrow is instant. It flows into my heart like thick black ink. Walt's voice seems far away.

"Billie's never talked about him since. I think she's blocked it out."

I'm back in the room with Walt, numb now. Walt's eyes are full of tears.

"The last time I saw you was a few moments after you were born. Billie was under. She'd become hysterical, so they gave her drugs to calm her down. I held you first. You were fiercely beautiful and so tiny. And so brave. You'd just lost your twin, and you were about to lose your parents. You were wrapped up in a hospital blanket. When I held you in my arms, I knew that giving you away meant giving away part of my soul."

Walt's voice comes in and out. My mind is focused on my twin. I had a twin. I had a twin. So I wasn't alone in there.

Walt is somewhere else, too. I come back to him as he talks. I'm with Walt now, in the hospital. He is a young man. I am a newborn, staring up at him.

"I held you tight, then I looked you in the eyes. Then I brought your little ear to my mouth, and I made you a promise. 'When you need me,' I whispered, 'if you need me, however many years from now, whatever I am doing, no matter what battle I am fighting, I will come to you.'

"Then I kissed you on the head and handed you back to the nurse and on to God only knew where.

"Then I walked past the room where Billie was lying in her drugged sleep, and down the brightly lit corridor into the nearest empty room, a small room at the end where they draw blood. And I closed the door and sat on a gray plastic chair opposite a clock with a crack in it, until the morning."

We sit, saying nothing, for two, maybe three minutes.

"Nobody told me I had a twin who died. But I knew. I must have done. That must be why I've been writing about it . . . here," I say. Trembling, I hand Walt the script of my play.

"Read this," I say, turning to the final page. "Please."

As it ends, only one of the two characters is left onstage. Walt reads the narrator's final words aloud. His voice sounds far away again.

"I hear a voice crying in the wind. It is the voice of my brother, drowning in a pool."

We sit for half an hour on the edge of my bed, on the multi-colored blanket Dad bought me when he visited Lesotho, saying nothing.

Walt's packing his luggage in his tiny pink hotel room. His flight leaves in three hours.

"Don't ever do anything that doesn't feel right because other people tell you you should. Trust yourself," he says. He keeps saying it. "You're the real stuff, kid." And then "Courage, kid. You're a warrior, kid. Courage."

We drive to the airport. My parking is terrible. I get the time wrong. We're two hours early. We check him in and then drive to the Green Man pub. I buy him some pork scratchings, a packet of prawn cocktail crisps, which he absolutely loves, and a ploughman's lunch. He eats everything but the pickled onion.

On our way back to the car, I sneak six packets of prawn cocktail crisps into the side of his bag and manage to zip it up without him noticing.

"I thought about you so much over the years," Walt's saying. "Wondering."

"Wondering what?" I say.

"When I held you in the hospital, just after you were born, I thought I saw something in your eyes that I'd not seen before."

"What?"

"My spirit, Pippa. For the past twenty-eight years, I've wondered if the child I gave away was the one child of mine who had inherited my spirit."

"And am I?" I say.

"God, yes."

Everything I hoped to find in my reunion with Billie, I have found in my reunion with this man. For the first time in my life I feel recognized. Validated. By someone who reminds me of me.

"Why are you crying?" he says.

"I've just found you and now you're going away on an airplane," I say.

"I will never go away again," he says. "I will always be here for you. Home," he says, laughing, "is somewhere where they have to take you in."

I withdraw instantly. "But you mustn't ever out of some sense of obligation, just to be kind or anything . . ." I begin, but, as I say it, I realize this is an old insecurity speaking that has no place here. That will, in time, go away. I know that this man is filled with the happiness I am full of.

"No unauthorized crying," Walt says as we wander toward customs. "You see, there are other people like you in the world," he says.

"I love you," he says. "I love the way you light up a room when you walk into it. You're a warrior. I love you, kid. Remember, there can be no courage without fear."

Chapter Twenty-six

I TELL NICK EVERYTHING. He replies immediately.

DATE: November 9
TO: pippa-dunn@hotmail.com
FROM: NickDevang@bankglobal.net

You remember that I met my father the year my mother died, and
that meeting him changed everything, just as meeting your father has
changed everything for you. But there is a difference.

What I have told no one, until now, is that when I found my father
he was living on a park bench in East London. His face was un-
shaven and his clothes smelled of stale beer. He told me he earned
his living painting on the streets. Literally. That day's painting had
brought him seven pounds fifty. He'd show me his work, only the rain
had already washed the chalk away.

He had been raised in foster homes in England and told me that
not knowing how he came to be was the great agony of his life. He
knew nothing about his parents, except that, owing to the color of
his skin, one of them must have been of Indian or Middle Eastern
descent.

He told me he had never left me and insisted my mother had
stolen me from him. He told me he had spent time in jail. He told
me he had once killed a man. He spoke of unfulfilled dreams, pov-

erty, cruelty, and sorrow. Then, turning to me with my eyes burning out of his weatherbeaten face, he urged me to get the hell out of England.

I didn't know how much of what he told me was true, and I never found out. I went back the next day with all the money I had, which at the time wasn't much, but he had gone. All that was left was a chalk painting of a river somewhere in India, full of the color, life, beauty, vibrancy that neither of us had ever found in England. A few months later I was contacted by a social worker who told me he had died of a heart attack, in a halfway house in East London. He was forty-six years old.

I became good—very good—at what I do, vowing never to let the poverty that had destroyed my father touch me, and as soon as I could I did, indeed, get the hell out of England.

I look at the faces of the people in the streets of Delhi, Mumbai, and Kuwait, searching for my father's face. Searching for my own. Sometimes I think I see it, and that is when I paint. It's when I paint that I feel I am connecting with the father he might have been.

Meeting my father gave me permission to become who I am. A nomad, perhaps. A traveler certainly. The main difference between my father and myself, of course, is that he had to steal to survive. And, unlike his son, never knew what it was like to travel on a five-star budget.

Love, Nick

And then, later, Billie calls and offers me a job, starting in the new year. She tells me she wants to spend a lot more time in Georgia to write and be near her father. If I will come to Art Buddies and help with the promotional side of things, it will free up her time to do just that.

"We don't have a lot of money, but you can work for me in return for room and board, and we'll pay you when we can."

I think of my dwindling bank balance.

"Billie, I'm not sure I can afford to do this."

"Oh, but you can." Billie's excited now. "Daddy told me that if you come to America he'll give you the second house!"

"Oh."

I think of the little light gray wooden house on the creek, a few miles from Billie's, that used to have tenants in it and now stands empty. You get to it by walking through trees and overgrown grass, about two hundred yards from the dirt track that, after a bumpy half-hour drive, leads to the nearest store. I picture myself working at the farm next door, stripping tobacco in the barn, with only dim memories of the days when I dated men who had all their front teeth.

"Billie, that's very nice of him, but I really don't think he should give me the house."

"If your grandfather wants to give you the house, he'll give you the house! It should bring in at least thirty thousand dollars, if you sell it. That way you're covered until we can afford to pay you."

Her enthusiasm is contagious.

"I do still have some money left on my credit card—and if I was sure I'd eventually be able to pay it off, perhaps I could afford another plane ticket."

"Honey, I'm offering you a job and a free place to stay just outside New York City. I really don't think you can turn this down. You'll be perfectly placed to pursue any creative endeavor you want. And you'll only be four hours away from your father."

When Charlotte calls and tells me she wants to sell the flat, I take it as a sign.

"But what about your career in advertising?" Dad says, when I tell him.

Wanting to put his mind at rest, I tell him Billie's job comes with a proper salary, and that she's not going to be there much anyway. Most of the time she'll be in Georgia, so I'll hardly see her.

"And Dad, if it doesn't work out—and of course it might not— at least I'll have a proper title on my CV," I say, running as far as I can with it.

"It does sound like a good opportunity," Mum says.

"Yes," Dad says eventually. "I suppose it does."

My instinct is screaming at me so strongly to go, it drowns out the guilt I feel. Almost.

Christmas and New Year will come as they always do with the usual round of drinks parties, present giving, and Scottish dancing. And no one will say anything more about it.

The night before I leave, I will get a two-line e-mail from Nick.

DATE: January 2
TO: pippa-dunn@hotmail.com
FROM: NickDevang@bankglobal.net

I consulted the I Ching. It said "The queen is returning to her castle."

WINTER

Chapter Twenty-seven

I THOUGHT WE'D SHARE MY ROOM," Billie says, pulling my suitcase along the corridor toward her bedroom in Adler. "This way we can lie in bed at night and talk, like girlfriends." After sharing dormitories for seven years, I hate lying in bed and talking "like girlfriends." I'd rather sleep in an airing cupboard.

But the simple fact of my sharing a room with her seems to make Billie so happy, and I'm relieved to be back in Billie's home after the torturously long security check at Heathrow and the cramped flight back to America. So I climb into my side of her enormous bed and fall asleep to the sound of Billie's voice telling me she's thinking of writing a book. "There you were longing to be a writer all your life," she says. "And now you've inspired me to become a writer too."

The next morning, after a breakfast of Slim-Fast, a kind of chocolate milk that Billie shows me how to make with ice, in a blender, I go into the sitting room to be officially introduced to Billie's creativity counselors, or, as she prefers to call them, art buddies.

My job will be to publicize Billie's workshops, because it's through the workshops that she gets most of her clients. For a fee, clients who have taken one of Billie's workshops can call Carol, Marvin, or Tom to talk about how their work is going. Billie determines who she thinks would be a good fit for them. If they're feeling insecure, their counselor will encourage them. If they're feeling blocked, their counselor will lead them through a series of creative visualizations, either in person or on the phone, until they are unblocked again.

Marvin is thirty, bald, skinny, and shakes my hand with the enthusiasm of a born-again Christian, because he is a born-again Christian.

"When Marvin's not counseling clients he acts as my secretary," Billie says. "Without him I'd be lost." She smiles at Marvin, who clearly has a crush on her.

Tom is about fifty and looks like the kind of well-worn New Yorker you read about in books. I like the way he dresses. His corduroy pants are scuffed at the knees and his lumberjack shirt is too big for his frail body. His eyes are young. It's only his body that looks old.

"I was introduced to Tom by his psychiatrist," Billie tells me. "He kept drinking and then blacking out in the middle of Manhattan. Then I gave him a job working for me, and the rest is history. Tom helps our clients with their time-management issues. All artists need structure. Isn't that right, Tom? *And* he's a world-class Scrabble player."

Tom and Billie play Scrabble every lunchtime, on Billie's bed. While they play, Billie makes phone calls to clients. Tom drinks strong black coffee with six sugars out of a dark green travel mug. He smokes two packs of Marlboro cigarettes a day.

Billie's clients are mostly people with regular jobs who want to learn to express their artistic side. She's very inspiring when she speaks. Tom tells me she could make Karl Rove believe he could jack it all in and become a sculptor if he just put his mind to it. His voice is deep and raspy. I notice his hand shaking as he puts his coffee down.

"And this is Carol," Billie says. "She came to dinner one night and told me she wasn't happy working at the library. So—ta da! I made Carol president of my company and made myself chairman of the board! All world-beaters need someone like Carol behind them, overseeing the organizational side of things."

Carol has an open, kind face and the clear skin and bright eyes of someone who works in a health-food shop. She's wearing a dark green pinafore dress with a light gray shirt underneath and a pair of flat brown shoes.

"My daughter's just like me, Carol! We're going to be one helluva team!"

"Good to meet you, Pippa," Carol says.

Billie is at the front door now, ringing a bell.

"Heathcliffe! Pandora! Mandlebeam!" At the sound of the bell, Heathcliffe and two large cats I've not met before come running up the stairs, cross the sitting room, and dash into the kitchen. One of the cats is orange and white, thin, and silky. The other is a fat tortoiseshell, with a weak hind leg and a gummy eye.

They run into the kitchen, jump onto the kitchen table, and start guzzling cat food from a cereal bowl next to someone's half-eaten bowl of Cheerios. Billie lets the cats eat off the kitchen table, rather than the floor, because she says it's easier to clean up that way.

Billie comes back into the sitting room holding a fork with a glob of cat food on the handle.

"My daughter's smart as a whip and as talented as I am, so she'll pick up most of it through osmosis."

Surrounded by Billie, Ralph, and my new colleagues, I think of the last time I heard the word "osmosis" and vaguely remember Miss Arbuthnott teaching it in biology. We used to call her Mrs. Tiggy-Winkle because she was round and motherly and used to scuttle from the biology lab up to the main school.

Billie's voice brings me right back.

"Pippa's background is in sales, so she'll be in charge of drumming up new business. I know she'll have some wonderful ideas."

Billie is so sure I'll be a great asset to the company, I'm starting to believe her. Carol and Tom shake my hand.

"That just leaves Cole. He's out getting supplies. We met at a conference a couple of months ago. He's going to oversee the financial side of things. He's a wonderful painter, and very spiritual."

As if on cue, the doorbell rings. In walks a tall man of about forty-five, with dark black curly hair and cobalt blue eyes, wearing a light blue vest and blue jeans. He's good looking, in a worn way. Sexy, even.

"Cole!" Billie says. "Meet my daughter!"

The phone rings. Billie goes to pick it up. I can hear her talking in the background.

"So you're Pippa," he says. "Your mother has told me all about you."

He's looking at me intensely. I feel naked. There's something about him that I instantly mistrust.

"Stop talking everybody and listen up!" Billie says, rushing back into the center of the room. She's put on a black sweater with a blue cat on it and is speaking as if she is performing for an audience. We all stop talking. Then she drops her voice. As I've told you before, you absolutely have to listen to Billie when she drops her voice like this.

"We have a crisis," she says.

Oh no.

"I've got to get back to Georgia right away." She pauses, to make sure everyone is ready to hear what she has to say. We are. Then, "Malice is holding Daddy prisoner. She's hidden Daddy's car keys, insisting he's too sick to drive up the mountain!"

"What are you going to do?" Tom says.

"I'm going to have Daddy back up that mountain by tomorrow afternoon."

Within minutes, Cole is helping Billie put her suitcase—and Heathcliffe—into the car. I watch Cole kiss Billie good-bye. I can't tell what kind of a kiss it is, because his long back is blocking my view. Maybe that's something Americans do to be friendly. Like the French. I'm not referring to a French kiss. The kind that involves tongues, etc. I'm referring to the cheek-to-cheek thing the French do when they say hello. Cole's kiss is sort of in the middle.

The other counselors clean up the coffee cups. Marvin hovers around me. He's obviously moved by my arrival. Finally he says, "God has brought you here, I'm convinced of it."

I cringe inwardly, as embarrassed by easy talk of God as I am by people I've only known a short while telling me they love me, and make an excuse to go into the kitchen.

"So, Pippa," Carol says, after Billie has left. Her voice is kind. "Welcome to the Billie Parnell Show."

Chapter Twenty-eight

THE NEXT DAY, Marvin sells me his brother's '86 Buick for five hundred dollars. I call it Earl Grey, because the name Typhoo's already taken. Following Marvin's turn-by-turn instructions on how to get there, I make the forty-minute drive into the heart of Manhattan, excited to be exploring New York City for the first time.

I know I'll probably be all right once I get into the city, because it's supposedly built on a grid and therefore quite straightforward—unlike, say, Canberra, in Australia, which is built in a circle and impossible to find your way around even if you've lived there for decades. I traveled around Australia when I was seventeen, in my year off between school and university. It's where I fell in love for the first time. With my cousin. We didn't have sex or anything, but I did learn about kissing lying down.

That's one advantage of being adopted. It's absolutely fine to fall for your cousin, because you're not blood relations. I've often thought it would have been nice if our love had lasted. Because then, if we'd got married and had babies, the babies would be blood relatives of mine and Mum's. Which would make me really related to Mum, if you see what I mean.

But the romance between Drew and me didn't last. I went back to university in England, and he became a park ranger in the Australian bush. Poor Drew. He really loved me, I think. And I loved him. And then I didn't. As I drive, I wonder if other people remember every detail about the people who stopped loving them first—and very little about the people they left brokenhearted.

The sound of horns hooting brings my mind back to the present. I read somewhere that it's illegal to hoot your horn in Manhattan. If that's true, then there are a lot of people breaking the law when I hit midtown.

I'm not a particularly good driver at the best of times. But when something makes me nervous—well, forget it. I try to do a three-point turn, just as my driving instructor taught me back in Kew. But this is not a peaceful, tree-lined street in West London.

I stall in front of a huge metal dumpster next to a barbed-wire fence. I get out and apologize. The horns hoot louder. Finally a parking-lot attendant takes pity on me and guides my car, backward, into his lot. I am surprised to note that he is wearing a bow tie, particularly considering the fact that his parking lot is nothing more than a forty-foot-square piece of concrete, surrounded by graffiti-covered walls, under open sky.

He tells me he wants forty-four dollars to park my car there. I check his face to see if he is joking. He isn't. But I'm grateful to him for rescuing me and impatient to see the city, so rather than spending hours trying to find a meter, I pay him. Then I sling my handbag over my shoulder and take my first walk through the streets of Manhattan.

I'd much rather walk through the streets below famous buildings than visit the buildings themselves. So, on my first trip into New York City, despite the fact that it's January and bitterly cold, I start walking. I head up Eighth Avenue, past the porn shops and the theaters and the subway signs with the letters *A, C,* and *E.* I stop for a few moments on the corner of Forty-fourth and Eighth. A subway train is passing beneath me, massaging my feet as it rumbles below.

The wind is fierce, and I'm grateful for the thermal underwear Mum sneaked into my suitcase and the Australian Ugg boots I've brought with me from England. My ears, however, are freezing, and I wish I'd brought a hat.

New York is alive with people selling things. Newspapers, umbrellas, coffee, gloves, watches, jewels. I stop at the Broadway Diner for a mug of hot chocolate with marshmallows floating on the top.

An hour later, heading along the famous streets toward what has to be Times Square, I notice a number of signs on a wire fence with Post No Signs stamped on it. "Jesus Saves," "Adali Snapple, the Best Flavors on Earth," "Thee Nail Salon—Manicure, Pedicure, for the Best Nails on Earth." I can hear Charlotte and Mum's voices in my head: "Why does everything have to be the 'best' in America? Why can't it just be good enough? Hmm?"

I stop at a pretzel stand and buy an enormous salted pretzel, which I cover with mustard from the squeezy yellow mustard container. It feels exotic and very American in comparison with Grey Poupon.

I'm fighting against the wind, passing a dark, narrow alley, finishing the last bite of my pretzel, when I'm startled by a tap on my shoulder. I turn around and see a tall, strong-looking man in a long black coat and black face mask staring down at me.

I won't mind giving him what little money I have, but I'd rather not be bundled into the back of a car and dumped dead somewhere north of 160th Street without my coat or my shoes, like the woman in *24*.

The man is holding my arm. I tell myself to stay calm.

"Hallo," I say.

The wind is blowing fierce and sharp, and I can't hear what the man is saying above the traffic. My scarf is flapping in the wind and I'm trying not to panic. His other hand comes toward me. He's holding something. A drug dealer. Stay calm, Pip.

"No, thank you," I say, "I don't take drugs, except for a cold. Sorry." I smile politely at him, pull my arm away, and start to walk in the opposite direction. Maybe he'll like my accent and let me go? He catches up with me, puts his arm around my shoulders, and pulls me into the alley.

I mean it when I say I won't mind giving him my money. When

I was about fifteen, I had my bicycle stolen. I knew the boys that took it—I saw them at the playground with it the following week. The white seat had been painted red, but it was definitely my bike. I went home and told Mum about it. She said, "Don't make such a fuss about it, darling. If they went to all the trouble of stealing it, they probably need the bicycle much more than you do."

Ever since then—well, I've seen her point. The only thing I'd really mind being stolen would be something I was in the middle of writing. Or my really comfy slippers. Everything else can be replaced.

We're protected from the wind by the alley, and I can now hear what the man is saying. "Your wallet," he says.

My first thought is to wonder why Americans insist on calling a purse a wallet and a handbag a purse. In England, a purse has a little metal clip and is used, mostly, for change. A wallet is flat. You keep your credit cards in it. They're completely different. Some Americans even go so far as to call a handbag a pocketbook, which is not part of the vocabulary in England. An educated guess might lead your average Brit to assume it refers to an A–Z, perhaps. Or one of those minibooks full of inspirational phrases that you can read on the loo.

My second thought is to remember that a magazine article I once read said that if you're approached by a mugger, just give him what he wants—don't put up any kind of fight, it's not worth risking your life. I reach into my coat pocket. Maybe if I give him the money, he'll let me keep my driving license. It would take me weeks to get another one, and I don't want to risk having to take a driving test in the U.S. It took me five tries before I passed my British test, and I'm sure the only reason I got through it is because I took Charlotte's advice: I resisted all urges to speak to the instructor, put my hair up in a bun, and wore a conservative-looking skirt with heels.

"Oh dear," I say, reaching into my pocket to give my purse to the man standing over me. "It doesn't seem to be—"

"Your wallet," he says.

I look into his outstretched hand. He's not holding drugs or a gun. He's holding my purse. "You dropped your wallet two blocks back. You gotta be careful, this is New York City."

"Oh!" I say, waves of relief washing over me. "Oh! I thought you were a mugger! Oh! Thank you!"

The man is taking off his face mask, which, upon closer inspection, isn't a face mask at all, but appears to be a balaclava, hand-knitted out of thick fluffy wool.

He has brown hair, beautiful soft brown eyes, and a kind, craggy, interesting face. He's lean and tall—about thirty-five or so—and he's laughing.

"Sorry," he says. "I didn't mean to scare you. My mom gave me this. She thinks I'll get frostbite if I don't wear it. I forgot I had it on." He smiles at me awkwardly.

"Here," he says, handing me his balaclava. "Take it. It's the least I can do after scaring you like that. Anyway, you shouldn't be walking around New York City in January without a hat."

His accent is gloriously, unmistakably from New Jersey.

"But I can't take your hat!"

"It's okay," he says. "I've got three more of these at home." His grin is impish and infectious.

I'm not sure which hole to put my head through. He takes off his gloves and helps me get it on. His hands are warm and big and steady. He stands back and looks at me. In my bright yellow coat and black balaclava, I look like an M&M.

"You look mean!" he says, smiling. "No one's gonna mess with you now."

My voice is muffled from inside the man's hat, which feels surprisingly soft against my freezing-cold face and smells pleasantly of man and aftershave.

He reaches out and tucks a strand of my hair into the hat. Then, he puts his gloves back on again and looks at his watch.

"I gotta get to work," he says.

"Oh," I say. "Well, thank you so much! My purse has everything in it. My driving license, my passport. British driving licenses don't have photo ID, at least mine doesn't. That's why I carry my passport with me. For ID. I need it when I go to the bank." I know I'm giving him too much information. I should let the poor man go.

"You're British, right?"

"Yup," I say. "Well, sort of." I stop myself before I start in on the whole story. "My name's Pippa," I say instead.

"Well, hi, Pippa," he says, smiling. "I'm Jack."

The wind is blowing his hair off his face, which I note is alive with merriment.

"I've got to get to work, but . . . well . . . look, don't get me wrong, I'm not trying to pick you up or anything . . ."

"Oh, good."

"But Friday nights are British night this month. Down at The Gold Room. I work there. It's between Third and Bleecker. Why don't you come on down sometime?"

"I'd like that," I say. "The Gold Room. Right. Got it. And . . . well, thanks for the . . . uh . . . gear!"

"You're lucky," he said. "I could have been wearing the hat with the little yellow duckies on it."

The wind has picked up again, and we part, waving heavy gloves at each other.

When I get back to Adler, Carol is waiting for me at the door. Billie made it to Georgia in time to tear her father away from a strongly protesting Molly Alice and drive him up to his cabin on the mountain. Earl died later that afternoon, lying in his recliner, looking out over the creek. The daughter he loved most was holding his hand.

My long-lost relatives have already started gathering. I am to get on an airplane and join them on Buck Mountain in the morning.

Chapter Twenty-nine

I'M SITTING IN THE BACK OF BILLIE'S CAR, sandwiched between Ralphie and my obese, manic-depressive aunt Marcie, while Billie careers down Buck Mountain at top speed toward the church. My aunt Octavia is sitting in the front next to Billie, telling me all about her daughter.

"Your cousin Augusta could be your double. She's got the red hair and the dimples when she smiles. Only she's got no arms and legs."

Rocks and dirt are spraying out from the side of the car.

"She lost her limbs the day she tried to kill herself. She threw herself off a bridge, but failed."

"It's the family mood disorder." Marcie's voice is as deep as a man's and she speaks very slowly. "It affects different family members in different ways."

Ralphie is staring blankly out of the window.

Octavia pulls out a gold-plated compact mirror and puts on some bright red lipstick, which is a challenge, because the road is bumpy and Billie's pushing seventy.

"I am just shocked at the way Molly Alice forced Daddy to have a traditional funeral and is just *refusing* to allow me to read my poem!" she says. Octavia has written a poem in memory of Earl entitled "My Father, My Self."

"She knows Daddy wanted us to celebrate his life, not mourn

it. Now she's finally got him where she wants him, she can control him," Billie says, taking a furious swig of coffee from her no-spill coffee cup. It misses her mouth and splashes, unnoticed, onto her coat. It smells of hazelnut. "Well, she can't control what we wear."

I am wearing a dark green chiffon dress of Billie's mother's, itchy and tight at the waist, and a pair of Billie's high-heeled velvet shoes. Billie and Marcie are both dressed in cherry red. Octavia is wearing a winter white cashmere suit. Poor Ralphie has been forced into a gold jacket and a red tie. We look like figurines on the top of a Christmas cake.

Unused to high heels, I hobble into Mapleville Episcopal Church behind Billie and Octavia, who stride in front of the rest of us, with their heads held high, wearing the only colored clothes in the church.

The right-hand side of the church is filled with about seventy of Molly Alice's family members. In the dim church light it's difficult to tell whether they're hunching their shoulders or a family with very short necks. Their black eyes dart suspiciously around the room. They look like a gang of moles. There isn't a blonde or a redhead among them. In the front right pew, Molly Alice is seated quietly next to her daughter, Lee, who is as tiny as her mother.

On the left-hand side of the church is Earl's family from his first marriage. Billie, Octavia, Ralph, Marcie, me, and, at the back of the church, a short, furry, red-haired man in his fifties who has to be my Uncle Irv, the convicted felon.

Octavia is sitting ramrod straight, with her poem folded on top of her white velvet purse. She is trying to catch the attention of the Reverend, who is trying to ignore her.

"Reverend!" Billie says. "Reverend!" Her words echo loudly through the church.

The Reverend Carpenter turns his attention to Billie and scuttles toward us.

Billie smiles at him. "You remember my big sister Octavia?"

"Tommy, I have known you since you were in shorts," Octavia

says, "and you will listen to me with something resembling respect. I would like to read a poem I have written about my daddy."

Reverend Thomas Carpenter's voice is strained, but calm.

"Octavia, we have been over this already. Earl's wife requested a traditional service, with no additional readings."

"Daddy would have hated that!" Billie is almost spitting. "You know that, Tommy!"

"There will be no poem," the Reverend says, all serenity gone. "Do you hear me? There will be no poem!"

"But . . ."

The Reverend Carpenter's green eyes bulge. He is trying to keep his voice low while his blood pressure visibly rises.

"Mrs. Parnell"—he is annunciating his words so carefully, he sounds almost British—"Molly Alice was married to your father for thirty years. She doesn't want to hear Octavia Stanford at her husband's funeral. She wants to hear Saint Luke."

Octavia draws herself up to her full height. "That's no way to speak to Earl's oldest living blood relative!"

But the Reverend has already left for the other side of the church.

Octavia is shaking. Billie's gone red. The service has begun.

"Amazing Grace, how sweet the sound . . ."

The accent doesn't matter. Anglican or Episcopal, the church service is the same on both sides of the Atlantic. Long, slow, dull, but comforting because, and perhaps only because, it is familiar.

But dull is not an adjective that can legitimately describe this particular service.

"We're not going to Molly Alice's reception after the service," Billie whispers loudly in my ear during the first reading. "Pass it on."

Next to me is Johnny Taft. Earl started him in business when he was eighteen and helped him buy a house on the mountain. He's a gentle, still, bearlike man who loved Earl. He is crying quietly.

I pretend I haven't heard Billie and stare at my hands, which are

clasped, tightly, in acute embarrassment, around the funeral program on my lap.

When the third hymn has been sung, Billie stands up.

"Reverend Carpenter, Molly Alice, friends, relatives, a word,
please."

Oh no.

There is a murmur in response to Billie. The Reverend stands.
Then sits. Then stands. Then sits again.

"I was the person holding Daddy's hand when he passed, and I
would like to say a few words if I may."

Billie bows graciously in Molly Alice's direction. Molly Alice
stares back at her, frozen. Billie's voice fills the room. Her tone is
soft, respectful, sincere.

"I know you're all going to go to Molly Alice's gathering on Pine
Drive after this funeral. And I can understand you would want to
do that, out of respect and all." She nods in Molly Alice's direction
again, smiling graciously. "But if, after that, you'd like to celebrate
Daddy's life in the way he wanted, with music, dancing, and poetry
written by a family member, I'd love you all to come on up to my
place on the mountain after the formalities are over."

She claps her hands like a child.

"I even have Daddy's favorite bluegrass band coming!"

And then, as if it's an afterthought, Billie turns toward Lee. She
is staring at Billie, blank-faced and still as stone.

"And, well, as we're all in God's house, I would like to take this
opportunity to say something to my half-sister Lee."

Her voice drops low, but every word echoes through the church.

"Lee, I love you! We may have very different mothers, but you
will always be my sister! And I want you to know that Daddy for-
gave you. Yes, he felt a little sad that you waited until the winter
of his final year, when his body was riddled with cancer, before
telling him. But both Daddy and I were so proud of the fact that
you finally found the courage to tell him the truth about your
sexuality."

Despite themselves, the congregation turns to stare at Lee, whose expression is still blank.

"Lee, Molly Alice, everyone, I'll hope to see you all later. And Lee, I want you to know that, in my house, you will always be welcome to bring your lesbian lovers."

The organist plays Bach's funeral fugue as the rest of the congregation scrambles to its feet.

Chapter Thirty

DATE: Jan 10

TO: NickDevang@bankglobal.net

FROM: pippa-dunn@hotmail.com

Dear Nick,

Thank you so much for your good wishes, which I have passed on to Billie.

Billie insisted we come straight back to New York after the funeral to start work. I think keeping busy is her way of coping. I wish there was something I could do to help her, but there isn't. Even working at this pace won't stop the sorrow coming. It's waiting for her, as sorrow always waits. Patiently. In the shadows.

Sorry. Don't mean to be gloomy. Both Billie and I are v. excited about the pending arrival of your paintings.

Love, Pip

Friday afternoon I'm in New York City putting up flyers for Billie's next workshop. The traffic going back to Adler will be horrible until much later, so I decide to take the man in the balaclava up on his invitation and go to British night at The Gold Room. It sounds like a fancy place, and I'm in my overalls, but so be it. At least they're the velvet overalls with the pretty buckles.

With visions of all the British friends I will have by the end of the evening, I enter the small, brightly lit bar with gold tables, bar stools, and a piano in the corner of the room. A fat, friendly waiter in lederhosen with a bell around his neck takes my coat, tells me he loves my accent, and points me toward the only available seat.

I perch on the gold bar stool, which is unusually high up, and look around. I note that half the people in the room are wearing lederhosen. The rest are dressed in long dresses with sequins and boas and wide-brimmed hats. All of them are men.

A man in a large white wig stands up at the microphone next to the piano and introduces "The Fabulous Sal," at which point the man who took my coat leaps toward the microphone. When he gets there he sings the song about the lonely goatherd from *The Sound of Music*. He yodels beautifully, in perfect falsetto.

Everyone in the room knows the lyrics and sings the chorus with him in tune and in time. I'm applauding and yodeling with the rest of them when I see Jack, who is also dressed in lederhosen.

"You came!" he says, hurrying toward me with a broad smile on his face.

"Yes," I say, laughing. Then, "Sorry. Bit underdressed."

"No, you look beautiful," he says.

I like being called beautiful, even if the chap saying it is a flaming homosexual wearing shorts in the middle of January.

"Are all these chaps British then?" I say. Jack looks at me for a moment, then he laughs loud and long.

"No," Jack says, finally. "We sing songs from British musicals on Fridays. Tonight's *The Sound of Music* and *My Fair Lady*. Sorry—again. I should have known you wouldn't know. The Gold Room is a cabaret bar. Which means most of our clientele are gay."

Two old men dressed in pink and purple boas stand up to leave, and Jack whisks me to their table, which is right at the front.

"What can I get you to drink?"

"Chocolate milk?"

He seems charmed by my choice of beverage. Good. I can be myself here. I start to relax.

The pianist starts to play, and Sal is talking now. "It's BRITISH NIGHT, ladies and . . . ladies," he says. "And we have a real live Brit among us. What's your name, sweetie?"

The adrenaline is up. I'm not going to be able to resist this.

"Pippa Dunn," I say.

"Can you sing?"

"Well, yes . . ."

"Know any *My Fair Lady*?"

I grin at him. "Oh yes."

"Come on up here!"

I leave my seat for the piano.

"Gorgeous outfit, darling. Where did you get it?"

"Harrods," I say. Everybody laughs.

I've never used a microphone before and tell him so. He shows me how. My hand is trembling slightly. But when the pianist starts playing "Wouldn't It Be Loverly," and I start to sing, the music takes me over, as it always has done. I've known and loved this song all my life.

All I want is a room somewhere,
Far away from the cold night air

The crowd stops talking and listens. Half of me is in the room, singing to Sal, Jack, and the cluster of handsome, gloriously clad gay men who are smiling up at me. The other half of me is back at boarding school.

It is my first day of term and I'm the new girl. I was a year and a half younger than the other girls in the dorm. Mum and Dad were moving again, and I somehow managed to pass the Eleven Plus when I was ten. "She's got a gorgeous voice! Come, Flora, listen to this!" Six girls are standing around my bed in their long flannel nighties. I am standing on the bed, high as a kite on the excitement of being at boarding school, just like the girls in the Malory Towers books. I'm singing them the same song I'm singing now.

Singing makes me feel connected somehow. At peace.

Now I'm back in the cabaret club again. At the end of my song the boys applaud wildly and ask for more.

"Who are you?" Sal is talking to me from the front row.

Good question.

"My name is Pippa Dunn," I say.

"Where are you from?"

They're all looking at me, waiting for an answer.

"Buck Mountain, Georgia," I say, in my poshest English accent. They all laugh and clap. "No, seriously," I say, "I came to America two months ago to meet the mother who gave me birth for the very first time. You see, I was adopted and brought up in England. Two months ago I thought I was English. But I'm not. I'm a redneck."

They laugh louder and clap longer. The guy at the piano starts playing "Redneck Woman." Unable to resist, I sing the lyrics in the most upper-crust English accent I can muster, and, to my surprise and delight, the crowd goes wild.

At one in the morning, I say good-bye to Jack, who gives me his address and phone number and tells me to call him anytime. I promise to come back to The Gold Room and sing again.

I drive back to Adler yodeling at the top of my voice. And as I yodel, in my mind the New York skyline transforms into the Swiss Alps. And the toll collector at the George Washington Bridge becomes a lonely goatherd shepherding his flock along their way.

Chapter Thirty-one

BILLIE AND I put moisturizer on our faces in front of her mirror. She won't allow me to use soap and water on my face in her house and insists that I adopt her nighttime skin-care routine, stage by stage. I've just told Billie I want to spend the weekend with Walt in Washington.

"But you only just got here!" Billie says, dabbing toner on her face in short, fast movements. "And it's a three-day weekend! I thought we could do something fun together. We could start by getting our hair sun-glitzed."

"We'll have lots of time to do things together, Billie, and I'll work hard for you, I promise. But first I really want to spend some time with Walt."

"Well, we'd all like to spend time with Walt, honey. But your father is a very busy man."

My heart thuds.

"He did say he'd love to see me," I say, sitting on the love seat next to her dressing table and watching her finish her routine. "In fact, he said that if I didn't come and visit him he'd come up here and put me in the car himself."

Billie tips the yellow Clinique bottle upside down and puts more moisturizer on her face.

"Well, honey, Walt is the kind of man who says the things he thinks other people want to hear. Why don't you spend this weekend in New York with me and go and see Walt in a month or so, when you're more settled?"

My need to touch base with Walt wins out over my guilt at disappointing her.

"I really do want to go to Washington, Billie. Just for a few days."

I think she's forgiven me, but just as I'm falling asleep, she turns over and says, "You're very manipulative, honey. But that's okay. I was exactly the same at your age. I love you. Good night."

The next morning, as I'm getting in the car, Billie says, "I may stop by and say hi to you and Walt on Monday. I'm not promising, but if I can get everything done . . ."

"That'd be lovely," I say, guiltily hoping she doesn't.

As I drive along the interstate between my mother and my father, the weather takes a turn for the worse. I call Walt on my cell phone. "The chap who filled my tank up with petrol said I'm probably about an hour away."

"Hope you've got some warm clothes, kid. It's colder than a witch's teat down here."

I have never had a good sense of direction. One summer Dad found me ten miles up the A23 looking for the sweet shop that was two minutes round the corner from our house. Dad knows that I am likely to get lost under the best of circumstances. My other father simply assumes I am competent in this area. He believes I can find my way to him by telling me to find the Washington Monument, turn left on Elk Street, and right at the light to the front of the Furama Hotel.

Four hours later, after an unfortunate detour in the direction of Lynchburg, I pull into the well-lit parking area of the Furama Hotel in Washington, D.C. Walt is downstairs in the lobby in a heavy coat. He almost drags me out of my car, tipping the valet to take out my luggage.

"Don't ever do that again."

We're standing on the smooth concrete outside the hotel entrance, which oozes safety and comfort. Walt has his hands on my shoulders, so I have to listen to him.

"For years I didn't know whether you were safe or in danger. I don't ever want to be in that position again. For God's sake, kid, where were you?"

I tell him.

"Pippa, if anything happened to you I wouldn't even know who to call."

"You'd call Billie, I suppose. And Mum and Dad, of course."

"I don't know how to reach them. I don't have their number."

"I'll give it to you," I say.

"You do that, kiddo."

Walt's apartment is a penthouse suite with cherry-red oak furniture, a thick light carpet, and huge glass windows looking out over Washington, D.C.

On the walls are pictures of Walt with Presidents Reagan and Bush. There are also prints of men in red coats and hard hats on horses. When Mum and Dad were living abroad, I used to spend long weekends away from school with my friend Amanda. Her father was the Master of Foxhounds, and they went hunting every Saturday. Groups of people in red jackets and hard hats, just like the ones on Walt's wall, gathered on horses on their gravel drive until a horn sounded. Then they'd charge off into the afternoon rain, chasing dogs chasing a fox. Amanda would ride with everybody else and I would follow on foot, in a sopping-wet parka and gumboots, counting the minutes until we could go inside the big old manor house and have tea and chocolate digestives by the fire.

Now I stand next to Walt Markham, looking out over the Washington Monument. He feels like my father. He smells like my father. I am no longer chasing foxes in a wet world where I do not belong. Here I feel at home.

Later we eat dim sum in a noisy Chinese restaurant by the Capitol.

"I've told my wife," Walt says. "I'll tell the kids soon."

My heart leaps. I can't wait to meet Walt's kids. Perhaps it's because Ralphie's so much younger than me that I don't really click with him, I'm not sure, but I'm hoping I'll connect with Walt's children on a level that's soul-deep. Or at least recognize them as my own kind.

"What did you say to Margaret?" I ask, trying to sound casual.

"I said, 'Margaret, you remember the baby that was given up for adoption twenty-eight years ago? Well, she's a little bigger now. And she's come to find me.'"

"Did she mind?"

"Oh, I don't think she minded the idea of you. It's Billie she's worried about."

The dim sum sticks to the roof of my mouth. I unstick it with a sip of hot tea.

"Why is she worried about Billie?" I say. "It's been decades."

Walt drinks the rest of his beer in one swallow.

Later, Walt takes me to a fancy hotel restaurant with a lobby to hear some jazz. We're sitting at the bar eating peanuts and drinking margaritas when a man walks into the bar. He's about seventy years old, tall and thin, with a long face and a long coat. He waves at Walt.

Slowly, carefully, Walt turns his back to block the man's view of me.

"Go to the ladies' room," Walt says firmly. "Now."

"But I don't need to!"

"I don't want this guy to see you. He's a spook."

I roll my eyes. Mum and Dad always used to accuse me of being dramatic. Now I know where I got it from.

"There's no need to be so dramatic," I say, in a voice that sounds exactly like Mum's.

"Go."

"Okay."

The bathroom has a comfy velvet sofa in it, a huge gold-plated mirror, and all sorts of makeup-related items girlie girls like to use. A hairbrush and comb, hairspray, hair gel, hair ties, Kleenex, Tampax, perfume, Q-tips, the works.

I spray a little perfume on my neck. I clean my ears with a Q-tip. I brush my hair. I sit on the couch. I brush my hair again. I sit down on the couch again. They have toothbrushes in individual packets, with the toothpaste already on them, so I brush my teeth. I look at my watch. Ten minutes. That's more than enough.

I leave the bathroom. The man is still talking to Walt. Walt is moving his hand behind his back in a subtle gesture clearly intended to send me back into the bathroom. But I don't feel like going.

"Hallo," I say, walking over to them, smiling at the man and holding out my hand.

"Hi," he says. He looks at Walt and back again at me.

"I'm Pippa."

"Pippa's a friend of mine," Walt says quickly. "She's here on a trip from England."

I don't know why I expected Walt to acknowledge me as his daughter, but I did, and for a second I feel dirty. Then years of British training take over.

"Very nice to meet you," I say.

"And you," he says. "You have such a pretty accent."

"I'm from England," I say. "Have you been?"

"Oh yes," he says. "My wife and I have spent a lot of time there."

"Really?" I say, in my most charmed voice. "How interesting! Which part?"

The man and I continue to have exactly the same conversation I have with every American of a certain age who has spent time in England. He and his wife just love England. They especially love it when the Brits call road bumps sleeping policemen. His great-grandfather was from a town just outside London called—now, what was it? Oh, if my wife were here, she'd know. That's right. Streath Ham. And isn't it funny that the hotelier told his wife, "I'll knock you up in the morning?"

When he leaves I turn to Walt and say, "He's not spooky. He's very nice."

"I didn't say he was spooky," Walt says. "I said he was a spook."

I look at him blankly.

"A 'spook' is a spy, Pippa," he says.

"Oh," I say. And then, "Do you know a lot of spies?"

There's an edge I've not heard in my own voice before. Who are you, Walt?

"I want to keep you out of all this."

"All what?" I say. "What?"

I can sense something I don't want to sense.

"What could he possibly do?" I say.

"Well, he could start by revoking your American citizenship," Walt says.

"Why on earth would he do that?"

"I'm not saying he would. But he could."

"No, he couldn't," I say, suddenly afraid. Suddenly aware of how attached to America I already am. It feels right for me, somehow. Accepting. Familiar. Big enough. Whatever threat this man represents now feels personal.

"No he couldn't. I was born here. No one can take my American citizenship away from me! My ancestors came over on the Mayflower on both sides! Hell, I'm an illegitimate daughter of the American Revolution!"

At this, Walt is unable to stop laughing, as is my intent. Then, "I get it, kid. I'd have come over too when I was your age."

"You're completely overreacting. He was very nice. He's been to Harrods."

The pianist is arriving now.

"Come on!" I say to Walt. "Let's get a better seat."

Everything is forgotten as the man at the piano starts to play. Music has always had the power to wash away whatever's going on for me. Even confusing, upsetting things.

When he is done, the piano man asks if anyone in the audience would like to sing. He starts to play again. I know the song. It's "If I Were a Bell" from *Guys and Dolls*. My adrenaline is up and I can't resist. Grinning at Walt, I stand up and start to sing. The people at the bar stop talking and listen. The pride in Walt's face has replaced whatever was going on earlier. When I've finished, Walt and the people who are left stand up.

"She's good!" the people say, applauding. "She's really good!"

"You're more than good!" Walt says. "I knew you were the real stuff! My God, kid, you've got a Broadway voice!"

I'm basking in his praise, and then Walt starts to laugh. The music and the margaritas and the euphoria that comes whenever I perform start me laughing too.

"You do know Billie wouldn't let you do that if she were here," Walt says as I sit down again. "She has to be the corpse at every funeral." Then, "How is she, anyway?"

The question is meant to sound casual. But something in his eyes tells me it's not. I respond in the way English people have responded to the "How is she?" question since the dawn of the English.

"She's fine," I say. And then, "She said she might stop by tomorrow, actually . . ."

Walt orders another drink and asks no more.

Back in Walt's apartment we both put our feet up on the oval glass table. We are both wearing odd socks. I'm telling him about everything I want to do.

"I've got all this extra energy, Walt, and now I know I've come by it honestly—well, there's so much I want to do! I'd like to be a writer of some kind, and sing perhaps, and help Billie with her company, and, oh, I don't know, I'd really like to try and *do* something politically."

"You've got the genes to do whatever you want, kid." His faith in me is catching and I'm on a high.

Now he's on the telephone in the kitchen talking to his mother, who lives on a golf course in Sarasota. That's what American grannies do, if they can afford to. British grannies stay in the houses they raised their family in and then get pushed off to an old folks' home in Bognor, where they live out the rest of their days being spoon-fed pink blancmange and getting sponge-washed by women in their fifties who sit them in front of very loud televisions and get irritated when they wet the beds.

"She's *exactly* like I was when I was her age," Walt says over the phone to his mother, who was only eighteen when she had him. "She's got our genes, Mother. And she's ready to fly."

Chapter Thirty-two

AFTER DINNER, Walt sits in his gray velvet armchair and I perch on the couch. He begins speaking with his face half in shadows.

"I wanted your mother as much as it is possible to want anyone," he says. "Hell, I was twenty-five and stuck in the wrong marriage, I was a sitting duck. 'Billie will destroy you,' Mother said, when she met her. And she did. But not in the way Mother meant."

Walt looks angry for a moment.

"They kept us apart. Oh yes, they did that." He takes another sip of whiskey and squints his eyes.

"You see, kid, Billie didn't destroy *me*—she destroyed the rest of the world for me. No one was ever as vibrant. Laughter was never again as helpless as it had been with her. And sex with any other woman never came close. I had to stay away from her in the end. Because you couldn't get too close to Billie without being burned."

As Walt is talking, the brown and blue pattern on the curtains seems to swirl a little. The whiskey is making my head fuzzy.

"You're the best of both of us, Pippa," Walt says, back in the room with me now. "You're as smart and alive as Billie was. As I was. I knew you'd be talented. With our ancestors you had to be. Hell, you've got generals, concert pianists, artists going back two hundred years. Even the governor of a state!"

We sit in silence for a minute. Then, "The old man used to say, 'Everything comes full circle.' That's for sure."

"I keep thinking of the night, long after it all blew up, after you were gone and Margaret had given birth to our second child. I'd pulled the chip and done the right thing, killing a part of myself in the process.

"I hadn't seen Billie in five years. I'd been driving myself as hard as a man can. Trying to forget. And, I might add, helping change the world in the process. A lot of Wall Street guys were running the world, and I went out to fight 'em by helping the conservative movement. Really we were Enlightenment guys who believed in God. We were not Jeffersonian. Some people called us extremists, but we weren't. You took what soldiers you could get.

"I'd been working like a dog and was home for the first time in days. At one a.m., the doorbell rang.

"'I'll get it,' I said to Margaret. I put on my slippers and went down the stairs to the door. It was raining outside, and someone was standing on our doorstep. My God. It was Billie. I let her in.

"I told my wife there was an emergency at work. I told her to go back to sleep. Your mother was wearing a yellow slicker and her hair was wet and her deep green eyes alight with mischief.

"'Hi Walt,' she said, smiling. 'I was passing through.'

"'You were passing through?'

"'I was passing through.'

"I pushed her into the library and shut the door. And while my wife and children slept upstairs I made love to Billie, on the couch, on the table . . .

"'I had to see you,' she said. 'You were forgetting. I don't want you to forget. I want you to long for me. So I came by. I don't want you to be happy without me.'

"'I'll call,' I said.

"'Every year,' she said. 'On her birthday.' She looked at me and I knew I would call. And then she was gone.

"We promised each other it would be the last time. I went back to Washington, started working, but then I'd smell her scent on a woman in an elevator—and my hand was reaching for the phone."

I am rooted to my chair, watching my father take this journey back to the most painful time in his life. He is not looking at me. Then he begins speaking again, as if to himself.

"I couldn't stand it. I couldn't stay away from her. I didn't.

"She came to me at home again. This time I introduce her to Margaret as a colleague." Walt's face is clenched in pain, his eyes squinting as he remembers.

"There's an intense beauty in her. And its opposite.

"It's the opposite that stops me saying to hell with it all, my career, my life, I'm going with the woman I love. There's something about Billie that's dangerous. I know this."

He's back with me now. The whiskey in his glass rocks to the left and right. We sit in silence. Than he looks at me and says, "Part of me feels we did the right thing. The other part of me yearns for the life I might have had with the woman I loved. And you. My precious child. My self, in female form."

His voice breaks a little.

"It was a terrible time, kid. Hell on earth. But never forget this. You were the product of a great love. The kind of love that only comes once in a lifetime. Every day I thought of you. Wondering where you were. Our child. Our baby. Our little baby girl."

His glass catches the light again. His face is relaxed now. His eyes are almost closed. He's speaking very quietly.

"The cherry blossoms had just come out when I left you both at the hospital. I had the top down on my convertible and remember every excruciating moment of my drive home. Agonizing about the harm Billie and I had done to each other. Wondering what harm we might have done to you. Joy and unspeakable sorrow and outrage. And those pastel trees."

Within a few moments he is asleep on the couch. I get up, cover Walt with a blanket, go into my room, and close the door. That night I am haunted by dreams of Walt and Billie. Billie is young, beautiful, desperately in love with my handsome, charismatic father. They're dancing together, unable to stay more than half an inch apart.

Then something else enters the dream. Something malevolent. It cuts the air between the two of them. Suddenly I am a babe again, cut off from my people, thrown, alone and whirling, into the dark blue night.

Chapter Thirty-three

THE NEXT MORNING, Billie calls. She's coming to Washington so we can spend some time together, "just the three of us." I do my best to savor the time I have left just with Walt.

We visit the Washington Monument and the National Gallery of Art. I help Walt a bit with his work.

Walt dictates letters much more slowly than I can type. The paper he gives me is headed "The Conservative Coalition" and has a post-office box address at the top and Walt's cell phone number.

Dear Kristoff,

After so many years of communism, we are all aware of the importance of the Ukraine in the world market and are sensitive to your current needs. We will be happy to raise your concerns next time we meet with the president.

Once we have you elected, we will certainly be able to help you in other ways.

Yours sincerely,
Walt Markham

Walt is impressed by the speed of my typing. I am impressed by my father. Instead of taking a break after recent losses in Afghanistan, he's already preparing to help the Ukraine.

Billie is running late. She's had her hair permed. Then she decided she didn't like it, so she had it straightened. Then she changed her mind again and had it re-permed. Then she had it "sun-glitzed."

"She's the love of your life," I say to Walt. "This is a historic meeting. You must dress for the occasion."

Walt puts on the red bow tie I bought him and a tux. We're sitting upstairs in Walt's apartment. Below us, Washington is drowning in rain.

The intercom buzzes. "I'll go and get her," I say.

I go down in the elevator. There, in the lobby, is Billie. She is wearing a cherry red coat. She's damp from the rain. She's not looking at me.

"I told Daddy I probably wouldn't marry again, but if I did, it would be Walt."

She takes off her red plastic rain hat, and shakes out her newly styled hair. The curls are even tighter than usual. She hands me the long, light tan camel-hair coat she is carrying.

"This is for you," she says. "You can borrow it until you go back to England."

When she says this, what I hear is that she wants me to go back to England. She doesn't really want me around.

I feel pain, instantly, in my chest, as if my heart's been hit with a hammer. Sometimes the hammer hits softly. Sometimes it hits hard. This time it hits hard, and I react, as I always do when I think someone's going to reject me, by resolving to leave them first.

Walt opens the door to his apartment and we walk in. We stand awkwardly in the middle of the room. Billie and Walt look at each other and say nothing. Then Billie walks toward Walt. Her voice is soft. "You look as handsome as ever, Walt," she says.

"Hello, Billie," he says. His voice has a crack in it.

She holds his hands in hers.

So, finally, here we are. All three of us, in the same room, at the same time. My mother, my father, and me. I stare at Billie and Walt. They are no longer ghosts. But I still can't quite believe they're real.

I've started to shake. I pull my sleeves over my hands so they can't see. I turn my back, pretending to look out over Washington. Actually I am looking at their reflection in the huge window. Despite her hair, Billie looks beautiful. Ephemeral, almost. And Walt is mesmerized.

What would it do to a family, I wonder, if the father fell hopelessly in love with someone else, but stayed with you and your mother anyway? I'm sure you'd feel it. It would be there, under the surface. You'd see sadness in your father—and hurt in your mother—you'd catch it, from time to time, and you wouldn't know why it was there. Even if they lied and said everything was fine, you'd know it wasn't.

Billie says it again. "You look as handsome as ever, Walt."

I can't tell what Walt is thinking. "Hello, Billie," he says again.

"Just going to the loo," I manage to mumble and walk quickly into the bathroom.

The hammer hits my heart like a metronome, in time with the raindrops on the window, over and over again. *Bang,* I am not wanted. *Bang,* I am not wanted. *Bang,* I am not wanted.

I turn on the tap so they won't hear my sobs. Twenty minutes later I somehow manage to walk back into the sitting room, tear-free and smiling, ready to spend time with the parents who gave me birth.

Billie and Walt get up late the next morning. Billie is wearing a shiny light blue nightie made of satin, and Walt is still in his blue toweling robe. He makes us eggs and bacon for breakfast. Billie has her hair in aluminum foil. "Marie told me to re-treat my hair two days after the perm," Billie says. She does not care that her head looks like a Christmas tree.

We spend the day hanging out in Walt's apartment. In the evening we watch *The Producers* with Zero Mostel and Gene Wilder. I have never seen it before. During the roof-garden scene, Walt and I are laughing so hard we literally roll on our backs on the floor. Billie is curled up in Walt's gray velvet chair, reading *Women Who Give Too Much.* "I prefer a more subtle kind of humor," she says.

When the movie is over, Billie kisses the top of Walt's head. Her perfume is sweet and strong and displaces all other smells from the room.

"Shall we keep her?" Billie says to Walt, smiling.

"I think the real question," Walt says, quietly, "is, will she keep us?"

When Walt shows me photographs of people on his side of the family who look like me, and explains who's who, Billie keeps coming into the sitting room and then leaving again. Finally she comes in, stands behind the couch, and starts running her fingers through Walt's hair. "Let's go to bed, honey," she says. "Pippa's tired. I'm tired. It's late."

Billie and Walt go into the bedroom and close the door.

I walk into the kitchen. My heart hurts terribly, and then the numbness comes back, stopping my tears. Which is a good thing, because the sign on the wall next to the fridge says "Crybabies will be shot."

The next day, Walt says he has to go out for some kind of meeting, on which he does not elaborate, and Billie and I find ourselves alone together. I am feeling everything, and therefore nothing.

"What is it, honey?"

The words are almost impossible to say, because I am so afraid of the answer.

"Are you sure you really want me here?" I ask her, finally. "Wouldn't you prefer me to go back to England? So you and Walt can be together? Without me?"

Billie looks genuinely astonished.

"Is that what you really think, honey?"

"Well, yes. And it's hard because—well, you've had years to get together with Walt, but I've only just shown up."

"Oh, honey," Billie says. Her face is full of love. She pushes my hair out of my face and tucks it behind my ears.

"It's not Walt I want to be with," she says. "It's you."

The place where the hammer hit almost stops hurting. But not quite. I want to believe her. I look at her face. Her eyes are certainly full of love for me.

For a second, she is the mother who used to float above me when I was sent to stand under the clock at boarding school. Caring about me first. Loving me first. I drink in her next words, because I so want to believe them.

"I can't get enough of you," she says. "Don't you ever think, for one second—now, look at me honey—don't you ever think for one second that just because Walt and I . . . well, don't think for a second it means I don't want you. Because I want you more than anything in the world! You coming to live with me, and work with me, so we can really spend some time together—well, it means the world to me!"

I'm staring at my long-lost mother. I see nothing but love in her eyes.

"You are very much wanted." As she says the words, the tightness in my chest loosens.

"Really?" I say, laughing through my tears.

"Oh yes, honey. Yes, yes, yes, yes, yes!"

She takes me in her arms. And I stay there, wishing, not for the first time, that Billie wouldn't wear quite so much perfume.

Billie has to get back to New York for a meeting. I am to follow the next day. The moment she drives off, Walt and I run upstairs, turn on the video of *The Producers*, and watch it again, laughing even harder the second time. We don't talk about Billie's visit.

Walt gives me the glass ball with snow in it that he keeps on top of his television.

"Here," he says, "take this. My father gave this to me when I was a child. It is something that is truly mine."

When you turn the ball upside down, snow falls over skaters with scarves and hats on, and there's a wizard in it too. When I turn it upside down I'm taken back to the night Billie and Walt met. They are skating around the ice rink at Rockefeller Center, holding hands and laughing. When I hold the glass ball, I am skating with them, invisible, waiting for their love to grow too strong to resist. So I can be born.

At five o'clock the next morning—I'm leaving early to beat the traffic back to New York—I accidentally drop my bag and the glass ball smashes to the ground. I can't stop myself from crying. The noise wakes Walt, who comes running out of his room.

"I broke it! I'm so sorry!"

Walt crouches down on the floor, picking up the pieces of glass.

"Don't cry, Pippa," he says. "Don't cry."

His voice has a rough kindness about it that makes me cry more. I'm inconsolable. We are both crouching, picking up the pieces, my tears splashing against the broken glass. Then Walt points to the wizard and smiles.

"See, kid? You've released Merlin. The magic is out in the world now, Pippa. You've set him free."

"Have I?" I say.

"You have," he says firmly.

A warmth creeps back into my soul. I stop crying and leave with a sense that, in spite of my usual clumsiness, I have just done something magical and good.

Chapter Thirty-four

Back in New York, Billie starts training me in earnest. In addition to writing press releases and promoting Art Buddies, my job is to help out wherever else I'm needed.

I spend a morning helping Tom explain to his oldest client why a tuba solo inspired by Stravinski's *Rite of Spring* might be a hard sell to colleges.

I spend an afternoon listening to Marvin encouraging a Christian poet to consider paragraphing when he takes dictation from God.

And Billie calls all her friends and tells them how wonderful I am when I answer the phone by mistake and manage to talk a failed sculptor out of suicide by promising to exhibit his clay ears at Billie's next workshop.

Billie fills every spare minute giving me advice. "The way you stay organized? Get a headset! That way, when you're on the phone talking to the boring people, like the tax man or whoever, you can get the chores done at the same time, see?"

I'm particularly impressed by the way she solves the "it must be around here somewhere" problem. She simply buys more of each thing. For example, she has ten pairs of glasses—two for each room—so she doesn't have to waste time looking for things.

By the end of January, Billie has handed a lot of her workload over to me and has begun research for her book. The working title is *Are They Nuts? Identifying Mental Problems in the People Around You.*

"Half the people around me are mentally ill in one way or another," she says to someone on the telephone. "Tom's obsessive-compulsive. My brother's a pathological liar. You know about Malice and poor Lee. As for Marcie, why she's practically psychotic!" She sounds delighted.

And then the CD with the photographs of Nick's paintings arrives. The moment I see them I can sense their power. They are erotic and angry and, above all, alive.

The pictures are of a man and a woman, somewhere a long way from America. The man is part Indian, tall, handsome, elegant, and looks like Nick. It's hard to tell where the woman is from. In one painting she looks like she could be from the Middle East, in another she could be from India, in another she could be English. It's the same woman each time though. She is achingly beautiful and dressed in a light purple sari covered with little round mirrors. There are flecks of red in her hair.

In one painting, the man and the woman are making love in a street full of strangers. There's violence in the air—and boys, girls, men, women doing ordinary things, pushing carts, walking down dusty roads, biking, eating. In the background they're running from an American tank that's on fire. But with all the activity in the painting, it's the man and the woman you can't take your eyes off.

I'm still staring at the paintings when Billie comes into the room. She looks at them one by one, with intense concentration. There are fourteen in all.

"He's wonderful," Billie says, finally.

"Really?" My heart soars.

"Yes, honey. And the paintings are sexy and shocking and topical, so they'll sell."

Most of the time Billie has so much on her mind when she's talking to you, you know she's thinking about something else at the same time. On this occasion, though, her focus is entirely on me.

"Are you in love with this man?" she says.

"I think so." Saying it aloud brings relief. "I feel linked to him somehow. It's hard to explain. I can't stop thinking about him. He feels a part of me. I . . . I understand him. And he me."

Billie looks at the paintings again. Then up at me.

"Honey," she says, "I've yet to meet an artist with this kind of talent who isn't entirely wrapped up in themselves," she says. "I'm sure all the encouragement you've given him has meant a lot to him. But what does he give you?"

I look at her, astonished.

"Everything!"

The phone rings, the moment is over, and Billie goes to pick it up. When she comes back in, Billie's focus has transferred to her poppy red lipstick, which she puts on at her makeup table. Once her lipstick is on, she swivels her stool around to face me.

"You're beautiful," she says, gently. "Like my mother. Only you don't think you are."

This is true. Walking next to Mum and Charlotte all my life, I've felt like a human Tigger—tall, ungainly, bouncy, and a bit of a pain. Certainly not beautiful.

"You could have any man you want," Billie says, "if you used your power. But you don't believe you have any, so you don't. And that makes you so vulnerable, honey."

Then she takes off her glasses and, on her way out of the room, says, "But he is a wonderful painter, and I know someone who can help him. I'll call Edelman."

"Who's Edelman?" I say, following Billie as she moves at top speed down the corridor toward the kitchen.

"He owns four of the top galleries in New York," she says. "If Edelman likes him, Nick will be made."

I rush to the computer to e-mail Nick. He e-mails me back right away.

DATE: Jan. 30
TO: pippa-dunn@hotmail.com
FROM: NickDevang@bankglobal.net

Dear Pippa,

    I knew in the moment I met you that you were to be a player in my life. I had no idea how important a player you were to be.

    Ideas for new paintings are exploding inside me. I'm up all night watching them take shape on canvas. And it's all because of you.

    The universe has spoken. We can no longer put off our meeting. I will come to you soon.

Love, Nick

Chapter Thirty-five

B Y THE START of my second month at Billie's I've settled into a kind of routine. My weekdays are spent working for Billie and e-mailing back and forth with Nick. On Saturday nights I visit The Gold Room, where Jack invariably coaxes me on stage. It happens so frequently, before I know it, I'm putting together an act.

Meanwhile, back in Peaseminster, life goes on much as before.

Little Tew
Peaseminster Pass
Peaseminster, Sussex, England

Feb. 12

Darling Pippa,

Lovely to hear it's all going so well!

Exciting news from our end. The Peaseminster Scottish Country Dancers have been asked to perform a demonstration dance at Tewksbury Hall in May for none other than Princess Anne! Your father has decided to have everyone dance a medley with a royal theme including the Duke and Duchess of Edinburgh (reel), the Balmoral Strathspey, and Holyrood House (reel).

Apparently Princess Anne not only sings the "Flower of Scotland" at the start of rugby matches, she also dances a lovely Petronella and likes to join in. So once we've finished the demonstration, your father plans to bow graciously to Princess Anne and invite her to take my place on the dance floor. I shall discreetly return to my seat just moments before.

Charlotte and Rupert's skiing trip to Courcheval was mercifully unaffected by the lack of snow, owing to snow-making machines.

Must go, lots of love, Mum

Even though Earl is gone, Billie spends every other week in Georgia writing her book and keeping watch on Malice. When she's there, she calls me in the early morning. It amuses her greatly to open with, "This is your mother speaking."

Whenever she calls herself my mother, my heart hurts, because it feels like she's just shot Mum.

"Why don't you call yourself Billie?" I say, lightly. "Rather than 'Mother.' I'll only get confused."

"But I am your mother."

"Yes—I know you are—of course you are, but, well, I'm used to calling Mum Mother, that's all . . . I guess—well, I guess, well, it just doesn't feel right. It's hard to explain, but . . ."

"Honey, did I ever tell you your great-grandmother shot a man?"

Bam. She's done it again. Gone off on a tangent the moment I try to tell her something she doesn't want to hear. As usual, the tangent's so interesting I forget what it is I've been trying to tell her.

"She did, you know. Your great-grandmother shot a man. In the leg. The sheriff let her off. As she said, 'If he had been a friend, he'd have walked right in. But he rang the doorbell, so I shot him.'"

After only two months of my working for her, Billie's business has doubled, thanks, in part, to the interview I managed to get her in *Art Today*. But it's been over a month since Billie sent the CD of Nick's paintings to Dwight Edelman and we've heard nothing. When I ask her when we're likely to hear she keeps saying, "Honey, these things take *time*!"

• • •

DATE: March 1
FROM: NickDevang@bankglobal.net
TO: pippa-dunn@hotmail.com

Dearest One,

   I've got a business meeting in NYC on the fourth. I have to be in
Singapore on the fifth, so I can only manage an hour. Meet me by
the ice rink at Rockefeller Center on Wednesday at 12:30. We'll have
lunch at the Sea Grill.

I let out a whoop. "He's coming!" Carol and I have just finished putting Billie's press release together and we're down in the office.

   "Who's coming?" Carol says, laughing.

   "Nick's coming! On Wednesday! He's coming! I just wish we had
heard from Edelman!"

   I run up the mud-covered hill to Billie's mailbox to see if there's any
news from Edelman. There are a few patches of snow under the trunks
of the still leafless trees, but spring doesn't feel all that far away.

   Billie's mailbox is stuffed with the usual catalogs wrapped in
plastic. I pull the catalogs out and rifle through them. Still nothing
from Edelman. I head back into the office and Carol hands me a letter, dated two weeks before.

February 15

Dear Ms. Parnell,

Thank you for your inquiry. Unfortunately, we are unable to take
on new clients at this time.

   Sincerely,
   Dwight Edelman

"I'm so sorry, sweetie," Carol says. "I thought you knew."

   Carol looks as if she is debating whether or not to say something
more.

"I don't understand," I say.

Carol walks out into the corridor and makes sure that Billie is still upstairs in the kitchen, on the phone. She shuts the door.

"Pippa, I know how you feel about Nick and . . ."

"And what?"

She's looking at me directly now.

"Dwight Edelman is one of the busiest art agents in the world," she says. "He doesn't represent unknowns."

"Does Billie know that?"

Carol doesn't say anything.

"Does she even *know* him?" I say, already feeling Nick's heartbreak.

"Billie met Dwight Edelman once, fifteen years ago, in AA."

"But she gave the impression she knew him well! And . . . and she told me she thinks Nick's wonderful!"

"She tells all the artists they're wonderful. And she gives the impression they're the only wonderful ones. That's how she keeps her clients. You know how insecure artists can be. Pay an artist a compliment and he's yours for life."

There's a bitterness in Carol's tone. Either I haven't heard it, or I haven't noticed it before.

"But Nick's not a client."

"No. But she'll do what she has to do to keep you."

I stare at Carol for a second. She's not smiling. My mind is spinning, my mouth has gone dry, and I feel sick.

"Is none of it true? Any of it?" I say.

Carol doesn't speak.

When I get angry, which doesn't happen very often, I'm filled with a sudden burst of extra energy that, on this occasion, propels me up the stairs to the kitchen, where Billie is now cooking scrambled eggs.

"Billie, why didn't you tell me about the letter from Edelman?"

She doesn't even look up.

"What letter from Edelman?"

"This one," I say, holding out Nick's rejection letter.

"Oh *that*," Billie says, glancing at the letter quickly before breaking eggs into a pan. Half of one of the egg whites ends up on the stove.

I suddenly see myself in the kitchen at home, doing the same thing. I hear Mum's irritated "Oh *dar*ling" and, for the first time, understand that it's not so much the spills themselves that are annoying, it's the fact that Billie never cleans up after herself. Which means that if I don't want to get salmonella, I'll have to do it.

"I'm a busy woman, honey. I don't remember exactly when the letter came."

"But Nick's been waiting to hear about this for weeks!"

"Well I *know* that!" Billie says, turning to me. "But I don't have any control over Edelman. All I can do is show him the work. The rest is up to him."

"But you said you'd help him!"

"Honey, I've been out of the mainstream art business for twenty-five years!" She sounds indignant. As if she never said she could help Nick and I am being unreasonable for suggesting she could.

Billie slaps the now-scrambled eggs onto a piece of burned toast and starts eating.

"But—you're Billie Parnell! You discovered Marfil! And you love Nick's work. Why don't *you* represent Nick?"

"I'm fifty years old. I don't schlep anymore. I'd rather do laundry. Besides, if Dwight doesn't like him—well, Dwight *is* the art world these days."

"But he's so talented," I say.

"Honey, so are a lot of people. I mean look at Cole. He's prodigiously talented, and he can't get an exhibition either."

Surely Billie can't think Cole's bad Andy Warhol knockoffs are in Nick's league. There's nothing original about Cole.

Nick has been painting like a madman, despite his fear of rejection, because I've given him hope. And now his hope is gone. I feel like a murderer.

"Anyway, as I've been trying to tell you, Nick just called," Billie says.

"What?"

"I'd have told you sooner if you'd let me speak, but you tore in here in such a fury, I didn't get a chance! Besides, I was sort of enjoying watching you. I've never seen you this angry before. You were *magnificent*!" She's filled with pride, for God's sake.

"Billie!"

"Nick's meeting's been brought forward to tomorrow. He wants you to meet him at the same time, same place. I told him that of course you'd be there."

"Tomorrow!" I say. Then, "Nick's coming all this way because he thinks Dwight Edelman is going to represent him."

"Oh, I don't think that's the only reason he's coming, honey," Billie says. Then, turning to me, smiling, cute, knowing, she says, "It'll all work out as it's meant to. You'll see."

Then she puts the pan in the sink "to soak" and picks up the phone.

That night I toss and turn with the kind of ghastly embarrassment that keeps you up all night and, just as you're falling off to sleep, makes you cringe and groan so loudly, you wake yourself up again.

Chapter Thirty-six

AFTER MY SLEEPLESS NIGHT, the drive into Manhattan toward the man who has sustained me over the last few months feels like a dream. I wonder how much he's changed in the seven years since I've actually seen him. I wonder, too, if our physical attraction will have grown too strong to resist.

My heart's beating extra fast as I walk down the promenade off Fifth Avenue toward the ice rink where Walt and Billie skated together nearly thirty years before. I'm wearing the Chanel suit a hopeful Charlotte sneaked into my suitcase, with a note attached saying "just in case." The silk lining feels soft against my legs. At Billie's insistence, I'm also wearing makeup, a gold necklace, and a pair of Billie's high-heeled shoes, which click on the marble ground past Botticelli, L'Occitane, and Le Chocolatier.

Nick told me once that he loves expensive chocolates wrapped in gold foil. "They remind me of a beautifully dressed woman," he said. "They need to be undressed before they can be tasted." Personally I'd prefer a Kit Kat, but they're not for me, so I go into the chocolate shop to buy him some.

"*La plus délicieuse femme à New York se trouve ici dans mon magasin de chocolats!*" The man behind the counter is smiling at me.

"*Merci,*" I say.

"*Une americaine qui parle français?*"

Not quite American.

I walk over the circle where they put New York's most famous Christmas tree and head toward the ice rink. Flags from different nations standing proudly around it make me think of the UN, which Dad calls "our one true hope for world peace" and Walt calls "a bunch of mewling foreigners."

Billie's pointy shoes are slightly too small. I'm wishing we'd agreed to meet somewhere I could wear sneakers and am feeling as disturbed as I always do at the thought of people spending hundreds of dollars on a pair of shoes just because they can, when I see Nick walking toward me. He's looking impossibly elegant in a dark green Versace suit.

I'd forgotten how beautiful Nick is. He's Omar-Sharif-when-he-was-young beautiful. That beautiful.

When he reaches me, he doesn't say anything. Instead he simply looks at me. Intense. Serious. I return his gaze. We don't speak.

He's wearing the sort of aftershave that makes me want to make love with him immediately. Certain aftershaves have this effect on me. If I knew how to seduce a man—which I don't, because that would require making the first move, which would involve the risk of rejection—I'd happily seduce any man wearing this particular aftershave. Just about anywhere.

I wish, suddenly, that I were the sort of woman who could smile enigmatically, take him by the hand without saying a word, and lead him to the nearest hotel. But I'm not. So I break the silence, kiss him on both cheeks, and say, "Hallo, Nick." And then, "Here, I bought you some chocolates."

Nick takes the chocolates, places his hand in the small of my back, and leads me toward the elevator that takes us down to the Sea Grill.

We order a deluxe plate of sushi for two. Our table looks out onto the ice rink and the magnificent golden statue of Prometheus that seems to fly above the skaters whirling in the cold winter air.

"You're staring at that statue as if you recognize it," Nick says, finally.

"I'm thinking about what it stands for," I say, turning back to him.

"It makes me think of you, breathing life into your wonderful paintings." My heart is beating extra fast. I'm going to have to tell him.

We're looking into each other's eyes again. His are almost black.
I'm about to begin, when Nick says, "I had a fascinating talk with
your mother. She sees you, you know," he says. "The real you."

"I know."

"And she's terribly proud of you. I adore her for that," he says.
"And also because she told me how much she loves my work," he
says, smiling. Then, "It's like a dream come true, all of this. You—
and the fact that the woman who discovered Marfil sent my work to
Dwight Edelman."

I can't bear it any longer.

"Edelman can't take you on, Nick." I finally manage to blurt it
out. "I'm so, so sorry."

One of my chopsticks falls on the floor. I bend down to pick it up,
aware that I am blushing, which never looks good on a redhead.

A waiter arrives at our table at lightning speed, bringing me a new
set of chopsticks. Nick hasn't moved. Nick and I are so alike, I know
the rejection is killing him. He'll hide it, of course, as well as I do.

"He—he thinks you're brilliantly talented and absolutely loved
your work, but he just can't take any new clients on right now."

The kind people on earth—like the polite people—are liars.

"You mustn't let this discourage you, Nick. You need to paint,
it's part of who you are, you mustn't, mustn't, mustn't let this stop
you painting!"

His gold watch and white shirt seem to shine in the reflected
light. I've finally run out of words.

"Have you finished?"

"I think so." I can't look away. Nick takes my hand across the
table. It's cool and strong against mine. I want to lift his hand to my
face and kiss his palm.

"It's all right, darling," he says. "Billie told me everything."

I look at him carefully. He's not smiling bravely to cover anything up. He's genuinely amused. Relief fills me instantly.

"And you're okay with it?"

"More than okay," Nick says. "I adore you for trying to protect me. But I know it's a numbers game, and so does your mother."

"Is that what she said?"

"Yes! And she also told me that she would hook me up with someone else who she is sure will take me on."

"Really! Who?"

"You, my love."

"Me?"

"When I called yesterday, Billie started raving about you. You're a genius, apparently, capable of anything you set your mind to—you do, after all, have her DNA. She was exactly your age when she got Marfil his first break. She's sure that if anyone can get me my first break in today's market, it'll be you."

"But . . ."

"Come on, Pip! Billie knows, I know, and you know that you were the top salesperson when you sold advertising in London. You're gorgeous, frighteningly intelligent, charming, as English as the fucking queen—and you know how they love that over here. You need money. I need an agent. If you get me an exhibition, I'll pay you twenty percent commission out of my take. On everything."

"But I don't know anyone in the art world."

"Pippa, your mother is Billie Parnell! *Carpe diem!* It's a chance for both of us. Come on, love. You'll blow them away, I know you will. Tell me you'll do it. Say yes."

A feeling of warmth and excitement swims into the heart of my being.

Of course! It's part of the plan. It's part of our destiny.

"Yes," I say, finally.

"Say yes again," Nick says softly. "Say yes to all of it. Say yes to me."

It's time for Nick to leave to catch his plane, so we head back out onto the busy New York street.

I can hide the fact that the air has gone out of my lungs. I can hide the fact that I want him to kiss me more than I've ever wanted anything. But I can't hide the fact that my hands are shaking.

When he sees this, Nick takes me by both wrists, his fingers curling tightly around them, like a bracelet that's slightly too tight, and pulls me closer toward him. We stare at each other, not saying a word. We dare not kiss. If we start, we won't be able to stop.

In my mind's eye we're naked on a bed together, somewhere far away. Crumpled white sheets. Sunlight peeking through the shutters. A plate of half-eaten fruit by the bed.

And then we're back on Fifth Avenue.

"Soon," Nick whispers.

"Yes," I whisper back.

"Good-bye, darling," he says finally. Then he kisses me on the cheek and disappears into a cab. The cab is quickly swallowed up by the traffic. I stand on tiptoe trying to keep my eye on it, but within moments he is gone.

Later that evening, as we're playing a late-night game of Scrabble, Billie says, "You know, a part of me feels a little jealous."

"Of what?"

Billie laughs gently.

"Oh honey. You have no idea, have you? Of your youth, honey. Of your talent. Of your prospects. Of this wonderful opportunity you have to represent Nick."

"Billie, if you want to represent Nick, that's completely fine by me!" All that matters to me is that Nick gets the exhibition he so richly deserves. I think of The Gold Room and the act I'm starting to develop. "I've got lots of other things to do. And you're much more qualified than I am."

"Honey," Billie says, "I love you. And I'm happy that Nick wants you to do this. Really I am. You'll get him an exhibition eventually, I just know it. And then both you and Nick Devang will be made."

SPRING

Chapter Thirty-seven

BILLIE WANTS ME TO GO and visit her sister Marcie, who is back in the mental hospital. The thought terrifies me. If I don't go and see Marcie, I can continue to tell myself that Billie is exaggerating and that really the aunt I met at Earl's funeral is absolutely fine. So I tell Billie I've got too much work to do and can't go. Billie is not pleased.

"You can't escape the family mood disorder just because you were raised somewhere else," she says, putting fake tanning lotion on her face without looking in the mirror. "You can't escape the addictions either. You have got to stop this *thing* you have with denial. Your daddy's an alcoholic, I'm an alcoholic, and my daddy was an alcoholic. Which makes you an alcoholic."

"But I don't drink," I say.

"It's the combination of the addictive personality and the mood swings that cause things like Marcie's psychotic breakdown," she says, ignoring me. "You can self-medicate the family mood swings by taking half an antidepressant just before bed. I'll give you some of mine."

Coming from a "pull yourself together, stiff upper lip, don't make a fuss" culture, I'm disturbed by the thought of taking any sort of prescription drug, let alone without a prescription. So I flush the pills down the loo.

The tanning lotion has been absorbed by now, and Billie's face looks lightly tanned, apart from the inch nearest her hairline, which has turned orange.

I've never thought of myself as suffering from "mood swings" or depression. Except when there's something real to be depressed about. And then—well, isn't sometimes feeling low part of being human?

I try not to think too much about the things Billie says these days. Instead I try to think about Nick, work on my act, and find myself reading Mum's letters with a wistfulness that's brand-new.

Little Tew
Peaseminster Pass
Peaseminster, Sussex, England

March 23

Darling Pippa,

Rehearsals are going well for the big event, however there has been a slight development. It appears Princess Anne asked the organizers if there would be any sword dancers present!

As you know, Scottish country dancing is quite different from Highland dancing, but your father has nobly stepped forward to save the day. He's hard at work learning how to do a sword dance, which he will perform in Princess Anne's honor at the end of the event. Solo!

Marjory was here this afternoon and says you must go up the Statue of Liberty and take a boating trip around New York on the Circle Line.

Must go, lots of love, Mum

March 24

Dear Mum and Dad,

I haven't managed to get to the Statue of Liberty itself yet, but the pic on the back of this postcard shows exactly what it looks like when I drive past at night.

Everything is going swimmingly. Lots of love, Pip.

P.S. Freezing cold weather here.

P.P.S. Please give Boris a hug from me.

Some New York art galleries are ostentatiously modern and sparsely furnished. Some are a hundred years old and sparsely furnished. All have beautifully dressed receptionists who look at me with absolute superiority and say, "I suppose if you really want to, you could leave your card."

It's the end of March and the day starts off relatively warm, so I leave Adler-on-Hudson for New York City in a short skirt and jacket, with the photographs of Nick's paintings. I'm hoping that dressing like a real New York businesswoman will help me get past the "perhaps if you leave your card" stage.

But March weather in New York can be as unpredictable as the weather in England—well, anytime. The difference being the extent to which the weather changes. In England the weather will go from sunny, to cloudy, to raining several times a day. But the temperature won't change at all. And the British rain, like British bathroom showers, rarely comes down much harder than a drizzle.

But when the temperature drops in America, it really drops. By two o'clock, the New York City sky is spitting ice and I feel like I'm being shot at. I've no money for a taxi, my car's half a mile away, and I'm so cold my legs feel like popsicles.

Realizing I'm close to Jack's building, I walk down Seventh Avenue to Twenty-second Street and ring Jack's bell.

"Hallo?" I say.

"Who is it?"

"Pippa."

"My favorite British redneck? Come on in."

Jack buzzes me in and I carry my sopping-wet handbag through his lobby, which is warm and quiet and smells of polished wood. As I enter apartment 1B, I leave my handbag to drip-dry next to his umbrella rack. The tiny studio apartment is tidy and peaceful and dark.

In the center of the room is a big bed, with a forest green quilt and forest green pillowcases to go with it. Opposite the bed are three tall oak bookcases, neatly stacked with hundreds of books and videos.

There's a fireplace with a hand-carved mantelpiece above it. On the mantelpiece are a few photographs—of Jack and his parents, it seems. And a silver urn, which Jack later tells me contains the ashes of his dead dog. Against the other wall is a comfortable-looking couch, also forest green. In the far corner of the room, next to a window with dark green blinds, is a small kitchenette. And Jack.

I am intrigued to note that Jack is ironing a sheet.

"Sit down. Make yourself comfortable."

"Oh—no—thank you—I've got to run," I say. "I just wanted to warm up for a bit."

There are burglar bars on the windows, behind the blinds. They don't go up and down. Instead they curve elegantly outward, to make room for an air conditioner.

Jack puts down his iron and looks at me. I couldn't get into New York for last week's open mike because of the weather, and I haven't seen him in two weeks.

"You've lost weight," he says bluntly. "Too much, as a matter of fact. You look like a freezing-wet ferret."

"Thanks," I say.

"Let me rephrase that. You look like a beautiful, freezing-wet ferret."

"Thanks," I say, laughing. "I think."

Jack unfolds a hand towel and gives it to me.

"For your hair," he says.

I dry my hair with the towel, which, not surprisingly, is forest green.

"I was just wondering if I could borrow a pair of trousers," I say.

In the manner of a man who gets this kind of request every day, Jack walks to his cupboard and takes out a pair of neatly folded jeans with a crease down the center of each leg.

"Sure," he says. "I'll go into the bathroom while you change."

"No—I can use the bathroom."

"It's no problem, Pippa," he says and disappears behind a dark green door.

Looking around the walls of his immaculate studio apartment I see posters of some very familiar faces: Peter Cook and Dudley Moore, Monty Python, even Reginald Perrin.

"No Benny Hill?" I call out, relieved.

"Can't stand Benny Hill," he says, out of the bathroom now. "But I love John Cleese. My uncle introduced me to British comedy when I was a kid. I've been hooked ever since. Ricky Gervais really cracks me up."

I'm standing in the middle of his sitting room, holding his jeans around my waist. They're far too big. Jack takes off his belt, threads it through the hooks, and does it up on the tightest hole. It's still not tight enough, so he folds the top of the jeans over. I can feel the tension that has been gnawing at me for the last few weeks leave my body. I like the way he smells. But he's definitely gay. He irons his sheets.

I'm about to leave when I see an electric keyboard in the large cupboard in the corner of the room.

"Try it out," Jack says.

I sit down at the stool and play a few chords. I've always loved the way piano keys feel against my skin. Smooth and hard and part of me.

"So, Pippa, why are you wandering around Chelsea in an ice storm in a short skirt and high heels?"

I play another chord and start to sing.

I went into three art galleries in Manhattan,
It was bloomin' cold, and I didn't have my hat on.

Jack laughs. "You still got the hat I gave you?"

"Yes, but it didn't really go with my outfit."

"You looked cute in that hat. Like a very sexy bee."

I smile. Gay men and fashion. I play a couple more chords:

My buddy thinks I look
Like a very sexy bee,
Ah—baby—let me tell ya—
A-what you mean to me
Allyoop. Allyoop.

Jack laughs.

I'm warm and relaxed and at ease in Jack's home. Soon I'm singing a rock-and-rollish sort of chorus, thanking Jack for lending me his clothes, riffing on ice, snow, cold, tights, and freezing legs. Some of it's good, some of it's definitely second-rate, but Jack joins in, and we end up playing like lunatics. His hair flops over his face in time to the music.

When we stop playing I sit back and almost fall off the piano stool. I like the feel of Jack's body next to mine as he catches me. Yes, I like the way he smells.

I have a theory about sexual chemistry. I think if you feel it with someone, then they feel it too. That's why it's called chemistry. There'd be no spark if the energy wasn't coming from two different places.

On this occasion I doubt my theory for the first time. I'm being ridiculous. The man is gay, for goodness sake. And he's not Nick.

"Hey, that was great!" Jack says. "Where are you going?"

"Home," I say. "I've got a lot to do."

"What do you have to do, Pippa Dunn?" Jack's voice is soft and slow and sexy.

There's an air of nobility about Jack. And something else. A nurturing quality perhaps that reminds me somehow of Mum.

I can keep charming, witty, handsome, sexy, even dangerous men at a distance. But kindness floors me every time.

And so I put down my bag and sit down on Jack's green sofa and accept the cup of tea he offers me.

And then, because he asks me about what I have been doing at the art galleries, I tell him about Nick.

Jack's eyes are soulful, there's no other word for it. And I am

relaxed. And I've had a chocolate muffin and half a plate of Fig Newtons. There's a fire burning in his fireplace. My cup of tea is made
with milk and two sugars, just how I like it. And the green tartan
throw on his green flowery couch reminds me of home.

Jack is sitting cross-legged at one end of his couch, and I am sitting cross-legged at the other. As I talk to my new friend about Nick,
I'm so relaxed, for the first time, I find myself telling another person
what being in love has been like for me, for the past ten years. I tell
him how every time I fell in love before I met Nick, I was terrified
whoever-it-was would leave me.

"And did they ever leave you?" Jack asks.

"No. I left them first."

"No man in their right mind would ever leave you, Pippa
Dunn."

Silence between us.

"Can I have another Fig Newton?"

"Sure," says Jack, pushing his plate toward me. "Have mine."

I start dipping them into my tea.

"Finally, I concluded that the key to dealing with a fear of abandonment is to date people I don't like, so if they do leave me, it
doesn't matter."

"That's funny," Jack says, writing it down.

"And just when I thought it was all completely hopeless," I say,
happily, "I refound Nick."

"More tea, dear?" Jack's fake British accent is surprisingly good.

"Yes, please." My God. He's got a Brown Betty teapot. "All that's
missing is the tea cosy," I say.

Nope. Out comes a tea cosy with a picture of a thatched cottage
on it, from the drawer under his sink.

He refills the teapot, puts the tea cosy on the teapot, and pours
fresh tea into the cup.

"So, let me get this straight. You figured you'd date Miles because you'd be in control because you were the gorgeous one and he
was a dog?" Jack says.

I nod, in shame. "And I was in control! For months! Until I slept with him."

"It took you months to sleep with him?"

"Well, yes. That way I kept the upper hand."

"Poor bastard."

"And then we went to Venice. And I couldn't resist him anymore, because it's impossible not to make love in Venice. And then the power shifted, or so I felt, and the panic set in."

I check to see if Jack is laughing at me. He isn't.

"And it got really bad. Just like it had with the others. Only this time it was with someone I wasn't really in love with. I mean I was, in a way. But in another way I wasn't. It's hard to explain. We didn't click. Not really. But then I guess—well, I guess I'm used to loving people with whom I don't really click."

"Sounds complicated," Jack says.

I look for impatience in his face. I don't see it. Then, softly, he says again, "No one in their right mind would ever leave you, Pippa Dunn."

We continue sitting together, cross-legged on the sofa, Jack and I, in the silence of his dark green apartment, sipping our tea.

Jack's feet are long and thin, just like him. He's wearing a pair of black socks, jeans, and a green T-shirt. And he doesn't seem to mind anything I've just told him.

"But you and this Nick—you feel it's different, right?"

"Right."

"You've waited long enough. I hope he's the one for you, Pippa, really I do."

"He is, Jack."

Silence in the room again. Peace. I feel as if I've just taken off a pair of too-tight shoes that I've been wearing for a very long time.

Half an hour later I put on my yellow sweater. Jack reaches into his second drawer and hands me another balaclava.

"I've got to go," I say. "Lots to do."

"I hope your mother and this incredibly lucky Nick guy are paying you well to do all this work for them," Jack says.

"Well, not yet, but I'm in training for Billie. And I'm working for Nick on commission. When I sell his paintings I'll be rich. And then we can be together. Then he'll give up banking and come and paint here in New York. Probably in a loft or something."

"Well, bee-girl," he says, "if that's what you want, I hope you get it."

Then Jack crouches down and runs his hands down the side of the pants he's lent me, and turns up the bottoms.

"A perfect fit," he says.

"I've really got to go," I say, heading quickly toward the door.

"Pippa," he says, "I've got every episode of *The Office* on DVD. You can come over and watch them with me anytime you like."

"The British version?"

"Of course. We can watch one now, until the rain stops, if you want." His brown eyes have green in them. I hadn't noticed it before.

I long to stay. The whirlwind I've been carrying in my head for weeks has calmed down completely, and I'm suddenly terribly tired. But I have been imposing on Jack's kindness long enough. The only thing worse than a woman unburdening her problems is a guest who will not go.

"Oh no, thank you, I couldn't possibly. Thanks so much for the trousers," I say. "And I'm sorry for—well—rabbiting on and on."

"You weren't rabbiting," Jack says.

"And thanks again for the trousers. I was just so cold. Awfully kind of you. I promise to get them back."

I dash out the door. As I leave, I notice that the walls of Jack's lobby are also painted green. The cornices are glossy white. It looks like the inside of Restoration Hardware.

Behind me I can hear Jack laughing quietly.

"Pippa?"

"Yes?" I say.

Jack's holding the door to his apartment open with his foot and dangling my handbag from his left hand.

"Your purse?"

"Oh," I say. He hands me the handbag. It's no longer wet, and he's done the zipper up.

"Sorry. Thank you," I say. But why, oh why, call it a purse? It makes no sense. Handbag makes sense. I turn round to put him straight, but he has gone.

Chapter Thirty-eight

IT'S SIX O'CLOCK in the morning and I'm woken by the sound of the phone. It's Billie, calling from Georgia.

"This is your mother speaking!" she says, her voice loud in my ear. "You know what she's done now, don't you?"

It takes me a second to tune in.

"Who?"

"Malice of course."

Of course.

"She's stolen my passport."

Oh no.

"She came up the mountain in the middle of the night and stole it."

"Why would she do that?"

"She hates me," Billie says.

I want to believe her. But Billie loses things all the time, just like I do. It's genetic.

A seventy-five-year-old woman who has just lost her husband doesn't drive twenty miles up a mountain in the middle of the night to sneak into her stepdaughter's house and steal her passport. I can picture Billie picking it up by mistake and throwing it away with a pizza container.

"Have you checked the trash?"

"Of course I've checked the trash!" I can hear her scrabbling about in the trash. Then, a few seconds later: "And it's not there!"

She sounds accusing. As if it's my fault. I recognize the tone of voice. It's the same tone I've used all my life when I can't find something.

"I can't find my hairdryer!" I'd say to Charlotte, late for work.

"Have you looked on your dressing table?"

"Yes. And it's *not there*!"

"Here you go," Charlotte would say, patient and kind as always. "You can borrow mine."

I might refuse to accept responsibility for the fact that I've lost my hairdryer, or my bra, or my shampoo, or my hot water bottle, or my swimming costume, or my keys, or even my passport—but I wouldn't go so far as to accuse an old woman of driving twenty miles up a mountain in the middle of the night to steal something I can't find. Would I?

Will I?

I'm thrashing about in Billie's ocean, afraid of currents I can't see, searching desperately for the woman I want Billie to be.

Sometimes I see glimpses of her. When she insists we all stop work and play a game of tennis "because life is short and it's a beautiful day." Or says something wonderfully encouraging that gives me the confidence to keep working on my act.

But then she says something like, "Your uncle's a sociopath. They think that might be genetic, by the way," and the mother I longed for disappears into the ocean again and becomes a devouring sea monster, waiting to pull me under.

My days are now accompanied by a growing pain in my chest that will not shift. It feels like a kind of sorrow, and it weighs me down. I know it's illogical and I feel guilty for feeling it, so I carry it inside me, hidden from the world.

I tell myself that the reason Billie never asks me anything about my life in England is because it's too painful for her to hear about the life I've had without her in it.

But I have had a life without her in it. Only the people who could remind me of who I used to be are a world away.

Little Tew
Peaseminster Pass
Peaseminster, Sussex, England

April 2

Darling Pippa,

Your father has been practicing and practicing his sword dance, and he's coming along quite well.

He's been improving his turn-out with an exercise called the Froggy Sit. This involves lying on his tummy, putting the soles of his feet together and pressing down on his knees. I stand next to him and press down when his feet or hips are tempted to pop up off the ground.

He's in the kitchen, practicing with two ties, using the towel rail as a bar. I can hear him now, as I write. "Pas de basque, pas de basque, change, leap, change, leap."

We've bought him a lovely new sporran for the big day, and his kilt is at the cleaners.

Must go, lots of love, Mum

Art Buddies
54 Route 8
Adler, New York

April 7

Dear Mum and Dad,

How lucky the Peaseminster Dancers are to have someone prepared to rise to the sword-dancing challenge! I'm sure Dad will be spectacular!

I told my friend Jack about your upcoming event. He's never been to a Scottish dance, but he did say he used to sing the

"Bluebells of Scotland" around the piano when he was little.

It reminded me of the time in Singapore, when Mrs.
Yanter—was that her name? The one who was married to the
Swiss man with the long beard?—when she played Scottish songs
all afternoon and then dived into the swimming pool.

I've got a meeting at another art gallery this afternoon.
Fingers crossed!

       Lots of love, Pip xxx

P.S. Is there any chance at all you could send me a jar of Dad's
homemade marmalade? You can't get good marmalade over here,
and I do miss it.

Chapter Thirty-nine

Pippa, I know how Billie feels about having you home.
But how are you doing in all this?" Carol's voice sounds casual.
We're sitting on the couch after spending the afternoon stapling Billie's latest mailing together.

"I'm fine," I say. And then, "I look at Billie. And I know we have the same hands. I hear her, and I know we have the same laugh. But—well, Billie keeps saying I'm exactly like her. But I'm not. Am I? Not that that would be such a bad thing," I say, quickly. "I mean, look at what she's achieved."

It's cool in the room, but Carol is blushing. Her tone is reluctant when she does finally speak.

"Half of the things Billie tells you about herself aren't true," Carol says.

"Like what?"

"Well, pretty much everything she's told you about Marfil."

"But she discovered Marfil!"

"Yes, she did. But she didn't 'make' Marfil. Tom Sniffen did that. And Billie worked for Tom as his number two, not his partner, as she tells people. And she didn't leave because she wanted to. She left because she got fired. She was drinking to dull the pain. It hurt her a lot when her husband left her. And it hurt Sniffen a lot when she showed up tanked to work."

"Oh."

Carol is about to say something else when Billie walks into the room. She's carrying some shopping. When she sees us sitting on the couch, she stops.

"Well, hi," she says sweetly. "Don't you two look cozy."

"We were just having a little talk," Carol says.

"About what?"

"Just some publicity ideas I have," I say, quickly. "I thought I'd run them by Carol. Let me help you with the shopping."

"Why don't you run your 'publicity ideas' by me?" Billie says. "I'm your mother."

"I hope you don't think . . . ," Carol says.

"I'm her mother!" Billie says, turning to Carol with a viciousness I've not seen before. "How dare you try to take my daughter away from me? After everything I've done for you! How *dare* you? You've been trying to muscle in on my territory with her ever since she got here."

"Billie, she wasn't muscling in," I say. "There was no muscling."

"You are *my* daughter. Not hers," Billie says, turning to me, eyes blazing.

I take Billie's shopping into the kitchen. When I come back into the sitting room, Billie is yelling at Carol.

"I am *not* a narcissist! My mother was a narcissist, so I know. Why, to say that *I'm* a narcissist—why, that's just nuts! How dare you try and turn my daughter against me! How dare you!"

Billie fires Carol immediately and then storms back into the sitting room.

"What did she say, honey. Tell me! What did she say?"

Billie is clearly used to this kind of drama. Right now she looks like she's almost enjoying it. I am not.

But I do feel terribly sorry for her.

"What did she say to you?" Billie says, shouting now.

"She didn't say anything," I say, not wanting to hurt her. "Honestly. Nothing at all."

"Carol's jealous. She doesn't have a daughter of her own, so she's trying to take mine. Oh, honey, I don't think I could stand losing you again. I need a hug!"

I don't feel at all like hugging her. But I don't want to hurt her feelings either. And so I let her close her arms around me. They make me think of the jaws of one of those big yellow trucks with jagged metal teeth that picks up a car and crushes it so it can never run again.

On my birthday, Mum, Dad, Charlotte, Rupert, and Neville, who are all down at Little Tew for the weekend, put the phone on speaker and call me to sing "Happy Birthday."

"Your father's sword dance was a hit!" Neville says.

"Was it?"

"It really was, darling!" Mum says. "Princess Anne absolutely loved it and your father danced like a real pro!"

"Which means back straight and not looking down! Pas de basque, pas de basque, change, leap, change, leap," Dad chimes in. Everybody laughs.

"And Princess Anne talked to him afterward for at least three minutes," Charlotte says.

Neville makes a neighing sound.

"Stop it, Nev!"

"Are you doing anything nice tonight darling?"

The only person who knows it's my birthday is Billie of course. She's ordered in an ice cream cake, which we're going to share with Ralph and Tom. Then, later, Billie is taking me to see a show.

"I'm going to see *Pajama Game*," I say. "On Broadway."

"Oh what fun! Who with?" Mum says.

It'll only be a half lie. If he knew it was my birthday he'd insist on doing something to celebrate it.

"Do you remember I told you about my friend Jack?"

Chapter Forty

WALT CALLS and announces he's coming to New York. I'm to meet him at the Waverly Bar on East Seventy-third Street at two thirty sharp. I haven't seen Walt since Billie told him she didn't find cowardice very sexy. This was in reference to the fact that Walt kept saying he was going to tell his other kids about me and then not doing it.

The bar is full of shiny dark wood and powerful-looking older men drinking whiskey and smoking cigars. As I enter, I can see Walt sitting at the end of a long drinks table next to four other men. I've never seen him so well dressed. He is wearing a beautifully cut suit, a pink and yellow tie, and appears to be holding court.

He sees me, looks surprised, stands up, kisses me on both cheeks and says "Pippa!" Then, before I can say, "But you said two thirty sharp," he turns to the men with an expression of regret and says, "Gentlemen . . ."

I see a look of anger cross the men's faces. As Walt introduces us, I learn that two of the men are from the Ukraine. Two are from Afghanistan. The man sitting next to Walt has piercing black eyes that glitter in the artificial light.

"Surely you don't have to leave just as things are getting clarified, Walt?" he says. His Ukranian accent is thick.

"Marin, forgive me, but my daughter is not a patient woman and so, if you'll excuse me . . ."

"I'm so sorry," I say, "I can always go and come back again . . . I didn't mean to interrupt."

"Not at all," the man says, looking at Walt. "Your entrance was so perfectly timed, it could have been orchestrated."

Walt is signaling for the check.

Marin smiles, "Please sit, Peppah. While we wait for the check at least."

There's a large bowl of cashew nuts in front of me. I hand the nuts round just as Mum and Dad trained me to do. As young children, Charlotte and I were instructed to "circulate with the eatables" at embassy parties. And we would, of course, dressed in little embroidered dresses with black velvet hair bands from Harvey Nicks.

The man pulls out the chair next to him and I have no choice but to sit down.

"Your father is an enigma, Peppah. I find him so hard to read."

Walt presses my hand under the table. Be careful.

"You know him so much better than I do of course," the man is saying. "Was he always this way?"

I look at Walt. He is clearly enjoying himself. Whatever game he is playing, I can play it too. Keen to show Walt how cool I can be, I turn to the man, smile sweetly, and say, "He hasn't changed since I was a child."

Now the men are talking amongst themselves, in another language. Now someone's saying something about how good a Ukraine-Afghani company will be for international relations.

Now one of the other men is saying something about the fact that despite the tragedy of it, sometimes good things can come out of war.

Finally the check arrives and we all shake hands.

"Perfect timing, kid," Walt says quietly into my ear as we're leaving the bar.

Then Marin turns toward Walt to say good-bye. There's a hardness in the man's eyes that chills me. "Peppah, it was a pleasure," he says, kissing my hand. "Walt. Until next time."

As we walk away, Walt keeps saying, "We pulled it off, kid!"

"I didn't have anything to do with it," I say, delighted that he is delighted.

"Yes you did," he says. "You arrived at just the right time. Ten minutes later and it might have been a different story."

He doesn't expand on why, and I don't press him.

Walt's brother Ben is due to meet us for a late brunch at the Gordon Grille. Walt has only just told him about my existence and some of the story behind it.

Ben is older than Walt, by about ten years, and does something important in the military. He is very tall, and extremely handsome, with auburn hair, an air of authority about him, and eyes the same shape as Walt's and mine.

As soon as he walks into the restaurant I detect something in the way Ben looks at me that I do not like. Hell, he's looking at me like I'm some sort of loose woman or something. Like I'm the illegitimate daughter of his brother's mistress. A rush of anger hits me in the chest.

"I'm very pleased to meet you," I say, with my back ramrod straight, smiling at him with all the British cool I can muster and holding out my hand to shake his. I will not bloody let him treat me with anything other than respect.

"Walt has told me so much about you."

Responding to rudeness with extreme politeness is an old trick employed by English people, reputable and otherwise, for hundreds of years, and it works again here.

His expression changes instantly. Good. He's ashamed of the way he looked at me and backtracks fast.

Two minutes later he's at the edge of his seat, exactly where I want him. Riveted, respectful, charmed.

"And so, here I am," I say. "Walt told me I belong in America, and he was right. I love it here."

I have Ben under my spell. Sorry if it sounds immodest, but, as Charlotte always says, when I choose to turn my charm tap up to full, no one can resist me.

We all order *moules marinière*. We all dip our bread into the sauce. We all put the empty mussel shells on the side of the plate we're eating from rather than in the bowl.

"This kid is you Walt! In female form!"

Later, when Walt has left the table to go to the loo, Ben says, "Your father is a great man."

"Yes," I say, "I know that. I'm just so sorry that, because of me, he never ran for Congress."

Ben laughs. "Is that the reason he gave you?" Ben laughs again, until he has tears in his eyes.

Ben cannot stop laughing.

Like the men in the bar earlier, Ben's laughter disturbs me—like an unidentifiable sound in the middle of the night.

It's one o'clock in the morning and I don't feel like going home yet, so I head for The Gold Room. The bar is empty apart from Jack, who is clearing up.

"Come for a nightcap?" he says.

"Yes."

"Everything okay?"

"Fine," I say.

"You sure?" He's looking at me closely.

"Yup."

Jack brings me a glass of chocolate milk.

"Pippa," he says, "if you ever want to talk about anything, anything at all . . ."

"There's nothing to talk about," I say.

Even if I was American, and used to talking about what I'm feeling, I don't understand any of it. So how can I possibly articulate it without sounding like a lunatic?

Jack doesn't press me, and I'm grateful for it.

When he's done clearing up, Jack walks me to my car.

Chapter Forty-one

ALONE IN THE HOUSE when Billie is in Georgia, I *almost* welcome Cole's company. But not quite. He reminds me of a piece of transparent, uncooked white fish that's ever so slightly off, you can almost see all the way through it. But not quite.

But Billie has appointed Cole the new president of Art Buddies, so I do my best to listen and learn from him. Cole seeks out my company, and in a low, monotonous voice, tells me about his terrible childhood. When he was five, he was made to eat his own shit by his babysitter. The fact that I am disturbed by his dark, sad stories seems to please him.

"When are you going to open up to me about your childhood?" Cole says, quietly. He's convinced I'm hiding some terrible dark secret. I hate to disappoint him, but I just can't think of anything. The time Dad shouted at me for drawing on my bedroom wall seems rather tame.

"Your mother told me you were sent to boarding school," he begins.

Not for the first time I try to explain that sending your kids to boarding school is just part of the British culture. Something the British do because they genuinely believe it's the best thing for their kids. It was just incidental that I hated it. "It wasn't exactly *Oliver Twist*," I say. "We didn't have gruel or anything."

"Yes, but how did you feel? I mean, you were abandoned by your birth mother. You must have felt abandoned again by your adoptive parents. That must have hurt."

I look at him, astonished. This man, who I don't really know, wants it to have hurt. I can see how he operates. He asks sensitive questions until he finds a woman's most vulnerable area, convinces her that he's got the panacea for that pain. Then he makes his move. He feeds off people's misery. My initial mistrust of him has turned to intense dislike.

While Cole was being forced to eat shit by his babysitter, I was sitting on the roof of our Land Rover driving through the Tsavo game park, looking for elephants, hippos, giraffes, and getting back to our campsite to find that the monkeys had taken our red washing-up bowl high into the trees.

I take refuge in old childhood memories, while Cole talks on. I remember walking across the rope bridge in the jungle in Ghana, a hundred miles outside the nearest town, rocking back and forth above a huge ravine, safe in the knowledge that I was with Dad, so of course nothing bad could happen.

It all seems worlds away now. Sliding down the side of Green Gable in the Lake District on tea trays, past sunlit streams, emerald green moss, fences dotted with old man's beard, and magnificent northern skies. Orchestra practice, proper tea parties, walks to historic castles and down country lanes, Mozart, Gilbert and Sullivan, and Flanders and Swann's "The Gasman Cometh" blaring through our house. And, of course, the incessant Scottish dancing, which, right now, I miss terribly.

"They didn't even raise you themselves," Cole is saying quietly. "They sent you off to boarding school. That must have hurt. Talk to me, Pippa."

I wonder for a half second how many British people have put on a kettle to extricate themselves from unwanted conversations. Millions, probably. "It's four o'clock," I say, sounding exactly like Mum. "How about a nice cup of tea?"

Cole's expression is dark and sullen. He is glaring at me from the couch.

"Well, I'll make one for myself then," I say, smiling at him cheerfully as I leave the room and head for the kitchen.

So Mum and Dad sent me to boarding school. Because their parents were sent to boarding school, by parents who'd been sent to boarding school before them. It's something the British do.

The problem with facing a long buried truth in one area of your life is that truths about other areas of your life, that you've been lying to yourself about for years, start popping out at you, making you jump.

I've suppressed my memories about boarding school for years. That rigid, enclosed world of bells and rules and corridors that smelled of beeswax. If you were more interested in climbing trees than talking about shades of nail polish, St. Margaret's could be a cruel, lonely place.

The Billie I know would have defended me when the teachers sent me to detention for sitting by the stream at midnight because I wanted to see the baby owl. No. The Billie I know would never have sent me there in the first place. The Billie I know would have wanted me with her. I'm sure of it.

But, goddamn it, I'd rather have five years fending for myself in a girls' boarding school than eighteen years of neglect from an alcoholic mother, who would have been so caught up in herself she wouldn't have even noticed I was there.

I have to believe that, because to do otherwise would open the door to an unbearable sorrow.

Standing in Billie's kitchen, looking out over the Adler Bridge, I think again of the Billie who used to live in my head. The sweet, understanding, empathetic, ethereal mother who loved me, focused only on me. One hundred and twenty per cent "there."

And then the tears start crawling down my cheeks. Because I can no longer pretend that the mother I have found is anything other than who she is.

I think about calling Mum and Dad, but they'll be asleep by now.

Disturbed, I look around Billie's kitchen. My world—my England—has gone. I am alone. Powerless. Trapped in a dark house by a river, peopled by broken souls.

It's the middle of the week, but with nowhere else to go, I head down to The Gold Room. The downstairs bar is quiet, so I head upstairs to open mike night. Instead of my prepared material, I perform an improvised song, to a made-up rock-and-roll melody I can't seem to get out of my head. It's midnight. My audience consists of Jack and a prostitute and her john, who get up when I am done, giving me my first standing ovation.

As usual, Jack walks me to my car.

DATE: May 3
TO: pippa-dunn@hotmail.com
FROM: CharlotteDunn@Harrods.co.uk

Dear Pip,
　　Don't forget Mum's birthday on the 6th. R and I went to hear Handel's Water Music at the Royal Festival Hall and bought her a pair of Too Hot to Handel oven gloves. What a hoot! Love, C. (Sent wirelessly by BlackBerry handheld.)

Chapter Forty-two

I'VE BEEN RUNNING AROUND all day with no time to eat anything other than M&M's. I'm at the YMCA putting up a poster for Billie's workshop. I slip on the newly washed staircase and fall on my head. I know I've just fainted because when I come to the walls are moving. I hold on to the banister and pull myself up. I look around to see if there's anyone who can help.

"I'm so sorry," I say finally to the man with a mop, "but could I trouble you for a towel or something? My head seems to be bleeding."

The man puts me in a taxi, which takes me to St. Vincent's Hospital. There's a long line of people waiting in the emergency room. I don't have health insurance, and blood isn't gushing out of me, so the woman at the counter says it could be hours before I'm seen.

The hospital is noisy and dirty. There are sick people lying in the corridors on metal trolleys. There's no peace, just rushing and noise and fear. When I fell off my moped and cracked my head open one summer, I was seen immediately at Peaseminster General, glued back together, and given a teddy bear to take home as a present. I suppose, not for the first time, that it's American health insurance companies who are behind the lie that a government-sponsored health-care system is always a mistake.

When I sit down, I pass out again. Then a man in a nurse's uniform is putting a plastic thing round my arm and taking my blood pressure. I still feel dizzy.

"What is the name of the president of the United States?"

"George W. Bush. Unfortunately."

Later, after he gives me a shot of some kind, a doctor appears with a chart, tells me I've got a concussion, and asks me where I live. When I tell him, he tells me I mustn't drive for at least twenty-four hours and asks me if there's someone I'd like to call.

The only phone number I can remember is Billie's in Georgia.

"Thank God you called!" Billie says, as she's picking up. "Malice has been into my house again. I can't find my wallet anywhere, and before you say anything, *yes* I've checked the trash. I'm going to ask Johnny Taft to have a look around next time he's working on her house. I'll just bet he finds it stashed away somewhere with my missing passport."

I hold the phone away from my throbbing head. My heart sinks. I bring the phone toward my ear again. Billie is still talking.

"I just wish that woman would let things go and learn to live in peace with the fact that I am not leaving! She can break into my house, put barbed wire between our properties, blacken my name around town, but she is not driving me off the mountain!"

"Of course not," I say. But I don't want to soothe Billie. I want her to soothe me.

My hand is shaking and my head aches. I get off the phone as quickly as I can. There is someone else I can call.

Jack arrives at the hospital within fifteen minutes and takes me back to his apartment in a taxi.

"I'll take the couch," he says. "You take the bed."

I lie down under Jack's comfy sheets and fall asleep. When I wake, I can see Jack's face in stripes, lit as it is by the city light coming through the spaces in the dark green blinds. I can see fairy dust in the yellow light. Tonight his studio apartment reminds me of Badger's house in the *Wind in the Willows*.

I've been given some pills by the doctor to help me sleep. The doctor told Jack to wake me every two hours, to make sure I don't slip into a coma.

Now he's gently shaking me.

"You okay, Pippa Dunn?" His brown eyes are filled with concern. I look at him for a moment and try and sit up. My head is throbbing.

"Ow."

"Here." Jack has some ice in a plastic bag. He holds it against the bruise on my head.

"That better?"

"Yes," I say. The ice helps a lot. I lie back down again. When I come to, Jack is sitting on his couch, reading a book. He's wearing a pair of gold-rimmed glasses. Sensing I'm awake, he looks over at me.

"You okay?" he says again. I look at the clock. Two more hours have passed. "Must have been a bad dream," he says. "You kept shouting about someone called Walt."

"Oh."

We don't say anything.

"What's going on?" Jack says quietly.

"Nothing. Really." I try to smile, but my face hurts.

"This Walt fella giving you trouble?" His expression is serious.

I smile at the thought of my powerful birth father being referred to as "this Walt fella." Like he's a hoodlum or something.

I don't say anything. Jack's voice comes in again.

"So who is this Walt?"

Jack is almost smiling. Patient. Waiting in the night for me to speak.

I can't. The thought of formulating words about Walt and the rest of it hurts too much.

The pills the doctor gave me are making me very sleepy. I give in to the overwhelming need to rest, sensing Jack close to me as I go back under.

The next morning, while I'm still lying in bed, Jack feeds me some yogurt and a banana in a green ceramic bowl. Then I fall asleep again. I sleep on and off, in two-hour intervals, through the next day and night. When I'm awake, I'm aware of Jack, sitting on his couch, only feet away.

"Don't you have to go to work?" I say at one point.

"I called in. Told them you'd had a fall. They told me not to even think about coming back until I was sure you were okay."

Then I'm under again.

It's nine o'clock on a Thursday morning before I can get out of bed without my head hurting. I've been at Jack's house since Monday afternoon.

If I disappeared from my English life for three days, the police would have been called by now. But here no one knows what's happened. Billie is in Georgia. Carol has left the company. I'm avoiding Cole anyway, Marvin's on sabbatical, and Ralph's down in Georgia, training with his mother.

I told Billie Ralph seemed very interested in cartoons. "Really?" she said. "I had no idea!" She promptly set up an animation department at Art Buddies for Ralph to run. He now spends his days giving advice to would-be cartoonists, and Billie is giving him more attention than she has in years. I'm sure Billie isn't exaggerating when she says he's doing brilliantly.

Hungry, I sit on a wooden chair at a green wooden table in Jack's tiny green kitchen. Jack's wearing a sleeveless white vest, a light blue apron, and a torn pair of jeans. He's staring into his tiny refrigerator, underneath his tiny kitchen sink.

"Now that you're awake," he says, "we can have a full English breakfast."

He takes some eggs, bacon, and a grapefruit out of his tiny refrigerator.

"Ah. I have got tomatoes," Jack says, in an English accent. "I'll fry them up for you the English way."

"Have you been to England?"

"Never been anywhere outside the U.S.," Jack says, lighting his tiny stove with a long wooden match. "My mom's parents were from Scotland, though. She came over to New Jersey from Glasgow when she was six years old.

The picture of a six-year-old packing her bags and moving from Scotland to America on her own makes me giggle. And then laugh. "Not on her own," he says, laughing with me. "With my grandparents, of course."

The bacon smells delicious. Jack puts it on some paper towel to get rid of the grease and puts it on a plate in front of me.

I savor every mouthful, while Jack tells me about his family.

It feels almost unreal, to be eating an ordinary breakfast, with an ordinary man, who has nothing whatsoever to do with Billie. I eat all the bacon, three eggs, two pieces of toast, and a hot cinnamon pretzel, which Jack has bought fresh from the bakery on Seventh Avenue. When I am done, Jack washes the dishes, then, still in his apron, he sits opposite me and hands me my third cup of steaming-hot coffee in a dark green mug.

"How you feeling now?" he says.

"Oh, much better. Thank you so much, Jack."

"No problem."

There's no chaos here. Only calm.

"My friend Elfrida's looking for a roommate," Jack says.

"Really?" I wonder if it might one day be possible to return to a normal life with a roommate in it.

"I could tell her you were interested if you want."

If only.

"That's so kind of you, Jack. But I don't think I can leave where I am."

"Why not?" he says. His eyes are steady.

I can't tell him I have no money to pay rent. If I do I'll have to explain that I'm still working for Billie for room and board only. I just want to be normal, just for these few moments. Like

I used to be before I made the phone call that changed my life. I was Pippa in those days. Just Pippa. I want to be just Pippa right now.

"It's a long story," I say to Jack, finally.

"Well, I'd like to hear it," he says. His body is tense. I'm feeling tired again.

"Do you mind if I lie down for a few more minutes before I leave?" Without waiting for a reply, I move over to Jack's wonderfully comfy couch and fall asleep again.

When I wake up, I can hear Jack taking a shower. I put my clothes on. He comes out of the bathroom naked, apart from a dark green towel wrapped around his lower half. Then Jack tells me he'll drive me home.

"No, really . . ."

"I'm driving you home."

We walk over to Thirty-second and Twelfth, and get into my car.

On the ride back to Billie's house, Jack and I don't speak. It's a comfortable silence. The kind you have with someone you've known for years.

Saying good-bye to Jack as he heads off toward the train that will carry him back to New York, I feel a tug that takes me by surprise. And I realize that I love this man. Not in the romantic sense, of course. Not in the way I love Nick. But I do love him.

An American would probably tell him this, but in this matter I am as English as Mum. Besides, it would only make him feel obligated to say it back, opening us up to ghastly embarrassment the next time we see each other.

So instead I just say, "Thank you again!"

Feeling woozy, I try to pretend I am somewhere other than this dank, neglected house, with its dirty carpet and the smell of cat food. I lie down on Billie's bed and fall asleep.

I'm woken by a phone call from Nick, calling me from somewhere at three o'clock in the morning, his time. My idea for a Middle Eastern series has had him painting all night, despite the fact that he has an early meeting tomorrow. I tell him I can't wait to see the new paintings. He hangs up, before I've had a chance to tell him about my fall.

Chapter Forty-three

THOSE FEW NIGHTS AT JACK'S are the first I've spent away from Billie's house in the four and a half months I've been living there. When I enter her house again, the feeling of disquiet that has been growing steadily stronger is now telling me clearly what I need to do. After days of working up to it, when I finally tell Billie I want to move to New York City and sell ad space for money, she kicks the Korean pedicurist in the face.

"Stop right there!" Billie says, holding her freshly manicured hand up like a crossing guard and turning to me intently. "Stop right there!"

It's nine thirty in the morning, and we're the only customers at Nails 4 U, which is a relief, because Billie is speaking very loudly.

"I can see what's going on here," Billie says, "and I am not going to allow it. You, my dear, talented child, are on the verge of real success. No—don't interrupt me! You are on the verge of real success. I will not let you sabotage yourself."

"But I'm not—"

"Honey, don't interrupt!"

The pedicurist is now giving Billie an unusually vigorous foot rub, and Billie's massage chair is on high speed so her entire body is shaking as she speaks.

"What kind of a mother would I be if I let my only daughter sabotage herself? You cannot possibly afford to move into New York

City or anywhere near it without working two or three jobs. And if you work all hours, your act will suffer."

We're both done at the same time. The Korean girls help us down from our chairs with our toenails still wet with fresh polish.

Usually we sit for ten minutes under a little foot fan until our toes are dry. But this time Billie and I walk straight outside in our free flip-flops, with the tissue paper still woven between our toes. We waddle across the parking lot, like penguins in intense conversation.

"Self-sabotage is common in people of our nature. We like the initial excitement, but once things are really getting going, we sabotage ourselves. You don't want to sabotage yourself now, do you, Pippa?"

"Well, no . . ."

"You can't go back to advertising sales," Billie says emphatically, swerving into her driveway. "You know you hated it. Promise me you won't sabotage yourself by rushing off and getting a job in the city before I've talked to Cole."

She's stopped the car, and she's looking at me.

"Besides," she says, "I've only just found you again. I'd miss you so! Promise me?" she says.

"I promise."

When Cole calls me into his office a couple of days later, he's sitting on a chair with his feet up on the desk. He's put a new after-shave on and has some kind of smelly gel in his hair. On both sides of the Atlantic, I have been astounded by men who think adding gel to their hair improves their appearance. It doesn't.

"We've made thousands as a result of the publicity you've been doing," Cole begins. "Billie and I have been talking, and we'd like to start paying you to go even more full out on promotion."

I know Billie's big annual workshop is coming up in two months' time. Billie charges five hundred dollars a head. For the past few years she's had twenty attendees or so. The room they rent has the capacity for a hundred.

"How about six hundred a week, for three weeks?"

I do the math.

"Okay," I say. "If you're sure the company can afford it." It doesn't seem like a bad solution to my problem.

"We can, kiddo."

I've got three hundred more dollars left until the limit on my second MasterCard is reached. If I'm careful, I should be able to make it last until I get paid. Then, if I borrow from my Visa card, I'll have enough money to put down a deposit on an apartment in the city. It feels like a perfect arrangement.

For the next three weeks I make calls and write press releases for Billie and walk out of the room whenever Cole walks into it.

At the end of the three weeks, during which time Billie's workshop fills to capacity for the very first time, I go to Cole and ask him for my check.

Billie is in town and looking up at me from behind her laptop. "What check?" Billie says.

"Very funny, Billie. The check for all the promotional work I've been doing."

Billie looks confused. Then she looks over at Cole.

"Wow!" Cole says. "Now you want money? In addition to a free place to stay?" There's something in his eyes that's daring me to continue.

Billie puts down the lid of her laptop and says, "Pippa, honey, you know we don't have the extra money to pay you for promotion!"

I feel as though the world has tilted under me. I am slipping around in mud, trying to find a foothold.

"Pippa, I thought giving you a free place to stay and free food in the refrigerator was payment enough! Most kids in America pay their parents some kind of rent—you agreed to do promotion in return for food and rent, right? You know we have debts and salaries to pay."

"I'm sorry, Billie, but I really did need a job. And I was going to get one and then Cole called me into the office and specifically said you had eighteen hundred dollars allocated—"

"What?" Cole looks indignant. "I hate to say this, Billie, but I didn't say I'd pay her anything."

"Now, honey," Billie says, enjoying the drama of the moment, "I know you're in a tough spot financially . . ."

I'm sinking further.

"And I know you're dealing with a lot, and I understand why you'd lie about this, really I do, I'd have done exactly the same at your age, but we just don't have the money to pay you!" Billie's voice is sympathetic. The house Billie told me my grandfather was leaving me hasn't been mentioned since.

I look at Cole, whose expression is unreadable. I look at Billie.

"Do you honestly think that I would lie about this, Billie?" I ask her.

"Oh, look at that dear little face. It doesn't make me love you any less, honey! I will never abandon you again honey, no matter what you do!"

"It's not that, Billie. It's—do you really think, for one second, that I'd try and cheat you? I've never cheated anyone in my life!"

"Oh, honey!" Billie has tears in her eyes. "When you first came you were so darn British, you wouldn't tell me how you felt about anything. Not ever. But now . . . Oh, honey! I am so proud of you. You've just told me how you really feel! And telling people how you feel—well, that's what we in America call intimacy. And until now—well, I don't think you've ever had real intimacy in your life."

I can't move.

"It's okay to be human, honey," Billie is saying, her voice low and soft. "I would have done exactly the same thing at your age."

"I'm sorry," I say, stepping away. "I was under the impression I was being paid to do this. I, um, I need a job, you see. I haven't got any money left."

"But what do you need money *for*? You've got a roof over your head, there's always a jar of peanut butter in the refrigerator."

"Uh, petrol, I mean gas. I need money for gas," I say, struggling to stay calm. "And getting into the city. And . . . and parking tickets . . . and going home to England."

"You want to go back to England?"

"Yes, for a visit."

"But your cabaret career!"

"Billie, I haven't seen my parents in months."

"Well, why don't you ask them for some money?"

"I've never asked Mum and Dad for money. I've supported myself since I was eighteen."

"Well, it's quite natural for parents to help their children, you know. Here's a hundred dollars, honey. No, don't say anything, I'm happy to loan it to you. You can pay me back when you can."

I stare at Billie's money, trying to wake myself up from this. Then, leaving the hundred dollars on the table, I turn my back and leave the room.

SUMMER

Chapter Forty-four

AT ELEVEN THIRTY on a windy, rainy night in June, I've just come offstage at The Gold Room when Jack hands me the club phone. He's wearing a freshly ironed white shirt and smells of Tide.

"Your mother called. She said she's got something important to tell you, and would you please stop avoiding her calls."

The brief respite from the constant ache, afforded by the laughter, has gone.

"So, now she's calling the club phone?"

"Uh huh," Jack says.

"Bugger, bugger, bugger."

Billie's been in Georgia for almost a month, but now she's back. I won't be able to avoid her now anyway, so I might as well get it over and done with. There's a hurricane coming, so I'd better not leave too late. Jack is looking at me closely.

"Pippa," Jack says.

"Yup?"

"What's going on?"

"Nothing," I say. I look up at him and smile my most charming smile. "Can I finish the tin?"

Jack passes me the tin of Nesquik. I scrape the chocolate out of the bottom and mix it with the teaspoon of milk that's left.

"That stuff about you being adopted? That true?" says Sal.

"Yup."

"No shit!"

"No shit."

"So you're really a redneck?"

"No," I say. "Well, my birth mother's from the South, but she's not a redneck. She's actually a creativity counselor. And very brilliant. I call her a redneck at the start of my act because it's funnier. More of a contrast, you know?"

"So all that stuff about coming to America to find her is true?" Sal says.

"Yup."

The door to the club opens, bringing in a gust of wind. The rain is pelting down now. It's time for me to go.

"So, in your act, why don't you talk about what that was really like? Meeting her, I mean?" Sal says. "You could write songs about it!"

For a second I'm silent.

"Yes, why not?" Jack joins in, cleaning up the glasses, despite the fact that he's not actually working tonight. "Why don't you talk honestly about what's really going on?" There's an edge to his voice.

Dammit. I'm not going to cry. You don't cry at the club.

"Because it's not funny," I say.

I rummage about in my coat pocket for a dollar, lay it on the bar, sling my backpack on my back, and head out into the storm.

I've driven an hour and a half to get to the club for my eight minutes onstage. I'm a paid regular on comedy night in the upstairs theater now, which means I get ten dollars a set. I arrived late because of the rain and had to park in a garage, so I have to give the parking guy thirty-eight dollars for one hour. Plus tax.

By the time I start driving, there are deep puddles on the road and the rain has gotten heavier. The windows are steaming up, so I turn on Earl Grey's heater, which starts up with an unhealthy roar. I turn my cell phone back on and check my messages. There are six, all from the same sweet, strong, excited southern voice.

A bad weather advisory warning sounds on the radio. The roads are slippery and I notice that I'm the only car on the road. But I know if I drive slowly I'll be all right.

The wind is so strong, the Adler Bridge seems to sway against the sky, which is the color of an aging bruise. The lights are bright and the river is black and wild.

As I slip turning right I hear Dad's voice in my head. It's clear, strong, and English.

"Don't forget, Pippa, always turn the wheel in the same direction as the skid."

For a second, Dad is teaching me to drive again, on a narrow country lane just outside Peaseminster. He's tense, speaking in monosyllables as I brake too hard and then take off again with a shudder. Thoughts of Dad are always accompanied by a sticky sense of guilt these days, so I push them out of my head.

Suddenly I hear my other father's name, on a news bulletin, on NPR. *"Washington lobbyist Walt Markham and CIA operative Marin Talenski—"* Then there's interference.

I'm filled with relief. Walt didn't return my last phone call, and now I know why. It's not because he's left me again. It's because he's been busy. He's been doing something so important, it's on the news!

The radio sputters on again: *"—are under indictment for fraud. Reports say that while the men lobbied for U.S. funding for electronic voting machines in the newly democratic Ukraine and Afghanistan, they failed to mention that the only company capable of producing such machines in the area was one in which they had a significant financial stake."*

The father I traveled the world to find has been arrested, and they're editorializing about how terrible it is that he should pretend to be trying to help the people of Afghanistan, when really he was working for huge personal profit.

"No!" I shout. "That's the opposite of who he is! That's not him *at all*!" My wheel hits a slippery patch. Dad's voice in my head has been blocked out by the sounds on the radio. I turn my wheel away from the skid, and the car heads toward the river.

I've had close calls a couple of times, at night, on wet roads. The first time was driving from London to Edinburgh. It was cold and I turned the heating up to full. Miles fell asleep at the wheel, and we spun off the road toward a cliff. The spinning seemed to take forever.

"Are we going to die?" I said to Miles.

"I think so," he said. But we didn't, thanks to a well-placed rock.

I'm not scared, because I know it's not my time to die. Not for years yet. I'm going to live to be a very old woman. I've seen it, in my mind's eye. I shall eventually die of a bad cough when I'm well into my nineties. And during the last few months of my life, I shall receive visitors lying down and insist they tickle the soles of my feet with a feather.

Tonight, the spinning seems to take forever. The car grows strangely silent. I feel as if I'm floating above it, watching myself trying to turn the wheel. When the car stops spinning, I get out. A man in a truck is coming toward me.

"You okay?"

"Fine," I say.

He pops the hood and looks in. He's a small, wiry man, with a weather-beaten face and a Spanish-sounding accent. "If your engine's gonna blow, that would be the time to do it. Looks like it saved your life."

"Yes," I say. So it seems that everything has some perks. Even driving a car that desperately needs servicing.

The man tows me to Billie's house. The closer we get to Adler-on-Hudson, the heavier my heart feels.

When I get to the house, Billie is waiting for me just inside her front door.

"Oh, honey! I've missed you so much. I need a hug!" I walk into her arms, feeling the little energy I have left leave my body.

"Walt managed to get a message to me," she says. "They've got him under house arrest. He doesn't want you to call to check on him because he doesn't want them to know about us, in case they use it against him in some way."

"But is he okay?"

"Honey, your father will always be okay."

Yes.

"Will you sleep in my room tonight? Please? Cole and Ralphie are away, and having you near me will make me feel so much better."

My heart sinks further.

"Okay," I say.

"I used to have to handle family dramas alone. But now I have a daughter—well, I feel so much better having someone else here with me now. You've filled me up, honey."

I put on the purple silk pajamas Billie brought me from Georgia and fall asleep to the sound of Billie's voice.

When I wake up two hours later, Billie is lying on her side of the bed. Asleep, she looks sad and young. She has sweet-smelling cold cream on her face and foil in her hair and her breathing is light.

I creep out of bed so as not to wake her and walk down the corridor to the kitchen. The rain has stopped falling and the moon is full. The cats wake up and jump on the kitchen table. I give them some milk, make myself some chocolate milk, and pad into the office. I turn on the computer in search of a message from Nick. Nothing.

Suddenly afraid of the silence, I go into the sitting room and turn on the television. During the last few months, I've watched late night specials featuring serial killers who have found God. And I've watched American soaps, featuring unrealistically beautiful people, with lovely hair, who have lots and lots of sex. Unlike the people in *EastEnders*, my favorite British soap, which features people with no money and desperate lives.

Tonight I watch a rerun of something called the *Robin Byrd Show*, which is hosted by a half-naked woman with gigantic plastic breasts. From another channel I learn where to get a miracle mop and a tap light. I learn how to get a perfect bottom in just two minutes a day. And I watch Anthony Robbins, mesmerized by his teeth.

I go back to the computer. Still no message.

DATE: June 10
TO: NickDevang@bankglobal.net
FROM: pippa-dunn@hotmail.com

Dear Nick,

How are you?

                                                              Pippa

An hour later I check again. Nothing.

The moon looks malevolent, and tonight I am afraid of the dark.

"Billie's deluded. She's going nuts." Carol's words ring in my head. "She makes people crazy. The healthy ones stay away."

Something ugly sits heavy on my chest, making it impossible for me to move.

The office has blue gray paint on the walls, which is peeling near the ceiling. The carpet is stained and smells damp. There are papers everywhere and dirty coffee mugs with an inch of stale milk into which I've stubbed out cigarettes.

I lie down on the floor, my knees curled up to my chest, breathing heavily. My head is resting on one of Billie's sweaters, which smells too strongly of perfume. I don't want to smell her. I throw the sweater aside, lay my head on my hands and close my eyes.

I dream of Billie again. She's breaking into my old apartment in London and smashing everything—photo frames holding pictures of Mum and Dad, my piano, the Chinese warrior chess set that I bought from the Kowloon market in Hong Kong. Then she holds up a photo of my sister and my mother, saying, "You don't look like these people! You look like me! You look like me! You look like meeeeeee!" Now she's dancing, whirling round and round. I try to wake myself up. I hear Jack's voice in my head.

"Why don't you talk about what's really going on?" His face is still, strong, thoughtful, kind, and quiet in the midst of the chaos.

The next morning, I pick up the phone and, with the remaining balance on my credit card, I book a flight home.

"You're coming *this* weekend?" Mum says. "Right! We'll meet you at the airport."

"No, no, don't, Mum, you'll be stuck in traffic for hours," I say. "My flight gets in just after rush hour. But if you don't mind calling a taxi for me . . ."

When I tell Billie I'm going, she's packing for Georgia, rolling her clothes and stuffing them into her suitcase at a furious pace.

"But the workshop's only a month away!" Billie says. "And what about Nick Devang?" Then, pouting, she says, "And what about me! I'll miss you, honey!"

"But you'll be in Georgia and won't see me anyway. Besides, I'm only going for a week, Billie!"

"Ohhhh!" she says. "I didn't realize." Then, in a calm, reasonable voice, she says, "Well, of course nothing could make me happier than knowing you're going to visit your adoptive family in England for a week. Now come and give your mother a hug."

Chapter Forty-five

THANKS TO THE TRAFFIC, it's ten thirty at night, and the lights are off in the kitchen when I finally arrive at Little Tew. I walk through the dining room, breathing in the smell of my parents' house, clean, old, as comforting as the sound of the grandfather clock and the wooden cuckoo that will pop its head out in half an hour.

Mum and Dad are in the little sitting room at the back. Dad is asleep in the maroon leather chair that Granny H. had in her house when she was alive. Mum is curled up on the sofa, shoes off. The fire is going strong. Dad must have been chopping wood recently, as the wood basket next to the fireplace is full and several extra logs are neatly piled up next to it.

They've obviously fallen asleep in front of the telly. Mum stands as I come in, smoothing her pale blue cashmere sweater. She smiles sleepily at me.

"Hallo, darling," she says, kissing me on the cheek. She smells of Mum. And ever so faintly of the lavender soap Charlotte gave her last Christmas.

"Hallo, Mum," I say.

"Hallo, Pip," Dad says. He looks awfully sleepy, too. Tucking in his shirt, he pats me on the shoulder.

"Good flight?"

"Yes," I say.

"Good film?"

"I watched several actually. *The Queen* was especially good. Gives you a completely different perspective on the whole Diana thing."

"Yes," Mum says.

My new green suitcase from Target is standing at the bottom of the stairs. It's enormous. I thought it was a good deal, getting that much suitcase for twenty-five dollars.

"Good God," Dad says, picking up my suitcase, "I thought you were only here for a week!"

"Sorry, Dad. I couldn't decide what to bring, so I brought everything. I'll take it up."

"It's all right," he says, unable to keep the irritation out of his voice. "I'll do it."

He's almost sixty. He looks a little older than he did six months ago. The suitcase bumps up behind him, stair by stair.

"Do you want anything to eat?" Mum says.

"It's all right," I say. "You must be tired. Why don't you go upstairs to bed, and I'll see you in the morning?"

"I think we will, darling. Do you mind?"

"Of course not."

I do mind. I mind terribly that they would rather go to bed than break their usual bed-by-eleven-o'clock routine and spend a little time with the daughter they haven't seen in six months. I mind that they accepted my offer to get a taxi from the airport, rather than have them drive all the way to Heathrow at rush hour.

Neville calls it Ping-Pong. His theory is that Mum and Dad want to pick me up at the airport as much as I want to be picked up at the airport. But because we're always putting the other person first in our family, we try and guess what the other person wants to do. And we never tell anyone what we want to do, in case there's a clash with what the other person wants to do. For a second Billie's voice rings in my head.

"Would it be so terrible if you just told them the truth?"

I consider the thought for a second. And then dismiss it. I've spent the last six months thinking about Billie and what she thinks about things. I'm only in England for one week.

Mum and Dad are in their immaculately tidy bedroom, which looks out over the South Downs. I can hear them talking quietly as they get into their double bed, which is tiny by American standards.

Mum and Dad change their bedroom wallpaper every five years or so. Right now, the room is light blue. They still have sheets and blankets, rather than duvets. In the middle of the blanket is a safety pin, put there by Dad, to make sure Mum doesn't take more than her share of the covers. Their clothes are all hanging up, or carefully folded and placed in the correct drawers.

Dad's shiny cedar dresser is on the right-hand side of the room. On top is a shoe horn, a comb, a wooden clothes brush with dark brown bristles, and green and silver nail clippers.

Mum's shiny cedar dressing table is on the left-hand side of the room. On top is the same Mason Pearson hairbrush she's had for thirty years, a bottle of Christian Dior perfume, and a light blue makeup bag, containing powder, pink lipstick, blue eye shadow, and a little blush from Boots, which she only puts on for parties.

After devouring three pieces of toast and marmalade and drinking a glass of milk, which, after months of Skinny Cow 2 percent, tastes rich, creamy, and delicious, I go upstairs to my bedroom.

Mum and Dad have put new curtains up since I left. They're green, and they have ruffles and a peach lining. Mary Wesley, Anne Tyler, John Fowles, and Jane Austen are among the paperbacks on the chest of drawers. The books are neatly stacked, in order of height, between two metal bookends. Dad has put my suitcase on the wooden suitcase stand by the bed.

I hear Mum's feet padding gently along the corridor, past the enlarged photograph Dad took of Charlotte and me skiing ten years ago, in the Pyrenees. And a more recent one of Mum sitting on a cairn, with Boris, somewhere in Scotland. She looks quintessentially, gloriously, utterly English in her green anorak, brown corduroy trousers, and walking boots, with her dog by her side.

Popping her head around the door of my room, Mum hands me a hot water bottle in the panda bear cover I gave her last Christmas. She's wearing her Marks and Spencer nightie—the light blue one with the white ruffle round the collar—and a comfy pair of light green slippers.

"It's lovely to see you darling," she says, blowing me a kiss. "Sleep tight," she says.

"Sleep tight, Mum." I listen to Mum pad back along the corridor to her room.

I am much more tired than I realized. Perhaps because this is the first time I've felt truly relaxed since I went to America. Except for that one time at Jack's. Actually, those two times at Jack's. Before I can work out how many times I've been to Jack's, I am asleep.

Thanks to jet lag, I'm awake at four o'clock in the morning, so I go downstairs to make myself some more toast and a cup of tea. Boris is lying in his dog basket under the kitchen table, but gets up, tail beating against the kitchen floor as I feed him some of my toast and Dad's homemade marmalade.

The pink and yellow pottery mugs from Greece are still hanging from the hooks under the kitchen cabinet next to the window. The tartan drying-up cloth is still folded over the rail by the sink. The white electric kettle is still in the same place, next to the tin of Earl Grey tea. The yellow ceramic pot with SUGAR written on it is still next to the slightly larger pot with FLOUR written on it in the same lettering.

Mum's new Too Hot to Handel oven gloves are hanging where her blue and white checked ones used to hang, on the hook next to the oven. The plastic rotary in the cupboard is still home to the salt and pepper holders, the Ryvita, the marmalade, the honey, and probably the same jar of Marmite I ate from before I went to America. Yes. Everything is still here. Reassured, I kiss Boris good night and head back upstairs to my room.

Five hours later I can hear Mum and Dad's voices coming up from the porch. I used to come home from university and sleep for days. Dad's always complained about it.

"She's still asleep." Dad sounds put out.

"Sssh, darling. She's exhausted. She's lost so much weight. She's tiny and terribly pale. Can't you tell how tired she is?"

"Yes, but she's only here for a week. And she's come to see us, not to sleep!"

I walk into the large, drafty bathroom at the end of the corridor, with its claw-footed white iron bath and hundred-year-old copper taps. In a reluctant concession to modern life, Mum and Dad installed one of those plastic showers the English are so fond of, that eventually dribble lukewarm water over you after you've let it run for at least five minutes. I choose, instead, to have a bath.

Drying myself with Mum's soft cream towel, I turn on the electric heater above the mirror and, feeling cozy and warm, look out over the Sussex countryside, soothed by the quiet.

When I come downstairs, Dad announces he's going on a sponsored bike ride to raise money for the Sussex Historic Churches Trust. "Why don't you come with me, Pip?" he asks.

I really just want to spend the day at home. In fact, I'd rather do just about anything than spend a day biking around the English countryside in the rain. But Dad looks so hopeful, and I haven't seen him in months.

"I'd love to," I say.

I put my packed lunch in the dark brown wicker basket attached to the handlebars of Mum's light blue Raleigh bicycle and follow my Scottish father on his black Raleigh bicycle past hedges and tractors and trees, along the narrow country road, and down the hill into Peaseminster. He's wearing waterproof trousers, a blue windbreaker, and the baseball cap I brought him from New York. I'm dressed in Mum's blue windbreaker, which has a hood.

As we come into town, Dad shouts, "Coming through!" to anyone within five feet of him.

I follow him through Peaseminster's tiny cobbled streets, past the little shops with Wall's ice cream signs outside. We bike past Muriel's Cream Teas, Pickwick's Bookshop, Mary's Coffee Shop, and in and out of alleyways, through the ancient streets, from church to church. The town is one of England's oldest and has no less than twenty churches. The average congregation numbers about twelve, which is quite large for the Church of England.

Old women with blue hair sell cups of tea and orange squash for fifty pence each every fifth church or so. They sit behind little tables, under umbrellas, counting change and trying to keep the plastic cover that's supposed to keep the rain off the tea from blowing away in the wind.

"You remember my daughter, Pippa," Dad says to the old women whenever we pass by one of the sodden tables. His face is wet and red and his eyes are alight, alive from all the exercise. He's smiling. Charming them all. "She's here for a week," he says, biking past. "From America!"

"Must be lovely to have her home!" they call after us.

"Yes, it is," he says. "It is."

Dad doesn't stop for a rest, and I dare not ask for one. Somehow I manage to keep up with him as he bikes up hills, through woods, past streams and the duck pond, where small boys in green Wellington boots are feeding yesterday's toast to the ducks. Dad only stops when he sees an ill-placed Coke or beer can. Then he sighs loudly and gets off his bike. Then he puts the offending article in the plastic bag, which hangs from the handlebar of his bike specifically for that purpose and takes it to the nearest bin.

We've been biking for six hours when we reach the chapel at Gately Castle. It was built in the twelfth century. The dark gray gravestones are covered with moss and weeds. And everything—the grass, the air, the inside of the church, which was built out of damp, old stone—smells of England.

Dad knows exactly when each church was built and who built it.

"The only good thing about religion," he says, "is the architecture."

At last we reach our final destination, Peaseminster Cathedral, with its great arches, domes, and the crypt in which the first earl of Peaseminster is buried.

I was confirmed in this cathedral. All the confirmation candidates, as we were called, were driven by our parents and godparents into Peaseminster from St. Margaret's in our white confirmation robes. After the service, a huge tea was laid on for all the parents back at the school, complete with sticky currant buns, chocolate cake, and help-yourself Ty-phoo tea, which we poured into thick-rimmed white ceramic teacups from enormous silver urns.

Today a boy's choir is rehearsing Mozart's "Ave Verum" in the loft above us. I'd like to go up and see them, but a light-blue velvet rope at the bottom of the stone spiral staircase stops me.

"I've stopped going to church," Dad says, as we're on the final stretch, headed home. "I've decided it's all a load of rubbish."

"But you've been church warden at St. Luke's for years!"

"That's only because they needed a good accountant. They've got an American vicar now. One of those bouncy evangelicals. He's got everyone playing guitars and throwing their arms up in the air left, right, and center. I can't stand the music."

On our way home, Dad and I sing all our favorite songs, from "What Shall We Do with the Drunken Sailor" to "Loch Lomond." Dad's rich baritone voice blends with mine, loud and clear against the traffic:

> *By yon bonnie banks and by yon bonnie braes,*
> *Where the sun shines bright on Loch Lomond*

Where me and my true love were ever wont to gae,
On the bonnie, bonnie banks o' Loch Lomond.

At supper, Dad and I devour several helpings of Mum's steak and kidney pie, then polish it off with a bowl of treacle pudding and custard.

"You can always count on a twenty-mile bike ride to help you get over jet lag," Dad says, patting me on the head. "That was fun, Pip. I'm off to bed."

Chapter Forty-six

"MUM AND I were wondering how you were doing for money," Dad says the next morning. I've slept through the night until ten o'clock and feel rested for the first time in months.

"Fine," I say.

"We were wondering," Dad continues without pause, "because, according to your June credit card statement, which we opened by mistake before forwarding it to you, you owe MasterCard three thousand pounds."

My first thought is to be thankful that he didn't open May's by mistake. It was five thousand last month. I borrowed money from my Visa credit card to pay it off.

"You know what the credit card people want you to think, don't you? They want you to think it's free money. Well, it's not free money!"

"Yes, Dad, I do know that," I say, feeling about twelve years old again.

"They're charging you hundreds of pounds in interest!"

"Yes, Dad, I know."

"So why don't you pay it off?"

Dad looks utterly bewildered.

I'm cornered. There is no way out here. "Because I can't. Okay, Dad? I can't."

"Just put twenty percent of every paycheck aside . . ."

"Dad, I don't have a paycheck."

"What do you mean you don't have a paycheck?"

"Dad, Billie doesn't have enough money to pay me. So I'm working in lieu of rent."

"She's making you work for rent?"

"Well, yes. All American kids pay their parents rent."

As soon as it's out of my mouth, I wince. Luckily, Dad doesn't seem to notice what I just said.

"I'd have thought after everything . . . well, she might bloody well spring for that!"

Dad gets up, storms into his study, and comes out with a checkbook—one of the new ones from the NatWest Bank, with furry little beavers on it. He hands me a check for three thousand pounds. "Here you are, Pip," he says.

"Dad, I can't take this!"

"Take it," Dad says.

I'm mortified. Ashamed. Embarrassed. Relieved.

Charlotte and Rupert throw me a Friends of Pip party on my last night at Rupert's flat in Kensington Gardens. It's filled with familiar faces from the world I knew before I found Billie. Charlotte's hair has grown longer now, but is still cut in a trendy bob, shorter at the back.

Charlotte expresses her excitement at seeing me by cooking huge amounts of food. Only Charlotte could keep a cream silk dress clean while making forty-four profiteroles, by hand, without an apron.

"Who'd have thought it, Pip?" she says, spooning the gooey mixture into tidy little eatables. "You, a singer and performer. In a club in New York City, no less! You must meet so many interesting people."

Because Charlotte and Rupert seem to find it so exotic, I tell them all about The Gold Room, and the open mike competition I've entered.

And, for that evening, even though everything has happened,

it also feels as if nothing has happened. I am standing in an over-crowded London kitchen, drinking warm Budweiser with drunk English people I went to university with. Everyone's as pleased to see me as I am to see them.

"Life is dull as ditchwater without you around, Pip," Neville says. "I haven't been on an all-day pub crawl to ease the heartache of whichever poor sod made the mistake of falling in love with you in yonks. London has become unutterably boring."

And Miles is there, standing next to a bowl of Twiglets and a sensible-looking woman, who Neville tells me is a physiotherapist from Gloucestershire. I'm surprised to note that the man who once could have destroyed me by so much as looking at another woman could be holding on to one in front of me a year later and I'd be more interested in the Twiglets. She looks nice. She's probably do-mesticated, too.

I have nothing left but a feeling of mild affection for Miles. I've often thought that the moment you realize you've fallen out of love is far more exhilarating than falling in it, and I think it again now.

"Hallo, Miles."

"Pippa." We kiss twice on each cheek. "This is Clare."

"I've heard so much about you," Clare says. "You sound so *interesting.*"

There was a time when I would have cringed at this. There was a time when I wished, more than anything, that I could be less *interesting* and just blend in. Not anymore.

Clare's utterly sweet. She'll be perfect for Miles. And then we're interrupted by Jan—and Fiona and Fiona and Fiona.

"Pippa!" Fiona says. "Pippa!!!!! Pippaaa!!!" Her long white arms curl around my neck. "How's America?"

"Oh, full of Americans," I say, "but apart from that it's fine."

It's a cheap shot, but guaranteed to make everybody laugh. When they do, I feel like a traitor.

"I've no idea how you can even think of living in that country," someone says, burping. "Everything's so excessive. The Americans always have to have the biggest car, or the hottest weather, or the biggest trade deficit."

"And they can't talk properly, either!" someone else chimes in. "They can't even ask for a glass of water! Last time I went to New York somebody actually said, 'Do you want to hydrate yourself?'"

Everyone guffaws. I'd forgotten how snobbish the British are about Americans. The put-down is delivered with an air of absolute superiority, which is ironic considering the fact that so many of their paychecks come from American companies.

Now one of Rupert's cricketing buddies is talking about an encounter he had the week before with that eternal target of British mirth, a lost American tourist.

"I wanted to say, 'Noooo. We don't pronounce the "ham" in Buckingham Palace!'"

"Why didn't you?" I say.

He burps. "Why didn't I what?"

"Why didn't you say, 'We don't pronounce the "ham" in Buckingham Palace'?"

"Pippa!"

"I'll tell you why," I say. "Because what you British call politeness is really a kind of cowardice."

"*You* British?" Fiona says, laughing, "Oh come *on*, Pip. Next you'll be telling me you love everything about America, including its appallingly imperialistic foreign policies." She's a little woozy, and I love her, but she looks so smug about it, and I just can't stand it.

"As opposed to what? Nonimperialistic British foreign policy? Wasn't it *we* British who marched into India and Africa and said, 'Now listen here, you little brown buggers, we're white, and you're not, therefore we're going to take over your country'? At least George Bush can be excused for being too stupid to understand the consequences of what he was doing when he went into Iraq. Tony Blair's smart as a whip."

"Blair's an idiot!"

To most of the Americans I know, Blair looks like a genius next to George Bush.

"At least we march against the war in this country, Pip, even if the bloody government doesn't take any bloody notice," Fiona says.

She's right to point this out. Nobody marches in America much. We send e-mails. It satisfies the impulse to protest without requiring any actual effort.

I wonder, not for the first time, what happened to the children of the Americans who took to the streets in protest against the war in Vietnam.

"Bloody Blair," Fiona says. She can't stand him. No one can stand him. But she is distracted from her tirade by Neville, who kisses her neck and pulls her off into the sitting room.

Later, when pressed, surrounded by four Fionas, one Neville, one Rupert, and a Max, I say, "There are lots of good things about America."

"Like what?"

Like the fact that I can do what I'm doing, performing in night-clubs, without anyone questioning me in any way. I'd never have been allowed to set foot on a comedy or cabaret stage in London. My accent's too posh. No one would have let me get past the "fuck off back to your Cordon Bleu cookery" attitude, despite the fact that I really can't cook.

I've spent the last few months feeling homesick for England, but by the end of the evening, I feel homesick for the United States. Where I can be completely myself because no one has any precon-ceived ideas about me at all. Where the school I went to is irrelevant. Where no one cares who I vote for. Where enthusiasm is considered a good thing. Where everyone's far too wrapped up in their own lives to care whether or not I have any fashion sense.

But the people standing in this London kitchen have made up their minds about America, and they're not going to change them. And so, to keep the peace, because it's easier, when they ask again,

"What's good about America?" I take the easy way out and say, "George Clooney and . . . well, George Clooney."

The next morning, I call Mum and Dad from London as I'm leaving for the airport and tell them I'll be back soon. Dad picks up the extension.

"It was lovely to see you, darling," they say.

"It was lovely to see you, too."

That's not true either. It wasn't lovely at all. It was far too short a visit, and with so much left unsaid, painful, difficult, and complicated. But it's what we say to one another, because we're English.

Charlotte and Rupert drive me to Heathrow, and I get on a plane and go back to America.

Chapter Forty-seven

I GET BACK TO A MESSAGE from Walt, who is no longer under house arrest: "They dropped the case. It was politically motivated, by the damn liberals of course."

When I call him back, he tells me his wife is away visiting family in Canada. I am to spend the weekend with him at his house in Marsama Beach, a charming, still relatively unspoilt seaside town, about an hour south of Washington.

His wife fell in love with the area years ago. He agreed to buy the house and let her raise the children there, as long as he could base himself in Washington. He promised that if she ever really needed him, he would come. Otherwise he would fight his battles in Washington and elsewhere and see the family when he could.

Walt is in the kitchen, cooking mussels in a marinara sauce when I arrive.

The blue and pink Cape house has white shutters and a white picket fence around it. It's less than a hundred yards from a small sandy beach, with tufts of light green grass growing out of the sand, and half a mile from a small jetty, with a rowboat tied to it.

The furnishings in the house are simple, and very old American. Light spring colors, lots of patchwork, and sparse wooden furniture. It's clean and bright and puritanical in feel.

I'm particularly intrigued by the jar of Noxzema by the sink. I've never used soap out of a jar before. It feels soft against my skin and smells of antiseptic. There are handmade blue and white patchwork quilts on every bed. At the corner of the bedroom is an old wooden rocking chair. I feel as if I've walked into another century.

Margaret's kitchen leads out into a small backyard, where there's a hose neatly coiled, hanging on a nail. I can picture Margaret insisting her children wash the sand off their feet after coming home from the beach, so they don't bring it into the house. Just as Mum would do.

Walt shows me pictures of his children when they were very young, along with their blond haired, blue-eyed, elegant and beautiful mother. No wonder Walt couldn't choose. She was a knockout.

When Walt shows me photographs of his children, I find myself staring at his daughter Ashley. She has copper red hair, just like mine, and looks very like I did when I was the same age.

In one shot, she's running around in a little white dress with a green silk sash. I wore one just like it when I was a three-year-old bridesmaid for the Luttman-Johnsons.

In the next photograph, Ashley and Edwin are playing with a black Labrador, just as I used to play with Boris's predecessor, who was also a black Lab.

"She looks exactly like I did when I was five, and six, and seven!" I say. "And—oh, look! I had a haircut that made me look like a monk when I was about thirteen too! Oh Walt," I say, turning to my American father. "When can I meet them?"

"Soon," Walt says.

He's been saying he'll tell them "soon" for nearly six months now. The knot inside me pulls a little tighter.

The next morning Walt comes downstairs, wearing an oversized T-shirt and his boxer shorts. He looks old and smells of sleep and sweat. His nose is crusty and even halfway across the room I can tell his teeth are badly in need of brushing. We eat waffles and bacon.

Later we go on a walk by the beach. "Do you prefer the beach or the mountains, Pippa?" he asks.

"I like both."

"Thought so," he says.

Walt wants to show me where his father is buried, in a beautiful graveyard by the sea surrounded by lots of other dead people from Marsama Beach. We go to see his grave.

I have no feelings about the man who was my grandfather, because I have never met him. He does not seem real to me. But I stand dutifully next to Walt as he stares at a piece of stone sticking out of the ground with tears in his eyes.

Later we walk down toward the jetty, next to a dark gray wall covered in seaweed.

Walt points to a teenage boy wearing a pair of white shorts and a dark blue sailing sweater. "That's a Kennedy," he says.

"How do you know?" I say.

"Look at the coloring," he says, as if he were describing a horse. "And the shape of the chin. You usually find them up at the Vineyard. That one's probably down here visiting Uncle Ted."

When Walt pulls into his driveway we notice another car parked outside.

"It's your brother." Walt says. "Quick. Get down!"

"I'm sorry?" I look at Walt to see if he's joking. He isn't.

"Get *down*!"

I crouch under the dashboard in Walt's car as Edwin gets out of his car. I hear Walt laugh and walk quickly across the path to his son. Their voices fade as he takes Edwin into the house.

I'm kneeling on the floor of Walt's car, next to an old newspaper, Walt's orange Orioles jacket, and a Styrofoam coffee cup from the 7-Eleven.

I feel dirty. Insignificant. Unwanted. Second class. A secret that needs to be shut away. A problem that needs to be managed. For the first time since I arrived in America, I feel like an old-fashioned, bona fide bastard.

Finally I hear Walt and Edwin come out of the house and what must be Edwin's car drive away.

When Walt opens the door to his car, he is laughing. "That was close, kid. You got your quick reflexes from my side of the family. Useful on the baseball field. Useful at times like this."

I can't speak. And I can't stop the tears. Walt stands at the door of the car.

"Come on out," he says. His voice is gruff. "Get out of the car."

My foot has gone to sleep. "I'm sorry," I say, stamping my sleeping foot, which is being attacked by pins and needles now. "But I thought you were going to tell him about me. *Them* about me."

"I will handle this. I will tell them soon."

I no longer believe him.

My leg is now bearable to stand on. I look up at Walt, pull my shoulders back, and stop crying.

"You've been saying you'll tell them soon ever since I met you." My voice is polite and cool.

My American father is entirely unused to being challenged, and he doesn't like it. But something shifted when he hid me in the car. I may be his bastard, but I'm sure as hell not going to let him treat me like one.

"It's a bit hypocritical, isn't it?" I say, ignoring his nonverbal signals to shut the hell up.

"What?" Walt says.

"You spend your life lambasting the liberals for their lack of morals and family values and talk a lot about integrity—your own, mostly—and then you shut your own daughter in the goddamn car because you're too much of a goddamn coward to tell your son about the existence of his own sister!"

I've gone too far. But I don't care.

"I hate it that you shut me in the car! I hate it! And I hate it that you're a goddamn fucking Republican!"

Walt doesn't move and neither do I. When he speaks his voice sounds far away. It's not a voice I recognize.

The words hang in the air.

"If we'd been liberals, we wouldn't have hesitated," Walt says.

"What are you talking about now?" I say. "Nothing you say ever makes sense."

"You owe your life to the fact that we were Republicans."

"What do you mean?"

"If we were liberals, you'd have been aborted. Don't you dare question my integrity again," says the stranger in front of me.

I walk into the house that Walt shares with his wife, get my handbag and my keys, and, leaving my overnight bag and clothes behind, without saying a word, or looking behind me, I get into Earl Grey, and head back to New York.

In the car, the anger that has been building slowly inside me comes out in the most curious of ways. Instead of screaming, hitting the steering wheel—or the road at a hundred and ten miles per hour—I start writing a song. I can't get the tune out of my head, and I sing it to myself over and over again until I know I won't forget it. Now all I need are the right lyrics.

And then I have them. I stop the car on the shoulder of the freeway to write them down. The only paper I have is a bag from Dunkin' Donuts, but paper is paper.

It doesn't feel like I'm writing. It feels like I'm taking dictation.

By the time I'm back in New York, I have a new act.

Chapter Forty-eight

I**T's STANDING ROOM ONLY** for the finals of the open mike competition at The Gold Room. I'm onstage and I've done well with my old material. Now it's time for the new. I tell them I was adopted. I talk about finding my birth mother. Then I talk about Walt.

"My birth father is a Republican who supports the Christian Coalition," I say. "In fact, I am the product of one of his Christian coalitions." The audience laughs.

"I've always thought of infidelity as wrong, because it means betrayal of the most hurtful kind possible. But if my birth father hadn't cheated on his wife, I would not exist. So, if there are any couples here this evening having a secret extramarital affair, I encourage you to breed."

While the audience is laughing and cheering, the prerecorded backing music starts to play. This isn't a song written by someone I don't know. This is a song written by me, when I was hurting so badly I thought I might not make it through.

The tune starts softly, I speak over the first part, in my English accent, sounding a bit like Noel Coward. While I'm explaining that I was adopted in England and raised to be a lady, the tune is sedate. Polite. English.

The moment I tell them I found my mother in Georgia, the tune becomes a wild piece of pure rock and roll, and I roam the stage, like an American rock star. My body is free. My voice is strong. I'm well and truly out of the proverbial bag.

> *I'm a rock-and-roll redneck*
> *I've gone completely wild*
> *Once an English lady,*
> *Now a bastard child . . .*
>
> *If you treat me like a bastard,*
> *Then I'll be a bastard,*
> *Yes, I'll become a*
> *Bastard Chiiilllllllllllllddddd*
> *YeaaaaaHHHHHHHHHH*

At the end of the song, the crowd goes wild. Jack runs up to me as soon as I get offstage and, glowing with pride, says, "You did it!"

There's a talent scout in the audience that night who invites me to take part in a competition on cable TV. The first prize is five thousand dollars.

All the stars seem to be aligning and so, determined to get things moving for Nick, too, I revisit every gallery in SoHo. It's a sweltering hot afternoon in July, and I've been walking for hours. I find myself opposite the famous Souk Gallery. The sign on the door says Closed, but the door is slightly ajar and so I go in.

The receptionist isn't at her desk, but the air-conditioning is world-class, so I decide to wait. The only other person in the gallery is an old man sitting on a trendy glass bench. He's looking at one of the most extraordinary paintings I have ever seen.

The painting has a subtle, raw sexuality about it. There's a juicy nectarine in the foreground just within grasp and some eggs pressed hard together within a knotted handkerchief that folds around their curves like a teasingly revealing shirt. The heat of the scene makes an oil can flood over. In the background is the most mesmerizing view of what looks like the French countryside, painted in vivid green against a light pink and violet sky.

The sexuality in Nick's work is overt and shocking, but it doesn't hold anything like the power of the painting in front of me.

I know I am looking at the work of not just a good painter, but a great painter. It's the kind of painting that makes you want to step into the world within it and close the door on this one.

"It's a Simon Gales," the old man says.

"It's extraordinary," I reply, continuing to stare at the painting.

"Yes," he says. "It brings me profound peace, while making me question the world I live in at the same time. I love to sit here and just spend time with it."

"I can see why," I say. We look at the painting in silence.

"Are you an artist?" the man says, after a few minutes.

"Oh no," I say. "I couldn't whitewash a wall. I'm here because— well, I suppose I'm an art agent. Of sorts. I've spent the last few months trying to get an artist friend of mine an exhibition, but so far, no luck."

Then, because he seems genuinely interested, I tell him about Nick.

"If I could just find a gallery that would take Nick's work, it would give him the encouragement he needs to jack in the bank and spend his life doing what he truly loves."

"Are you doing what you truly love?"

"Knocking on the doors of unbearably superior gallery owners who won't even glance at Nick's portfolio? No, I hate it. But I promised Nick I'd help him. Anyway, it's just a sideline really."

And then, because he really wants to know, I tell him about the writing and performing I've been doing. As the afternoon turns to dusk, he asks me why I came to America, and I tell him, and he listens with interest.

When the old man asks to see Nick's paintings, I get out the transparencies and show them to him.

"What do you think?" I say, finally.

"I think he's a lucky man to have found you," he says slowly.

The man looks at the paintings again.

"There's a ruthlessness in his work. A kind of cruelty," he says.

I look at Nick's paintings again. I feel uneasy for a second. As if the images are trying to tell me something.

"I know there's darkness in his paintings," I say, finally. "But he isn't at all cruel in real life. He's absolutely lovely. Only he doesn't show it. He's terrified of being rejected, you see. So he does everything he can to stop anyone knowing how soft he is. He's a terribly kind man really."

He shakes his head. "No artist can hide his true nature. It's always in the work." Then the man turns toward me and I see his face full on for the first time. Tall, strong, old, and gray, he makes me think of a hawk that has flown over the entire world and seen everything.

Then he smiles and says, "You have come a long way, my dear. And the work is certainly interesting. Let's try and get someone out here to help you."

Then he stands up and walks slowly toward the reception desk and rings the bell.

A round woman with glasses and her hair tied back in a tight bun comes out from behind a glass door. She looks flustered as soon as she sees my new friend.

"Oh, Mr. Souk, I'm so sorry, I had no idea you were here."

She rushes around the reception desk and holds out her hands to take his jacket.

And I realize that the man I've been chattering away to is James Souk. Of the Souk Gallery. I feel like an idiot.

"Pam," Mr. Souk says, "please take Ms. Dunn and her transparencies to the back room. She has something to show you." Then he turns to me and says, "Ms. Dunn, if you'll agree to exhibit both series of Devang paintings at the Souk Gallery, we would be delighted to give Mr. Devang his first exhibition. Will Nick Devang's agent step into my office and negotiate terms?"

"Yes," I say, beaming. "She'd be delighted."

"I knew you could do it!" Nick says, calling me from a restaurant in Tokyo, thrilled by the news. "The exhibition must be a rip-roaring success."

"It will be."

"My loveliest girl, we are both destined to reach the top of our chosen fields. We must promise never to permit anything but the very best possible work from each other."

"We must."

Like Billie and Walt, before things went wrong for them, we will take New York by storm.

Chapter Forty-nine

THE LINEUP for the cable talent show consists of the Keenan Cowboys, a rap artist, a magician wearing an electric blue suit with silver stars on it, and me. I'm going to sing my "Rock-and-Roll Redneck" song while playing the piano. Only this time I'll have a live band, who I've been rehearsing with all afternoon. The song sounds great, except the drummer hasn't shown up. This matters, because there's a drum solo, during which I am to leave the piano stool and do a leaping, redneckish sort of dance.

With no drummer in sight, the director decides to cut my dance in the middle of the song. I'm devastated. I've been practicing it for days and have a really great moment where I reach behind the piano and put on sideburns. With the dance I've got a chance of winning. Without the dance there's no way.

I'm feeling horribly disappointed when Jack arrives with the rest of the audience and sits down at my table. I'm about to explain the situation when one of the band members shouts out Jack's name and starts clambering toward us, through television cameras, over cable wires, through the already drinking crowd.

"Jack Cain!" The man's almost shouting.

"Billy J?!" Jack says, standing up and laughing. The two men are slapping each other on the back like old friends, which leads me to conclude that they are old friends.

"Hey," Billy shouts to the guys in the band, "it's Jack Cain."

"You still playing, man?" Billy J. says.

"No," Jack says. "I quit a few years ago. It's been a long time." Jack's eyes are alight.

"Can you help us out? Our drummer hasn't shown up."

"Well I dunno . . ."

"You were a *drummer*?" I say, turning toward Jack.

"Come on, Jack. We're playing this great new song by this cute new British chick." Billy's winking at me now.

Jack throws his head back and laughs and laughs.

"Oh man, Pippa, you got a drum solo in this now?"

I'm beaming. "Yes!"

"How long we got?"

"About fifteen minutes. And we're going up live."

"Hey! Brian! Ben! Richie! Jimmy! Look who's here! It's Jack Cain."

Suddenly the table is surrounded by men in their late thirties with long hair who drag Jack up onto the stage and sit him down behind the drums. Jack picks up the drumsticks.

"I know the song," he says. "It'll be fine."

The men go to their positions onstage and start playing the show's theme tune. When it's time for me to go on, I'm excited. And alive. And on edge. And I know it's going to be a good set. And it is.

When its time for the drum solo, I jump off the piano stool and reach behind the piano, where I have hidden my special sideburns. I've got special glue stuck to the side of my face, so the sideburns will stick on at a touch. With my hat on, I suddenly transform into a real redneck. Billie, Walt, and the pain that accompanies me everywhere are forgotten. As I jump and whoop and leap in a redneckish way across the stage, Jack plays the drums like a wild man.

The drumsticks have become a part of his body and they move together to the frenzied rhythm he's creating throughout the room. It's hot under the lights. Half the buttons on his shirt have come undone and Jack's hair is plastered against his face.

At the end of the song, the whole crowd jumps to its feet.

Now we're offstage. A woman I've not seen before has put her arms around Jack's neck.

"Jack! I haven't seen you since you broke up with Lisa!"

"How is she?" Jack says.

"Good—great! Got kids now, you know."

"Hey!" I say, shouting across the room. "Hey! I thought you were gay!" The words come out without my thinking about them. And when I realize what I've said, it's too late to take them back.

Jack stops kissing the woman's cheek and is looking at me.

"You thought *what*?"

I walk quickly over to where Jack is standing.

"So, you're not?" I say.

I try to take my eyes away from Jack's, but I can't. He is looking into mine with an expression I can't quite read. He's covered in sweat, and very, very sexy.

"You had a girlfriend?"

The woman is saying something, but neither Jack nor I hear her.

"Yes," he says.

"But I thought you were gay." Oh God, Pip, shut up.

Jack looks perplexed.

"You thought I was gay."

"Well, yes."

"Why?"

"Well, you iron your sheets. And you work at The Gold Room. And then there's the Harvey Fierstein quote on your fridge."

"What?"

"'Never be bullied into silence.' The Harvey Fierstein quote."

"I tore that out for you, Pippa."

"You tore that out for me?"

"Whatever—or whoever—has been stopping you singing about what was really going on, well, that felt like bullying to me."

"Oh."

We're still looking at each other. The rest of the room isn't there.

"So, you're not gay?"

"No," he says. Still now. "No. I'm not. Never have been. Not going to start now."

The moment is broken by the emcee, who comes over to hand me my check.

"You should have some of this money, Jack," I say. "I wouldn't have won without the drum dance."

"No," he says, his eyes still on me. "Use it to move into the city."

I write a letter to Billie and send it to her in Georgia, where she is spending the rest of the summer.

July 20

Dearest Billie,

I will never be able to thank you enough for welcoming me so fully into your life. And I want you to know that I will always deeply appreciate everything you have done for me, from your generous, loving action in giving me up when I was a baby to really being there for me when I needed you most.

Right now, though, I am in very real need of some time to absorb everything that has happened and have decided to move into New York City. Even though I know it will be hard for you, I would be so grateful if you would respect my very real need for "space." I promise to call you as soon as I can.

It doesn't mean I don't love you. I think it has something to do with my need to figure out a way to integrate everything I've learned into my new identity.

Please try to understand.

I'll leave you my phone number and address of course. I

promise there will never be another day of your life when you do
not know where I am.

        With all my love, Pippa

Jack rents a truck, drives it out to Adler, and helps me lift my garage-
sale couch and my suitcase onto the back of it. I follow in Earl Grey.
And as I do so, the tightness in my chest begins to loosen, and I start
to feel like myself again.

Chapter Fifty

ELFRIDA'S APARTMENT is on the second floor above a restaurant on Union Square West, right next to the farmer's market, with a marble bathtub so tall you have to climb into it, like a Roman.

My windowless bedroom has a loft bed, under which Elfrida has put some curtains, to create a dressing room that doubles as a closet. For the first time since I arrived in America, I have my own space, somewhere that has nothing whatsoever to do with Billie. I start having moments in my day when I do not think about Billie or even Walt, who I haven't heard from at all.

The feelings I have for them have become a brown muddy thing that I keep in a box on a mantelpiece. When I'm feeling strong enough, I take them down and feel a bit more of the pain that I do not understand. Then, when it becomes overwhelming again, I put it back in the box on the mantelpiece, next to the silver cuckoo clock and the yellow ceramic pig Charlotte gave me on my thirteenth birthday.

Like every genuinely gorgeous American woman I've ever met, Elfrida thinks she's ugly and is obsessed by how much she weighs. She wants to fall in love, but her Norwegian boyfriend went back to Norway, her day-job boss is married, and the guy she likes in her theater group hasn't made a move yet. She thinks he might be gay. I think she might be right. But then again, I'm not exactly batting a hundred in that department.

I solve Elfrida's imaginary weight issue by eating most of her chocolate, which she keeps in the freezer, under her bed, and in glass jars behind the kitchen sink.

As far as men are concerned, I keep trying to sell her on our mutual friend Jack.

"He's a really good man," I say. "He'd treat you beautifully. And he's funny and kind, not to mention cute. And he cooks and he irons and he cries whenever he remembers his dead dog, so you know he'd be a wonderful father. And he's calm and he's someone you know you could trust with the really important things. He's sexy, too— and absolutely not the kind of guy to cheat on his wife. He'd be perfect for you."

"He'd be perfect for you," Elfrida says. "If you weren't in love with the infamous Nick."

I can't pretend I haven't thought about what it would be like to be with Jack. But I've come too far to settle for a man just because he makes me feel safe.

"It's not just Nick," I say, pouring dinner into large red plastic cups. We recently discovered Carnation chocolate meal-in-a-drink. It only has a hundred and fifty calories and contains all the nutrients you need for a well-balanced dinner.

"I've had tea with the Governor of Hong Kong. Jack's never been out of the United States. He would never fit into my world."

"Pippa, you don't fit into your world."

"But I can. Therein lies the difference. You should see me at Henley. I can blend in with the best of them."

"What's Henley?"

"It's a town by a famous river in England where people in fancy hats go to watch people race boats, while they sit on the side of the river on a grassy bank drinking Pimm's."

"You're into rowing and Pimm's?"

"Not at all. But that's not the point. What I'm trying to say is that Nick and I—we come from the same world. We want the same kind of things. Nick wants to go down the Amazon, and so do I. He's traveled all around the world, and so have I. He reads Rudyard Kipling, and he knows what I'm talking about when I refer to Blue Peter. Actually he probably doesn't, scrap that. But he's—well, we're adventurers, Nick and I. We're not the type to settle."

Now Elfrida and I are ready for the garlic cloves we roasted in the new convection oven that she ordered from the Home Shopping Network.

"I like Mozart. Jack likes rock and roll."

"But you *write* rock and roll. You *sing* rock and roll."

"True."

We spread the garlic clove on two Carr's water biscuits and bite into them.

"Deeelicious," we say, in unison.

"You're out of your mind," Elfrida says.

"And so's Nick. And that's why he's right for me."

"No matter," Elfrida says, when we're done with dinner. "Jack's a lost cause anyway."

"But he said he wasn't gay."

"It's not that. He's been in love with someone else for a while now."

It would be supremely unfair to allow any feelings of jealousy. And so I don't.

"Really? Who is she?"

"He won't tell anyone. And you can't probe Jack."

"True," I say. And then, "So, you're not interested in Jack?"

"Not in that way," Elfrida says. "It would be like dating my brother."

"Okay," I say, curiously relieved. And I'm pleased for Jack. Really. He's met someone. Good. Good, good, good, good, good.

Jack and I can stay friends. Because we're both in love with other people. It's good to have got this sorted.

So now I know that Jack is helping Elfrida paint her bedroom walls from maroon to cream because he's her friend, not because he wants to date her. Soon he's going to start working on her ceiling. So he'll be around a lot.

Chapter Fifty-one

JAMES SOUK encourages me to generate all the preshow publicity I can for the exhibition—"An artist only gets one chance to make a first impression," he says—and Nick and I are in contact almost every day.

"I'm inviting all the bankers," I tell him. "And the Brits. According to the embassy there are one hundred and fifty thousand of them in the New York area."

Nick can't make it to New York before the exhibition, which is scheduled for October, but we're thinking of rewarding ourselves with a trip to Rome, perhaps, in November. If the exhibition goes well, we might go to Athens too.

I have days when I am almost happy.

I have moments of lightness. Sometimes I have moments of hilarity. Like the moment Elfrida and I discover that what we thought was a mouse under the stove is actually a dirty sock.

And then the phone rings. And it's Billie. In an instant the pain is back and the joy has gone.

"I know what this is all about. You're testing me, honey. Well, I'm not going anywhere without you," Billie is saying. "Without you I carry around an empty space inside me. Just talking to you helps a little, but seeing you would put cupfuls of joy back into me. I'd feel full again. You said you were going to call!"

By the time I put the phone down my hand is shaking.

"Hey," Elfrida says, on her way back up from the laundry room to which she has delivered the dirty sock. "Are you okay?"

"I'm fine," I say.

I'm *not* going to burden my friends with this.

It's bad, but not as bad as it was. I'm not in Billie's house anymore. I'm no longer alone. I have Elfrida, and Jack, and, of course, my Nick.

DATE: August 5
TO: pippa-dunn@hotmail.com
FROM: NickDevang@bankglobal.net

Released from your prison you reached out and released me from mine, and I adore you for it. One of the things that's stopped me painting in the past has been the sense of isolation that painting brings. Knowing that you have been there, encouraging me, doing everything you can to bring my art into the world, has somehow made it all possible. I adore you. And I want you. In every way.

Love, Nick

I'm getting paid five hundred dollars a gig on Saturday nights now. I have to perform outside Manhattan to get that kind of money, but Earl Grey drives me safely out to Brooklyn and New Jersey, getting me home by one or two in the morning.

Whether I collapse on the couch or in my bed, at eight o'clock on Sunday mornings, the phone rings. And it's always Billie.

"When are you going to call me?"

"I just need some time."

"How much more time to you need? You've had six weeks!"

If I give in to her, and go and see her, she'll start pulling me to her again. I won't be able to resist. I'll lose the tentative grip I have on becoming Pippa again. A different Pippa from the Pippa I was before, but Pippa nonetheless. I'll be drowning in the mud again, with no way out.

I tell Billie I have a lot to think about and ask her to please give me some time. She says she understands and promises to wait for me to call her.

But then, as I'm padding across the floor to the bathroom to brush my teeth the following morning, the phone rings. And it's Billie again. And I'm plunged back into the bog.

"Ralph's moved over into publicity, and he's doing wonderfully well. We're making a profit this year. You can come back anytime. We can pay you anything you want."

"Billie, it's not about the money. I just can't. I'm busy here. I—"

Now her voice turns.

"I've been reading about adoptees and their issues. Whatever kind of family you went to, you've all got issues!"

I've been at the gallery, going over the list of people to invite to the exhibition. We're getting close now, and there's a lot to do. I want Nick to take New York by storm.

When I get home, the phone rings and it's Billie. I find I can distance myself a little if her voice isn't in my ear, so I put the phone on speaker. Then I put down my bag and sit on the floor next to the phone.

"I love you so much, Pippa." The pitch of her voice goes from low to high. "And you're hurting me so badly."

"What do you want me to do?" I say.

"Well, for a start, I'd like you to do what you say you're going to do! You said you were going to call me for my sausage stew recipe, but you never did!"

The words, in all their absurdity, hang in the air.

"I've been busy, Billie."

"I feel like a dictionary."

"A dictionary?"

"You walk into my life, make me fall in love with you, get the information you need, and then you walk out again. You are not the only one with abandonment issues."

"I'm so sorry."

"I love you, Pippa!" She's shouting now. "I want you in my life! And I want to see my grandchildren! They are my grandchildren, goddammit! How can you deprive your children of their grandmother in this way?!"

"But I don't have any children."

"I know you don't have children, what are you, nuts? I'm talking about when you *do*! I loved my grandparents so much."

And then ten minutes of memories of her childhood at her grandparents' estate. My arms are wrapped tightly around my knees now. My head is buried in them too. The same body that took a tough Saturday night crowd by storm two nights before is now curled up in the fetal position next to the phone. The darkness is back.

And then Billie changes tone.

"I went to the adoption agency. I wanted to find out what happened. I figured you must have been abused or something, to be having this much trouble with your adoption."

I'm not having trouble with my adoption, I want to shout. *I'm having trouble with you!*

"I figured something must have happened to you in the foster home for you to have all these issues. But they said it was a nice foster home. So you just got problems. So, deal with them, honey! You gotta work them through! Just like I worked mine through in AA. Becoming an alcoholic was the best thing that ever happened to me." And then she tells me, as she has told me time and again, about how her alcoholism started soon after she gave me away.

I sense someone standing in the door to the kitchen. It's Jack. I have no idea how long he's been standing there. He's looking at me with an expression I don't recognize. I can't move.

"You can love your adoptive parents and me, you know," Billie is saying. "It doesn't have to be one or the other!" And then, when I don't reply, she says, "How can you be so cruel?"

"I'm so sorry, Billie. I'm so sorry."

"Well you should be."

"And I am."

I can't stop the shaking and I still can't move. Jack walks over to the phone. Solid. Sure.

"Billie?"

"Who are you?"

"I'm a friend of Pippa's. She's very upset."

"*She's* upset?"

"Yes. And she needs to hang up now. Good-bye."

And with that, Jack puts the phone on the cradle.

"Has this been going on a long time?" Jack's eyes are dark with fury. "Has it?"

"Jack—you just—you just hung up on her."

"It wasn't hard," he says. "You just close your hand around the phone and put it down." He isn't smiling.

From the look on his face, I can tell that he heard it all. My cover is blown. The Pippa Jack knows isn't what she seems. Underneath, she's a heaving, porous mass of mess. The darkness is winning. She's going under.

"How long have you been there?"

"Long enough."

A siren screams past on the street outside. Jack comes over to me and helps me up off the floor.

"You must think I'm a terrible person, causing her so much pain."

I can see Jack choosing his words carefully.

"Pippa," he says, his voice straining in anger, "you're not the one who's only thinking about herself here. Do you *really* think it's fair of her to lay this huge guilt trip on you?"

I look at him. "Maybe not, but . . ."

"But nothing," Jack says. "But fucking nothing."

A few moments later, we're standing next to the phone, my friend and I, as close as it is possible for two people to stand together with all their clothes on.

And then the phone rings.

"Let the machine pick up," Jack says.

We wait for the needy southern voice, but it doesn't come.

Instead the voice is young and male.

"Hi. I hope I've got the right number. This is Walt Markham's son Edwin speaking. I'm—uh—I guess I'm Pippa's brother."

"Edwin?" I say, picking up the phone.

"Hi sis," the voice says.

"Hi," I say, feeling a huge sense of relief. Then again, "Hi."

"Can you meet me on the corner of Thirty-fourth and Sixth in an hour? I'll be the redhead in the Orioles hat."

"Yes!" I tell him. And then, "Me too."

I put down the phone, grinning.

"Jesus!" Jack says. "It's one helluva rollercoaster you're on here."

But, seeing the joy in my face, he's smiling as I go.

Chapter Fifty-two

IT'S A WINDY DAY, and Edwin isn't there yet. I crouch down beside a dumpster for shelter and wait. A shadow blocks the sun. I look up. Edwin is standing in front of me. He is tall, with a face that looks remarkably like mine.

"So," he says, "I meet my sister for the first time ever, and she's sitting by a dumpster." I jump up.

"Hi," I say.

"Hi," he says. We laugh.

"So, the cat's out of the bag," he says.

"Meow."

We stare at each other. His hair is my hair, only short. His face is my face, only male. He's taller than me and clearly shares my lack of interest in fashion. We're both wearing jeans, a sweatshirt, and, as anticipated, an Orioles baseball cap.

"Why did he tell you now?" I say, finally.

Edwin smiles. "He doesn't like my girlfriend. So he said all mistakes have consequences, some of them serious. Then he told me about you."

Oh. Well, at least he told him. My joy at meeting a sibling who I already recognize completely is far stronger than anything else.

"Were you surprised?" I say.

"Not really," he says. "I always knew there was something. Dad was never all that happy, especially at holiday times. Your mother must have been something special. Dad's not really the affair type."

"Yes, I think she was," I say, picturing the two of them, for a second, as they were, forbidden to love each other, but loving each other anyway.

"Now I know why Dad used to want to know my girlfriends' birthdays," Edwin says. "He wanted to be sure I wasn't dating my sister." With New York City rising above us, we start laughing like hysterical children.

"When is your birthday?" I say, back on the street as we head toward Times Square.

"September sixth, nineteen seventy-eight."

"Mine's April twenty-sixth, nineteen seventy-eight." We grin. "Must have been an active year."

"So we're Irish twins," he says.

"I guess so," I say. He looks at me closely.

"How do we know he's dead?" Edwin says.

"Who?"

"Our brother."

Our brother. Edwin's brother and mine. Walt has told him about my twin. Our brother. I am no longer alone.

"Why would they lie about it?"

"Have you seen the death certificate?"

"Do dead twins have death certificates?"

"Dunno. Did he have a birth certificate?"

"If he did, I haven't seen it. I haven't seen my birth certificate either, for that matter. I'm not allowed."

"What do you mean?"

"I was adopted. I'm not allowed access to my original birth certificate in the U.S."

"No shit?"

We walk around New York and talk and talk. About politics, justice, Walt, me, him. And our sister Ashley. She works with children with special needs.

"Does she know about me?"

I watch something tighten in him. "No," he says.

"Are you going to tell her?" I say.

"I can't. Dad made me promise."

"Why?"

"Something to do with Dad's theory that boys handle tough things better than girls."

"So your dad has made you promise to keep my existence a secret from your sister?"

"Our sister," he corrects me. "God, but you're so like her!"

"Is she sane?" I ask.

"Hell no!" he says, grinning.

Edwin stays overnight on my couch. I'm tired when I climb up the ladder to my loft bed, but I don't sleep well. I dream of a sister with only half a face, and I wake with a start.

I can see Edwin is awake too, because his eyes are open.

"You okay?" I whisper. There's pain in his eyes. Keeping other people's secrets hurts. He doesn't say anything. I turn onto my back and stare at the glow-in-the-dark stars Elfrida stuck on the ceiling above me, wishing there was something I could do to help ease his burden.

Edwin and I go out to breakfast at the Cornelia Street Café in the West Village. We both order the fried eggs with roasted garlic cloves.

"Growing up, Dad loved playing hero to everyone but his family," he says. "You didn't miss much. He drank a lot, and he ignored my mother, and he was never there."

That makes sense.

"He played hero to me, I think. At least for a little while. When I met him, well, to me he was the perfect father I'd dreamed of all my life."

"I'll bet he loved that!"

"Yes, I think he did," I say, suddenly missing the father I had so wanted Walt to be.

"When did you last see him?"

"It's been a while," I say. I haven't heard from Walt since I left Marsama Beach.

There's understanding in my brother's twinkling eyes. Behind his smile is the kind of depth that can only come from pain. He knows how much I'm hurting over Walt. I don't have to say a word.

I wonder why it is that I recognize Edwin completely and Ralph not at all. Is it just because we're so close in age, or have I really inherited more of Walt's genes than Billie's?

"I've got some news. It's not good," Edwin says once breakfast is over.

"Okay."

"Dad's had to go away for a while."

"What do you mean?"

"He's going to be out of the country for a while. That's all I know."

I wait for more. There isn't any.

"Do you have any idea what, exactly, he does for a living?"

"No." Edwin laughs. "He's never really talked about it. Dad's always been an enigma. He likes it that way."

"Well, at least he bequeathed you to me before he disappeared again."

"Yeah," Edwin says. Then he laughs again and says, "So, now I have a sister who says 'bequeathed.'"

When I say good-bye to this funny, familiar brother of mine I'm hit by a profound sorrow. In the hope that it'll help me figure out where it's coming from, I start walking around the city.

By the time I reach the Hudson River, I realize that Edwin's arrival probably means that I've seen the last of my father.

I know Walt loves me. But Walt's image of himself as a great man is as important to him as breathing. When the child who most resembles him called him a coward it must have shaken him to the core. Walt has spent his life—and probably made his living—keeping secrets. Other people's, as well as his own. Honest, direct communication is not something he values or is familiar with. Much easier for him to cut me off again than deal with the "me" I have become.

Having finally found out the truth about the people I came from—not just the parts that are easy to deal with, but all of it—I find I can't lie to myself anymore. About anything. I can't lie to other people either.

What Walt doesn't know—and what I didn't know until this moment—is that the profound disappointment I feel doesn't make me love him any less. Perhaps, in a way, it makes me love him more. If Walt can be imperfect, then so perhaps can I.

Walt doesn't know how to say he is sorry. But I do. I am English after all. So I stop at a phone booth and leave him a message. I don't tell him I love him. I'm still way too English for that. I don't say good-bye either. Instead I say, "I'm just calling to let you know that it's okay by me for you to be human, Walt. I understand all of it. And—well—thank you for sending me Edwin."

Chapter Fifty-three

WHEN I FINALLY GET BACK to my apartment in Union Square, I'm too exhausted to think anymore and realize I have lost my keys. I try calling Elfrida but she doesn't pick up. I bang on the door for half an hour but she stays asleep.

I go back downstairs to where Farik the doorman is sitting in his usual place by the elevator, chanting the Koran. I ask him if he has a spare key to the apartment. He shakes his head to indicate a negative answer to this and keeps chanting.

"Well, please will you help me bang on the door to try to wake Elfrida up?"

He stops chanting long enough to tell me that, according to the Koran, when people are asleep, they are in a holy state and that you should therefore never wake a sleeping person.

"You will sit next to me until the morning," Farik says, pointing to a grubby-looking chair in the corner off the hallway.

I bloody will not. I look at my watch. It's 1:34 a.m. Who can I call at this hour?

Fifteen minutes later, I'm standing outside Jack's apartment. His hair is tousled and he isn't wearing a shirt.

"Come in," he says.

"I'm so sorry to wake you," I say. "I'm so sorry. I . . . well, thank you."

"How did it go with your brother?"

"Great. He's great."

Half naked, Jack looks as sexy as Harry Connick, Jr., when he took off his shirt in *Pajama Game*.

"Do you have something I could sleep in?" I say. I don't want him thinking I'm here to sleep with him. Because I'm not.

Jack gets a pair of sweats out of an immaculately packed drawer and hands me a T-shirt. "You can change in there," he says.

He shuts the door to the bathroom behind me. I put on his sweats and T-shirt and open the door.

"Are you going to sleep in your shoes?" he says.

I stare at the sneakers on my feet. I never wear socks. I'd like to say it was a fashion choice, but the truth is I can never find them. There are consequences to this.

"I really think that, as your apartment is so small, I should keep my shoes on."

Jack looks blank. This clearly isn't the moment to be British.

"My feet stink," I say. "If I'm going to take my shoes off, I'll need to wash my feet."

Without a word, Jack opens the bathroom door again. I roll up Jack's pants and get into his lime green bathtub to wash my feet. When I turn on the tap, instead of the bathwater, Jack's powerful shower rains down on me in a torrent. I let out a little scream.

"Everything all right in there?"

"Uh, not really," I say.

"Can I come in?"

"Okay."

I'm standing in Jack's bathtub, in his soaking wet T-shirt and sweats. I wait for the tone of irritation, but it doesn't come. Actually Jack is laughing, and, as seems to be his wont, handing me a towel.

"I have a wide selection of T-shirts, ma'am, if you insist on wearing clothes in ninety-degree weather."

"I do," I say, padding after him.

"Thank you so much," I say as he hands me a Ray Davies T-shirt and a pair of green boxer shorts with monkeys on them.

"You're welcome so much," he says.

"I don't want to keep you up," I say, after I've changed.

I'm looking at everything but Jack, who is still half-naked.

"Here, take the bed," he says, finally. "I'll take the couch."

"No, no, I can't do that. You take the bed."

"Take the bed, Pippa."

I'm lying, once again, between Jack's crisp green sheets. Only this time I don't have concussion. I try to think of Nick. But I can't. I can think of no one but the man lying six feet away from me. He is overwhelmingly sexy without his shirt on. His eyes are filled with kindness and humor and fondness for me. He might be in love with someone who isn't here, but he is not gay.

I have never made the first move with a bloke. Ever. But suddenly I am tired of the way I have been. Tired of being passive. Tired of just responding to events. I want to initiate something. I'm an American now. It's time to come right out with it. So I say, "Is the sofa comfy?"

"Uh huh." Jack's voice is deep in the dark.

"How's your back?"

"Okay."

"It doesn't hurt on the couch, then?"

"What?"

"Your back."

"Nope."

Jack doesn't say anything. Then, "Pippa?"

"Yes?"

"Do you want me to get into bed with you?"

"Yes."

And he does. And we lie next to each other in the dark of Jack's tiny apartment, not moving for a few moments, my friend and I.

We are both in love with other people. I'm safe. He's safe. It's not a betrayal of Nick. Not really. I mean, Nick and I haven't slept together yet. Not yet.

"I'm glad you're not gay," I say.

Jack laughs quietly. And then, slowly, in unison, we turn toward each other in the dark, and we kiss. Jack's lips are soft and full and he smells wonderful as always. Jack. Jack. My dear friend Jack.

And then he's not my friend anymore. He's a sexy, irresistible, demanding man who is clearly capable of devouring me. And he does. And then I find myself burrowing under what the English would call a duvet and the Americans would call a comforter. And then I find him.

"Pippa?"

"Yes?"

My voice sounds muffled from under the sheets.

"Are you sure about this?"

"Well you've had a shower, haven't you?"

He laughs, but only briefly, because then we're somewhere else, Jack and I.

Later, wrapped tightly in each other's arms, we sleep deeply until the morning.

I wake up to the first sense of peace I've had in years. It's not just the fact that Jack is, without a doubt, far and away the most unselfish lover I have ever had. Or that I climaxed three times in a row.

It's also because the panicky feeling isn't there. I know Jack's not going anywhere. At last, at long, long last, I can lay down my guard and relax.

And then my cell phone breaks into this perfect moment. Perhaps if I hadn't picked it up, things would have turned out differently. But I have not yet learned that there are times in life when one should pick up one's cell phone, and other times when it's best to just let the damn thing ring.

Chapter Fifty-four

THE VOICE AT THE END of the phone belongs to the new receptionist at the Souk Gallery. She has exciting news. Nick Devang—*the* Nick Devang—is in the gallery and looking for me.

"He's *gorgeous*," she says breathlessly. "He was wearing a gold silk suit! I think it was Armani!"

Well done, Nick, I think. You've just turned the image of the starving artist on its head.

The receptionist goes on. Nick wants to meet me at the entrance to Central Park at three.

My soul mate—the man I am destined to love—is in New York. And I am in bed with my best friend.

Heart beating, I turn off the phone and glance over at Jack, still naked, tousled, sexy, there.

Nick's finally come for me. What have I done?

"What is it?" Jack says.

"I have to go," I say, avoiding Jack's eyes. "Nick's in town."

Jack doesn't say a word.

My overalls are still stuffed into the towel rack in Jack's bathroom in a horribly crumpled state. If I hurry I'll have time to go to Filene's Basement to pick up something other than Jack's Ray Davies shirt and sweats to wear to meet Nick. I scrabble about in my bag. I've got a stick of lipstick somewhere. That'll have to do.

I look over at Jack again. I want to get back into bed with Jack. But Nick's words ring in my head: *Avoid safe places. They are so very hard to escape from.*

"Last night was—well, amazing," I say to Jack. "But . . ."

Jack's face is completely without expression.

"I know you're in love with someone too, Jack. Or I'd have never let last night happen. You are, aren't you?"

Please say yes. Please!

"Yes," Jack says, still not moving.

Jack is lying on his bed, hands behind his head, staring at the ceiling.

"Thank God for that!" I say. "No one who ends up with me is going to get away without doing at least some Scottish dancing. Can you imagine how ridiculous you'd feel in a kilt?"

I still can't read the expression on Jack's face.

"Dear Jack," I say, kissing him softly on the cheek. "Thank goodness we are in love with other people. You and I—we could never work." And then, trying for a joke that comes out all wrong, I say, "You need to be with someone who's prepared to clean the fridge. I need to be with someone who knows how to make a long-distance call to London."

I look at Jack's face. It's still without expression.

And then, feeling like a heel, I leave Jack lying naked on his bed and head out of his apartment and up Seventh Avenue, calling the gallery on the run.

"Where's Nick staying?" I say.

"The Waldorf," the receptionist tells me.

The Waldorf. Of course. Nick's chosen the hotel where my parents first met. Where else? Everything is coming full circle. I can't wait until three o'clock to meet him in Central Park. I'll surprise him at the hotel.

Thank God he's here. One more night like the one I've just spent with Jack and I'd never have escaped.

Avoid safe places. They are so very hard to escape from.

Nick's arrived just in time. And he's right. And the reason they're so hard to escape from is because they make you feel at home.

I'm destined for adventure. I mustn't settle for anything less. Not after the journey I've been on. I'm ready for true love now. I'm holding Nick's hand and I'm ready to jump, whatever that means. Nick's at the Waldorf. I need to get to Nick.

Bugger Filene's Basement. I'll go in Jack's sweats. I doubt I'll be keeping my clothes on for long. I've come a long long way. I'm ready for a man like Nick now, and he has finally come for me.

The hotel's huge marble pillars are holding up the famous golden ceiling high above exquisitely carpeted marble floors. I hope that my accent and my brightest smile will cause the man to overlook the way I'm dressed and give me Nick's room number. As usual my accent does the trick.

I ring the bell to room 1406. No one answers. There's a painting on the wall, in the hall, of a hunting scene. I wonder if it was hanging there the night my parents met, in this same hotel, twenty-nine years before. If it was, I wonder if they noticed it. I wonder if Billie and Walt felt back then the way Nick and I feel today. Caught in the kind of love that's verging on obsession.

I ring the bell again and hear footsteps approaching the door. It opens.

"Hallo?"

The woman is Indian, like the woman in Nick's paintings. She has the same delicate beauty and is dressed in a dark green and gold sari. She has flecks of red in her hair and a luminous stillness about her. In comparison I feel loud and big.

"I'm looking for Nick Devang."

"Oh, yes, please. Please. Come in." Everything about her is gentle.

"My name's Pippa Dunn," I say, catching sight of my hair in the mirror. It's sticking out. At a right angle. I look preposterous. "I'm Nick's . . . agent."

"Pippa! Oh how wonderful to meet you! Nick has told me all about you. Come in. I'm Aradhana."

"Hallo," I say.

We sit on the sofa, embroidered in gold and black, and drink tea from a silver teapot, served in thin rimmed cups. The painting on the wall behind her is of another hunting scene. This time dozens of men in hunting hats and red coats are surrounded by beagles. It looks like an original, but it can't be. Walt has the same painting on his wall in Washington.

"We haven't seen Nick in two weeks," she's saying. "We thought we'd join him here in lovely New York. The hotel said he's expected back some time this afternoon," she says. She's handing me a sandwich with no crusts on a silver tray.

"Nick is so thrilled about all the developments," she says. "He was so excited when he heard from your mother!"

"Really?"

"To be working with the genius who once represented Marfil! It means so much to him. He speaks of nothing else."

"Mina! Nicholas!" Two tiny children aged about three and five come into the room, followed by another woman—clearly their nanny—in a sari. The boy is dressed in a light blue suit and the girl is wearing a little gold dress. They have beautiful brown eyes and they are shy and achingly beautiful.

"They look just like him, don't you think?" she says.

I do.

"Hallo," I say, rummaging in my handbag for some chocolate. Two pairs of tiny hands reach out and take my emergency Hershey bar and yellow box of peanut M&M's.

The nanny is smiling. Aradhana is smiling. She looks radiant and so proud of her Nick.

I cannot destroy her happiness. I will not.

"Aradhana, it is wonderful to meet you at last," I say. The lie takes everything I have. Then I tell her I have an urgent appointment and need to go.

"Nick will be so sorry to have missed you," she says.

I bet he will.

She has such gentleness about her. Oh, oh, oh. He's married. With children. Oh, what a fool am I.

I smile at her again because her peace of mind depends, entirely, on her not knowing why I am here.

"I so hope we can see you again while we're in town," she says. "Perhaps we can do something together, with the whole family?" Her voice is soft and sweet.

"That would be lovely," I say.

"Perhaps we could take one of those boat trips around Manhattan," she says. "What do they call it?"

"The Circle Line."

"Yes," she says. "The Circle Line."

I walk away from the Waldorf realizing what a total fool I have been.

The Nick I built up in my mind wasn't any more real than my idealized birth parents were.

But oh! The sense of betrayal! How it stings!

With it comes the first sense of absolute clarity I've had since I landed in America, and I know what I must do.

Still wearing Jack's clothes, I find Earl Grey and drive straight to Billie's house. Only this time I am not coming as Billie Parnell's daughter. This time I am coming as Pippa Dunn.

Chapter Fifty-five

A T THE END OF THE DRIVE, Billie's house looks dilapidated and dark. The smell of dirty carpet and general neglect hits me hard as I walk through the door.

"Billie?"

She's wearing purple overalls and a red shirt. Her lipstick hasn't quite reached the edge of her lips and she's carrying a huge pile of papers. Heathcliffe rushes past her, tail stretched toward the ceiling. One of the tiles on her ceiling has come loose and fallen to the floor.

Her earrings tinkle as she turns her head toward me.

"Honey!"

We stare at each other for a second, Billie Parnell and I. We've come a long way since our first meeting. We still look the same, pretty much, and yet we're no longer looking at our selves reflected.

"Well, hiiiii!" Billie says.

I walk across to the couch and sit down on the edge. The light isn't working and I can smell cat food as usual. No need for small talk. I'm an American now. I can come straight to the point.

"Have you been in touch with Nick?"

She's standing by the door to the kitchen. Her laughter breaks through.

"Oh honey, I have missed you so much." She's delighted I'm there. She moves toward me for a hug. I'm not giving in to it. Not this time.

"Have you been in touch with Nick?" I say again.

She stops and walks toward the window to put the papers down.

"Have you told Nick you're going to represent him?"

I hope that I've misunderstood what Aradhana was saying. I want my suspicions to be a mistake. But as I watch her debate whether or not to tell me the truth, I know that I am right.

She turns toward me, eyebrows raised. "Well, clearly you know I have, or you wouldn't have come storming in here like Boadicea with PMS. I love watching you when you're this angry! You remind me so much of Mother, who . . ."

But this time I refuse to let her sweep me away on one of her tangents.

"Without consulting me, Billie? Goddammit, will you just stay on the subject just this once?"

Billie stops talking.

"Why didn't you tell me, Billie?" My voice is calm and clear.

"Well, I tried!" she says, finally, in an utterly reasonable tone. "Really, I tried. But it's real hard to consult someone who won't pick up the phone."

"What did you say to him, Billie?"

"I don't remember exactly . . ."

"Billie!"

"Well, I might have said that you were a little disorganized. Well, you are, honey! I mean you could sell sand to the Arabs, but organized you are not. And . . ."

"*And . . . ?*"

"And I might have said something about experience counting in these things." Then she says, "It was Nick who asked me to represent him, honey, not the other way around. And I only agreed for you."

"What?"

"You've done some good work here, honey, but I know how to take someone like Nick and turn him into a star. I did it with Marfil, and I can do it with Nick. I talked with him at length about it only this morning. Isn't that what you want? For Nick to be a star?"

She's pacing now. Excited.

"Of course, I still want you on the team, whatever Nick says. We'll be a mother and daughter team. We'll set up a new agency and call it Parnell and Dunn. We'll split the commission. I don't mind, honey, you have done a lot of the legwork."

I stop trying to get a word in and just watch her. She is telling me she's taking half my commission and implying that she's doing me a favor. She and Nick plan to tell James Souk they'll take the next set of paintings elsewhere unless he doubles his price.

On top of that, if I want to be paid half the money I'm owed for almost a year's work, I'll have to work with her. And she's packaging all of this as something good. Fascinated, I watch her convincing herself that it's all in everyone's best interests. She really seems to believe what she's saying. Actually I don't care about the money side of it. I'm making all the money I need from performing now. And I'm strangely relieved about Nick. But I do care about James Souk.

And the fact that I've allowed myself to be so blatantly used is killing me.

"Did you know Nick was married?" I ask Billie.

Billie's quiet.

"Did you?"

Billie's sitting down now. "No, honey. I didn't." I look at her face. I believe her. All that time and energy spent dreaming about Nick, thinking he wanted me, when all he wanted was a break.

"His wife's beautiful. And Indian. And . . . and . . . and delicate!"

"Oh no. Not delicate."

"Yes," I say. "Delicate."

"Oh, honey."

She takes me in her arms. And for a second I am still.

"Oh, baby, you're so hurt." She's right. I am hurt. And I'm humiliated. Above all, I'm furious with myself for being such an idiot.

"Nick Devang has played you beautifully," Billie says finally. "But if he were a nice guy, well, he wouldn't be able to paint like that, now would he? The biggest mistake you could make now would be to drop him. That is exactly what he wants. He could have any agent he wants now he's got the exhibition, believe me, honey. At least you've learned one of life's most important lessons. Never mix business with pleasure."

Has it been pleasure? Or obsession? I'm not sure. It certainly doesn't feel like pleasure now. The betrayal stings me again, like a hard, unexpected slap.

"Oh, honey! That face! That dear little face!" Billie's sitting next to me now, holding me like a child. "You'll move on. I did. It happens." She's soothing me with her movements, rocking me back and forth. Then she wraps me in the throw from her couch and I sit, clutching my knees to my chest, staring out at Billie's sitting room, broken.

"Now you stay here," she says, "and I'll go make us something to eat. God, it's just so wonderful to see you."

"I feel like such a pillock," I say, as Billie comes back into the room.

"A what?"

"Never mind." It is time to stop trying to explain British expressions to the Americans. Particularly ones I've never understood myself.

Wrapped in the blanket, I sink into the couch that hasn't been cleaned in twenty years. Billie suddenly seems so reasonable. So certain that this is a good way forward. If we set up Parnell and Dunn, I won't have to do it all on my own anymore. Perhaps we could figure out a way to represent Nick together. And eventually there'd be other clients too.

Billie has dimmed the lights, and the sitting room doesn't look as depressing as it did earlier. Billie is singing "Someone to Watch Over Me" in the kitchen. She may not be the mother I wanted her to be, but she is my mother. It's time for me to grow up. It's time to accept her the way she is.

And thus I might have stayed, had Heathcliffe not decided to jump on Billie's desk and knock over a pile of papers.

Listening to Billie's voice, I get up off the couch and pick up the papers that have fallen on the floor. That's when, between two pages from an Ethan Allen catalog, I see a return airplane ticket to London, dated a month before.

"What's this?" I say.

Billie has stopped singing and is balancing two mugs of tea on the baking tin she is using for a tray.

"It's a plane ticket," she says. "You can see that."

Billie puts the tea down on the table.

"To London?"

"Yes." She sounds much too casual.

"What were you doing in London, Billie?"

"Honey, you know London is one of my favorite cities to walk around."

"Billie."

There's a pause. And then, in the patient tone of an adult talking to an unreasonable child, Billie says, "I went to see your parents."

"You did what?"

"Well, you weren't returning my calls. You even blocked my e-mail. I was worried about you."

"So you went to see my parents?"

"I can't lose you again, honey. Don't you understand?" She looks like a perplexed angel.

"I *understand* all of it," I say. "Your sorrow, your aching heart, your longing for me. And I'm sorry you have suffered so. Really I am." The anger rises up and bursts out of me. "But I didn't give myself up for adoption, Billie. I didn't leave you. You left me!"

"And now you're punishing me for it!"

"When will you get it into your head that I am not punishing you for giving me up for adoption? I'm grateful! You know that! I've thanked you for it a thousand times. The reason I don't want you in my life now is because being around you makes me miserable. And I don't trust you. I've tried to trust you, but time and time again you've shown me that I just bloody well can't!"

Finally. It's out.

"But I'm *family*!" she says.

"I didn't come to America to swap families, Billie! 'Oh, thanks for the nappy changing, and the education and the skiing holidays Mum and Dad, now I'm buggering off to join my real family.'"

"So, you feel a sense of *duty* toward them?"

"No, Billie. I love them. Mum, Dad, and Charlotte are my family. They always have been. I have loved them all my life and I always will. And it's not the kind of love that hurts me either! It's the kind of love that feels like love!"

"But . . ."

"But nothing, Billie! They are my family. Which, again, wasn't my choice. It was yours."

"Well," she says, "Welllllll. Well, your parents don't want you behaving badly toward me."

"What?"

"They raised you to be considerate about other people's feelings. And they said to me—listen to me, Pippa—they said to me that you could spend Christmas and Thanksgiving with me, and they could have you in the summer. They said that, honey."

"Billie, I'm not up for shared custody! I can make my own decisions! I am twenty-nine years old!"

"Don't you have any feelings for me at all?"

The anger subsides as suddenly as it came. Billie looks like a child again. I walk toward her.

"How could I not feel for you?" I say, gently. "God, giving up a child would hurt any woman terribly. How could it not? I know you suffered. And I know my finding you has brought up all the feelings of loss you've buried for so many years. I know that. And I feel for you. Really. I'll always be grateful for the way you welcomed me, and encouraged me, and made me feel wanted. It would have crucified me if you'd said you didn't want to see me. But Billie," I say, "I wasn't away on vacation."

There's quiet in the room. Billie walks toward the window. Then she turns toward me with an angelic expression on her face and says, equally gently, "It's time to come out of denial, honey. You don't belong with those people anymore."

"Those people?"

There's no point in continuing. The anger is back.

I start to leave, but Billie keeps talking.

"I told your mother it's time for her to let you go."

I stop. "What?"

"She can't understand you the way I understand you, because she's not your real mother. To make you feel a failure because you were untidy, when really you were just wildly creative, well, I don't care how you paint it, abuse is abuse!"

"No! Tell me you didn't say that to Mum, Billie! Please, Billie! No! What have you done, Billie? What have you done?"

Suddenly I'm running out the door.

"Don't leave me again, Pippa." She's pleading now. Shouting. "Don't leave me again!"

"Oh, for fuck's sake, Billie. I didn't leave you. You left me! YOU LEFT ME!"

I run down the stairs to the lower floor and bang on Ralph's bedroom door.

"Ralph? Will you drive me to the airport?"

"Where are you going?" Billie says, following me as I head toward the car.

"I'm doing what I should have done a long time ago. I'm going home."

"But what about Nick?"

"Fuck Nick."

"Pippa!"

"You go on the Circle Line with Nick and his delicate wife and gorgeous little children. I'm going home."

Chapter Fifty-six

I DON'T WANT YOUR MOTHER," I say to Ralph, who drives the
road between Adler and JFK even faster than she does. "Despite
her endless protestations to the contrary, she's not my 'real' mother."

"Okay, okay," he says. His face is young, and he's laughing.
"Man, you women really know how to sling shit, don't you!"

We're driving at eighty now. He is his mother's son.

"Way to go, bro."

We get to the airport and I run through the doors. A British Air-
ways flight has just left. There's another flight in an hour. I'll manage to get on it with just enough time to buy a toothbrush, some
respectable looking clothes, and an overnight bag from duty-free.

"Ralph, thank you."

"Hey, I'm cool," he says. And smiles.

"Good luck, Ralph."

An American voice booms out across the airport. "You are not
required to give money to solicitors. This airport does not support
their activities." I can't help laughing. Because even though I'm an
American now, I'll always be English too. And, to me, a solicitor will
always be a solicitor. Not a solicitor, if you know what I mean.

And then I'm on the airplane, and the whirlwind's back. Billie
has said the one thing to Mum and Dad that I never, ever wanted
them to hear.

I'll never regret finding and coming to know my birth parents.

The parts of me that no one else recognized, they recognized. The talents I knew were within me, they validated. I'll never again have to answer the doctor's "What's your family medical history?" with "I was adopted. I don't know."

But if Billie has hurt Mum and Dad in any way, how will I ever forgive her?

I turn my attention to the Virgin Atlantic flight attendant who's asking me to buckle up. They're all wearing red skirts and white blouses and remind me of the girls I used to see around the streets of Peaseminster, who wore makeup and highlighted their hair and knew all about the latest bands and sold me Tampax at Boots. They still look nothing like me, but I find their familiarity comforting.

I've been caught up in a whirlwind, far, far away. As I travel across the ocean, my love for the country and the family I left fills me completely. I'm being pulled back to England with the same sense of urgency I felt when I left it.

Tears start to trickle down my cheeks as I think of Jack, who I could have trusted. He was right there. Lying right next to me. And on top of me. And underneath me. And I ran, instead, toward a man who didn't really exist.

I have behaved appallingly to the one man I've ever known who I could have truly trusted. And therefore truly loved.

The flight attendant offers me an apple juice and several extra napkins.

"Thank you," I say, blowing my nose loudly.

I yank my mind back to the present. Billie has been to visit Mum and Dad, leaving God knows what damage in her wake. Oh God. What has she done?

Keeping a low-level panic under control as best I can, I walk quickly toward the exit, hail a taxi, and ask the driver to cover the roads between Heathrow and Peaseminster as fast as he can.

As we drive, I realize I am looking at England like an American.

Taking note of the cute little cars, and the cute little roads as if for the first time.

The taxi has a little place between the front seats for Murray Mints. The taxi driver leans back and offers me one.

"Thanks."

I bite into it.

"Did you chew that?" he asks, chuckling.

"I did."

"Better have another one then." He hands another back to me. I pull the wrapper off with my teeth and pop it in my mouth.

"Remember the commercial on the telly about the Murray Mints?"

I do. It seems a lifetime away from where I have been. Another world, which was not supposed to collide with this one.

We say the line in unison: "Never Hurry a Murray."

The difference between the old Pippa and the new is that I'm not going to waste any more time thinking there's something wrong with me for not being able to suck my mints for hours. It's as much a part of who I am as my red hair, pale skin, and fondness for chocolate.

When I get to my parents' home all the lights are out. Mum, Dad, and Boris, the worst guard dog on earth, are fast asleep. I reach under the flowerpot by the front door, take the spare key from underneath it, and, tapping in the alarm numbers, enter the house.

The fourth stair board creaks as I creep quietly up to the second floor, just as it always has. I walk quietly past the room where Mum and Dad are sleeping, down the corridor to my room, and fall fast asleep.

I'm awakened by the smell of bacon frying. I look at my watch. It's three thirty in the morning in America. Which means it must be eight thirty here. From my bed I can see white clouds crossing the bright blue sky above England and the trees moving in the late summer wind. One of the branches hits the corrugated roof of the pool house. First it taps the roof, then it makes a scraping sound, and then there's a three-second gap before it starts again.

I get dressed and head down to the kitchen. Dad is reading the

Times and Mum is getting a jar of Chivers marmalade down from the kitchen cupboard.

"Hallo, Mum," I say from the top of the stairs.

"Pippa!" she says, dropping a spoonful of marmalade onto the kitchen table. "Darling!"

Dad looks up from his paper and starts laughing.

"What a lovely surprise!" Dad is patting me on the back, and Mum is kissing me on the cheek.

"Hi, Mum! Hi, Dad!" I say.

"What a lovely surprise!" they say again.

And it is.

I've been so far away. And now I'm back. And my beloved parents are still here. Nothing has changed in their world. They are still doing the same thing they've been doing since I went away.

They woke up at six. Dad went downstairs and made Mum a cup of tea and brought it upstairs on a tray with two Garibaldi biscuits, otherwise known as squashed flies. After listening to the World Service and reading the paper, Mum went down to the kitchen, still in her dressing gown, and made Dad a cup of coffee. In the royal wedding mug. Which they bought from the village fête in Barnfield twenty-five years before. Charles and Diana look young and in love, and the whole country believed it would last forever, because they wanted it to.

"What a splendid suitcase," Dad says, when he sees my smart new plaid suitcase with buckles. "Not too full either. Well done, Pippa!"

Dear Dad. It doesn't take much. They seem okay. But are they really? My heart is pounding.

"How is everybody?" I say.

"Oh fine," Mum says. "Charlotte and Rupert spent last weekend in Cornwall eating scones and clotted cream. This weekend, they're biking it all off in Wales. They'll be so happy to see you!"

I open the door to the bread bin, take out a thin piece of Waitrose whole wheat bread, and put it in the toaster. Then, waiting for

the toast to pop, as casually as I can, I ask them if they've had any
visitors.

"Mary came yesterday," Dad says. "She's been feeling low since
Mabel got mangled, but your mother cheered her up no end."

New York has guns. Peaseminster has farming machinery. Mary's
friend Mabel was killed by a combine harvester one sorry afternoon
last May.

"Any other visitors?" I say, waiting.

"Only Poppy," Mum says. "To talk about the village fête. We're
thinking of having an egg and spoon race next year."

"Farted up a storm all afternoon!" Dad's hooting with laughter.

"Alas-*dair*!" Mum says.

"Anyone else?"

"No," they say.

"Is anything wrong, darling?" Mum is looking at me carefully.

"Yes."

Dad, stands up, folds his newspaper under one arm, and signals
to Mum that he's going into the next room to listen to some music.

"Bring your toast and Marmite out onto the porch, darling,"
Mum says. "We can talk there."

I put my toast on the Peter Rabbit plate I've used since I was a
child. I carry it through the house, past the Oriental carpets and the
wooden cedar chest to the porch, and sit down on the wicker chair.
Mum has re-covered the cushions since I was last there. I can smell
freshly picked tomatoes ripening in a bowl next to the swimming
pool heater.

"Mum," I say, sitting down. "Are you all right?"

"Of course I am, darling. Why wouldn't I be?"

"Well, Billie told me she came to see you . . ."

"Ah," Mum says.

She takes off her sunglasses and turns toward the garden. A tiny
robin is hopping around one of the croquet hoops trying to pick up
something off the grass, I can't see what.

Mum turns back toward me.

"Did she come here?" I ask.

"Yes."

"When?"

"About a month ago."

"Oh Mum. Why didn't you tell me?"

"Probably for the same reason you haven't told us about what's really been going on with you." She's stating a fact. There's no criticism in her tone. "I suppose I didn't want to worry you."

My throat constricts. *She* didn't want to worry *me*?

"What happened?"

Chapter Fifty-seven

D AD AND I had been to see the Saturday matinee at the Mari-
ton," Mum says. "It was a very interesting play about Isadora
Duncan. The one people always used to say you reminded them of."

"The one who got strangled by her scarf?"

"Yes, that Isadora Duncan. Well, anyway, I drove your father
home afterward. And then, because we were on Weight Watchers
and I didn't feel like cooking, I popped down to Sainsbury's to get us
a Lean Cuisine for supper. They're so good, especially the ones with
salmon and rice in the white sauce."

"Mum."

"Sorry. When I got back home there was a red rent-a-car in the
driveway."

"It's Billie's favorite color," I say, trying to keep things light, despite the fact that I am terribly afraid of what I am about to hear.

Mum tells me she walked into the kitchen and saw Dad talking
to a woman in white furry boots and a multicolored jumpsuit.

"Although she looked awfully familiar," Mum says, "I couldn't
think where I knew her from. She said 'hallo' in a pretty southern
American accent, with such a friendly smile. I said 'hallo' back, of
course.

"And then I noticed your father jabbing the air behind her back
with his finger. Honestly, Pip, for a second I thought he'd gone quite
barmy. And while your father was jabbing the air like a lunatic, the

woman was hugging me and telling me she would have called, only she didn't have our number.

"It's funny. It wasn't the accent that made me realize who it was. It was the expression on her face when she told me she got our address from the back of one of your letters."

Mum doesn't look traumatized. She looks intrigued. "When you were about four years old, and trying to charm me after doing something you knew was naughty, you used to look at me in exactly the same way. And that's when I knew who it was.

"She has your dimples, you know," Mum says.

"She'd say I have hers."

"I suppose she would." Mum takes a sip of her tea and carries on.

"When she got out her cigarettes, I thought your father was going to have a fit. So I told him to go and read the paper, led her out to the porch, and opened a window. Her cigarettes are very thin, aren't they?"

"They're called Eve," I said. "They're menthol."

"Not like Dunhill then? I do miss my ciggies you know. If your father dies before I do, I'm going to start smoking again."

"You never told me you missed smoking!"

"Can't tell you everything now, can I?" Mum smiles, pleased that she has shocked me a little.

"Anyway, then Billie said, 'I'm here to talk about my daughter.' It was odd, hearing another woman talk about you as her daughter."

"Just odd?"

"Well, yes. I mean you are her daughter, darling. And—well—no. It didn't bother me. In fact I was fascinated, if you really want to know. I've never seen anyone who looks even slightly like you before. It gave me an idea of what you might look like twenty-five years from now."

"So it was interesting?"

"Very. We *have* wondered about the people you came from, Pippadee. It's only natural."

"Well, why didn't you ever say so?"

"Probably for the same reason you didn't tell us you wanted to know who they were. We wanted to protect you, I suppose. We didn't want to bring up things that might upset you."

Ping-Pong again. There I'd been for years, longing to talk to my parents about it all, but not, for fear of upsetting them. There they were, for years, feeling the same. Neither of us doing anything about it for fear of upsetting the other. How absurdly, entirely, utterly English.

Mum and I sit still for a moment. The moment between us feels honest and clean.

"She kept calling me Jemima," Mum says suddenly.

"Jemima?"

"Yes. And she kept taking tiny puffs of her cigarette while she paced around the room. Just like you did when you used to smoke. It is 'used to,' isn't it?"

"Yes," I say. "I stopped when I realized that even though she claims to only have one or two, Billie smokes a pack a day. I didn't want to be like her."

"I suppose every difficult situation has its perks."

"Yes."

Mum is leaning back in her chair, as relaxed as I am tense.

"Then Billie turned toward me and told me you were dead."

"What?"

"That's what I said. But she told me she didn't mean it literally. She meant it metaphorically. She said she felt that you were cut off from an important part of yourself, and that it was crucial—for your development—that you spend more time with her than you have been recently. In order to fulfill your potential as a creative artist, I think she said. I must confess I was so relieved you weren't actually dead, I didn't take much of that part in."

"Oh, Mum!"

"It's all right, darling. Really. It was fine. Then Billie told me how much you love each other. And then she became quite fixated on the puffin."

Granny Dunn found a puffin dead on a beach somewhere in 1936, brought it home, and had it stuffed. It's been sitting on the dark brown armoire in the dining room ever since.

"'Oh how sad!' Billie said. 'To stuff a bird and leave it in a glass case like that!' Do you know, I'd never thought of it as sad before. But she was so convincing, suddenly I felt quite sorry for the puffin. Almost guilty—as if I'd killed the puffin myself. Even though I knew perfectly well the puffin was dead as a doornail before Granny Dunn found him."

Mum puts her teacup back into the saucer with a satisfying click and continues with her tale.

"Billie's mind was darting around from topic to topic, just like yours does, darling. She said she thought our garden had a 'wonderful contained beauty'—I think those were the words she used. Perfect for people of our nature. She compared it with her garden in Georgia, and told me how much you both loved the wildness of the Blue Ridge Mountains.

"I was particularly intrigued by her curly hair, which is a lovely color and bounced rather charmingly as she spoke. She's very animated, isn't she?"

"Yes."

"Oh, and guess what she did with the bourbon biscuit I offered her?"

Mum is actually giggling.

"She scraped off the choccy cream in the center with her teeth— just like you do! Amazing!"

I hadn't thought about this part of it. That Mum and Dad might have wondered, too. I look for signs of upset in Mum's eyes. There's nothing there but curiosity and—yes—glee, glee, glee.

"Then Billie thanked us for being wonderful parents to you. And then she said it was time for us to let you go. She said we were adult women. She said there was no point in sugarcoating things, and she was going to get straight to the point. And then, after meandering quite charmingly around several subjects for a minute or so, she told me I didn't understand you like she understood you, because I'm not your real mother."

My heart is beating fast. She did hurt Mum. Oh God.

"And then she asked where you were. That's when I realized she wasn't being truthful about how inseparable you were. I imagined that you probably needed some time and were therefore avoiding her. But it was quite clear she didn't want to give you any time and was trying to find out where you were. With everything you've had to absorb during the past year, I thought she was being unspeakably selfish."

"Oh, Mum."

"But I thanked her for coming to see us and told her how grateful we are to her. And we are! Oh darling, if it weren't for Billie . . ."

"Yes."

"Anyway, I assured her that we only wanted what was best for you and that if you wanted to spend time with her, of course that would be fine with us.

"And then she said, 'So you won't be pressuring her to come back to England?'

"I told her that, in my experience, putting any sort of pressure on you to do something you don't want to do only causes you to do the opposite. And that you probably just needed a little time to sort yourself out. She looked relieved for a moment. And then, as suddenly as she appeared, she left."

The story is over. I look across the porch at the mother I've known and loved since I was a child.

"Mum," I say, with a lump in my throat, "you are my real mother. And nothing could ever change that. If . . . if I could have designed you myself, I couldn't have done a better job."

Mum's smiling at me, with a twinkle in her eye. "Well, that's lovely, darling, and thank you for saying it. But the last part's not strictly true, is it, Pip?"

"Well—well, if I could have designed you myself you might

have been playwrights—but, but—no, Mum! No! If I could change a thing I wouldn't. I love you so much, Mum."

"I know that, darling. But I also know that love doesn't come in amounts. I know that you loving Billie doesn't mean you'd love us any less."

"But I don't love her," I say, appalled at myself for saying it aloud. "I know I *should*. And I feel dreadfully guilty about it, but I just don't. I've tried to. And I thought I did for a while. I've told her I do. And maybe I do in a way. But—well, the truth is being near her is confusing and—well, immobilizing. And I can't live a happy life if I can't move, Mum."

A furious fly is buzzing around the chrysanthemum pot.

"It's awful, Mum. I'm awful. But when I'm near her I—well, I just can't feel for Billie the way she wants me to feel."

The fly has found its way out of the porch window now and is headed off toward the swimming pool.

"And I know how terrible it must have been for Billie to have to give up her baby," I say. Saying this, thinking this, has become a sort of mantra.

"Yes," Mum says. Her tone is firm now. "And being given away by your mother must have been terrible for you, darling. You were tiny. A babe. You'd only just been born."

Now Mum has tears in her eyes too. "We were so happy to have you darling. And we believed that adopting a baby would be exactly the same as having one of our own. But that wasn't true, was it? Especially for you."

"No."

"Darling Pip, you've spent all this time thinking about Billie's feelings and no time at all thinking about your own. Billie was a grown-up. She made a choice. You were a tiny little baby. You had no choice. It must have been far, far worse for you."

Perhaps.

We sit for a moment saying nothing. The garden stretches out behind us in the afternoon sun.

I sit hopelessly, looking at Mum.

"I wish . . ."

"You wish what, darling?"

"I wish I could find a way to give her some of what she wants from me."

Dad has been standing by the door. In a tone that's as gentle as it is gruff, he says, "It's not your burden to carry, Pip. It never has been."

I catch my breath and stay very still. I've never heard Dad speak in this way before. Ever. Mum is equally still and, I am certain, as surprised to hear Dad's words as I am.

"You're not Superwoman, you know," Dad says.

I smile inwardly at the expression, knowing he'd never have used it if he hadn't been forced to watch *Superman II* when Marjory's grandson came to tea.

"You've had a huge amount to deal with, Pippadee," Dad continues. "You wafted off to another country, into a very complicated situation, with no support whatsoever, an ocean away from everyone you knew. Good God, it was like throwing yourself off the high trapeze without a net! Meeting Billie and Whatshisname as a grown-up meant you've had to completely reassess who you are. While dealing with what must have been overwhelming emotions. That would be difficult enough for anybody."

I dare not move. Dad's voice sounds reassuringly Scottish as it comes to me through the afternoon air. His hand rests steady on my shoulder.

"Add to it this, this—how can I put it? This hole Billie has inside her, that she's been asking you to fill. Well, it's not fair of her to expect you to do that, Pippadee. It's not your responsibility. It's hers."

The knot inside me loosens a little.

"The years we're granted to live on this earth are few and precious," Dad says. "You have a right to live them happily. You don't have to carry Billie's burden, darling. It's not your burden to carry. Put it down, Pippadee. Just put it down."

With that, the father I thought didn't understand me at all pats me awkwardly on the shoulder and goes back into the house. Mum doesn't move. But I detect a little extra light in her clear blue eyes.

And then something happens. Inside me. There's another shift. The thoughtful words—spoken by the father who fed me, loved me, and nurtured me when my other father could not—open the doors to the sense of peace I've been aching for all my life, which floods into the heart of my being. With my father's words, the thick, ugly knot of guilt inside me finally comes untied.

And everything I've been holding in for so long, in order to protect people who did not need to be protected, finally has permission to come out. And I start to cry. Mum sits next to me and hands me Kleenex after Kleenex from the yellow tissue box, which Dad has brought into the porch from the top of the downstairs loo. Dad appears at the porch door every so often, checks to see if I am still crying, and then disappears back into the house.

And then, as the afternoon turns into the evening, I tell Mum everything I've told you, about Billie and Walt and my life in New York. When I tell her about Jack, her expression changes slightly.

The early September sun is setting over the wheatfield behind the house now, and it's getting a little chilly. It'll soon be time to go in.

"Do you remember, when I was little, when I used to be frightened of monsters under the bed?"

"Yes," Mum says, laughing. "Until we turned the light on and your monster turned out to be the pile of clothes you'd inevitably left on the floor."

"Well, finding out the truth about Billie and Walt has been a bit like that, I think."

Mum smiles. "Then it's been a good thing, darling."

"Oh yes, Mum. Yes! If I hadn't found them, I'd never have known what to do with the parts of me that are so different from you, Dad, and Charlotte. Now I know the people I've come from—well, now I can be wholly me, instead of just half me, if you see what I mean."

"Yes," Mum says. "I think I do."

Through the glass I can see Boris trotting through the sitting room toward us. When he gets to the porch door he whines once, thumps his tail, turns around and lies down on the mat, with his head on his paws, waiting.

"And Jack's been there all along, hasn't he, Pippa?" Mum says. "The one steady thing in the midst of the chaos."

"Yes."

"He sounds even tidier than I am!"

"Yes," I say, almost laughing. "I think he is. And he seems to like tidying up after me!"

Mum laughs. "He sounds perfect for you!"

"He is Mum. He was. And not just because of that. He's—he's the kindest man I know—and wise too. I feel at home with him. Rather, I did. But I've ruined everything, Mum. I'm an *idiot*."

I start crying again as I tell her everything that's just happened with Jack. Well, almost everything. She is my mother after all.

Finally we go inside and have supper. While I was bawling on the porch, Dad, who never cooks, had made chicken with parsnips, peas, and roast potatoes. And for pudding he's made a chocolate cake—with extra icing—from an old World War II recipe he found in the *Peaseminster Post*.

After supper, I go upstairs to bed. I don't wake up again until eleven o'clock the following morning.

Chapter Fifty-eight

I$^{\text{T'S A RAINY AFTERNOON}}$, and Dad's got his old slide projector out. We're in the sitting room watching slides of Mum and Dad's first trip across America in a red Chevrolet, a year before I "arrived." Mum's serene and graceful and beautifully dressed, with her straight blond hair pushed back in a light blue hair band. Dad's hair is blond too. He looks young and handsome. He's wearing a green tartan beret and smoking a pipe. And looks—well, extremely Scottish.

Both of them are three years younger than I am now. They assume that conceiving a child of their own will be easy. They don't know, yet, that they will have to go through the agony of discovering they can't have children of their own. They don't know, yet, that they will be adopting me.

In the next set of slides, I'm a bawling infant.

"That's you, Pip. Outside the adoption agency," Dad says.

"No, it's not, it's the foster home," Mum says.

In the next picture, I'm looking up at my new mother with a peaceful expression on my face. I do not look pained, or unhappy. I look cozy in Mum's arms. Safe.

Mum is beautifully dressed, in an elegant blue and white dress this time. Her hair has been styled in a pretty blond flip, and she's wearing red lipstick. Dad's wearing a tie and an elegant suit. His hand is reaching out for mine.

Mum chuckles. "The first thing Granny H. said was, 'Look at her red hair, all spiky, sticking up like a little bird.'"

"That's exactly what Billie wrote in the letter, just after she had me," I say, "the very same phrase." It's a huge relief not to have to censor myself anymore.

"You looked just like Woodstock! From the Peanuts cartoon!" They giggle.

I look at the pictures I've seen many times before. Only this time, I know who the baby Pip looks like. She looks like Walt and Edwin and Ashley, and a bit like Billie too. She still looks nothing at all like the parents who adopted her.

In the following picture, I see a little red-haired girl, impeccably dressed, holding her ice cream cone reluctantly out to her father, who's taking a big lick of it. In the next picture, she's in a paddling pool with her little sister. In the next, she's running naked around an English garden, in and out of croquet hoops, surrounded by doting relatives drinking tea.

In the next, she's eight years old, camping in the Serengeti game park. There she is surrounded by other half-naked children, building the dam in the river where the hippos bathe, down the hill from where Charlotte and I got charged by the elephant.

Then there's a picture of Charlotte and me sitting on the roof of the Land Rover as it drives bumpily along miles and miles of narrow, dusty African roads.

"Couldn't do that now," Dad says. "Much too dangerous. Probably get killed. By people," he adds, to clarify.

I look at my parents, holding hands in the dark of their sitting room in the south of England. They have never kept secrets from anybody. They have never made promises they did not keep.

"Do you think you'll move back?" Mum's not pressuring me one way or the other. She just wants to know.

I smile. "I don't think 'Rock-and-Roll Redneck' would go down all that well in England," I say.

Then Mum says, "And your lovely Jack lives over there, doesn't he?"

At the mention of his name my heart flips up, around, and back down again with a thud.

"He's not 'my Jack' Mum. Besides . . ."

"Besides what?" Mum and Dad are both looking in my direction.

"Well, even if I hadn't blown it completely, he's in love with somebody else. And—and we're from completely different worlds. He'd rather stay home and eat Fig Newtons than go camping!" I say, waiting for a reaffirming "Good God!" from my father. It doesn't come.

Mum looks perplexed. Finally she says, "What's a Fig Newton?"

"Squashed figs surrounded by squashy biscuit," I say, missing Fig Newtons, too. Wishing I could go back to the first time Jack and I ate Fig Newtons together, knowing everything I know now, about Nick, about Jack, about myself. And start again from there.

But I can't. It's too late. And even if, somehow, our night together put him off this other woman . . . well, I behaved appallingly. He'll certainly prefer the other woman now. I hate her almost as much as I hate myself for pretending, to both Jack and myself, that our night together wasn't perfect. I feel like I'm going to cry again.

Dad looks at me across the light from the projector, which beams from the back of the sitting room to the screen he's erected at the front. Dust particles swim in the light. All's quiet, apart from the whirring of the projector and the sound of the sitting room curtain moving slightly in the breeze.

"Do you know what I think?" Dad says, adjusting the focus on a slide of Mum and Charlotte playing Snap and drinking mango juice with the Morton-Pecks.

"What do you think, Dad?"

"I think that the greatest adventures are the subtlest."

• • •

Charlotte and Rupert hurtle down to Peaseminster the moment they learn that I'm back.

Over the next few days, we settle back into our old familiar rhythms. Charlotte and Mum take me shopping for a bridesmaid's dress and ask my opinion on the seating plan for Charlotte and Rupert's wedding. They'll be getting married a year from now, so according to Charlotte there isn't a whole lot of time.

As I try to express interest in the dresses she wants me to try on, Charlotte keeps asking me if I'm all right and I keep telling her I'm fine—old habits are never entirely broken. The main difference, perhaps, is that during the past year I appear to have lost the art of hiding what I'm really feeling from both myself and the people I love. And I no longer feel that it matters.

Chapter Fifty-nine

O N SATURDAY NIGHT, Mum, Dad, Charlotte, Rupert, Neville, and I are invited to go Scottish dancing at the village hall. For the first time since I can remember, I am actually looking forward to it. Dad wears his kilt and a sporran. Mum lends me her spare tartan skirt. The average age of the Scottish dancers is about seventy-five. There are about forty of them. Thirty-four women and six men. Dad is one of them.

"Come along, Pip, set to the left then to the right." We're dancing the Hamilton House. I am out of time, but loving being here.

"I'll tell you the secret to Scottish dancing," says an earnest, moon-faced woman with dark hair and a soft voice. Her face is right up against mine. "You need to count, you see. I still count, even though I'm an expert."

I count throughout the next dance and do slightly better.

A tiny woman with a platform shoe on what I later learn is a wooden leg comes up to me.

"How lovely for Gemma and Alasdair to have you home. What is it that you do in America?" she asks.

"I sing songs to drunk people in nightclubs," I say, smiling.

"How interesting!" Mary says, clapping her hands together in delight. "What sort of songs do you sing?"

"Well, recently I've been writing my own."

"Oh, how marvelous!" she says, looking quite flushed. "How exciting!"

"It's great fun," I say happily. "Writing songs is like writing lots of little plays."

"Oh, I never thought of it like that," Mary says. "How *interesting*. Well done!"

The music is starting from the other end of the room. Dad's voice is booming over the microphone. "Places please, everyone!"

"Now," Mary says, eyes alight, putting one of her arms around my back and holding my arm out with her other arm, "this next one's one of my favorites. It's a strathspey, a nice slow one. Would you care to dance? I'll be the man."

"I'd be delighted," I say, as she leads me across the floor.

Later Mum tells me that Mary lost her leg in a dreadful car crash in which her husband was killed. Terrible things happen to British people as often as they happen to Americans. The main difference, I think, is how people handle them. The British don't tend to talk about horrid things that happened in their past. And Americans do.

Mary, I later learn, hasn't spoken about the accident since it happened. She went on to become headmistress of St. Bart's and, to quote Mum, "led a very successful life." Mary doesn't like to talk about her emotions any more than Mum does. Of course it doesn't mean she doesn't have them. To me, Mary is living proof that denial, as a way of coping, is wildly underrated.

Mary whisks me around the floor as my father barks instructions over the microphone and a science teacher in a green kilt plays the bagpipes very loudly, walking with absolute precision up and down the hall. To my surprise, I no longer want to run from the wailing music. Instead I really hear it, as if for the first time. Something deep inside me has awakened. For the first time I recognize the beauty in the ancient sound.

Only a year ago I would have done everything I could to have avoided this evening. Tonight, despite the ache in my heart over

Jack, I am managing to savor every minute. When Colin Dykes spends half an hour telling me about how astounded he is by the size of American pancakes on a recent trip to Florida, I actually listen to him. American pancakes *are* huge compared to British pancakes; it's really quite funny. I enjoy every slightly stale Hula Hoop and every sip of lukewarm orange squash.

When Marjory and Poppy come over to talk to me, I do not run away at the first excuse. Instead I share their indignation about the cost of sausages at Marks and Spencer and try not to giggle as Poppy farts in time to Strip the Willow.

I used to feel threatened by this world. Now I don't. Now I value everything about it. Because I nearly lost it.

As my strathspey with Mary comes to an end, there is a tap on my shoulder.

"Excuse me," the man says. "May I have the next dance?"

I turn around and, for a second, the room stands still. Because there, standing in front of me, is Jack. My American Jack. Dressed, it seems, in my father's spare kilt and sporran and a beautifully ironed white shirt.

"Ralph told me what happened with Nick. And where you were. I somehow worked out how to call the UK," Jack says.

Somehow I manage to speak.

"Oh Jack, I'm so sorry . . ."

"When I somehow managed to get through, I had a long talk with your mother. And your father. And your sister. And your cousin Neville. Who said, and I quote directly, 'I've never seen her so miserable. For God's sake get yourself on a bloody plane and get over here.' Then your mother got back on the phone and said, 'What he means, Jack, is that we'd be delighted if you'd like to join us at next Saturday's Scottish dancing party. If you're not too busy, of course.'"

I look over at Mum, Dad, Charlotte, Rupert, and Neville, who are watching from the side of the room, looking absurdly pleased with themselves.

"I like wearing a kilt," Jack says, grinning broadly. "I have to get one when I get back to New York. It'll help me fit right in with all the other gay guys."

"Oh Jack, I'm so sorry!" And then, hardly daring to believe him I say, "But what about her?"

"Who?" Jack looks genuinely confused.

"The woman you've been in love with for a long time."

I think I know the answer now. I hope I know the answer.

Jack looks as Scottish as my father in his kilt and white shirt, and handsome as hell.

"She's standing right in front of me," Jack says, softly.

The bagpipes are playing "Loch Lomond" now, but all I can hear and see is Jack.

"Pippa, it's you," he says. "It's always been you." Jack's voice is hoarse. "I was only half alive before I met you."

"But I've behaved so terribly! I've been so preoccupied with— well, everything but you. Oh Jack, I'm so sorry!"

Jack's hand is shaking. I take it in mine and kiss his palm, closing my eyes with relief. When I open them, Jack takes my hands in his and says, "You needed to find out the truth about who you came from, so you could really know yourself. So you could move on, honestly, with the rest of your life. It took everything you had to survive this without going under. But you did. And now look at you."

We're standing very close now, in the corner of the room. I can't speak.

"I love everything about you, Pippa," Jack says. "I love the way you light up a room whenever you walk into it. I love your wit and voice and your charm and your kindness and your absolute bravery in the midst of total confusion. I love the fact that you have no idea how beautiful you are. I love your energy and your light and . . . and I love the fact that you are predictable only in your unpredictability. Most of all, Pip, most of all, I love your kindness," he says, smiling. "And, of course, your legs."

Jack puts his arm around my back and pulls me closer to him.

"I've not been able to think of anyone else but you since the moment I picked up your purse on the streets of New York," he whispers into my ear.

"You said purse and not wallet," I whisper back.

"I did."

The joy is back. It's back, back, back. It's swimming back into me and filling me with love for the man standing in front of me. And when we kiss, I know that the journey I've been on has somehow freed me up to love him back. Fully. Totally. As he deserves to be loved. Without any kind of fear.

We've joined the other dancers now. Jack looks darkly handsome in the evening light. I can hear Poppy whispering to Marjory.

"He looks just like that American actor, doesn't he?"

"Exactly like him. You mean Al Pacino."

"No, the other one."

"Which other one?"

"Tom Conti."

"He's not American!"

"Yes, he is." I can hear Poppy's fart from across the hall. I swear I can.

Their voices fade into the background. Jack is laughing. His arm feels strong in the small of my back. His face is close to mine. He smells just like Jack—this kind, wise, sexy American in a skirt, who has somehow found his way into this ordinary village hall, in an ordinary part of England, because he loves me.

"Pippa! Jack!" Dad's voice barks into the microphone a moment later. "This is supposed to be the Gay Gordons, not a Viennese waltz!"

The other dancers are heading toward the stage. Jack and I are dancing toward the door. As we glide past Mum, Dad, Charlotte, Rupert, the piper, and Neville, who is charming Poppy's very pretty daughter, in my mind's eye I can see the parents who gave me birth. They're young, beautiful, hopelessly in love, and dancing across the lobby of the Waldorf Hotel, in a world right next to this one. And then, the ghosts disappear, taking with them the remains of the whirlwind that has blown through me for so long.

Now Jack and I are walking through the front door of the village hall and out into the English air. And as we turn toward each other I feel nothing but profound love for the man standing in front of me. And, of course, the soft kiss of the English rain.

Acknowledgments

It is my privilege to thank my agent, Jennifer Joel at ICM, for her unwavering faith and smart, solid advice at all times. My brilliant and sensitive editor Marysue Rucci, for knowing exactly how to get me to make it better. David Rosenthal, Virginia Smith, Loretta Denner, Amy Ryan, Tina Peckham, Katie Sigelman, Victoria Meyer, Rebecca J. Davis, Leah Wasielewski, Catherine Casalino, and the entire team at Simon & Schuster.

For their encouragement, without which the early pages would still be in a box somewhere: Peter Buckman, Lynn Franklin, Marie-Louise Hogan, Melanie Rockcliffe, Katinka Neuhoff, Leslie Farrell, Clare Foster, Karen Hayes, and Jim Keenan.

Thanks also to Jane Byron, Suzanne Folke, Linnea Hasegawa, Anne Luttman-Johnson, Kate McAbe, Judith Schwartz, Liz Stein, Philip Thurston, Barb Valenti, Victoria Whelan, BritishGiftBaskets .com—and the Scottish connection, Alyson and Isobel Dewar, Jean McKirdy, and Rob and Brigid Whyte.

Thank you to the artist Simon Gales for the use of his name and his work.

Thank you to my friends Pam and Rysuke Hasegawa for giving me the keys to their house, so I could write uninterrupted.

I would also like to thank my birth parents for the precious gift of life.

And Mum and Dad, for showing me how to live it happily.

About the Author

Alison Larkin was born in Washington, D.C., and spent her childhood in England and East and West Africa. After graduating from London University and the Webber-Douglas Academy of Dramatic Art, she played classical roles on the British stage, then moved to America and became a stand-up comic. She appeared regularly at The Comic Strip in New York City, The Comedy Store in Los Angeles, and on *Late Night with Conan O'Brien* and *Comic Relief*. She also appeared on Broadway in the Royal National Theatre's production of *Stanley*. Her unusually wide range of voices can be heard in dozens of cartoons and movies, from work by Robert Altman to *The Wonderful World of Oz* and *The Wonderpets*.

Combining stand-up comedy and theater, the author's internationally acclaimed one-woman show, *The English American*, premiered at the Edinburgh Festival's Assembly Rooms, headlined at the Soho Theatre as highlight of the London Comedy Festival, and has been seen in concert performance around the world.

Alison Larkin lives twenty-five miles outside New York City with her husband and two young children. Visit her website at www.alisonlarkin.com.

The
English
American

Questions for Discussion

1. In what ways is Pippa American? In what ways is she English? Do you think there are national characteristics unique to Americans? If so, what are they?

2. How much of Pippa is nature, how much is nurture and how much is individual choice? What do you think about this question in relation to yourselves?

3. How effectively does the author use humor in the book?

4. What is your favorite scene in the book, and why?

5. How does the author explore themes of fantasy and reality in relation to Pippa's relationships, both romantic and parental?

6. If Pippa decides to stay in America and marry Jack, what do you think she will miss most about England?

7. How do you think Pippa's journey frees her to be herself?

8. How do you feel about Billie? If you could give her advice about how to help her daughter before she meets Pippa, what would be your list of Dos and Don'ts?

9. How do you feel about the way Mum responds when Pippa tells her that she feels she needs to find her birth parents?

10. Has the author been successful in showing why Pippa's need to search for her birth parents is not a rejection of her adoptive parents?

11. In what ways are Walt and Dad similar? In what ways are they different?

12. How does Pippa change from the beginning of the book to the end?

13. Are you one of the 60 percent of Americans who have a personal connection to adoption? If so, what has your experience been? Has the book changed the way you view the needs of the people in your life who have been touched by adoption?

14. On pages 56 and 57 and in her "DNA Song," (www.youtube.com/alisonlarkin), the author makes it clear she is alarmed by the fact that adoptees are the only U.S. citizens unable to routinely obtain their birth information. Because knowledge of one's medical history can be lifesaving, this exclusion raises significant human rights concerns. How do you feel about this issue?

A Conversation with Alison Larkin

In what ways are you and the main character, Pippa Dunn, similar? And in what ways are you different?

Pippa has long red hair and is achingly beautiful. I have mid-length blond hair and can look quite cute on a good day. Neither Pippa nor I care about what we're wearing and we are both impulsive and chronically untidy. Like Pippa, I was adopted in America as an infant and raised all over the world by tidy, loving English parents. Like Pippa I adore my adoptive parents despite the fact that we are very different.

Like Pippa, when I found my birth parents—who are free-spirited and artistic Americans—the discovery answered key questions about myself. It also brought me closer to my adoptive parents, as is usually the case.

However, while Pippa's emotional journey in many ways mirrors my own, I'm not a cabaret singer, my birth mother doesn't run a company called "Art Buddies," she doesn't live in Georgia, and my birth father isn't a neo-conservative, enigmatic, politically involved business man. The mysterious Nick, who seduces Pippa via e-mail, didn't exist in my life—although he may have existed in my dreams. My dad isn't short, my mum isn't blond, and I don't have a non-adopted sister, a dog called Boris, or a penchant for Fig Newtons. The list goes on and on. In other words, it's fiction.

You were a classical actress and playwright in England. Soon after meeting your birth mother you became a stand-up comic in New York. How did this happen?

A few weeks after meeting my birth parents, in the throes of "I've just found out I'm really an American" euphoria, I found myself in New York City. I stood up at a comedy club and, in my very English accent, I said "Hallo. My name is Alison Larkin and I come from Bald Mountain, Tennessee." The audience laughed. I didn't know anyone else in New York and they felt like friends, so I kept getting up onstage and telling them a comedic version of what was going on in my life. I quickly discovered that the beauty of stand-up comedy is that you can say anything you want, as long as you make it funny.

When people found out that I was telling the truth about meeting my birth parents, they'd ask questions like, "What was it like meeting your 'real' parents?" and "Why would someone from a happy adoptive family want to *do* something like that?" My one woman show—a combination of theater and stand-up—was my answer to both these questions, plus a good excuse to crack lots of jokes about England and America.

So with young children and a busy speaking and performing career, why did you decide to write a full-length novel?

There's only so much you can do in seventy-five minutes onstage, and the show only skimmed the surface of the bigger, funnier, more authentic story I knew I wanted to tell one day.

People have no idea of the huge internal and external obstacles that face adopted people who decide to try to find their birth parents. In today's culture, adopted people tend to be portrayed as victims at best or serial killers at worst. (Or they're just presented as rather blah—like the adoptee in Mike Leigh's otherwise excellent film *Secrets and Lies*, which told the birth mother's story authentically and sympathetically—and presented the adoptee as completely together and unaffected by what I knew to be an intense, life-changing experience for myself and other adopted people I know.)

I was completely fed up with what seemed to me to be a lack of empathy and understanding for what the adoption-and-reunion journey might be like for the adopted person him- or herself. I had a growing sense that if I could create an appealing, funny, authentic, vulnerable adopted heroine/narrator—and take the reader with her on her journey in an entertaining, accessible way—people might start to really "get" what it might be like, from an adopted person's point of view. I started with the premise of my autobiographical one-woman show and jumped off into fiction from there. Instead of presenting the adoptee as yet another victim, I wanted to create a realistic, accessible adopted heroine at the center of the kind of book I like to read.

And what kind is that?

The kind that keeps you up at night because you *have* to know what's going to happen next! I don't have time to read much now that I have kids. When I do read, I'm either on a plane or about to go to sleep, so a book has to grip me totally from page one if I'm going to have a chance of finishing it. It also has to have short chapters!

How do your parents, birth and adoptive, feel about the book?

My English parents have "accidentally" left copies of *The English American* in hotel rooms while on holiday in Singapore, France, and Scotland. My birth father slips the cover of *The English American* over whatever book he is reading when he's on an airplane and makes a point of laughing uproariously. When the book was featured in *Vogue*, my birth mother marched the magazine into bookstores all over the South and showed it to bookstore owners so they could be sure not to run out of stock.

Mum does not express any fear when Pippa decides to go off to find her birth mother. Why did you write her that way?

I wanted to portray an adoptive mother who puts her child's needs before her own. The English mother in the novel, like my own adoptive mother, is a wise and inherently unselfish person. Instead of making Pippa feel even more guilty than she does already, she gives her vulnerable, overloaded daughter what she truly needs to grow up—that is, the emotional space to go on her journey. This is, to me, an act of genuine love and it plays a large part in finally enabling Pippa to come into her own. I have heard from many adoptive parents who tell me that they have found her example to be helpful and inspiring.

What kind of reactions have you had from members of the adoption community?

Adoptive parents tell me they no longer feel threatened by the thought of their son or daughter going to find their birth parents. Birth mothers tell me the book helped them understand just how much the child they relinquished will have to integrate after a reunion—and why this may take years. I have also heard from countless adopted people of all different cultural backgrounds who tell me that Pippa is "them."

Is the way Pippa approaches her love life at the beginning of the book typical of adopted people?

I can't speak for everybody, of course, but I have heard from many adopted people of all different cultural and ethnic backgrounds who tell me they strongly relate to the fear of rejection that prevents Pippa from being able to fully trust her early boyfriends. Like many of my non-adopted readers who experienced some kind of abandonment in childhood, they find hope in the fact that once Pippa finds the truth, which leads to the uncovering of her authentic self, she is finally able to love without fear.

Were you hesitant to meet your birth parents? Why did you wait until you were 28?

As Pippa says at the start of the novel, "I think everyone should be adopted. That way you can meet your birth parents when you're old enough to cope with them." It's a joke, but there's truth in the second line. It's a huge thing for any adopted person to even think about and not something I felt anywhere near ready to deal with emotionally until I had dealt with the pesky task of growing up.

Do you have any regrets either way?

I certainly don't regret finding my birth parents any more than Pippa does. However, I do regret the fact that I did not have adequate professional help at the time. I feel so strongly about the importance of this that I've put a comprehensive adoption support referral page on www.alisonlarkin.com, to help adopted people who are even thinking about embarking on this challenging journey. The page also includes referrals for adoptive parents and birth parents.

How has your sense of humor helped you through all the revelations of being adopted and then with meeting your birth parents?

I rely on my sense of humor as much as I rely on my right arm and my eyesight. When you can laugh in the midst of even the most painful of situations, it releases something. It helps you through.

At what age did you recognize that you had talents as a writer/comedian/actor?

I've written and performed ever since I can remember. When I was seven I performed *My Fair Lady* in a drafty bathroom in Yorkshire one wet summer holiday afternoon for my parents and their friends. (We were in the bathroom because the farmhouse didn't have heating except for a heated towel rail in the bathroom, thus it was the warmest room in the house.) This memory—altered to make it fit the story—made it into the book.

Why did you seek out your birth parents? Do you have an ongoing relationship with them?

I sought out my birth parents because, like Pippa, I wanted to reassure them that I'd had a happy life and because I had questions about myself and my origins that only they could answer.

Thankfully they were open to contact and 100 percent available when I needed them to be. They helped me understand and value the parts of me that were so very different from my adoptive parents. Even more important, I no longer have to say "I don't know, I was adopted" when a doctor asks me for my medical history—something that turned out to be critical when it came to the birth to my first child.

I have the greatest respect for my birth parents, but they didn't parent me day-to-day, so the word "parent" doesn't really feel right for me. I think of them more as friends. While I remain in occasional contact with them, it is my parents in England whom I think of as my parents, whom my children think of as their grandparents and whom I phone all the time and plan family vacations with.

How do you cope on the Fourth of July?

I'm never quite sure whether I should celebrate or mourn the shrinking of the British Empire. So generally, I wear black and eat a hot dog.

If you could leave your readers with one thing, what would it be?

British chocolate. I order mine at www.britishgiftbaskets.com.

What do you like most about living in America?

The fact that it is full encouraging, optimistic people who say "Go for it!" as often as folks back in England said "Ooooh, I wouldn't try and do that if *I* were you."

Are you planning a new book? If so, what is it about?

Yes! I am hard at work on my second novel. My new heroine, Annie Perry, fled to America years before the story begins because of something that happened to her in England—we find out what during the course of the book. She's older than Pippa—a witty, slightly eccentric Miss Marple type and she gets the love story, which is pretty epic and directly affected by one of the secrets at the heart of the book.

Do you consider yourself English or American?

I consider myself an American with a British accent, and a Brit with American enthusiasm levels.

Enhance Your Book Club

A FEW WORDS FROM ALISON:
I come from a performing background. When the comedy is working, you know it, because the audience laughs. When the story is moving the audience, you can hear sniffles right there in the room with you. Writing a novel is quite different. You work on it for months and months and eventually people read it, but you have no idea what they're thinking or feeling unless they tell you!

I love hearing from book clubs a) because it's great fun and b) because it always gives me a new perspective on what I have written. To invite me to phone into your book club, or let me know what your book club thought of the book, go to www.alisonlarkin.com and shoot me an email.

I have been delighted to hear that many book clubs have discussed my book over a cup of English tea. This is a fine idea. After all, T.E.A. could be seen as an acronym for "The English American."

You can find clear instructions on how not to make a cup of tea on page 94. Here are a few updates on Pippa's how-to suggestions.

Pippa's Perfect Pot of Tea

Put the kettle on. When it whistles at you, pour half a cup or so of the boiling water into your teapot (a Brown Betty or glazed china, ideally), twirling it round inside the pot before pouring it away. While you are doing this, treat yourself to a piece of chocolate, preferably Cadbury's from England, and hum one of Pippa's favorite songs from the book.

Dole out one heaped teaspoon of tea leaves—Earl Grey, Lapsang, or Darjeeling—one for each person and one for the pot, into the warmed teapot. The kettle will have reached a cheerful boil by this time, so pour the water over the tea. Take care that the water is not long boiling; over-boiled water results in a foul tasting concoction that could upset your friends.

Let the tea brew for anything from three to six minutes, but no longer, (see above.)

Give the tea a good stir and pour it, not forgetting the tea strainer to catch leaves; otherwise you'll find that people will spend more time picking the leaves out from between their teeth than discussing my book. If you take your tea with milk, you should add it to the cup, cold and fresh, before pouring the tea.

If you, unlike me or Pippa, are a woman with culinary energy, you might like to go all the way and serve the tea with toast and homemade marmalade. Here's my Dad's prized recipe for homemade marmalade, taught to him when he was a boy by his Scottish cousin Janie.

Seville Orange Marmalade

You will need:

A large stainless pan—for the quantities below I use one that holds 7 quarts.
8 pints of water
4 pounds of Seville oranges
2 lemons
8 pounds of white sugar
(These quantities can be halved if necessary)

Fill the pan with the water.

Cut the oranges and lemons in half. With a citrus reamer, extract the juice, saving the seeds and pith. Add the juice to the water, and tie the seeds and pith into a muslin bag.

Cut up the peel by hand or pulse it in a food processor.

Add the peel and muslin bag to the water and simmer them gently until the peel is tender—about 2 hours.

Take out the muslin bag and discard the contents.

Add the sugar, stirring until it's dissolved in order to avoid sticking and burning.

Bring the pot to a rapid "rolling" boil, until the setting point is reached—about 20 minutes. The setting point can be tested either by seeing if the mixture falls like a curtain from a wooden spoon or by putting a small amount on a chilled saucer and seeing if the surface crinkles when pushed with your fingertip.

Meanwhile, heat clean jars. Leave the marmalade to stand in the pan for 5 to 10 minutes, then fill the jars. When they feel cool, top the marmalade with waxed disks and add covers.

Instead of serving toast and marmalade, you might consider serving genuine British delicacies mentioned in the book! An excellent place to purchase these at a reasonable price is www.britishgiftbaskets .com. Their products include, but are not limited to, Ty-phoo tea, Scone mix, strawberry jam, chocolate digestive biscuits, Hobnobs, Maltesers, Crunchies, chocolate buttons, and penguins. The president of this company and the person who puts the groceries and baskets carefully together is my husband, who just happens to bear a startling resemblance to one of the men in *The English American*. (Guess which one!)

To further enhance your book club discussion, go to www.youtube. com/alisonlarkin, where you can watch:

1. Alison Larkin singing her DNA Song, echoing themes from *The English American*.
2. The ladies (and gentleman) of the AM Northwest's TV Book Club discussing Alison's book.
3. An interview with Alison from TurnHere films.

For additional information go to www.alisonlarkin.com.

Alison performs for a lot of charities and other organizations.
To book her as a speaker for your next event, send an email to
bookalison@alisonlarkin.com.